Nothing Between Us

RONI LOREN

BERKLEY BOOKS, NEW YORK

THE BERKLEY PUBLISHING GROUP
Published by the Penguin Group
Penguin Group (USA) LLC
375 Hudson Street, New York, New York 10014

USA • Canada • UK • Ireland • Australia • New Zealand • India • South Africa • China

penguin.com

A Penguin Random House Company

This book is an original publication of The Berkley Publishing Group.

Library of Congress Cataloging-in-Publication Data

Loren, Roni.
Nothing between us / Roni Loren. — Berkley trade paperback edition.
pages ; cm. — (A loving on the edge novel ; 7)
ISBN 978-0-425-26857-5 (softcover)
1. Triangles (Interpersonal relations)—Fiction.   I. Title.
PS3612.O764N69 2015
813'.6—dc23
2014035755

PUBLISHING HISTORY
Berkley trade paperback edition / January 2015

PRINTED IN THE UNITED STATES OF AMERICA

10   9   8   7   6   5   4   3   2

Cover art: Sunlit blinds © Patryk Kosmider / Shutterstock.
Cover design by Diana Kolsky.

continued . . .

FALL INTO YOU

"Steamy, occasionally shocking, and relentlessly intense, this book isn't for the faint of heart. But with fiery, emotional characters and their blisteringly passionate relationship, it is also one that isn't easily forgotten."   —*RT Book Reviews* (4½ stars)

"Fast-paced and riveting with clever plot twists. Loren writes vivid descriptions, and *Fall into You* is a hot erotic romance."
                                                              —*USA Today*

"*Fall into You* is an erotic romance with heart and serious heat, one that I could not put down. I adore Grant and Charli, and think they may be one of my favorite couples of 2013."
                                                —*Romance Novel News*

MELT INTO YOU

RITA finalist for Best Contemporary Single Title Romance

"Quite a ride. The story is heartfelt and pulls you into the relationships with the characters. *Melt into You* takes the traditional version of romance and twists it so that the idea of three individuals in a relationship seems perfectly right."   —*RT Book Reviews*

"Roni Loren's books are masterful, story-driven, sensual, and very erotic . . . Definitely one of my have-to-get-as-soon-as-possible series!"   —*Under the Covers Book Blog*

"Loren does an incredible job portraying the BDSM lifestyle in a sexy and romantic way . . . Loren should definitely be put on the must-read list."   —*The Book Pushers*

CRASH INTO YOU

"Loren writes delicious, dark, sensual prose . . . Multidimensional characters, a very complicated relationship, and suspense combine to make *Crash into You* unique and emotional—an impressive debut from Loren."
—*USA Today*

"Revved up and red-hot sexy, Roni Loren delivers a riveting romance!"
—Lorelei James, *New York Times* bestselling author of the Mastered series

"Hot and romantic, with an edge of suspense that will keep you entertained."
—Shayla Black, *New York Times* bestselling author of the Wicked Lovers novels

"A sexy, sizzling tale that is sure to have readers begging for more! I can't wait for Roni Loren's next tantalizing story!"
—Jo Davis, author of the Sugarland Blues novels

"This steamy, sexy yet emotionally gripping story has the right touch of humor and love to keep readers coming back for a second round."
—Julie Cross, author of the Tempest novels

"Sexy as hell, gutsy as all get out—*Crash into You* has balls! . . . Loren understands the dark beauty of D/s and treats her characters with respect even as she takes them to the very edge of what they and the reader can handle. I can sum this book up in one word: Damn!"
—Tiffany Reisz, international bestselling author of the Original Sinners series

"A stunning first work. I read it straight through in one sitting, and I dare you to even attempt to put it down."
—Cassandra Carr, author of *Awakening*

Titles by Roni Loren

CRASH INTO YOU

MELT INTO YOU

FALL INTO YOU

CAUGHT UP IN YOU

NEED YOU TONIGHT

NOT UNTIL YOU

NOTHING BETWEEN US

Novellas

STILL INTO YOU

FOREVER STARTS TONIGHT

ACKNOWLEDGMENTS

Every book is a labor of love, and each story has its own unique challenges. For Colby's book, I knew I was taking on a big story line with a lot of moving parts (pun intended, lol), so I expected bumpy roads and blocks along the way. And boy, was I right. But I'm blessed to have people around me who keep me (somewhat) sane and who don't let me burn manuscripts when I'm convinced I've mucked it all up.

So, thank you to my writing support group—Julie Cross, Jamie Wesley, and Taylor Lunsford—who were always there with advice, cheerleading, and a sympathetic ear (or an emergency beta read) when I was fighting to get this book just right.

To my family, for always believing in me and what I'm doing. I never take that enthusiasm and support for granted.

To my son, for being patient with Mommy and making her laugh when she's in writer-deadline mode.

To my agent, Sara Megibow, for all your positivity and encouragement.

To my editor, Kate Seaver, for letting me take risks in my books and for uttering the sweet words (when I warned her this book was running long): "Don't worry about going over word count. Tell the story you need to tell. More words just means more for readers." Thank you!

And to my husband, Donnie, for being there always—for everything. Love ya, babe.

Nothing Between Us

ONE

Georgia Delaune had never been particularly drawn to illegal activity. Or taking risks. Or, okay, fine—sexually deviant behavior. She was woman enough to admit what this was. So finding herself hiding in the dark, peering around the curtains of her second-story window with a set of binoculars, should've tipped her off that she was officially losing her shit.

But since moving into the house on Fallen Oaks Lane six months earlier, she'd known this moment was coming. Before now, she'd convinced herself that she'd only been catching inadvertent peeks and unintentional glimpses. Her neighbor would surely shut his curtains if he didn't want to risk being seen, right?

She groaned, lowered the binoculars, and pressed her forehead to the window frame. God, now she was blaming the victim. *He gets naked in the confines of his own home. A home that's on a treed corner lot with tons of privacy and a seven-foot-tall fence. How dare he!*

This was so screwed up. What if he saw her? He could call the cops, and she'd be slapped with some Peeping Tom charge—or Peeping Tammy, as the case may be. That'd be an epic disaster. Especially when the cops found no information on a Georgia Delaune. Plus, afterward, she'd have to move because there'd be no facing her neighbor again. Not after he knew what she did at night. And there was no way in hell she was moving. It had taken too much time, effort, and planning to find this spot, to finally feel even a smidgen of security and safety. These walls were her only haven, and she had no intention of leaving them.

But despite knowing the risks, when she saw a lamp flick on and light glow in the window of Colby Wilkes's bedroom, she found herself dragging a chair over to the window and lifting the binoculars to her eyes. It took a second to adjust the focus, but when the lenses cleared, the broad, wet shoulders of her dark-haired neighbor filled the view. Her stomach dipped in anticipation.

He wasn't alone.

She'd known he had friends over. She'd seen the group going in when she'd closed her living room blinds earlier that night. Two women and three guys, plus Colby. Later, she'd heard water splashing and the murmuring of voices, so she'd gone into her backyard for a while to listen to the distant sounds of life and laughter. That world seemed so foreign to her now. Being surrounded by people, having friends over, relaxing by the pool. She couldn't see anything from her backyard. Colby's pool area was blocked by the house and bordered by trees. So she'd lain in her lounge chair out back, closed her eyes, and had imagined she was a guest at his party, that she was part of that laughter. And she'd also found herself wondering what would happen afterward.

Now she knew. Colby had stepped into his bedroom, obviously fresh from the pool with his dark hair wet and only a towel knotted around his waist. And he had company with him. One of Colby's friends, a tall blond guy who was also sporting a towel, had followed him in. And then there was a woman. She wore nothing at all. Georgia's lip tucked between her teeth, heat creeping into her face. She *so* shouldn't be watching this. But she couldn't turn away. She'd learned rather quickly that her dear neighbor, despite his affable grin, Southern-boy charm, and straitlaced job, was a freak in the bedroom. Threesomes were only part of it. The man was dominant to the core. Considering her last relationship, that alone should've turned her off, sent her running. Guys who wanted control. Fuck, no.

But the first time she'd caught sight of Colby bringing a flogger down on a lover's back, Georgia had been transfixed. She'd been completely stuck on her latest writing project at the time. But after watching Colby drive a woman into a writhing, begging state, Georgia had gone into her office, opened a new document, and written until the sun had broken through the curtains the next morning. Before she knew it, her thriller-in-progress had taken a decidedly erotic turn. Thankfully, her editor had loved the new direction. So now Georgia, in her guiltiest moments, told herself these stolen moments at the window were all in the name of book research.

Yeah. Even her sleep-deprived brain didn't buy that one.

The guilt wasn't enough to make her stop, though. Especially now when Colby was grabbing for the knot on his towel. She held her breath. The terry cloth fell to the floor at Colby's feet, and everything inside Georgia went tight. *Holy heaven above.* She'd watched—oh, how she'd watched—but never before had she been able to see everything in such intimate detail. The binoculars transported her, took her by the hand and dragged her into that room with those strangers. Colby was right there in front of her—strong, beautiful, aroused. His hand wrapped around his cock and stroked ever so slowly, taunting her with unashamed confidence. No, not her. The woman. God, Georgia should look away. But need rolled through her like thunder from an oncoming storm, her fingers tightening around the binoculars.

The other man had stripped, too, and although he was gorgeous in his own right with his polished, camera-ready good looks, Georgia was drawn to the rough-around-the-edges brawn of her neighbor. Every part of Colby hinted at the wildness he hid beneath his surface—dark wavy hair that was a little too long, the close-cropped beard that shadowed his jaw, and a body that looked like he could bench-press a Buick. He was the opposite of the pressed and creased, Armani-clad businessmen she'd been attracted to in her former life. He was the guy you'd be wary of on first glance if you ran into him in a dark alley—the cowboy whose hat color you couldn't quite determine straightaway.

Perhaps that was why she was so fascinated with him, despite the fact that he was a man who wanted what she could never give. She'd learned that danger often hid behind the gloss of an urbane smile and perfectly executed Windsor knot. Colby was none of that. But regardless of the reason for her mixed-up attraction, she couldn't stem the crackle of jealousy that went through as the other man laced his fingers in the woman's hair and guided her to take Colby into her mouth.

The view of Colby's erection disappearing between the lips of some other woman was erotic. There was no denying that. But it also made Georgia's jaw clench a little too hard. She could tell, even from the brief moments she'd been watching, that this woman belonged to Colby's friend. They were a couple and Colby the third party. But it still activated Georgia's *He's mine, bitch!* reflex.

Georgia sniffed at her ridiculous, territorial reaction, and tried to loosen the tension gathering in her neck. *Sure, he's yours, girl. You can't walk down the street without swallowing a pill first, much less start something if he were even interested in the weird, spying chick next door.*

But she shoved the thought away. She didn't want anything tainting these few precious minutes. This wasn't about finding a hookup. Only when she stood at this window did she feel even a glimmer of her former self trying to break through. This was her gossamer-thin lifeline to who she used to be, to the capable and confident woman who would've never hidden in the dark.

Before long, the blond man eased the woman away from Colby and guided her toward himself, taking his turn. Georgia tilted the binoculars upward, finding Colby's face instead of focusing on the scene between the other man and his woman. What she found lurking in his expression wasn't what she expected. There was heat in Colby's eyes, interest for sure, but as she stared longer, she sensed a distance in those hazel depths. Like he was there with them but other . . . separate. Alone.

It probably was only because the other two were a couple. Or maybe it was Georgia's mind slapping labels on things to make herself feel better. But regardless, it made her chest constrict with recognition. She didn't know what was going on in his head. Or how seeing his friends together made him feel. But she knew loneliness. And for those few seconds, she was convinced Colby did, too. She pressed her fingertip against the cool glass of the window, tracing the outline of Colby's face. Needing to touch . . . something.

The glass might as well have been made of steel, the yards between the houses made of miles.

But she couldn't walk away. The night went on and there she sat, watching the three lovers move to the bed, the woman being cuffed to the headboard. The two men lavished her with hands and mouths and tongues. It was like watching a silent symphony, the arching of the woman's back the only thing Georgia needed to see to know exactly how these men were affecting their willing captive. The melancholy feelings that had stirred earlier had quickly been surpassed by ones much more base and primal. Georgia's body was growing hot and restless, her panties going damp.

When Colby braced himself between the woman's thighs and entered her, Georgia trained the binoculars on his face, unable to handle the image of him having sex with another woman. Her mind was developing quite the ability to focus on the fantasy and block out the unwanted parts. She only had a view of Colby's profile, but she watched with rapt attention as his jaw worked and his skin went slick with sweat instead of pool water.

Without giving it too much thought, she braced one elbow on the window ledge to hold the binoculars steady and let her other hand drift downward. Her cotton nightgown slid up her thighs easily. Somewhere her brain protested that this was wrong—sick and sad. She had a perfectly functioning vibrator in her bedside drawer. She had an imagination strong enough to fuel an orgasm without doing this, without watching the man next door screw another woman. But her starved libido didn't seem to give a damn about morals or ethics or pride right now. There was need. And a solution. Simple as that.

As Colby's lips parted with a sound she could only imagine,

Georgia's fingers found the edge of her panties and slipped beneath the material. Her body tightened at the touch and the little gasp she made reverberated in the dead silence of the guest bedroom. Colby's head dipped between his shoulders, and Georgia imagined it was her he was whispering passionate words to. That deep Texas drawl telling her how good it felt to be inside her, how sexy she was, how he was going to make her come. He would be a dirty talker, she had no doubt. No sweet nothings from Colby Wilkes.

She closed her eyes for a moment as she moved her fingers in the rhythm of Colby's thrust—long, languid strokes that had a fire building from her center and radiating heat outward. It wouldn't take long. Her body was already singing with sensation, release hurtling toward her. But she wouldn't go over alone. She forced her eyes open, the binoculars still in her grip, and found Colby again. His dark hair was curling against his neck, sweat glistening at his temples. He had to be close, too. Every muscle in his shoulders and back had tensed. All of her attention zeroed in on him, and in her mind, the touch of her own fingers morphed into his—his hands and body moving against her, inside her.

Every molecule in her being seemed to contract, preparing for the burst of energy to come. Her breath quickened, her heartbeat pulsing in her ears. And right as she was about to close her eyes and go over, Colby jerked his head to the side toward the window. His heated gaze collided with hers through the binoculars—a dead-on eye lock that reached inside Georgia and flipped her inside out. *He knows.*

But she was too far gone for the shock to derail her. Orgasm careened through her with a force that made the chair scrape back across the wood floor. She moaned into the quiet, the binoculars slipping from her hand and jerking the strap around her neck. The part in the curtains fell shut, but she didn't notice. Everything was too bright behind her eyelids, too good, to worry about anything else but the way she felt in those long seconds. *Enjoy. Don't think. Just feel.* The words whispered through her as her fingers kept moving, her body determined to eke out every ounce of sensation she could manage.

But, of course, the blissful, mindless moments couldn't last forever. Chilly reality made a swift reappearance as her gown slipped back down her thighs and sweat cooled on her skin. She sat there, staring at the closed curtain and listening to her thumping heart. Colby *couldn't* know, right? His gaze had felt intense and knowing because the binoculars had made him seem so close. But her window was dark, her curtains darker, and the moon was throwing off enough light that it would make the glass simply reflect back the glow.

But her chest felt like a hundred hummingbirds had roosted there, beating their wings against her ribs. She wet her lips and swallowed past the constriction in her throat. She had to look. Would her neighbor be striding over here to demand what was going on? Would he be disgusted? Embarrassed? Angry?

God, she didn't even want to think about it. She wanted to turn around, go to her bedroom, and hide under the covers. But that was all her life had turned into now—hiding. And though she couldn't fix that situation, she refused to create another one. So she forced herself to lean forward and peel the curtains back one more time, leaving the binoculars hanging around her neck.

What she saw made the hummingbirds thrash more. Colby wasn't in the room anymore. His friend was now with the woman in the bed, and both seemed totally absorbed in each other. Did that mean that Colby had left and was heading this way to confront her? She was about to go downstairs to check the yard but then paused when she realized nothing had changed about the view. Nothing at all. If Colby had been concerned about a nosy neighbor, he hadn't bothered to close the curtains or warn his friends. Surely he would've done that.

She sat there, debating and worrying, but soon Colby returned to the bedroom. The man and woman had finished. Colby had on a pair of boxers and had brought clean towels in for everyone. He didn't look concerned. He didn't glance over at the window. He seemed perfectly relaxed as he helped uncuff the woman's hands, kissed her forehead in a friendly gesture, and then left his friends to sleep alone.

Georgia let out a long breath, sagging in the chair.

He didn't know.

She should stop taking this risk—throw away the binoculars, put a bookcase in front of this damn window, and stop while she was ahead.

But she knew she wouldn't. She would find herself here again.

Because if she didn't have her secret nights with Colby Wilkes, what was left?

Four walls, long days, and fear.

She needed this. She just had to make sure he never found out.

TWO

october 31

Right before quitting time, Colby got a visit from the Grim Reaper. Colby looked up from his desk at the hooded head peeking in through his doorway. "You know where Dr. Guthrie is?"

The sullen voice sounded appropriately grim for the costume. Colby put aside the student file he'd been making notes on. "He had to leave early because he wasn't feeling well. Were you supposed to meet with him today?"

The reaper shrugged and pulled his hood back, revealing the face of junior Travis Clarkson. "Yeah. But if he's not here . . ."

Colby could hear the indecision in the drift of Travis's voice. If his counselor wasn't here, he had the right to skip his appointment, but Colby sensed the kid needed to talk. He'd heard there'd been a bullying incident this morning and that Travis had been the target. Unfortunately, not an uncommon spot for Travis. Poor kid came from one of the wealthiest families in the area, but money couldn't fix his acne-prone skin, his crippling social anxiety, or the resulting depression it caused.

"Come on in and grab a chair, Travis," Colby said, keeping his voice casual. "There's only a half hour before the bell. You can skip the rest of study hall and chat with me."

Travis shifted on his feet in that awkward way teen boys did when they hadn't quite grown into their new longer limbs. "I don't want—you look busy."

"Nope." Colby stretched his leg beneath his desk and sent the chair in front of it rolling toward Travis. "I was just finishing up some notes. You'll save me from boring paperwork."

Travis tucked his hands in the robe of his costume and shuffled in. He glanced around at Colby's office, his eyes skimming over the shelves of books and the few photos he'd kept from his music days. "Your office is different than Dr. Guthrie's."

No shit. That was because Guthrie liked to pretend he was Freud himself instead of some guy working at the pedestrian institution of Graham Alternative High School. Guthrie's office had a plush couch, hunter green paint over the cinder-block walls, muted lighting, and a freaking desk fountain. If smoking weren't banned in the building, Colby had no doubt the school psychologist would have a pipe hanging from his mouth during sessions. But Colby had learned that the last thing these kids needed was to walk into something that looked like a therapist's office. In fact, he spent most of his sessions with his students doing something active while they talked. It was amazing how a kid could open up if he was shooting hoops and not being stared at when he answered personal questions.

"I like to keep things simple."

Travis went to the wall to get a closer look at a photo instead of immediately sitting down. "Is that you and Brock Greenwood?"

"Yeah," Colby said. "I played with him in a band when we were younger. Of course, back then, he wasn't *the* Brock Greenwood. Just a guy who could sing his face off. You listen to country music?"

Travis turned away from the picture and lowered himself into the chair. "I listen to everything. I like mashing shit—er—stuff up on my computer. You know, making things that don't seem to go together blend."

Colby smiled. "Really? That's cool. I can't be trusted with all those music programs. I have a friend who does it and he's tried to teach me, but he's declared me a hopeless case. Just give me my guitar and a blank piece of paper to jot down lyrics."

"Old school."

"Or just old."

Travis almost smiled—something Colby wasn't sure he'd ever seen Travis do—but the kid seemed to catch himself before he let it break through. God forbid he let the school counselor know he liked talking to him. "You still play?"

"I do. I play a few gigs here and there. Nothing serious. It's a good way to relax—playing without any pressure attached to it."

Travis nodded. "Yeah, I get that. But I can't really imagine getting onstage as being relaxing. I like the behind-the-scenes stuff. Putting on my headphones . . . I don't know, it's like a switch that shuts out the world and transports me somewhere else, another life."

"An escape."

"Yeah," he said, rubbing his chapped lips together. "That's what I like. That escape. Nothing else matters when the music is playing."

Colby leaned back in his chair and hooked his ankle over his knee, understanding that desire but also hearing the loneliness lacing Travis's words. "Ever thought about pursuing a career in that? Sound engineering or music producing?"

Travis glanced up, his face a bit haunted—although that could've been the whole Grim Reaper look he had going on. "I've thought about it. But my parents would shit a brick—sorry."

Colby waved a hand, dismissing the language. The kid was talking, he didn't care if he slipped up and cursed.

"They hate me fooling around with my computer. They think it isolates me or whatever. Like if I just stop doing that, suddenly my life will be all Friday night football games and proms and crap." He sneered. "They can't see that those things aren't options for me even if I wanted them. Maybe they should be the ones on medication. They're delusional."

Colby rubbed a hand over the back of his head, choosing his words carefully. It was always a fine line when kids complained about their parents. If you took the parents' side, the kid shut down. If you undermined the parents and agreed with the kids, you helped justify behavior that might not be one hundred percent healthy. "Sometimes it's hard for parents to see the benefit in something that from the outside looks like wasting time. If they don't share that passion, it can be hard for them to understand."

"They just wish I were someone else." His gaze dropped to his hands, which were fiddling with the strap of his backpack. "I don't really blame them."

Colby hid his frown. "Would you want to be someone else if you could?"

He twisted the strap around his fingers. "Maybe."

"And who would you be?"

He grimaced. "I don't know. Someone who could ask a girl out without getting pit stains in front of everyone."

"Is that what got Dalton and his friends after you today?"

He chewed his lip and gave another shrug.

"Would you want to be him?" Colby asked, picturing Dalton Wiggins—Mr. Popular, lead shit-stirrer at Graham High. And a kid who had an irrevocably broken home life that Colby would wish on no one. Of course, no one here knew that except him since Dalton only shared that stuff in the privacy of his counseling sessions with Colby.

"Fuck, no," Travis bit out. "The guy's a jerk. But if I looked like him, I wouldn't act like he does. I'd just, I don't know, use it for good."

Colby lifted a brow. "For good?"

"For girls," Travis supplied, a little smirk touching his lips.

Ah, it always came back to girls. "So what happened today when you asked that girl out?"

"She started out being nice about it—even though she was going to say no. I could tell. They always say no. But when Dalton walked up and teased me about sweating, she just kind of looked embarrassed. And like . . ." His jaw clenched. "Like she felt sorry for me."

Colby's chest squeezed. Damn, this kid couldn't catch a break. He was probably one of the smartest students in the school. His test scores were always off the charts. He was only here at Graham because his depression had become debilitating last year, and he'd missed too much school. One day, he'd probably be some brilliant engineer, rich off his ass, clear-skinned and sought after by droves of the fairer sex. But Colby knew the future seemed so damn far away when you were a teenager. "Travis—"

"I just want the crap to end, you know? Like, can they cut me some slack for one goddamned day? You know how hard it was for me to get the nerve to ask Mallory out?"

"I'll make sure and talk to Dalton about his behavior. He's already on warning and is close to getting kicked out if he keeps it up. We'll make sure you can come to school without having to worry about bullies."

Travis sniffed. "Someone else will just replace him."

Colby flinched, knowing that was probably true. "How about we—"

The bell rang, startling them both.

Travis jumped up, slinging his backpack over his shoulder. "I gotta go."

"Hey," Colby said, standing. "Wait, you don't have to—"

"I need to pick up my sister at her school. If I'm late, my mom will be pissed."

"Travis, I want to make sure you're okay after what happened today. If you want to talk some more, I can—"

"I'm fine." He pulled his Reaper hood over his head again. "Happy Halloween, Mr. Wilkes."

Colby opened his mouth to say something else, then shut it when Travis disappeared into the now-bustling hallway. Colby sat back in his chair and rubbed a hand over his face. Monday he'd pull Travis out of class for a full session. At least with the weekend, the kid would get a break from school for a few days.

And after today, Colby could use one, too. He packed up his things and headed out. He had a party to host. And a bet to honor.

He wasn't looking forward to the latter.

———

"Damn, Colby, you were supposed to dress up. Where's your costume?" Kade asked when Colby opened the front door to let his two friends in a few hours later.

Colby lifted his plastic ax to his shoulder. "Don't fuck with me,

Vandergriff. I have weapons. And Paul Bunyan could totally kick a zombie's ass. One swing to the head and you're done."

Kade grinned a macabre, dead man's smile and stepped past Colby into the house, carrying grocery bags. "So I guess this means you lost the bet with Kelsey and Wyatt?"

"I was hustled. I had no idea that girl was so good at pool."

Tessa, Kade's girlfriend, was fighting a smile beneath her black lipstick as she followed Kade in. "Evening, Mr. Lumberjack."

Colby groaned and cocked his head toward his ax. "You're lucky you're good-looking, zombie girl."

For months, members at The Ranch, the BDSM resort Colby worked at on the weekends, had been calling him The Lumberjack behind his back. He hated the nickname, and now it was definitely going to stick. Especially after he saw Kade set down his bags and snap a pic with his phone. It was probably spreading through their network of friends like a virus as they stood there.

Tessa handed him a plastic-wrapped tray of red and green Jell-O shots that were shaped like brains and tilted her head to give him another once-over. "Don't worry. It's a good look for you. Very rustic. I'm sure you could head out to The Ranch and have a crowd of submissives volunteering to play Babe the Blue Ox for you tonight."

He laughed and took the tray from her. "There's nothing sexy about an ox."

Plus, he had no desire to go to The Ranch tonight. He'd been working there for a few years now as a trainer. It was what he did for a little fun and a lot of extra money. And normally, Halloween was one of his favorite nights to go out there since no one knew how to do deviant costumes—or the *treat* part of the trick-or-treat equation—like kinky people. But the enjoyment had been draining out of his time at The Ranch over the last year, and it had started to feel like work instead of an escape. He couldn't pinpoint what had shifted. But lately, the dynamic of training someone as a business arrangement had sucked a lot of what he loved about kink out of the experience. He used to get a high from sessions. Now too often he felt hollow and exhausted by the end of them. Even when he was with someone off the clock, it still felt like a transaction instead of a connection.

In fact, the last time he remembered having a really good time with anyone was the night he'd helped Kade give Tessa her threesome fantasy. It'd been a fun and sexy night with friends. But Colby had known then it would be a onetime thing. His best friend had been stupid in love with the girl already—even if the idiot hadn't realized it at the time. And though Colby was always up for a little fantasy and fun, he knew better than to mess around with friends once things got serious. Kade hadn't even had to say it. Colby knew Tessa was completely off-limits now.

Which was fine with him. Tessa was great—beautiful and smart. But there was no doubt she was meant to be with Kade. The two lit each other up in a way that had Colby more than a little jealous. And damn, when Kade and Tessa had fallen into their dominant and submissive roles that night they were all together, it'd been something to behold. The air had seemed to vibrate with the energy between them. That was how it was supposed to be. That was where the kink transformed into something bigger than hot sex and dirty words. It became sacred. Colby couldn't remember ever being with anyone who flipped his switch like that. That night, more than anything else, had made him start to question his job at The Ranch.

He liked having the extra cash but not enough to stick around if the role had lost its shine. The submissives he worked with deserved better than a guy who was becoming more and more tempted to phone it in. He planned to talk to Grant, the owner of The Ranch, about stepping down as soon as he'd secured the full-time counselor position at Graham.

But regardless of his own issues, he was thrilled for his friend. Kade had found exactly who he needed. Tessa was it for him. They all knew it, and somehow, they'd all moved past any potential awkwardness from their one night together without much effort. Mostly because Kade was so damn cocky he didn't know how to be jealous.

Colby carried the tray of wiggling brains into the kitchen.

"Well, I think you brought enough alcohol to tank the whole neighborhood. I approve."

Kade tucked a few bottles of wine and a twelve-pack of beer into the fridge, his shredded zombified suit swinging with the movement. "Jace, Evan, and Andre said they'd pick up pizza on the way. Kelsey's bringing candy to hand out to the kids, and Wyatt's contributing his top three horror movies of all time for us to choose from."

"Sounds like y'all have got it all covered. I should play host more often. I didn't have to do anything but open the door."

"Your place is the best for Halloween. Kids aren't even allowed to trick-or-treat in my or Wyatt's neighborhood. It's ridiculous."

Colby sniffed. That was because his friends were loaded and lived in those swanky neighborhoods with coded gates and a mile between the damn houses. The kids would pass out from exhaustion by house number three.

Colby had gotten used to being one of the few of his friends who wasn't rolling in cash. He'd saved up a lot of money from The Ranch and had invested the money he'd made from his brief music career early on, so he did well for himself, better than most. But he tried to be smart and not live lavishly. He didn't need—or want—that castle on the hill. What he had now was a thousand times better than the broken-down rental house he grew up in. He had a nice home with a pool. Quiet neighborhood. And privacy. That was all he required.

Kade shut the fridge. "You know the kids aren't going to understand your costume, right?"

"I'll tell them I'm an ax murderer," Colby said, lifting up the plastic wrap on the gelatin brains and snagging one. He popped it in his mouth.

"Believable. You're the type. The friendly neighbor who disappears for long stretches of time on the weekend with implements of torture in his truck. Deviant bastard."

Colby grinned. "Takes one to know one."

"So you have a hot date coming over tonight?" Kade asked, helping himself to one of the shots.

"Nah, I'd figured me and your brother could represent the dwindling singles population in our group, but I heard he sprained his ankle yesterday. So I guess I'll just flirt relentlessly with everyone else's women to keep myself entertained. Your girl did say my outfit looked good on me."

"Uh-huh. Unless you plan to use that ax tonight, I wouldn't recommend treading in my territory."

Colby chuckled. "Look who's developed a possessive streak."

"Damn straight." Kade nodded toward the window, where rays of dusky sun were stretching over the side yard. "What about your hot neighbor? She doesn't look like she has any big plans tonight."

Colby leaned forward on the countertop, squinting at the view through the window. His neighbor, Georgia, had ventured out of her house with a package in one hand and gardening gloves in the other. He walked toward the window, following her with his eyes, and propped his shoulder against the frame. It was such a rare occasion to see Georgia outside that he had to take the time to savor and appreciate the view.

She was obviously prepared to get dirty. She'd tied a purple handkerchief around her head to keep her curly halo of black hair away from her face and was wearing threadbare jeans and a faded White Sox T-shirt. But hell if he could imagine her looking any better. Something about the way those jeans hugged her curves and sat just a little too low in the back, exposing the dip of her tailbone and a swath of creamy cocoa skin, had everything else fading into the background.

She headed toward the side of her house, peeking over her shoulder more than once as if she were waiting for someone to show up in her driveway. She couldn't be worried about trick-or-treaters yet. It was still too early. A guest, maybe? But no one was there. And Colby would bet money that no one would be coming. Georgia never had visitors—unless they were only stopping by while he was at work. His gut told him that wasn't the case.

She plopped the package next to her herb garden, kneeled in the grass, and took one last glance toward the front yard. When she seemed assured she was alone, she put on her gloves, pulled a ball of wired plastic pumpkin lights out of the box, and leaned forward, bracing on one hand and stabbing a stake into the ground with her other. Her jeans sank lower down her backside.

Now that was a sight Colby didn't need to see. Georgia on all fours, the barest peek of her ass taunting him and sending his thoughts in a decidedly X-rated direction. Damn, what he wouldn't give to end his night with that view, his hands spreading over those flared hips.

But he knew it would never fly. Georgia Delaune was like some mysterious, uncharted island. One with tall, craggy, stay-the-fuck-back rocks around the perimeter and no lighthouse. Not that she'd ever said a cross word to Colby, but he'd gotten the message just the same. He'd tried to flirt with her when she'd first moved in and though he could tell she wasn't . . . unaffected by him, he'd felt that thick wall rise up between them. Since then, he'd had the feeling that, for whatever reason, he'd been given the *Look, but don't touch* label in Georgia's head.

Because, God knows, she *looked*—and had seen way more than he'd ever allowed anyone outside his circle to see. But he liked it too much to make her stop.

His neighbor thought she had a secret.

Colby knew better.

"Earth to Colby?"

Colby snapped out of his spinning thoughts. "What?"

Kade lifted an eyebrow. "I said why don't you go over and invite her to the party? It'd be a neighborly thing to do."

Colby snorted. "Neighborly?"

"Fine. Fuck neighborly. How 'bout this? You've been working your ass off. You look exhausted. And I think you need a little fun in your life. Go invite hot neighbor chick over and have some. We promise to behave—mostly."

"You totally should," Tessa said with a sage nod from the doorway of the kitchen. Colby hadn't even noticed her come in. "That lumberjack getup is like girl Kryptonite. She'll say yes. Plus, we could use another woman around here to even out the testosterone."

Kade sent his woman a narrow-eyed glance. "Girl Kryptonite?"

Tessa shrugged and with her tattered dress, it reminded Colby of one of the walking dead from the old "Thriller" video. "Just saying. It's an empirical observation." She headed over to Kade and slipped her arms around his waist. "But don't worry, I'm, of course, into blond, blue-eyed zombies."

Kade kissed the top of her head. "Yeah, you're kinky like that."

Colby smirked. Ten seconds, tops. That was how long he'd give it before his friends would have black lipstick all over each other. He turned back to the window to leave them to their own devices and watched as Georgia lined her garden with the pumpkin lights. Her movements were efficient and her posture stiff, like she was performing a duty instead of something she wanted to be doing, which was kind of strange considering no one *needed* to have Halloween decorations. But she seemed determined to get them set up.

He should probably leave her to it. He'd tested the waters with her before only to find them chilly and uninviting. He wasn't one to chase. If someone wasn't interested in what he was offering, so be it. Plus, he rarely hooked up with anyone outside The Ranch. The vanilla world really had no place for him. But as he watched Georgia lift her hair off the back of her neck and listened to Kade and Tessa kissing behind him, the pang of want went through him.

What did he have to lose? Unlike a random girl he met somewhere, Georgia *knew* what he was. She might not understand the extent of it, but she'd seen it with her own eyes. He'd seen her curtains twitch and sway on that night he was with Tessa and Kade. And he'd watched those same drapes move late at night when he undressed in his bedroom or when he brought someone home. Either the woman was terrified of him and documenting all of his deviant acts in case he turned out to be a serial killer . . .

Or she was turned on by it.

Tonight, he planned to find out.

It was about time he paid another visit to that isolated island of hers.

———————

The fading sunlight felt good on Georgia's skin. That was what she focused on—the warmth of the late-afternoon rays, the tickle of the fall breeze against her neck, and the smell of the rosemary and thyme growing in her small herb garden.

But only paying attention to those pleasant things took effort. It meant ignoring the prickling of nerves that was an ever-present companion when she was out in the open. She was getting better at handling the anxiety each time, though. That was something. Even on the days she found it more difficult, she forced herself out at least once a day anyway to keep the promise she'd made via Skype to Leesha, her friend and therapist. Baby steps. That was what Georgia was relegated to. But at least they were steps.

Georgia got the string of pumpkin lights all lined up and turned on. She smiled that they were working but quickly realized they only illuminated a bunch of weeds that had popped up since the last time she'd cleaned the garden. Damn. Well, what did she have but time? The kids wouldn't be coming around for candy for a while still. And even then, she didn't plan on opening her door. She'd bought a big bowl and made a sign that said Help Yourself to put out on the porch. So she went to work weeding the garden.

She'd never been particularly into yard work before moving to Texas. It was hell on the nails, and she used to care about shit like that. But now it had become an outlet for her—one where she could let her mind wander and relax. Grab and yank, grab and yank. In a way, it was like meditation. And tonight she could use a bit of serenity. It would be a late night of hearing unfamiliar noises outside.

She pulled at a stubborn weed, but it didn't give. And it was blocking one of her pumpkin lights. That wasn't going to work. With a huff, she put her other hand at its base and got into a squat to tug harder. The roots didn't want to release but she was determined to get it out of there, so she gave it one last yank. The weed came free and sent her sprawling backward, a trail of soil arcing through the air. She landed on her ass with an *oof*, and the dirt showered her shirt and jeans.

A shadow enveloped her. "And she's down for the count."

Her heart gave a start at the deep voice and the nearness of it. She scrambled, spinning around onto her knees and pulling the canister on her hip in an automatic gesture. But as soon as she had the pepper spray aimed, her subconscious thankfully processed the voice before her systems could go completely haywire. "Colby."

He had his hands up in a *whoa, there* gesture but didn't seem overly concerned, as if instinctively knowing she wasn't going to attack.

"Shit." She lowered her arm and let out a shaky breath. "Sorry. I—you must think I'm a lunatic."

He gazed down at her, blocking out the sun, and then put a hand out to her. "No, it's my fault. I didn't mean to startle you."

She eyed his hand, reluctant to even go there, but she didn't want to be rude. She put her hand in his large, warm one and he helped her to her feet. "Thanks."

He let her hand go immediately, as if aware that the contact made her nervous, and took a step back. "You okay?"

"Yeah, I'm fine. It's just . . . Halloween makes me jumpy." The excuse was lamer than most she came up with, but that was all she had at the moment.

He gave her a friendly smile. "I'm not sure pepper spray works on ghouls and ghosts, but it's never a bad idea to protect yourself. Did you hurt anything on the fall?"

"Only my pride." She glanced down and brushed the dirt off her ratty clothes. But it just made dark streaks smear over her shirt. Nice. She looked like she'd been rolling in the mud and he looked like . . . wait. She let her gaze travel over him again. He'd pulled a knit cap over his curly dark hair and had let his beard grow a little extra. And though it was cool outside, the red plaid flannel shirt and dark jeans seemed a little out of place for the night. Frankly, the whole rustic woodsman look was kind of working for him—and her—but she couldn't quite figure out if it was supposed to be a costume.

He must have noticed her perplexed expression because he smirked. "I'm supposed to be Paul Bunyan. If I had my ax or an ox, it'd probably make more sense."

She bit back a smile. Well, he was a giant of a man—well over six foot and broad—so it sort of made sense. "Right. That's . . . creative."

"I lost a bet."

A laugh escaped, the act feeling foreign in her throat. "Well, I guess it could be worse then. They could've made you wear a tutu or something."

"I don't know. I think my friend is bringing over a stuffed blue ox for me to carry around, so there's more humiliation to come," he said, hooking his thumbs in his jeans and making his shirt stretch across what she knew was a well-honed, to-die-for chest.

She had to press her tongue to the back of her teeth to keep herself from inadvertently licking her lips. *Don't think about him naked. Don't think about him naked.*

"So anyway, I was coming over to see if you'd like to play witness to that humiliation."

She blinked and her brain scrambled for a moment. "What?"

He cocked a thumb toward his house. "I'm having some friends over tonight. Nothing major, just pizza, movies, and a little alcohol in between handing out candy. If you're not doing anything tonight, you should come over."

She glanced down at the ground, that familiar push and pull yanking at her. The shadow of her old self leapt at the idea of going to a house party and meeting new people, at hanging out with the guy she'd been spying on for over a year now. Before everything happened back in Chicago, she'd never been an introvert. But that was then. She wasn't stupid enough to think she could handle this. She could already feel the electricity working through her, the nerves priming for fight-or-flight. If she attempted to go over there, she'd make a scene whether she wanted to or not. No. Freaking. Way.

He must've thought she was looking down at her clothes. "You don't need a costume or anything. It's going to be laid-back."

Was *laid-back* his way of saying all his friends would end up in bed together? Because she'd seen some of the parties at his house. But she couldn't imagine that he'd ask her to something like that. He didn't know her at all. And though she knew he was kinky, she got the sense he kept that side of himself very separate, only exposing it to a trusted circle. He did work at a local high school, after all, and had to maintain a certain image. "That's really nice of you to ask."

"So come," he said simply.

She forced a weak smile. "I'm sorry. I can't. I need to work tonight. I'm doing online interviews for a virtual assistant and . . . I'm not great with crowds anyway."

Shit. She hadn't meant to confess that.

His eyes narrowed as he studied her for a second. If he was trying to figure her out, she wished him luck. Most of the time, she couldn't figure herself out.

"All right." He gave a nod and she appreciated that he didn't push the issue.

That was one of the main reasons she'd managed to act halfway normal around her neighbor. Most men made her anxious these days. The girl who was never afraid to go after a guy and flirt could barely breathe when guys approached her now. But Colby seemed to sense her skittishness and always stayed a couple of feet away from her, giving her space, and he never got pushy about anything.

"I appreciate you thinking of me, though," she added.

His sexy half smile almost made her rock back on her heels, the sensual power of it like a physical blow. "You're easy to think about, Georgia."

Her stomach dipped.

He adjusted his knit cap, more dark hair escaping around the edges, and turned. "Invitation stands if you change your mind."

"Okay," she said, but it came out small, and she wasn't sure if he'd even heard her.

When he crossed the invisible line back into his own yard, she felt more alone than she had in a long, long time.

If he took one of those women at the party to his bed tonight, Georgia knew she would watch. And it might kill her. Because this time, she knew it could've been her.

But when she went upstairs late that night, Colby's curtains were shut tight.

THREE

At dawn Monday morning, Georgia shuffled to her living room with a steaming mug of coffee and a headache. She hadn't slept well, but she wouldn't be able to sleep anymore this morning. Once she was up, she was up. Plus, she had a video chat session scheduled this morning with Leesha, and they were supposed to discuss Georgia's progress now that the trial was only two and a half months away. Georgia blew across the top of her mug, but it was more a weary sigh than any attempt to cool off her coffee.

Progress. It was going to take Georgia the hour before the call to come up with things to list in that column. Everything was going so much slower than she, Leesha, or the prosecution had hoped for. The notion that she was supposed to get on a plane in January, fly back to Chicago, and face her ex-boyfriend, Phillip, was too much for her to think about right now. In the last six months, her biggest accomplishment had been managing to go back and forth to the grocery store without having a complete meltdown. Even in that, she wasn't a hundred percent successful every time. Last week, she'd left a basket of groceries defrosting in the middle of the store because she'd seen someone who looked like Phillip and had to run out to the car before she made a scene.

But if she didn't figure out a way to get herself to Chicago, functioning at full capacity, Phillip could walk. He'd murdered the person she'd loved most in the world, and he could stroll out a free man. The thought made her want to retch, but it was a real possibility. Phillip was a brilliant attorney and had hired an equally brilliant one to represent him. Most of the evidence was still circumstantial and Georgia's testimony was key. But if she got on the stand and freaked out, jurors would believe the things the defense attorney would say about her—unstable, overactive imagination, drama queen.

Not an option. If Phillip went free, she was done. Revenge would be swift and deadly at his hands. Or worse. He'd take her and not kill her at all. He'd try to *keep* her.

Georgia shivered and went to the front window to let in some light. There were too many shadows surrounding her all of a sudden. But when she cracked her blinds open, her breathing ceased, and she almost dropped her mug to the floor.

There was a man in her front yard. Fear swept through her in a rush. But before she could tumble into full-fledged panic, the man turned and she caught sight of his familiar profile.

Colby reached up toward the tree in her front yard and tugged something from it. Only then did she take in the rest of the scene, her tunnel vision widening out. Her front yard was a complete disaster. Toilet paper hung in sagging loops from every branch and bush, and the flowers around her tree were flattened into a brightly colored carpet.

Seeing all her hard gardening work dismantled had the fear morphing right into anger, helping her shake off the dark memories she'd been plagued by a few minutes before.

She set her mug down and went to her front door, unlatching the three deadbolts and deactivating the alarm before pulling it open. The sight was even worse outside. Her entire garden out front looked like a herd of elephants had trampled through it. "What the hell?"

Colby turned at the sound of her voice, his jaw set. "Morning."

She wrapped her arms around herself, remembering she was only wearing a thin robe. "What's going on?"

He dropped the pile of soggy toilet paper to the ground and took a few steps toward her. He was dressed for his morning run—baseball cap, track pants, and a blue Nike shirt. The man was like clockwork with his routine. Not that she'd noticed or anything.

"Apparently, some of the neighborhood kids decided to go on their own post-Halloween rampage and went a little overboard last night. My house got hit, too. When I came out, I figured it was probably a group from the school I work at targeting the staff. But then I saw your yard. My kids would know better than to tear up someone's garden. At least they better or I'd have their butts out here fixing all this."

She glanced over at his house and saw that it had gotten the same treatment. The white streamers of toilet paper billowed in the breeze. "Why are you over here, though? Looks like you have your own mess to handle."

He shrugged. "You work hard on your yard, and it'd be tough for you to reach this stuff in the tree. I figured I'd help."

"Thank you. That's really nice of you." She fought past her tendency to evaluate the kindness. She'd learned that a favor could be an aggressive move, a way to make someone feel indebted without permission. But every instinct told her Colby wasn't a danger to her. The man was dominant and a sadist, but he lived by a code. She'd done her research on his lifestyle and had seen it in action through the window—structured, practiced, controlled. He only hurt with consent. "Do you want some coffee? I just made a fresh pot."

He wiped his hands on his pants and smiled. "Sure, that'd be great."

She stepped back inside and put her hand on the door, giving him the subtle signal that he wasn't invited inside. No one was. "I'll grab some and bring it out to you. Cream?"

"No, black with a little sugar is fine."

She shut the door and locked it. With lightning-fast precision, she pulled on a pair of yoga pants, a bra, and a long-sleeved T-shirt, then made her way back toward the front of the house with two cups of coffee. Colby was sitting on her front steps when she walked out. He stood when he saw her and took the cup from her hand.

"Thanks," he said, leaning against one of the brick columns on her porch. "I usually don't let myself have one of these until I get to school."

She wrapped both hands around her mug, the heat warming her cold fingers and soothing her nerves a bit. This was just coffee with the neighbor. "If I don't have it within ten minutes of opening my eyes, I'm ruined for the morning."

He took a long sip and recoiled a bit. "Whoa."

She bit her lip, trying not to smile. "Sorry, I make the kind with chicory in it. My dad's originally from New Orleans, and I picked up the habit. I could get you some cream if you want."

He coughed, but his eyes were smiling. "No, I'll be fine. Just didn't expect that kick. That'll grow hair on your chest."

"I certainly hope not," she said, taking another sip.

He chuckled and his gaze drifted downward ever so briefly to the V-neck of her top, making her instantly aware. But as quickly as the glance was there, his attention was back on her face again. "So is that where you're from? New Orleans?"

The question was a simple one but held more drama than he could know. "No, my mom's a college professor, so we moved when I was little from New Orleans to Chicago once she landed a tenured position."

"How'd you end up here?"

This had been a bad idea. She knew her story, had it memorized for anyone who asked, but somehow Colby had her wanting to tell the truth. Something about him made her want to pour it all out there on her porch. But of course she couldn't do that. "I don't like harsh winters. And since I'm a writer and can work from anywhere, I figured I'd set up shop someplace warm with a low cost of living."

It all sounded logical. Of course, it was all bullshit except for the writer part. She was simply renting this place because a good friend had inherited the house from her grandmother and offered to let her stay there. She hadn't cared where she landed as long as it wasn't anywhere close to where Phillip would be. As soon as he was safely behind bars, she could return to her cute little house in

Evanston and start living again. Find that happy girl who used to have great friends and a busy social life.

"What do you write?" Colby asked, bringing her mind back into focus.

"Lately?" *Really hot, kinky scenes loosely based on my neighbor.* "I do freelance stuff for websites and am working on a novel. A thriller."

He couldn't know that she already had an ongoing thriller series published under the pen name Myra McKnight and that she made her living from that. As far as anyone knew, Myra had moved to some exotic island to write her next book about well-loved undercover agent Haven Fontaine and would be making no public appearances in the near future.

"Wow, that must be fun," he said, sounding genuine. "I'd love to—"

But his cell phone buzzed and cut off whatever he was about to say. He apologized and pulled the phone from the clip on his pants. He frowned when he read whatever text message he'd received.

"Everything okay?" she asked.

His laid-back expression had tightened into concern. He looked up, as if he'd forgotten for a moment that she was there. "Yeah, sorry, I think so. It's just a message from my boss. I'm going to have to get going. Something's come up."

"Oh, right, sure," she said, surprised at the disappointment she felt. It'd been a long time since she'd shared coffee with anyone. And sharing it with Colby had been more pleasant than she cared to admit.

He handed his cup back to her. "Hey, when I get home tonight, how about I help finish the cleanup and then we go grab a burger or something? I'd love to hear about your book."

The offer was *so* tempting, but he might as well have asked her if she wanted to accompany him to Paris for the night. Each was equally impossible unless she wanted to load up with her anxiety pills. Then she'd be no company at all anyway. "I'm sorry, I can't."

He tilted his head slightly, his expression more curious than anything. "Can't or don't want to?"

She looked away.

"Hey"—he touched her elbow gently—"either way, it's fine. I've noticed you don't go out much."

She pressed her lips together and forced her gaze back to his, then nodded. "Leaving the house is . . . difficult for me."

His eyes softened, and she imagined he probably made a very good counselor to the kids at his high school. Despite his seemingly rough edges and overwhelming size, there was something in that expression that held understanding and sympathy without judgment. He gave a little smile. "Well, maybe I'll bring the burgers to you, then."

She couldn't help returning the smile, despite knowing how bad an idea this was. She wasn't prepared or equipped to pursue anything with anyone—especially someone like Colby. But her mouth was working on its own volition. "Maybe I'll let you."

When she shut the door, she leaned against it and smiled. Maybe she would have some progress to report to Leesha after all.

Being called into the principal's office first thing in the morning was never a good thing. Not in Colby's school days and not now. So when his impromptu coffee date with Georgia had been interrupted by a text from Principal Anders, requesting that Colby come to her office before the first bell, an old knot of dread had settled in his chest. He'd wanted to call her immediately, insist on knowing what it was, so his mind wouldn't have to go down all the possible paths. But this was one of the few relationships in his life where he wasn't in the driver's seat. Principal Anders liked to do things her way. And her way was face-to-face meetings. He smirked to himself as he headed into the bathroom for a quick shower. She'd probably make an excellent domme.

But the amusing thought died quickly as he hurried through his routine and the possibilities of what she could want to see him about drifted through his mind. On the way to the school, he told himself it was probably just a request to fill in as a substitute for the day or something. That happened on a pretty regular basis. He wouldn't relish the duty today—he'd had a string of late nights over the weekend, starting with the Halloween party Friday night and then putting a new submissive training class at The Ranch through their paces on Saturday evening—but he'd do it. It was always easier when someone familiar to the kids was in charge of the class. The students were pros at steamrolling the inexperienced and unsuspecting substitutes the district sometimes sent them. The Graham Gauntlet. That was what the teachers called it behind the closed doors of the teachers' lounge.

But when Colby pulled into the half-empty parking lot and two Dallas PD squad cars were glinting in the early-morning sun, Colby knew his initial qualms had been well founded. Not that it was completely out of the ordinary to see cops at the school. Any high school had issues. An alternative school for kids who'd gotten booted from the main system had more. But there were no students in the building yet. School wouldn't start for another hour. So that meant something had happened over the weekend. Either someone had gotten arrested or someone—

No, he wouldn't go down that road yet. But the same sick feeling he'd had six years ago filtered through him, making his few sips of coffee burn in his stomach. Though it had been a different city and a different school, that day had been all too similar. Early-morning call. Cops. And questions for Colby. Only then, there had been an urgency to everything, a crackling frenzy. A feeling that something could still be done to help. Nothing had. In the end, a student had disappeared in the night—a vulnerable seventeen-year-old kid who'd sat silent in every form of therapy but who had opened up to Mr. Wilkes, his music teacher, and had shared things Colby hadn't been prepared to handle. He'd tried to help, but he'd fucked it up.

The student had eventually been labeled a runaway, but most of the staff knew that wasn't likely. There'd been a note. A missing gun. A good-bye to the world.

So the cops had closed the book, stopped the search. And Colby had been left with the eat-you-from-the-inside guilt that he could've done more. That it was his fault. He'd resigned his position, knowing that the school would've encouraged him to do so even if he hadn't volunteered. There'd been whispers of lines being crossed. After that, he'd moved to Dallas and had gone back to school to get his master's in counseling, vowing that next time he'd know how to handle a kid who needed real help.

Now another ominous morning. Another call. And more cop cars.

He sent out a silent prayer to the universe as he climbed out of his truck and headed inside. *This will be just another ordinary day.* Maybe if he said it, it would make it true.

But it wasn't.

Principal Rowan Anders was wearing her solemn face as she invited Colby into her office, her usual everything-in-place appearance loose at the edges, like she'd gotten ready in an even bigger hurry than Colby had. The school psychologist, Ed Guthrie—or Dr. Guthrie, as he so often reminded his students and colleagues—was already there, peering over at Colby from one of the chairs as Colby took a seat.

"What's going on?" Colby finally asked, done with thick silence.

Rowan tucked an errant blond hair back into the clip that was precariously holding it up and sighed. "It's Travis."

The name and her tone had his stomach tumbling. "What's wrong?"

She pressed her hands to the top of her desk. "Around eleven last night, he took a handful of his mother's sleeping pills and cut his wrists with his dad's hunting knife."

No. Colby's chest seized at the information, shock and heartbreak colliding. "Is he, did he . . ."

Principal Anders took a breath and kept talking. "He's still alive. His father woke up with indigestion later that night and went to get antacids out of the downstairs bathroom. He found Travis lying in the bathtub, unconscious and bleeding. Thankfully, the cuts hadn't been deep enough to kill him quickly, so the ambulance got there in time. He's had his stomach pumped and he's lost a good bit of blood, but they think he's going to be okay—physically at least."

"Christ." Colby breathed a deep, bone-shaking sigh of relief at that outcome and rubbed a hand over his face.

Rowan's shoulders lifted and dipped with another long exhale, and that was when Colby felt the shift in the room. This wasn't just a meeting to inform him about one of the students. He could see the businesswoman mask slide over her features. "Colby, I understand that you were the last of the staff to talk to Travis on Friday."

He blinked, caught off guard for a second. "Yes, we had a short session before the last bell."

"Can you tell me what happened in your meeting with Travis?" she asked as she straightened a few papers on her desk without looking at them.

Colby rubbed a hand along the back of his neck, still trying to get his heartbeat to settle after worrying he'd lost a student. On Colby's left, Dr. Guthrie gave him a sidelong glance.

Colby ignored the stench of judgment he could sense wafting off the other man and focused on his boss. "Travis was supposed to have a session with Dr. Guthrie but since Ed was out that afternoon, I offered to talk with him instead. I knew Travis had been having trouble with a few of the other kids, and we discussed that. He was down and frustrated, but nothing that sent up any red flags."

"Did he inform you that he'd gone off his meds?" Ed asked, his voice cool.

Fuck. "No. But I didn't ask."

"Why not?" Principal Anders asked.

Ed's eyebrows quirked up, and he leaned forward in a way that said, *Yes, Mr. Wilkes, please share with us how completely incompetent you are.*

Colby resisted the urge to throat-punch the guy. The jerk had always seen himself as far superior and had been against Colby's more down-to-earth approach with the kids from the start. "The session was informal since we only had a few minutes and I didn't have his file. Plus, Travis and I haven't talked in an official capacity before, and I needed to build some trust and rapport. If I had jumped right into questions about medication, he would've shut down."

Ed sniffed and Principal Anders gave an unreadable nod. "Did you notice any danger signs, anything that gave you pause?"

Colby thought back to Friday. The kid had looked tired, a little beat down by the rough week, but nothing out of character from what he'd seen of the kid before. The only thing out of the ordinary had been that Grim Reaper costume. Looking back, maybe that had been a clue. But there'd been at least three Reapers roaming the halls that day. It wasn't an uncommon costume. "Nothing that made me overly concerned. He told me about his altercation with Dalton earlier in the day. He talked about how he liked to create music on his computer. We discussed how things like music can be a nice escape from stress sometimes."

"What did he say to that?" the principal asked.

"He agreed. He said"—Colby replayed the conversation in his mind, that hollow-stomach feeling returning—"he said he craved the escape."

Ed grunted. "This is why I should never take an afternoon off. How did you not see the signs, Wilkes? Did you ask him if he had a plan for an escape?"

Colby's hands curled around the arms of the chair, but he forced himself to keep his voice even. "It wasn't said like that."

Principal Anders frowned. "Colby, I'm sure you're well aware that if a threat or plan for suicide is shared, we are legally bound to break confidentiality and report it."

Colby counted to three in his head before responding. "Yes, of course. I've already done it twice this year when students have admitted thoughts of self-harm. That was not the case on Friday."

"Travis told his parents this morning that he talked to you, that he told you he wanted it all to end," she continued.

Colby frowned. "The bullying. He said he wanted the *bullying* to end."

God, *had* he missed something? It'd been late on Friday. He'd had a busy week with a number of small successes with his students. But he'd also been tired and a little distracted, knowing he was hosting the Halloween party that night. And Travis had rushed off. Maybe he hadn't listened closely enough. Maybe he had missed the signs. Maybe he should've run after him when he'd bolted.

Principal Anders smoothed the papers in front of her, her mouth pinched. "Colby, I'm sure you did what you could. You do a good job here, and I know the kids connect well with you. That's why I've been trying to get you bumped up to full time. But the school district is going to get heat for this. Travis's parents are well-to-do and were already annoyed that their son was in an alternative school after things didn't work out at his private school. The cops said the words *lawyer* and *negligence* were already being thrown around at the hospital. You know how sensitive these things are for the school district."

Colby could feel it, the anvil hovering above his head.

"So, until an investigation has been conducted, I'm going to have to put you on leave."

Bam. Flattened. "Rowan, you can't think that I'd—"

She lifted a hand, cutting him off. "If lawyers get involved, they'll dig. They'll pull all of your background, your work history."

Cold moved through him.

"The incident with that student at your previous school"—she glanced down at her notes—"Adam Keats, is sure to come up. I know this is a different situation, but from the outside, it could look bad. Like a pattern."

He shook his head, too gutted to respond. Even thinking about Keats again was too much to handle. But that wasn't the only problem with someone poking into his background. Colby had a side job that would make every school board member's head explode. He'd be fired faster than he could spell *BDSM*.

"Dr. Guthrie will take over your caseload for now," Rowan continued, all business now. "We'll bring in extra help if needed. But we have to show that we are taking immediate action and looking into the matter. And you should know, the school district may decide that our students should only be seen by a psychologist instead of splitting the caseload between you and Dr. Guthrie. You know that's not my opinion. I think you add a different perspective and approach. And frankly, the kids here need all the resources they can get. But I might not have a say if Travis's father really kicks up dust."

Colby caught the barest hint of a smile in his periphery. That fucker Guthrie was probably preening with glee on the inside. He'd never wanted Colby here. He'd wanted a promotion and a raise, not a counselor added to the mix. So from the very beginning, Guthrie had made it clear what he thought of "a washed-up musician counseling young, vulnerable minds." The ire had only grown when it'd become obvious that the kids gravitated more toward Colby's no-nonsense approach than Dr. Guthrie's cool, clinical tactics.

Now all of Colby's students would get moved to Guthrie's caseload—temporarily in the best-case scenario, permanently if Colby's position was eliminated altogether. The thought made him want to throw things. The faces of the students he counseled each week flipped through his head like a slide show on fast-forward. Kids who had come to trust him, kids who had made hard-fought progress, kids who didn't need another change in their already unstable lives. Kids who were a lot like him when he was that age.

He wasn't under the impression that he was the only one who could help them. But knowing that he *could* be the one was what got him up every morning, what kept old demons at bay.

But he hadn't helped Travis on Friday. Just like he hadn't helped Adam Keats. Maybe he'd gotten too confident that he knew what he was doing.

"I understand," he said, the fight draining out of him.

Principal Anders gave another terse nod, as if putting a period on the end of her declaration. "Thank you, Colby. Hopefully, this won't go too far or for too long. His parents are understandably upset and panicked. They're going to want to find blame everywhere else. We're the easiest targets."

No, *he* was the easiest target. And maybe it wasn't unfounded. He should've asked Travis about his medication. He should've grabbed his file to see if there were any hot points to check in on. Maybe instead of trying to put him at ease by getting him to talk about music, he should've asked him different questions. "I'll get my files and go over them with Dr. Guthrie so he can be up to date on my students."

Guthrie slapped his thighs and stood. "No need. I've already had them moved to my office. Your students will be shifted onto my calendar starting today."

Well, wasn't he the eager beaver. Apparently, Rowan had called him first and had everything taken care of before Colby walked in. It was like being fired only without the pink slip. Everyone knew it was going to happen except you.

After Guthrie strolled out, Colby stood and headed for the door.

"Colby?"

He looked back to Rowan. She'd stood as well and her cool principal mask softened into one more human. "For what it's worth, I know that if you had suspected he was in real trouble, you would've reported it."

He nodded.

But he heard what she didn't say. *Maybe you should've suspected.*

They were words he'd heard before.

FOUR

"You playing tonight, Wilkes?"

Colby looked over to the left at the man who'd leaned against the bar and posed the question. Jenner Bodine smiled back at him, toothpick clenched in his teeth. Colby took another sip from his whiskey. "Nope. Jus' drinking. You?"

Had his words slurred? He couldn't tell anymore.

"Yeah, I'm onstage next. Filling in for an act that had to cancel." He glanced out at the empty seats in the bar. "I hate playing on Mondays. Only the real dedicated drunks show up on a Monday."

Colby raised his glass in salute.

Jenner laughed. "Wow, the hard stuff, huh? I don't think I've ever seen you with anything but beer."

Yeah, and Colby's brain was feeling the effects. He could handle his liquor, but he'd been here since early afternoon and things were getting a little fuzzy around the edges now. Good. If there was ever a time to get shit-faced, it was the day one of your students almost fucking died—and you realized it might have been partly your fault. All he kept thinking about was how if Travis's father hadn't chosen Thai food for dinner that night, Travis would've been dead this morning. A sixteen-year-old kid. Dead. Two days after a session with Colby.

God. He rubbed a hand over his face. Was he that fucking blind? That useless? He'd been too wrapped up in his own crap and missed danger signs with his little brother all those years ago. Then he'd screwed things up with Adam Keats, and the kid had disappeared. Now this. Maybe he should just stick to his guitar and his job at The Ranch after all. Everything else he touched seemed to go to shit.

Colby tapped the bar and motioned for Lenora, the bartender, to pour him another. She grabbed the bottle of Jack Daniel's but frowned at him before she poured. "Sugar, I know you're a big man who can take his liquor, and I'm guessing you had a real bad day, but you're going to be sick as hell if you keep going."

Jenner chuckled and gave Colby's shoulder a pat. "Looks like you're cut off, my friend. Now you'll have to sober up while you listen to my set."

Colby grunted but didn't protest for Lenora to pour. Even through his liquor-soaked thoughts, he recognized that she wasn't giving him a choice in the matter. She was a world-class flirt and would give any customer the sweet-as-MoonPies Southern girl routine, but she ran this bar with a nonnegotiable set of rules and would kick anyone out who gave her flak about it.

"A Coke then," he said, the words coming out slower than he intended.

"Now we're talking." She patted his hand and poured him a soda, then pushed a bowl of nuts toward him. "And eat something."

Jenner said good-bye and headed toward the side door that led backstage. Colby sighed and grabbed a handful of nuts, figuring he might as well stay to listen to Jenner play. The guy was a little more pop than country in Colby's opinion. Colby preferred playing stuff with an old-school flavor. But Jenner had a good voice and a knack for writing good lyrics. And what else did Colby have to do tonight? It wasn't like he had to get to bed early to be up for school tomorrow.

The thought was more than a little depressing. He had no idea what he was going to do with himself for the weeks that stretched out before him. He kept his life busy for a reason. If he wasn't working at school, he was at The Ranch giving training sessions or here at the bar with his guitar playing a gig. The thought of sitting at home and doing . . . he didn't even know what he'd do, made him want to crawl out of his skin. He pulled the straw from the glass and took a swig of his soda. He'd go crazy stuck in that house with nothing to do.

Stuck in the house. Something about the thought niggled him. He tried to pinpoint whatever it was, then gave up and pushed it aside.

It didn't hit him in that moment. It didn't even hit him for the first few songs of Jenner's performance. But when the alcohol started to filter out of his system and his mind began to clear, the thought circled back to him. Stuck in the house . . .

Shit.

He'd told Georgia this morning that he would bring burgers by. She'd barely accepted the invitation as it was, but now it was past ten and he hadn't even stopped by to tell her something had come up. Goddammit. He'd finally gotten his neighbor to agree to a semi-date with him, and he'd fucking blown it.

Way to go, Wilkes. He pushed away from the bar, relieved that the world tilted only slightly and that he was steady on his feet. "Hey, Lenora."

She spun his way. "Yeah, hon."

"I'm going to leave my truck in the parking lot and take a cab. I'll come by and get it in the morning, so don't tow me."

"Sure thing," she said with a smile. "Get some rest."

He stepped out of the bar, the brisk air sobering him even more. The street was mostly deserted. No cabs in sight. He should've known. This part of Fort Worth was honky-tonk party row on the weekend, but on a Monday night, it was a ghost town. He stuck his hands in his pockets and took a left down the street. He knew there was a Hilton a few blocks over, and that'd be his best shot at grabbing a cab.

The wind had picked up and was blowing along the sides of the buildings with a punch of cold. Thunder rumbled in the distance and promised a chilling rain. But the residual effects of the alcohol kept him warm enough for now. A few notes of music drifted through the air as people opened the doors to some of the bars and clubs. But as he neared the end of the second block, more than a snippet of a song hit his ears. Lonely notes of a familiar melody seemed to echo from far away and stopped him dead in his stride.

He glanced behind him, trying to pinpoint the source of the sound, but the sidewalks were empty. He closed his eyes, grabbing on to the faint sound of the song. Lyrics he should've forgotten by now filled in the blanks in his head.

The yellow tape winds
The signs all warn
Fingers grab and twine,
And everything is torn.
I'm a trespasser, never will I belong.
My life is off-limits, everything is wrong . . .

Colby opened his eyes and shook his head as a chill moved through him. No, it couldn't be. He must've had more to drink than he thought. He was so drunk he was hearing ghosts. Old demons were sliding out of the gutters and wrapping around him. He picked up the speed of his steps.

But as he moved forward, the sound of the guitar only got louder, the chords clearer. Like a man possessed, he took a sharp right, crossed the street, and followed the sound. The music grew crisp as he neared a closed record store. He turned another corner and found himself facing a small park. There was a statue of a horse at the center of a stone circle, and benches surrounded it. On one of the benches sat a guy with a guitar and full sleeve tattoos, playing a song that didn't belong to him.

"Hey," Colby called out as he walked into the circle. "What song are you playing?"

The guy glanced up for a second, his face in the shadow of the canopy of trees above him, and the music stopped. "Five bucks and I'll tell ya."

Colby peered at the open guitar case at the guy's feet. There were a few bills in it. "That's not your song to play."

"The fuck it isn't," he said, and started strumming again.

Colby stepped forward, his heartbeat pounding. "Tell me where you heard it."

"Price has gone up to twenty," the guy said, not even bothering to look up this time. Thunder rumbled closer now and a gust of wind blew over them, rattling the leaves above them.

Colby gritted his teeth and pulled his wallet out. He dropped a twenty in the case. "Tell me."

The guy's blond hair had fallen in his face, but Colby could see his smirk. "In my head. I wrote it, asshole."

Well, that just pissed Colby off. He kicked the guitar case shut with a bang.

The guy's head jerked upward. "What's your pr—"

But his green eyes went wide and his words trailed off as his gaze met Colby's.

For a second, the pieces didn't register, didn't fit together in Colby's fuzzy head. He just stared for a few long seconds. But when it all finally clicked into place, it was like a swift, hard punch to the gut. *"Keats?"*

That seemed to snap the guy out of his stunned state. He got off the bench with hurried movements and flipped open his guitar case to set his battered instrument into it. "No, man, ain't me."

Colby considered for a moment that he was seeing ghosts. He'd had a bad day. He'd had a lot to drink. Keats had been on his mind earlier. But when Colby gave the guy a longer look, he knew he wasn't imagining things. The boy he'd known had grown a few inches and had inked up his skin. His hair was longer and he was leaner than Colby remembered. Harder. But there was no doubting those pale green eyes or the awareness that had flashed through them.

This was Keats. Alive.

Keats yanked his case from the ground and hitched a backpack over his shoulder, turning to go. He took two steps before Colby had a hand on his upper arm. "You're just going to walk away?"

Keats tensed in his grip, and he turned cold eyes on him. "Unless you plan to throw more money at me, big man, I'm outta here."

Colby let his arm go but squared off in front of him to block him, the dominant side of him shimmering to the surface. "Keats, if you think you're going to blow me off and pretend you don't know me, I suggest you rethink that."

Keats's smile was wry even though fear flickered through his eyes. "Blow you? So that's what this is about? Not my thing, dude. But give me two hundred bucks and maybe I can forget that I don't like cock."

Colby stepped into his space, unsure what pissed him off more— that Keats was still keeping up this act or that what he said could be true—that the smart, quiet kid he used to know was now selling himself to keep afloat. He hoped to God Keats was just bluffing. But if the kid wanted to play this game, he could, too.

"Fine."

Keats blinked, the tough-guy face faltering for a second. "What?"

"Five hundred and you come home with me for the night."

"That wasn't the offer."

"You're going to turn down five hundred bucks and a warm place to sleep?" he asked, knowing Keats had no more than thirty bucks in his case and that the cold rain would start falling any minute.

"Nobody gives you that much money for nothing," he said, his expression tight. "And I don't fuck guys."

Even hearing the crass words roll off Keats's lips had anger welling in Colby. So he was going to keep this bravado crap up. Colby crowded Keats against the side of the bench, using his size to the fullest advantage. He knew he wasn't fighting fair. Keats was nervous even if he was trying to play it off. But there was no way in hell Colby was letting him walk away. If it meant playing as dirty as Keats was playing, so be it. He leaned in, meeting Keats eye to eye. "Do I look like someone who'd need to pay for a fuck?"

"Col—" he started, then caught himself. "Shit."

Colby smiled and backed off, victorious. He took the guitar case from Keats's hand, the burden of Colby's awful day lifting a little. The situation was beyond screwed up. Keats was on the street—or close enough to it to be busking in a park. He hadn't actually asked

him if he had somewhere to go. But he was alive. That was enough
to be thankful for. "Come on. Let's get a sandwich and get indoors
before the skies open up. I need to sober up before I can drive. But
when we're done, you *are* going home with me."

The nothing-bothers-me attitude dropped from Keats's expression and he looked . . . lost. "Why?"

"Do you have someplace better to go?" he asked, lifting a brow.

Keats's jaw twitched and he glanced away, the shame in his eyes
making him look more like the kid he used to know and less like—
Colby counted off the years in his head—the twenty-three-year-old
man he'd grown into. "Not if I don't show up with some cash in my
pocket."

"That's reason enough, then. I'm guessing five hundred will cover
you. Come on."

Keats followed him when Colby started walking back toward
the main road. He fell into step with him. "Your . . . family isn't
going to mind you showing up with some stranger?"

Colby peered over at him, the question catching him off guard.
"I live alone."

"Oh." Keats looked down. "That's cool."

Ah, hell.

This had trouble written all over it. Colby switched the guitar
case to his other hand and put some distance between the two of
them.

Line drawn.

FIVE

Georgia sat curled up in her living room, nursing a glass of wine and trying to plot out the next scene in her book on the legal pad propped on her lap. A rerun of *48 Hours* was on in the background, but she wasn't listening to it. Really, she hadn't been able to concentrate on much of anything all evening. Instead, her eyes kept drifting to her living room window. Colby had said he might bring over burgers tonight. All day she had stressed about it, wondering if she would be able to manage it. She knew she couldn't go over to his house, but she wasn't sure she could let him in hers either. Every time she thought about it, she got that electric feeling in her muscles—like they were all going to seize up at once.

But Leesha had been so enthusiastic when Georgia had mentioned the potential date-that-wasn't-really-a-date to her this morning. According to Leesha—in all her therapeutic wisdom—getting interested in a man was a "major" step in the right direction. It showed willingness to trust again and reconnecting to the outside world and blah blah blah. Georgia had zoned out a little on the therapist-speak. Even so, Leesha's excitement had been contagious, and Georgia had promised her she would do all she could to give it a chance and not chicken out.

So she'd started making plans to eat on the backyard deck. Her garden back there was quiet and the trees offered shade. She could control the situation there. But all the planning and worrying had been for naught. Colby hadn't come home at his normal time. And it wasn't like he had her phone number, so he hadn't called. So either something had come up or he'd simply forgotten. Or something was wrong.

She pushed the thought aside, frustrated that her mind always went there. *Hello, Paranoia, nice to see you again.* It was always there, waiting in the rafters and ready to pounce. Sometimes she wondered if Phillip had seared it into her psyche permanently, that there was no getting better for her, that he had killed the woman Georgia used to be spiritually even if her physical form had managed to survive. Maybe she was sentenced to a life inside these walls, watching the world go by through her windows and on her TV screen, and only going out when she popped a pill that made her thoughts go slow and sticky. She set her wineglass aside and pressed the heels of her hands to her eye sockets, the thoughts making her brain want to implode.

No, she wouldn't let that happen. She was trying to get better. She was going outside every day. She was doing her therapy. Hell, she'd held a full conversation with her neighbor today. Even Leesha was hopeful. Things were getting a little better, right? And once Phillip was put away for good, the fear would surely go away. Knowing that he was out on bond and could pop back into her life was what held her hostage. The chances were slim that he'd leave the state since if he tried, he'd be thrown in jail. But it was the existence of that minute possibility that she couldn't get past. Because she knew without a doubt that if he found her, there would be no escape this time.

A door slammed in the distance, making her jump and almost knock over her wine. She turned her head toward the window. Colby was back and someone was climbing down from the passenger side of his truck. Georgia shifted on the couch to turn fully around and watch. At least he was safe, even if the thought of him bringing home some woman had a different kind of feeling twisting in her stomach. But when his passenger came around the front of the truck, it was a lanky guy with shoulder-length blond hair. Not anyone she recognized from Colby's gaggle of friends.

Jealousy rooted down in her gut despite the fact that it was a guy. Georgia had watched Colby long enough to know he wasn't only into women. Though not recently, she'd seen him with a male lover once before. It had shocked the hell out of her initially. She knew gay or bisexual men didn't necessarily fit a stereotype. But Colby was the epitome of the Southern-boy alpha male—the last person she would've ever suspected. When she'd first watched him fool around with the guy, she'd expected to be turned off. She'd always dated what she'd thought of as "manly" men, ones who would've balked at the idea of touching another guy.

But she'd been floored by how hot it had been to watch Colby take over another man. It hadn't been effeminate at all. It'd been rough and sexy and intense. Transfixing. By the time the night was done, she'd been sweating, breathless, and out of her mind with all the . . . wanting. She hadn't quite understood her reaction, but she'd decided not to dig too deep into that one.

However, tonight she wasn't in the mood to watch. Her pride was dinged. She and Colby had made plans, albeit loose ones, and then Colby had blown it off and brought someone else home. It was probably stupid to feel any jealousy. She and Colby were just neighbors. It was only an offer for burgers. She probably wouldn't have even been able to invite him inside. But it didn't stop the feelings from surfacing.

She watched the other guy pull something out of the truck bed, a guitar case from the looks of it. Colby said something to him and then glanced toward Georgia's house. Instinctively, she ducked back. All he'd be able to see between her blinds was the ambient light from the television, but even so, Colby was already heading her way.

"Shit." She scrambled off the couch. She was still in her jeans and favorite pink cashmere sweater. Stupidly, she'd gotten a little dressed up for the night, even putting on some makeup. Of course, she probably had raccoon eyes at this point from rubbing them. She strode to the mirror above the small table in the entryway and ran her fingers under her eyes to clear the smudged mascara right before the knock hit the door.

She almost didn't want him to see that she was still fully dressed. She didn't want him thinking she'd been waiting like some forgotten girl on prom night. That gave him an edge, power. But she didn't have any choice. She checked the peephole to make double sure who was on the other side, then deactivated the alarm and undid the deadbolts.

She swung the door open, finding the hulking mass of Colby Wilkes filling the doorway. He looked nothing like the fresh and spry guy he'd been when he'd left that morning. His hair was disheveled, his eyes a little bloodshot, and his clothes looked like they'd been rained on.

"Hey," she said tentatively.

He gave her a brief up-and-down glance. "Good, you're still up. I saw the TV was on and took a chance."

"Yeah, I was just about to go up to bed."

Something flickered over his expression at that, but he shifted his weight, bracing his hand on the doorjamb, and the flicker was gone. "I just wanted to say I'm sorry I didn't stop by tonight like I said I would."

She shrugged. "It's okay. I didn't really know if you were serious anyway."

He sighed and ran a hand over the back of his head. "I was. But today has been . . . complicated." He glanced toward his house and the guy leaning against the side of Colby's truck. "And is still complicated."

"Everything okay?" she asked, eyeing Colby's guest.

"I don't know if it can be defined as okay, but I have things under control. Mostly."

"Who's the guy?" she blurted, then cringed when she realized how nosy she sounded. "Sorry, none of my business."

Colby rubbed his jaw, considering her. "He's . . . a guy I used to know and who needed a place to crash tonight. Long story."

The way he said it, the underlying current of regret in his voice, had her curiosity welling, but she kept her questions to herself. "Anything I can do to help?"

"Not really." His lip curled at the corner. "Having dinner with you tonight would've helped. I was looking forward to that. Rain check?"

"Sure, okay."

"Good. I'll hold you to that." He leaned over, cupping her elbow, and panic stiffened her for a second as he entered her space. But all he did was press a light kiss to her cheek.

He smelled faintly of maple syrup, but the rough brush of his beard against her skin sent a current straight downward. She had to bite the inside of her lip to keep from making a sound. He lingered close for a moment, and she swallowed hard. She could turn her head—just a few inches and those lips would be on hers. If she were her old self, she would've done it. That girl didn't cower. That girl took chances.

But that girl wasn't her. Not anymore.

He pulled back before she could even attempt to get the nerve. He gave her that heartbreaker smile of his, though she could see the tiredness and strain lingering in his eyes, and stepped back onto her porch. The whole exchange had her wanting to reach out, run her hands along his jaw, and offer comfort—possibly of the naked variety. But all she could do was tell him good night and close the door.

When Georgia went upstairs a little while later, she tried to walk past the guest room without stopping in. But it was a siren call she couldn't shut off. After slipping into her oversized nightshirt, she padded barefoot into the dark guest room. A few lights went on and off in Colby's house, but eventually he appeared in his bedroom doorway. He shut his door and leaned against it. He ran a hand over his face in a fuck-my-life motion. It was the first time she could remember seeing him look so beat down. He headed into his bathroom. She knew she needed to close the curtains and go to bed, but she remained in her chair, somehow feeling less alone sitting here instead of in her room.

A few minutes later, she was rewarded with the sight of Colby stepping out of his bathroom with only a towel around his hips. His hair was still wet and his skin still damp. She picked up the binoculars. Colby turned off the overhead light, leaving his bedside lamp on, and then he glanced toward her window. Her heart stuttered for a second, but his gaze moved away as quickly as it had come. He undid the towel, exposing a backside that could inspire her to take up sculpting as a hobby, and tossed the towel into a hamper.

When he turned to the side, her magnified gaze tracked down his profile, tracing along the lines of his nose and jaw, going over his honed biceps and the cut of his hip, and then hovering on the hand he'd just wrapped around his quickly stiffening erection.

A shiver went straight through Georgia. She'd never seen him masturbate. She'd long ago assumed he did it in the shower or something. But tonight it seemed he had other intentions. She couldn't pull her focus away from that big hand of his stroking upward. She could see the flesh start to broaden in his hand, the head going a darker shade.

But right when she was getting lost in the show, he moved out of the binoculars' view. She quickly adjusted the focus, unzooming, and gasped when she realized he was looking right at her. She jerked back for a second, that *caught!* feeling racing through her. But of course he couldn't see her. He was just looking that way. Maybe he was thinking about her? The idea sent warmth stirring low.

She held her hands steady on the binoculars, watching as something flared in his eyes—desire, need, maybe a little loneliness, all of it was in that look. But the moment passed and he turned away, grabbing something from a bedside drawer—a bottle of clear liquid. Without pulling back the covers, he stretched out on his bed and took himself in his lubricated hand, stroking in long, luxuriating motions.

God. Georgia was going to fucking lose it.

The tip of her tongue touched the center of her lip as she let the desire wake up her body. This hadn't been her plan when she'd sat down in front of the window. She'd only wanted to see what kind of "friend" Colby had brought home. But now there was no way she'd be able to sit here and watch Colby pleasure himself without relieving the tension building between her thighs.

She kept her focus glued to Colby as she pulled open the drawer in the table that flanked the window and pulled out the small vibrator she'd stowed in there. She slipped her fingers inside her panties. She groaned under her breath at the feel of her touch and how wet she was already. Watching Colby flipped her switch like nothing else, it seemed. She turned the vibrator on to a low setting, which sent a shudder of pleasure up her spine, but she forced her eyes to stay open. Colby had cupped his balls with one hand and was sliding his fist along his shaft with the other. He didn't look to be in any kind of rush, and Georgia imagined it was her there giving him that slow, sensual pleasure instead—teasing him until he begged for more. She knew he'd feel heavy in her hands and hot. She could only imagine how he'd feel sliding inside her. It'd been so damn long . . .

The slowly weaved fantasy made her sex clench around the vibrator and her thighs tighten. She wouldn't last long at this rate. Her heartbeat was already pounding right behind her clit, the demand for release building. Colby looked to be getting closer as well, his movements speeding up and his thighs flexing.

She couldn't wait for him. Her body seized around the stimulation and orgasm rocketed through her. She panted her way through the hills and valleys of it, tasting sweat on her upper lip. But right as she was drifting down from her quick high, she caught movement at the edge of her view. She swung her binoculars to the left.

Colby's door had cracked open. A guy stepped a foot inside and his eyes went wide with an *oh, shit* expression as he realized what he'd walked in on. She couldn't gather much about him beyond that he was relatively young and really surprised before he backed up. Everything was happening too quickly. But Colby hadn't noticed the intrusion, apparently too lost in his final climb to release. Colby's guest went to shut the door but then hesitated, leaving a crack where Georgia could only make out half his face in the low light. He seemed frozen there as he stared at the man on the bed. Colby came in a rush, his release landing against his stomach and chest, and the guy hurriedly shut the door before Colby opened his eyes.

Colby was never the wiser. But Georgia knew.

For once, she wasn't the only Peeping Tom in the neighborhood.

SIX

Fuck, fuck, fuck. Keats cruised back to Colby's guest room at warp speed, almost tripping over his feet in his effort to get the hell out of the hallway. That walk to the bathroom had not gone as planned. Apparently, it was the second door on the *left*, not the right. He shut his door silently and then collapsed against it, his blood pounding at his temples . . . and much lower.

He slid to the floor, clasping his hands behind his neck. Jesus Christ. He had stood there way too long. He'd been a half second away from Colby seeing him. That would've been fun. *Hi, thanks for giving me a place to crash tonight. No, don't mind me while I turn into a total creeper and watch you jack off.*

God, what the hell was wrong with him?

He hadn't been able to look away. It wasn't like he didn't know how jerking off worked. He was rather fond of it himself. But realizing he was seeing Colby Wilkes without the teacher façade, just the man—naked—had frozen him in place. All the mixed-up feelings he'd had back in high school had rushed back in a flash. Back then, when he'd heard through the rumor mill that Mr. Wilkes sometimes dated guys, his mind hadn't been able to let that go. Images had popped into his head unbidden and relentless—followed by fantasies he would've never admitted to out loud.

He'd used those fantasies on a constant loop to get off back then, only to follow up with all the guilt and shame that rushed in afterward. And here he was, twenty-fucking-three years old and those stupid teenage urges wanted to well up—that old inner voice calling him a fag and a cocksucker and disgusting. Words his father had supplied but Keats's brain had latched onto.

He tapped the back of his head on the door. No. That wasn't him anymore. He no longer believed that backwoods shit his father had pounded into him. People could screw who they wanted to screw. But he was straight. The weird fantasies about Colby had been a fluke, some wires crossing because Colby had been the only person he'd trusted, and he'd wanted to be closer to him—had wanted those student/teacher boundaries keeping everything formal to disappear. That was all. As soon as he left home, those mixed-up feelings had faded away.

Keats liked women, bedded them regularly, and thoroughly enjoyed it. Plus, he'd been on the streets long enough and had gotten sick of married guys in expensive cars propositioning him with a fistful of cash and a hotel room key. Those offers had cured him of any thoughts of bisexuality.

But when he'd seen Colby step into his corner of the park tonight, all of that aversion seemed to fall away. A deep, whole-body response had taken over his brain. Keats was good at telling people to fuck off. And he sure as hell didn't take direction from anyone anymore. But if Colby had taken him up on his sarcastic offer of a blow job for a couple hundred bucks, Keats would've gotten on his knees for him for no cash at all and figured out how to do it.

The thought scared the shit out of him. He should've never come here. He'd humiliated himself in front of Colby—well, Mr. Wilkes back then—once before, reading too much into things and making a fool of himself. That was enough for one lifetime. Plus, he knew that Colby had let him off easy tonight. They'd eaten at Waffle House in near-silence. But Keats had no doubt that the questions would come tomorrow. What Keats had done back then was unforgivable on so many levels. And Colby had taken heat for it even though the guy had done nothing wrong. Keats had seen the not-so-subtle references in the news coverage when everyone was looking for him back in

Hickory Point. The young music teacher had fucked up and crossed lines with his poor, innocent student. Ha. If they'd only known the real story.

But now Keats was going to have to deal with the consequences if he stuck around. *Fuck.* That was the last thing he wanted to face. He eyed the neatly made bed in the middle of the room. The damn thing looked so fresh and inviting. Since he'd broken up with his last girlfriend a few weeks ago, he'd been back to paying week-to-week at the Texas Star Motel with the cash he made from the day labor jobs he picked up here and there. But tonight his ex's punk-ass brother had caught up to him, demanding money *she* owed him. Keats hadn't known Nina was running pills for her brother—or taking them. It'd been one of the reasons he'd broken it off with her. But now she was telling her brother, Hank, that Keats had taken off with her stash. And Hank wanted his grand back.

Hank and two other guys had cornered Keats earlier that day, catching him off guard. Keats knew how to fight, but he also wasn't stupid enough to take on three dudes who were probably armed and amped up on crank. He'd handed over his rent money, and Hank had *kindly* offered to give him until Wednesday to make his next payment. Fucking psycho.

So now he had two days to come up with at least another couple hundred bucks for Hank and more for rent. And, of course, it'd rained this morning so the construction work he'd been picking up hadn't needed guys today, which was why he'd resorted to his old standby of busking in the park. Playing his guitar was what he enjoyed most anyway. But until Colby had come along, he hadn't earned enough to even pay for another week at the motel.

The cash he had made was tucked in his pocket. It was enough for one night at least. He could sneak out now and save himself the drama of tomorrow. It'd be a dick move, but he doubted Colby really wanted him staying there anyway. He'd taken him home out of guilt, like a stray. But if he left now, he would never know if Colby really planned on giving him five hundred bucks. That wouldn't fix everything, but it could go a long way for him right now. And he didn't have to do anything for it but sleep in a comfortable bed and have an uncomfortable conversation. That was worth it, right?

His stomach flipped over. Maybe not.

The smart thing would be to sneak out. Colby probably wasn't going to give him the money anyway. He'd probably want to turn him in to the police as a former missing kid or something. Hell. No.

He got to his feet, planning to grab his shit and get out, when there was a knock on the door. His heart jumped in his throat at the sudden sound.

"Keats?"

Shit. He sent a quick plea to the universe that Colby hadn't seen him standing in his doorway. "Uh, yeah, come in."

The door opened and Colby stood on the other side, wearing a white T-shirt and a pair of basketball shorts, his hair still wet. His sheer size had always done something to Keats—a few inches taller than he was and broad as hell. But now that Colby wasn't close shaven and had let his hair grow a little longer, the effect was even more potent—like an untamed version of the teacher he used to know. Add to it the hint of color in his face, warmth Keats knew was a post-orgasm glow, and Keats was completely fucking distracted.

Colby handed him a thick white towel. Clothes were folded on top of it. "I thought you might want to shower before bed. The guest bathroom should have shampoo and soap in the cabinet beneath the sink. Feel free to use whatever." He nodded at the clothes. "Those are probably going to be too big, but the shorts have a drawstring, so you should be able to tighten them."

"Thanks, you really don't have to do this. I mean, I have some extra clothes in my backpack." Though most of it was dirty. He had planned to go to the Laundromat this morning before his unfortunate run-in with Hank.

Colby frowned. "They're probably wet from the rain. Leave them out here in the hallway and I'll toss them in the wash. Then you'll have your own stuff for tomorrow."

"You don't have to do my damn laundry," he said, scraping a

hand through his hair. Colby being nice to him was making him feel like an even bigger shitbag for wanting to sneak out. "I can handle things. In fact, I don't even know why I agreed to come here."

Colby leveled a gaze at him. "I don't suggest you get any ideas about leaving tonight. We made a deal. I expect you to honor it."

Keats turned away, his defenses rising in response to that don't-fuck-with-me look Colby was so good at giving. "Like you're going to give me five hundred bucks for nothing."

"The house alarm is on," Colby said, sounding tired. "So I'll know if you try to leave. I don't make a habit of holding people captive without their consent. But tonight, you gave me that right when you took my offer. I bought your time. Now it's mine until morning. So take a shower, put your dirty clothes out here, and go to bed. You do that, and you'll get the money you were promised. I don't break my word."

The way he'd said *mine until morning* had Keats's traitorous brain spiraling down a forbidden path. He pushed the ridiculous reaction down and replaced it with a safer one—sarcasm. "What the fuck is that supposed to mean? You keep people captive often?"

The corner of his mouth tipped up, revealing a dimple hiding beneath the scruff. "Never mind. Good night, Keats."

Keats watched him stroll back down the hallway and grimaced. So much for his brilliant escape plan.

Colby leaned against his kitchen counter, sipping coffee and watching bacon fry. This was normally the time he'd be getting in to school to start his workday. But he'd apparently entered some other dimension. Not only did he have no job to go to this morning, but now he had a smart-mouthed houseguest sleeping the morning away in the other room.

Fucking Keats.

Colby had been so goddamned relieved to find out Keats was alive. But seeing this hardened version of him was difficult to stomach. The kid he'd known had been a gentle soul—smart and a little shy, talented as hell. The songs he'd written in high school had shown a depth and ability that Colby hadn't seen in anyone that young since. But all of it had gone to shit because of stupid mistakes. Mistakes by Colby with how he'd handled things, how he hadn't seen the warning signs that Keats was reading more into their time together than he should. Mistakes by Keats's jackass father, who'd made it his mission to make his son feel worthless. And mistakes by Keats, who had run away instead of trusting the people who were trying to help.

Now where that gentle soul had been was a world-weary, angry guy who seemed to barely be getting by but was too mistrustful to accept any help from anyone. The whole thing made Colby want to punch something.

He flipped the bacon and heard movement behind him. Keats shuffled in, wearing only the shorts Colby had lent him. The sight jarred him for a second. He kept expecting to see the boy but kept finding a grown man there instead. The tattoos he'd noticed on Keats's forearms last night went all the way up—full sleeves of colorful ink, framing a lean but defined torso. Colby cleared his throat and looked away. "Mornin'."

Keats's bare feet smacked over the ceramic tile and he pulled out a chair at the bar. "You're going to burn that bacon. Heat's too high."

Colby glanced back at Keats and lowered the flame on the burner. "Bacon expert?"

He shrugged. "I worked the griddle at a breakfast joint for a while. You ruin enough bacon, you learn the tricks. Low and slow."

Colby grunted and turned back to the pan. "I usually microwave it, but I'm out of paper towels."

"Microwave?" Keats's chair scraped the floor, and he walked over to Colby, putting his hand out for the tongs. "I got it. You have any eggs?"

Colby was surprised to have his formerly hostile houseguest offering to take over breakfast, but he wasn't going to complain. Cooking wasn't exactly his strong suit. He handed over the tongs, grabbed a carton of eggs and some butter from the fridge, and dug a skillet out. Keats got the other pan going in no time, cracking the eggs one-handed.

Colby slid into the spot behind the bar to sip his coffee. Watching Keats from behind, his face obscured, made it easy to forget who was standing there. The tattoos alone were something to behold. They weren't rush jobs; they were art. Expensive shit by the looks of it. From this distance, he couldn't tell what all of it was, but he could see trailing music notes and scrawled words—probably lyrics if he knew Keats. Colby's gaze traced over the words and lingered on the way Keats's shoulder muscles moved as he shifted his attention between the pans—efficient, almost elegant. Colby forced his attention to his cup of coffee.

Having a half-naked guy in his kitchen wasn't a new occurrence. Even though Colby tended to gravitate toward women more often than not, he'd figured out pretty early on in his life that he didn't fit into a narrow lane when it came to sexual preference. It took him a little longer to figure out that besides attraction he only had two true requirements when it came to his bed partners—submissive and tough enough to handle what he liked to dish out. What was below the waist mattered a lot less to him than what was in someone's wiring above the neck. That was what got his blood pumping.

But none of that mattered right now. Beyond the fact that Keats had declared he wasn't into guys last night, this was *Keats*. A twenty-something-year-old guy he'd pulled off the streets. A former student. Off-limits.

Keats dished up a plate of eggs and bacon for them both and then stood at the counter to eat instead of taking the chair next to Colby.

"Thanks," Colby said, stabbing a piece of scrambled egg with his fork. "This looks great."

Keats poured himself a cup of coffee and dumped in sugar and a little cream. "No problem. I figured someone who microwaves bacon can't be trusted."

Colby smirked. "Are you still working as a cook?"

His gaze shifted down to his plate. "Nah, I quit the diner a while back when I got a gig at a tattoo shop. That was a good job—decent pay and the owner did my ink on the house. But then he got sick and they had to shut down, so lately I've been doing construction."

They ate in silence for a few moments and Colby was trying to figure out how best to approach that looming elephant in the room when Keats pointed his fork at the window behind Colby. "So what's with your neighbor?"

Colby glanced over his shoulder to see Georgia in her yard, picking through the remnants of the toilet paper he hadn't gotten to yesterday morning. "What do you mean?"

He swallowed his bite of eggs. "Nothing, just saw you hightail it over there last night, figured I'd interrupted plans or something."

"I was supposed to help her finish cleaning up, and I was going to bring burgers over but . . . got sidetracked last night."

"By me?"

"Eventually by you. But by whiskey first. Had a shitty day at work."

"How come?"

Colby pushed at his breakfast. "A student attempted suicide over the weekend."

Keats flinched. "Sorry. He okay?"

Colby blew out a breath, not sure why he was sharing any of this with Keats but unable to stop. "Yeah, thank God. But I've been put on leave since I was the last one to counsel him. His parents want an investigation."

"Counsel?"

Colby took another long sip of coffee. "Yeah, I'm a school counselor now. I went back for my master's after . . . after I left Hickory Point."

Keats's head lowered and he picked at the food on his plate. They stayed quiet for a few more minutes until Keats shifted on his feet and cleared his throat. "You lost your teaching job because of me."

Colby leaned back in his chair, the past pressing down on him with that, smothering him in the bright, airy kitchen. "No, I resigned. I knew the rumors wouldn't stop. And really, I didn't want to be there anymore anyway."

Colby wouldn't tell Keats that he'd been physically sick with grief for months, torturing himself with the constant *what if*s, wondering what could have saved Keats, and knowing, deep in his gut, that he'd handled things all wrong. He'd seen too much of himself in Keats and had wanted to be there for him. But he should've known that offering that level of open conversation could be misconstrued by a confused kid. He hadn't kept the boundaries clear enough. And that last night, when Keats had asked if Colby was bi, Colby had admitted that the rumors were true.

Looking back, it had been so inappropriate to share that. But he'd seen Keats tearing himself up for feelings and urges he was having, using his father's hateful language as a constant internal soundtrack. He and his dad had had a huge fight that final night, and his father had threatened to send Keats to military school.

Besides the regular music classes at school, Keats had been taking guitar lessons two nights a week with Colby. But that final evening, he hadn't shown up for his appointment at the rec center where they met. Late that night, he'd shown up on Colby's doorstep instead, carrying his broken guitar. Keats's father had smashed his son's most precious possession against the wall.

Colby had made the fatal error of letting Keats inside. Keats had spilled everything about the fight with his dad. His father had found a sheet of lyrics Keats had written—a song called "Off Limits" that had made it sound like Keats was in love with a boy. His father had flipped his shit, called Keats every disgusting name in the homophobe handbook, and had told him he'd rather be dead than have a fag for a son. Even when Keats denied that the song had anything to do with that—that it was really about how everything he loved to do, like playing music, was off-limits—his father hadn't listened. His dad wasn't going to be satisfied until his artsy son turned into what he wanted—a tough-as-nails "man's man" who would follow in his father's and older brother's footsteps into the Marines.

It had taken everything Colby had not to drive over to Keats's house and beat the stupid out of Keats's father. How could anyone look at Keats and not see how talented and amazing the kid was? But he'd controlled himself and had tried to be there for Keats as a sympathetic ear and to offer a safe place for him to express his feelings. But when Keats had asked him point-blank about his sexuality, Colby hadn't been able to lie. Instead of saying that wasn't an appropriate question to ask him, he'd been honest.

Colby had long suspected the kid was confused about his sexuality, and he'd wanted Keats to know that if he felt drawn to both guys and girls, he wasn't alone, that it was okay to have the feelings he did. That being a "real" man had nothing to do with who you were or weren't attracted to. But while Colby was busy trying to be Mr. Save the Day teacher, he'd been too stupid to realize that Keats's confused feelings were a lot less hypothetical and a lot more personal. Not until Keats had leaned over to kiss him had Colby realized how wrong everything had gone.

And he'd handled the whole situation in the most immature and dangerous way possible, reacting out of fear, thinking of self-preservation first. He'd shoved Keats away and asked him to leave.

And Keats had. For good.

"So you left there and came here to be a counselor," Keats said, breaking Colby out of his reverie. "Glutton for punishment?"

He huffed a quiet laugh. "Maybe."

"And now you're on leave because some kid tried to off himself?" Keats shook his head and ate his last bite of bacon. "I guarantee you they don't pay you enough to be held responsible for the decisions of teenagers. I remember what I felt like back then. I didn't know which way was up. No amount of talking or intervention would've made me change my mind about running away."

"I don't believe that," Colby said. "I screwed things up that night. I should've handled it differently."

"No." Keats shook his head, his gaze shifting away from Colby's. "You did what you needed to do so that you didn't get tossed in fucking jail. I was messed up and terrified of what my dad was going to do. You were nice to me, listened to what I had to say, and seemed to give a shit. My head got all mixed up about it and I thought that maybe if I kissed you, you'd let me stay there and not send me back home. Plus, I think I needed to find out if what I was feeling was really attraction. You know, that maybe the reason I felt so out of place all the time was because I was into guys or whatever. But it was just reaching for straws."

Colby considered him. "Was it?"

He shrugged. "Yeah. I haven't wanted to kiss a guy—or do anything else with one—since."

"So I scared you off guys for good. Good to know," he said, trying to lighten the mood and chase away the dark memories.

Keats met Colby's gaze for half a second. But whatever he had planned to say never made it out. He grabbed his plate and turned around to rinse it in the sink.

When he spun back around, he hitched a thumb toward the hallway. "Thanks for the breakfast. I'm going to grab my stuff and get out of here. You don't have to pay me the money. You don't owe me anything. Never did."

Colby didn't have time to respond before Keats had disappeared from the kitchen. But no way was this going to be the end of it. He hadn't gone through the trouble of taking Keats home only to drop him back off on the street this morning. Colby followed him down the hallway and stopped in the doorway to the bedroom.

Keats glanced up after pulling his T-shirt over his head, his expression going wary when he saw Colby standing there. "What?"

Colby leaned against the doorjamb and crossed his arms over his chest. "What if I told you there was a way to earn that five hundred dollars? Would you feel better about taking it?"

Keats's gaze flicked down Colby's body almost too quickly to detect, but the color that instantly dotted his cheeks gave him away. Colby knew what thought had first crossed Keats's mind. That Keats thought Colby would even go there irritated him. What irritated him even more was the answering ping that went through him at the thought.

Fucking hell.

"What do you have in mind?" Keats asked, tucking his hands in the back pockets of his jeans and trying to look nonchalant.

That was the wrong question. Colby didn't want to admit to himself what had flashed through his head. But even if Keats wasn't straight, Colby was smart enough to know it'd be a bad idea on so many levels to cross any of those lines. Beyond the fact that Keats was a former student and almost a decade younger than him, he no doubt still had a mountain of issues plaguing him. The guy needed a break, not more complications.

Colby managed to keep his expression neutral despite his errant thoughts. "Come with me."

When he turned, he half-expected Keats to ignore him and stay behind. But to his surprise, without hesitation or questioning Colby's intentions, Keats fell into step behind him. "Aye, aye, sir."

Blind trust.

He hadn't earned it. Not after how he'd let Keats down in the past. But Colby made a promise to himself right then and there that this time, he would be worthy of it.

SEVEN

Georgia was cursing all high schoolers who ever lived and the manufacturers of triple-ply toilet paper by the time late morning rolled around. She'd worked for two hours in the yard, trying to get all the wet soggy mess out of her shrubs and trees, but it seemed like the stuff multiplied. And the damage that had been done to her flower beds—she couldn't even think about the work it would take to get them back in shape. But hey, at least she'd spent hours outdoors without any panic attacks. She'd take that as a win. But by ten, she'd given up the effort and had gone inside to shower and write for a while.

She'd gotten one chapter under her belt in record time. Her main character, Haven, and her partner on the job, Mario, were having all kinds of sexual tension in this book, which was fun to write. Haven had walked in on Mario, finding him tied up in his hotel room, courtesy of the bad guys. After making sure they weren't in any immediate danger, Haven had enjoyed his state a little too much and had toyed with him mercilessly. Her badass heroine was discovering her vixen side in this book, and Georgia had Colby and her midnight viewings to blame for it. But she liked the layers it was adding to Haven's character, so she was going with it.

After the chapter, she had taken a break to look through résumés for virtual assistants, but right when she was about to email one, the doorbell rang. As usual, the sound sent an arrow of nerves through her, despite the fact that she knew doorbells rang in neighborhoods all day long. Packages, people hawking services, people preaching their religion of choice. It was a world of activity the nine-to-fivers were never aware of. But even so, her mind automatically shifted from green to yellow alert. With a sigh, she pushed herself away from her desk and went to the front door to check the peephole.

But it wasn't a delivery from the UPS guy. Instead, a familiar face greeted her. One she was beginning to get used to. She unlocked everything and swung open the door.

Colby smiled from beneath the brim of a Billy Bob's cap. "Hey, neighbor."

"Hey," she said, returning his smile. "What's up?"

"Sorry to interrupt. I'm sure you're working, but I wanted to give you a heads-up instead of just going for it," he explained.

She tilted her head as she tried to decipher his meaning. "Going for it?"

Colby cocked his thumb to the left and another man walked up her front steps to join Colby. "This is my friend Keats. Keats, Georgia."

Her gaze jumped to the newcomer, any stranger stirring distrust in her. But she realized it was Colby's houseguest. The guy had tied his hair back with a rubber band, but there was no mistaking the sleeves of tattoos that covered his arms. It was something Georgia wouldn't normally find herself drawn to. She'd never had a bad-boy complex. Okay, maybe she'd harbored a brief crush on David Beckham once upon a time. Whatever. But hell if it didn't look exactly right on this guy. This very beautiful guy.

Eyes the color of sea glass met hers, but he didn't offer a handshake, his hands staying firmly tucked in his front pockets. "Good to meet you, Georgia."

His voice was deeper than she expected, melodic with a dash of Deep South drawl, like liquefied butter. She wondered if he sang as well as played that guitar he'd been carrying last night. She had the urge to demand he sing a few notes of something. "Same here."

"So," Colby said, putting a hand on Keats's shoulder. "I'm lending

Keats's services and mine today to help you get your yard back in shape."

"What?" she said, looking between the two of them. "Oh, no, it's fine. I've been working on it. You don't need to put yourself out—"

"Well, actually," Colby said, "you'd be helping us out. I'm on a break from work and being bored drives me nuts. And Keats owes me a favor and is happy to work it off here. But I wanted to make sure you were okay with that because it's your yard."

She licked her lips. This was so out of her comfort zone, but the guys would only be in her yard. And she knew Colby well enough to know that he wouldn't let someone he didn't trust around. "I— well, I guess I could use the help."

"Fantastic." Colby grinned, and even Keats managed a hint of a smile. "I'm going to leave Keats here to start pulling the trampled stuff out of the flower beds while I run over to the garden center to grab some new flowers. I know a guy there who will give me a good price."

"Colby, you don't have to—" she started.

He held up a hand. "Not a problem. I'm no longer convinced this wasn't some of my students. We're the only two houses that got hit on the block, and another teacher texted me this morning saying her yard had been trashed, too, so I feel partially responsible."

"It's not your fault—even if it was your students."

Keats sniffed. "Colby has a tendency to feel responsible for his students' behavior. I'm not sure there's any convincing him otherwise."

Colby's smile went flat, and Georgia's eyebrows lifted at the instant shift in mood. There was a story there, but it wasn't her business. "Okay, I guess I'll just say thank you, then."

"You're welcome," Colby said, his good humor returning, and just like the night before, he leaned over and pecked her on the cheek.

She was still standing there slightly stunned when he jogged down her front steps, gave her a wave, and headed to his truck. When he pulled away, she was left standing there with Keats, a perfect stranger. For some reason, she couldn't muster up any true concern.

He was a few years younger than she was but taller and obviously fit, so he could easily be a threat to her. But there was something deep in her gut that told her he meant no harm.

"So," Keats said, breaking the awkward silence, "I have some of Colby's gardening stuff. I can go ahead and get started if you're down with that."

She cleared her throat. "Sounds good, just give me a sec and I'll get changed so that I can help."

His gaze slid over her gray thermal shirt and jeans, male appreciation flickering in them before he could hide it. "It's okay. You don't have to get dirty again on my account. We saw you working out here earlier. I don't mind flying solo."

His little flare of interest surprised her after what she'd witnessed last night. She'd figured he was into guys. It also surprised her how much it pleased her to be on the receiving end of it. Especially considering the man who'd just left was who she couldn't stop thinking about—or watching. But regardless, she suddenly didn't want to go back and sit alone in her office. The completely out-of-character urge made a little flutter of adrenaline go through her—a happy one. Maybe the baby steps were working.

"How 'bout this?" she said, feeling a seed of confidence for the first time in a while. "I'll go make us some iced tea, you get to work, and then you can tell me how you know Colby."

His lazy smile made her stomach tighten a little. Damn, this one could probably singe the panties off a girl if he turned on the charm full throttle. "I'm not sure that's a story you want to know. But I won't turn down the company."

"Deal."

She told him she'd be a few minutes and went back into the house to brew some tea. When she came back out, Keats was already on his knees in her front garden, pulling crushed plants from the beds with hands that looked used to hard work. He hadn't noticed her come back out yet, so she gave herself a moment to admire.

Keats wasn't brawny like Colby, but she could tell he was strong, the muscles on his arms working as he pulled at the roots of the plants. And where Colby was dark scruff, Keats was smooth and golden. Not baby-faced but definitely a glimmer of youth still lurking there. If not for the wariness in his eyes, the ink, and those battered hands, Georgia's starved libido probably would've labeled Keats as too young and too pretty. But when those few edges were added to the mix, she found herself unable to drag her gaze away.

He glanced up, shading his eyes with his hand. "Everything all right?"

"Huh?"

"You have a funny expression on your face."

Ha. Yes, the expression was called *inappropriately turned on by a complete stranger*. She cleared her throat and shook her head. Her lack of sex life was officially making her crazy. "Everything's fine, just got lost in thought for a sec."

She walked over and set the glass of tea near him and gave him a pair of gardening gloves, then settled onto the porch steps so he didn't feel like she was hovering over him.

He wiped his hands on a rag and took a long pull from the glass, his throat working in a rhythm that made her forget not to stare again. When he lowered the glass, he smiled over the rim. "Thanks for this. I haven't had fresh-brewed stuff in a while. I sometimes bring the bottled kind on jobs, but it's not the same."

She turned sideways and leaned against the railing so she could face him fully and let the breeze hit her heated face. "What do you do?"

He put the gloves on to get back to work while he talked. "Lately, construction when I can find it. But I mostly do whatever anyone will pay me to do. Cash is cash, you know?"

She frowned. No, she didn't know. Her parents had given her a comfortable life when she was growing up. And she'd done well for herself with her writing. She wasn't wealthy, but money had rarely been a concern. "And you like doing that kind of thing? The construction?"

He shrugged and glanced her way. "I *like* playing my guitar. I like performing my stuff. But people don't pay me money for that. Fun stuff doesn't pay rent."

She sipped her tea. "You never know. Colby gets paid to play his music. I get paid to write."

He snorted like the thought was the most ridiculous notion ever.

"You seem too young to be so cynical."

Those clear green eyes lifted. "I'm not that young, Georgia."

The implication in the words was obvious, and she had to sip her tea again to hide her reaction. What was it about this guy that got her skin tingly? She felt like some desperate housewife flirting with the too-young gardener. Maybe it was just the residual hum after writing sexy stuff all morning. "How young?"

"Twenty-three."

Seven years younger. Not an eternity in years, but in life experience, probably a helluva lot. Damn, why was she even doing the math? It wasn't like she was going to invite him in for a quick midday romp on the couch. She didn't even have the guts to invite him in for iced tea.

When she didn't respond, he filled the space. "So what's the story with you and Colby?"

The shift in subject broke the tension and the eye contact. She rubbed her lips together. "What do you mean?"

"You know what I mean," he said, digging again. "Is he going to come stomp me with those big-ass feet if he catches me flirting with his woman?"

She lifted an eyebrow in playful challenge. "Are you flirting?"

He grinned. "I was thinking about it."

Oh, this guy was trouble—of the tempting sort. "We're just neighbors."

"Uh-huh. He must be a really friendly neighbor to go through this much effort to fix your garden."

"He is." She set her glass down. "But you would know that since you're friends with him, right?"

"No, we're not really friends."

She frowned. "What do you mean?"

He sat back on his heels and looked over at her again, the gleam of sweat starting to shine on his face. "He used to be my teacher back in high school."

"Oh," she said, the answer catching her off guard and her mind rewinding to what she had witnessed last night. "And you two have kept in touch?"

"No, I hadn't seen him in six years actually until last night. We kind of stumbled into each other," he said, sitting down in the grass and reaching for his tea again.

"And you just went home with him?" The words were out before she could stop them.

He paused with his glass halfway to his mouth. "It's not like that."

"I'm sorry, I didn't mean—"

"Colby took me home for the same reason he's out getting flowers for you now. Apparently, he likes to help."

"You didn't have a place to stay?" she asked, her tactful switch turning off at the thought of Keats needing the roof-over-your-head kind of help.

He picked at a blade of grass. "Work has been nonexistent the last two weeks because of the rain. Rent's past due. Not a big deal. I always figure it out. But Colby made me an offer I couldn't refuse."

"He's paying you to do this today, isn't he?" she asked, the pieces coming together.

"Yeah," he said. "But he would've given it to me with no strings. I'm just not into taking a handout."

Georgia sat there for a few long moments, considering Keats as he pushed himself back into a kneel and returned to the gardening. She had no idea why she felt so damn comfortable around him, especially when he'd been flirty with her. Even the seventy-year-old mailman, who was clearly harmless, had made Georgia nervous when he told her how pretty she looked one particular day. But something about Keats had her wanting to reach out instead of shrink back.

An idea was forming in her head—one that was completely off

the wall and out of her comfort zone. But it hit her with such force that it was impossible to ignore. Keats clearly was struggling and probably had issues of his own if he was living job to job. She knew desperate people could do desperate things—steal, lie, whatever it took to survive another day. A person like that wasn't someone she should feel so relaxed around. But long-dormant forces were rallying in her, pushing her toward the plan anyway.

She scuffed the toe of her tennis shoe along the porch railing, trying to talk herself out of it. But before she could get the words out one way or another, Keats yelped.

Her attention snapped upward to find Keats jumping up and shaking the leg of his pants. Fire ants were racing over him. She hopped up, knocking her glass over.

"Shit, shit, shit," he said, trying to shake them off, as they no doubt bit the hell out of him. "Get water. A hose or something."

Georgia glanced toward the side of the house, but her hose was tucked away in the garage since she'd had a sprinkler system installed. Without thinking, she grabbed Keats's arm. "Come on. Now."

In a rush, she shoved open her front door and led a cursing Keats inside. The downstairs bathroom didn't have a shower, so despite her hammering heart, she guided him upstairs. Ants were falling in a trail behind him, but she'd deal with that later. They got to the top of the stairs in record time. She shoved the door to the guest bathroom open and turned on the shower.

Keats was already jumping in despite the icy-cold water. "Fuck. They're going higher."

He went for the button on his jeans before Georgia could even process what he was doing. The jeans came off in a rush, leaving Keats standing under the spray in a pair of black boxers. He kicked the jeans to the other side of the tub, his motions frantic, and brushed at the ants with his hands.

Not knowing what else to do, Georgia reached for the handheld shower attachment, turned it on the blow-your-head-off setting, then aimed it at Keats's legs. Finally, the ants started to fall off and swirl toward the drain. But a few of them were determined to hold on.

"Shut the curtain," Keats said, his words frantic. "No way these bastards are going any higher."

"What?"

"Curtain," he said through clenched teeth, and she got it.

"Oh, right." She yanked the curtain closed and heard more wet clothes hit the bottom of the tub.

While more cursing ensued from the other side of the curtain, Georgia worked hard at not going into a panic. Someone was in her house. A man. Someone she didn't know. No one had been inside besides one repairman since she'd moved in. But the adrenaline pumping through her seemed less to do with her safety and much more to do with the fact that Keats was naked on the other side of that thin shower curtain.

She occupied herself with stomping the stray ants that had fallen onto the floor, while Keats washed off the last of the little demons. She rubbed the back of her neck, trying to fight off the tension, and heard a long sigh from Keats. "You okay?"

"Well, they didn't get to the no-fly zone, so there's that."

"Can you tell if you have a lot of bites? They're poisonous and too many can be serious and maybe you need a doctor and maybe—"

The curtain shifted, cutting her off, and Keats stuck his head out, a half smile on his dripping wet face. "All I need right now is a towel."

"Oh, right, sure." She opened the cabinet below the sink and handed him a fresh towel.

She turned to leave, but he was already stepping out of the shower before she got there. The towel was secured around his waist, but everything else was bare. A flash of desire stabbed her.

"I . . ." she said, searching for something to say and trying to keep her eyes on his face instead of on the smooth muscles of his chest and those tattoos that currently looked very wet and lickable. *Stop it.* "I think I have some cortisone cream around here. You're probably going to need it."

Keeping one hand holding the towel, he used the other to take the rubber band out of his wet hair. "Georgia—"

But before he could say anything more, there were heavy footsteps on the stairs and someone else calling her name. Her heart leapt against her ribs, and she stepped out into the hallway. Colby was trundling up the stairs, his features pinched with worry. When he saw Georgia, his fierce expression relaxed. "Jesus, I saw the door wide open and a broken glass and both of you were gone. I got worried. What—"

Of course, Keats took that moment to step out of the bathroom in his half-naked, still-wet ensemble. Colby's eyes went wide.

And everything came crashing down around Georgia.

EIGHT

"What the hell?" Colby didn't know what to make of finding Keats sopping wet and mostly naked in Georgia's hallway. He hadn't been gone *that* long. The guy couldn't work that fast, especially with someone as standoffish as Georgia. And if he'd managed to—

"Georgia," Keats said, his worried voice breaking through the theories racing around in Colby's head. "Are you okay?"

Colby followed Keats's gaze. Georgia had backed up against the wall, her eyes were closed, and her chest was moving at a way-too-rapid rate.

Keats put a gentle hand on her shoulder. "Georgia?"

She flinched at the touch and shrank back farther again, her palms pressing against the wall behind her. Keats moved his hand away, giving her space.

Colby inched closer. "Georgia, hey, sweetheart, it's okay. Are you having an asthma attack?"

She shook her head, a quick, darting movement. Her eyes remained tightly shut.

Keats sent Colby a what-the-fuck-do-we-do look, and Colby's training kicked in. "Keats, run downstairs and see if you can find a paper bag, something for her to breathe into. She's hyperventilating."

"Right." Keats snapped into action and jogged past Colby.

Sweat had broken out on Georgia's skin, and her chest continued to heave. Colby had dealt with this a few times before—recently, with a submissive trainee at The Ranch who turned out to be claustrophobic in restraints. "Georgia, I need you to try to slow your breathing if you can. Are you having a panic attack?"

A quick, tight nod. Her fingers curled against the wall.

"Okay, it's all right," he said, trying to keep his voice calm and even for her. "Keats is going to get something to help, but I want you to listen to me and try to take a deep, slow breath. You're okay. You're safe. Panic can't hurt you."

To her credit, she gave it a shot. He saw her puff up for it. But she was too far gone, and her breaths turned even more rapid. Tears slipped down her cheeks. Then she swayed on her feet, and he realized she was going down. He lunged forward and got his hands on her before she collapsed to the floor.

Her eyelids fluttered open, then shut again. She was still conscious, not deadweight in his arms, but she was probably dizzy as shit from the lack of air and the panic. "It's all right. I've got you."

He got his arms situated beneath her back and knees and lifted her against his chest. Keats charged up the stairs with an empty pharmacy bag. "Oh shit, did she pass out?"

"Not yet, but we need to get her lying down." He held her tight to him, but her body was still jerking with the quick breaths.

Keats hurried past him and pulled open the first door in the hall. But it was a linen closet. "We need a couch or a bed."

Keats swung open the next door, revealing a small guest room. "In here."

Good. That'd be better than invading her personal space in her master bedroom. But when he carried her in and saw a set of binoculars on a small table next to the window and a small bullet vibrator, he realized he'd seriously failed on the personal space issue. This wasn't just a guest room, this was *the* room—the one she watched him from. A twist of desire went with that image, his libido having no decency when it came to appropriate time and place to get fired up. But he ignored it and focused on the task at hand. Georgia needed to lie down and get her breath back. He'd worry about the awkwardness this might cause later.

The bed was made, so he laid her atop the mint green comforter, and Keats put the bag up against her mouth.

"Breathe, it's going to be okay. We've got you," Keats said, brushing her hair off her damp forehead in a tender gesture.

Georgia exhaled into the bag and blinked her eyes open long enough to give Keats a grateful look.

Colby frowned, a kick of jealousy going through him. Jealousy and something else. Watching the two of them share a little moment, Keats half dressed and Georgia lying in bed, had his thoughts going in a dangerous direction again. He shoved the thoughts aside. Clearly, it'd been too long since he'd had someone in his bed. His brain was in one-track mode.

Focus.

The sound of the crinkling bag was the only noise for a few minutes, but to Colby's relief, Georgia's breathing started to regulate. "That's it."

When the breaths became long and steady, Keats left the room for a minute. He came back wearing a fluffy purple robe and carrying a wet washcloth. He kneeled next to the bed and wiped Georgia's cheeks and forehead with gentle swipes, then folded the cloth and put it over her eyes.

Keats gave Colby a pointed look, then cocked his head toward the table. Colby didn't waste a second. He slid away from the bed and discreetly tucked the vibrator into the half-open drawer of the side table. He eased it closed, hoping Georgia would think that was where she'd left it. He had a feeling she'd be mortified if she knew what they'd seen.

He stepped back toward the bed just as she was lowering the bag and pulling the towel away. Her dark eyes were clearer than they had been, but the set of her mouth was weary, like all her energy had been sapped. "I think I'm okay now."

Colby reached out and gave her hand a squeeze. "Glad to hear it."

She slowly pushed up onto her elbows. Her gaze skittered over to the table behind Colby. Worry flared there in her eyes, but when she looked back to him and apparently read no awareness on his face, she relaxed a bit. He could almost hear her thoughts. *Phew, he hasn't seen them yet.*

She glanced at Keats. Her lips curved into a shaky smile when she saw him in her robe. "That's a good look for you."

Keats peered down at his purple ensemble and grinned. "I was having trouble keeping that towel on. I didn't want to make you hyperventilate again. Or traumatize Colby."

Colby snorted and she smirked. "That scary?"

"No, that impressive," he said solemnly.

Georgia pressed her hand to her forehead and shook her head. "Shameless."

Colby clamped his lips together, trying not to laugh. The shy Keats he'd known before had definitely left the building. He was charming the panic right out of Georgia.

Georgia peeked over at Colby and reached for his hand. "Thank you for catching me. They usually don't make me that dizzy. Everything in my vision flipped upside down."

He brought her hand to his mouth and pressed a kiss to the top of it. "Happy to help. Do you get those often?"

Her gaze slid away, but she nodded.

"I'm sorry if I startled you coming up the stairs. I thought something was wrong. I didn't realize what—well, I still don't know what was going on."

"Ants," Keats supplied. "A shit-ton of red ants attacked me in the yard. I must've kneeled in a pile. Georgia hustled me up here before the damn things could eat me alive. But they were all over my clothes so I had to strip them off."

"Oh."

"And I'm sorry about . . . all of this," Georgia said, sitting up in the bed. "It wasn't that you startled me. It's just"—her jaw twitched and she looked down at her hands—"I don't let people inside my house. I have . . . issues with that. I didn't think about it when Keats needed help, but when that part was over and you came up the stairs, it all hit me."

Colby kept hold of her hand, not entirely shocked by the revelation.

He'd realized early on that Georgia didn't like to leave her house. She didn't even step into his yard. So it wasn't too far of a stretch to realize her anxiety extended to people coming into her space as well. "I'm really sorry. I would've never come inside without permission."

She shook her head. "It's okay. This is beyond embarrassing. I hate what this does to me. I mean, normal people can have neighbors over."

Keats frowned. He probably felt the same way Colby did about the word *normal*. What the hell was normal? Fuck normal.

"But maybe this was good," she continued. "Like pulling off a really big Band-Aid. Because look, you're both still here, and I'm not a panting maniac anymore."

Colby could think of better ways to turn her into a panting maniac, especially with two guys and a bed—and maybe that vibrator, but he should probably be struck down for having that thought at the moment. "It's one way to do it. Like guerrilla exposure therapy. The room full of spiders for the arachnophobe."

She shuddered. "Yeah, I think I'll just keep my fear of spiders then, thank you very much."

Keats smiled. "Ditto. And add fire ants to that list. I've had enough exposure therapy for one day. A few more minutes with my pants on and I might have lost my ability to father children."

Colby chuckled. Fire ants in your underwear. Now there was a thought to inspire nightmares. He had a feeling he'd missed the ant version of the *Tommy Boy* "Bees!" scene when Keats had discovered he was being attacked.

"So," he said, standing up and putting his hand on the back of Keats's neck, making sure neither of them turned toward the binoculars. "How about I go grab this guy some clothes and we get out of your hair for a little while so you can rest?"

Georgia rubbed her hands on her jeans in what looked to be a calming gesture before she stood, revealing that maybe she wasn't as easy-breezy as she was pretending to be. "Yeah, okay. I have rogue ants to clean up anyway."

"Do you need any help?" Keats asked.

She reached out and squeezed his arm, giving him a warm smile. "No, you both have done enough. Thanks for not making me feel like an idiot."

When she leaned over and kissed Keats's cheek, Colby had to fight hard not to show his surprise. It was so un-Georgia-like. But she wasn't done. She stepped over to Colby, pushed up on her toes, bracing a hand on his shoulder, and gave Colby one, too.

It took everything he had not to put his hands on her and pull her closer, inhale that coconut scent he only got a brief whiff of during the kiss. "Our pleasure, gorgeous."

They all walked downstairs together, but soon Keats and Colby were back outside. Georgia locked up behind them, and Colby and Keats headed next door to get Keats some clothes. But as soon as they walked into the kitchen, Keats spun around and crossed his arms. The stance might have had a shot at looking tough if not for the purple robe. "Well, *that* was interesting."

"That's one word for it," Colby said, rolling the tension out of his shoulders. "Thanks for the towel thing, by the way. Saved a potentially awkward situation."

"No problem. I didn't want to embarrass her," he said with a shrug. "Not that she should be embarrassed—I mean, how hot is that? But you know how girls can be. And dude, the binoculars? Does that window . . ."

"It looks into my bedroom."

"Fuck," he breathed, putting his hand over his heart. "That's so damn dirty. I think I'm in love."

Colby laughed. "She's not spying on *you*."

"An epic tragedy," he said with a grin. "Maybe we should switch rooms. I'm happy to give her a show."

Colby leveled him with a look, and Keats laughed.

"No, but seriously, are y'all hooking up?"

Colby leaned against the counter. "At this point, we're just friends."

"So that's why you gave me the eat-shit-and-die look when you saw me walk out of the bathroom?"

Colby smirked. "No, that was my what-the-fuck look, not

eat-shit-and-die, there's a difference. I knew before today that Georgia had some issues with people being in her space. I guess I feel a little protective of her and when I saw you there in her house, practically naked, I had no idea what to think."

"I'm skilled, Colby, but not that skilled. Even I can't get a girl in bed that fast."

Colby laughed. "You're better than you think. She likes you."

"Maybe, but she *watches* you. And apparently enjoys the show." Keats lifted himself to sit on the island, apparently forgetting he only had a robe on or not caring. The flaps fell open, revealing his chest all the way to his navel, where a light trail of hair tracked downward. "Doesn't matter anyway. She thinks I'm too young."

Colby pulled his gaze upward and focused on Keats's face. His libido was already on a hair trigger today; he didn't need any extra encouragement. He had to keep reminding himself that this was *Keats*, his former student, a straight guy, and not some submissive at The Ranch trying to get his attention by parading around half naked. "You *are* too young."

Keats scoffed. "You're always going to see me that way, aren't you? The innocent, helpless student. Well, news flash, Teach. It's been a long time since you've known me. I'm far from helpless and definitely not innocent."

Colby laced his hands behind his neck and sighed. "Why does it matter how I see you?"

He shrugged, dropping some of the attitude. "I don't know. It just does."

"What do you want me to say, Keats?" he asked tiredly. "That you're a grown-up? That you're a man? That you're of fuckable age for my dear neighbor? Fine. You are. But that doesn't mean you still don't have a lot to learn."

Keats leaned back on his hands, preening like a peacock. "Yeah? And what exactly do you think I need to be taught? I haven't had any complaints from women."

Colby watched him, half amused by the cockiness. "Being a man has a lot more to it than knowing how to get someone off in bed. And I promise you, at twenty-three, you don't know how to do that as well as you could either."

He lifted a brow. "And you do?"

"You have no idea," Colby said smoothly. "But that's not the point. If you're going to chase after women in their thirties, like Georgia, they're going to want you to have some stability, some discipline in your life. And I'm guessing your current situation doesn't allow for much of that."

His jaw tensed and he looked down at the tie on the robe. "Yeah, well, the job market for a high school dropout doesn't exactly allow for a lot of stability—unless you run drugs, sell women, or like to suck cock for cash. I've heard those career paths pay well."

Colby gritted his teeth at that image. Thank God Keats hadn't resorted to those lines of work yet. "I get it. I know how shitty a situation you had growing up. But now you're an adult. Do you plan to live the rest of your life like you're doing? Just getting by week to week?"

The defensive mask descended over his features. "Did you forget who you're talking to? I ran away. This *is* my fucking life. That bed's already made."

"Bullshit. You can always change your direction." Colby should know. He'd done it.

Keats scoffed. "Right. Let me just dial up that fairy godmother, and she can wave a wand for me."

"Fine. You want a wand? Here it is," Colby said, crossing his arms and throwing down the gauntlet. "Come stay with me for a while."

Keats's eyes flickered with surprise, and he straightened. "What?"

"You heard me. I have an extra room. Use it."

"I can't do that. I'm not that kid looking for his teacher to solve his problems anymore. I don't want to be your charity case again."

Colby rubbed the spot between his eyebrows, pressure building there. "Look, Keats, I get the whole pride thing, but pride can birth stupidity. I'm offering help. Take it."

Keats slid off the counter and pulled his robe more tightly around him, closing off. "I need to get dressed."

"Keats."

"Thanks for the offer. But I just want to get some clothes on, get this garden done, and go home. I've got shit to take care of," he said, reaching down to scratch his calf.

Colby knew he'd reached the end of Keats listening to anything he had to say. He'd gone into shutdown mode. Colby glanced down when Keats scratched again, noticing for the first time the red, swelling bumps on Keats's legs and feet. "Those are getting worse. Are you allergic?"

"Not any more than anyone else." Keats reached down for bites on his other leg. "I'll be fine. Just let me throw on some clothes, and I'll meet you outside."

"No, if you come back out in the sun, they're going to itch even more. Why don't you take some antihistamines—there should be some in the hall closet—and then go soak your legs in cool water. I can finish up the rest."

"But you're paying me—"

"You've earned your keep. Consider it hazard pay for the ant bites." Reluctantly, he added, "And I'll be back in a while to bring you home."

But when Colby checked on him later to make sure the reaction hadn't gotten worse, Keats was sprawled across the bed in the guest room, sound asleep. The bites didn't look too bad, so Colby closed the curtains, threw a blanket over him, and let him sleep.

He lingered in the doorway for a moment more than necessary. Only a few more hours and Keats would be gone.

Colby didn't know whether to be relieved or damn disappointed. Fuck.

NINE

It's only a few steps. That was what Georgia repeated in her mind as she crossed the invisible barrier from her yard into Colby's, but nerves crackled through her like static anyway. After the incident from earlier, they had never really gone away. Beyond the residual effects of the panic attack, she'd been unable to stop wondering whether Colby had seen the binoculars in the guest room. He hadn't said anything or acted any differently than normal, but he was a counselor. Part of that job was keeping a poker face when you heard or saw outrageous things. That he might've discovered her secret had freaked her out to the point of nausea. So she'd given in and taken an anxiety pill, which combined with the drained adrenaline from the panic attack had promptly put her to sleep. When she'd woken up, her yard had been perfectly restored and Colby and Keats were gone.

She'd put in an emergency call to Leesha to offload everything that had happened that day. It was the benefit of having a best friend who was also a therapist. She could tell her things she'd be way too embarrassed to tell a stranger. But even so, it'd been a hell of a hard thing to admit aloud that she'd been spying on her neighbor. Leesha had hardly flinched and had assured her that, considering her *isolated* situation, it wasn't *completely bizarre* that she had resorted to that kind of behavior. Plus, she'd added that considering Phillip had watched Georgia without her permission, this was a subconscious way for her to feel in control—by being the one doing the watching. *Whatever.* Georgia had rolled her eyes and demanded that Leesha drop the therapist hat and be the girl she'd known since grade school. This wasn't a session.

At that, Leesha had broken into a conspiratorial grin, called her a dirty bird, and asked for a full description of how hot her neighbor actually was. Georgia had growled into the webcam. "Leesh, pay attention. He. May. Know. Did you hear that part? What the hell am I supposed to do? He probably thinks I'm some pervy stalker girl."

She'd shrugged. "Feel him out. Maybe he didn't see anything. And if you find out he knows, do the right thing and apologize."

So now it was time to do the right thing. And that thing involved moving out of her barricaded comfort zone and womaning up. She was trying to channel some alternative version of herself with each step. *I am strong. I am in control. I own this moment.* Goddamn, she sounded like that guy Stuart Smalley from the old episodes of *Saturday Night Live.* Pitiful. She clutched the casserole dish in her hands like it'd save her from some impending doom and kept putting one foot in front of the other. Only a few more steps.

The porch light was on and Colby's truck was still in the driveway, so she knew he was home. She had no idea if Keats was still there. Maybe Colby had taken him back home. She hoped not. She had a feeling Keats wasn't going back to a happy situation, and he'd been so kind helping her earlier today. She didn't want to think about him struggling to keep afloat. Plus, she'd never had a chance to ask him that question she'd started when the ants had attacked. Maybe she could help.

Her heart began to pound harder as she walked up Colby's sidewalk, but she managed to keep her breathing even. She pictured an aerial view of her house in her mind—one of Leesha's visualization exercises—and imagined her house was a green zone, the safe zone, that stretched to the edges of her property. With some effort, she pictured that circle expanding, the green creeping wider and enveloping Colby's yard and house. This was just an extension of her space, nothing to get freaked-out about. She prayed that the image would convince her faulty wiring that all was good in the 'hood.

When she reached the door without drama, she wanted to do a victory dance. But the harder part was yet to come. She balanced the dish in one hand and raised the other to knock. *Here we go. Be cool.*

Colby answered a few seconds later, barefoot in track pants and a snug white T-shirt, obviously fresh from the shower. He didn't bother hiding the surprise on his face. "Oh, hey. Everything all right?"

She stared at him for a few seconds, nerves stealing her voice, but she made herself swallow and speak. Unfortunately, everything came out at once. "Yes, everything's fine. I fell asleep and when I woke up, I saw the yard, and it's . . . beautiful. And I wanted to tell you that I really appreciate everything. Not just the yard but earlier. And I thought you might be hungry since you probably worked through lunch and so I made enchiladas. They're chicken, and you like burgers, so I'm assuming you're not vegetarian and—"

The slow, broad smile that crept onto his face stopped her mid-ramble. He leaned against his door frame, arms crossed over his chest. "You're on my porch, Ms. Delaune."

She pressed her lips together and inhaled a breath, trying to slow her heartbeat. "I needed to talk to you, and I wanted to thank you."

"I can't think of a better thank-you." He reached out and pushed his door open wider. "Want to come inside to do the talking?"

Her gaze darted past his shoulder, taking in the spacious living room behind him, all done in soft browns and tans. The TV played ESPN but the volume was all the way down and a half-full beer sat on the coffee table. It looked comfortable and welcoming. So much of her wanted to go inside. But she hadn't been inside another person's house in over a year, and it felt a little like standing on the edge of a cliff with shifting soil. "I'm not sure."

He reached out and took the casserole dish from her and set it on a table by the door. Then he held out both his palms to her. "Here, let's try this. I won't ask questions because it gives your mind too much time to analyze. Just listen and follow my instructions. If any of it becomes too much, you say *stop* and I'll shut up. Deal?"

She nodded, not giving herself time to think about it. "Okay."

"Now take my hands and step inside. It's getting cold outside and it's warm in here. I don't want you to be cold."

She placed her hands in his large ones, and he tugged her gently, easing her forward like a parent teaching a toddler to walk.

"Plus, I have no idea what temperature to cook this in the oven, so I need your help," he continued.

Another step.

"And God knows we don't want Mrs. Benson across the street gossiping about us, so we need to get where she can't see us." His dimple appeared.

Another step. She was inside. He bumped the door with his foot to shut it behind her. The click of it closing sounded as loud as a thunderclap in her head. Her fingers curled into his palms. "Keep talking."

"And for the record, I'm about as far from a vegetarian as one can get. I put meat on top of my meat."

She snorted.

"Right, good point, probably shouldn't talk about my meat."

Now she couldn't stop a laugh from bubbling up. She took another step. And another. She kept her gaze on Colby and that reassuring smile of his. Wood floorboards sounded beneath her shoes, then the soft hush of an area rug.

Soon, Colby stopped moving, but her momentum carried her forward another step into his personal space. He bent and put his lips close to her ear. "Congratulations, neighbor, you've made it all the way to the couch without a scratch."

She straightened and turned her head, surprised to see she was already in the middle of the living room and far from the front door. She'd only been watching him, focusing on his eyes and voice, and somehow he'd coaxed her all the way inside without her panic switch being triggered. She was in someone else's house.

And she was *okay*.

"Holy shit. We did it!" Her voice was way too loud but she didn't care.

"*You* did it."

"I can't even believe—thank you." Victory surged in her, and without thinking, she put her hands on his shoulders and kissed him right on the lips. *Smack!*

He stiffened for a half second, obviously caught off guard, and she hopped back, putting her hand to her mouth. "Oh crap, I didn't—I'm sorry."

He smiled and tilted his head in challenge. "Are you?"

She blinked. An auto-response jumped to her lips. *Retreat, retreat, retreat.* But she didn't let the cowardly words come out. She steeled herself, reaching deep for the old seeds of confidence, and held his gaze. "Okay, no, not really. I've kind of been wanting to do that for a while."

"Yeah?"

She rolled her lips inward, feeling giddy for some reason—probably some combination of residual anxiety and the rush of breaking that boundary and kissing him. "Yeah."

"Want to do it again?"

She laughed, but nerves were trying to push in. "I don't know, I mean—"

He reached for her belt loop and tugged her gently forward, his affable expression morphing into something far more intent as he looked down at her. "Because I'd like to kiss *you* again. Really kiss you. But I'm not going to until you tell me it's okay."

She nodded, trying to swallow past the fear bubbling up. "It's okay."

His hazel eyes searched hers. "Remember how I told you on the walk over here that you could say *stop?*"

She breathed through the butterflies trying to overtake her insides. "Yes."

He moved his hand to cup her jaw, his fingertips brushing gentle lines along her neck. The soft, simple touch had her ready to melt on contact. *God.* Every part of her felt so starved for touch it was as if her neurons couldn't make sense of it. Everything firing off in all directions—want, need, fear, anticipation. His eyes traced the curves of her face. "That applies to this, too."

With that, he lowered his head. The moment his lips touched hers she could tell that this was not going to be a quick peck like she'd given him. This was going to be so much better. Her eyelids fell shut as his mouth met hers with a gentleness that belied the intensity she'd seen in his eyes. The kiss was so tender, so softly sensual, that she thought she would die from the slow burn of the connection. Colby Wilkes, a man in no hurry. He teased her bottom lip with a playful tug and then took it between his. The tip of his tongue grazed the line of her lips, but he didn't push or deepen the kiss yet. It was a taste, a sip of what he could give her.

Her hands went to his chest, feeling the solid muscle and a quickly beating heart beneath her palms. His T-shirt curled in her fingers and a soft sound escaped her—her starved libido begging on her behalf. *Please, sir, may I have some more?*

He continued to kiss her, and the hand against her hip tightened as he guided her against him, bringing her body flush with his. That was when she opened her mouth to him, inviting a deeper, more all-encompassing kiss. Like walking into a bakery after a juice fast, she wanted to gorge on *all* the things, taste everything he could give her. Not just a sample. But after a gentle twining of their tongues, he eased back. "I can't tell you how long I've wanted to do that."

She blinked, off balance for a second, already missing the feel of his lips, the brush of his beard against her skin. *Please don't stop.* She feared if she paused, her broken brain would take over and ruin it. "You don't have to stop."

He smiled, that dimple flashing again, and squeezed her hip. "I do."

"Why?" she asked, her frustration flaring.

"Because you came here to talk to me," he said, lines of strain appearing around his eyes, proving that it wasn't exactly easy for him to dial back either. He pushed a stray hair off her forehead. "And I know it was a difficult challenge for you to come here. So if I push you too far too fast, the panic might catch up, and we'll do more harm than good."

"Sounds way too logical and smart," she declared. "I hate that."

He chuckled and put his hands over hers, which were still

clinging to his shirt. He lifted them and kissed her knuckles. "How about you tell me what I need to do with those enchiladas, then we'll talk? If you still want me to not stop later, I promise to throw all logic out the window."

"Deal," she said with a smile. "And it's twenty minutes in a three-hundred-and-fifty-degree oven, then a minute or two under the broiler at the end to brown the cheese."

"I can handle that." He released her and guided her down to the couch. "Sit and relax. I'll be right back. What do you want to drink? I've got beer, red wine, and soda."

"A beer would be great."

"You got it." He changed the station on the TV to one that played mellow contemporary music, then grabbed the dish of enchiladas and disappeared into the kitchen. The fact that he hadn't put on the country station made her smile because it was obviously for her benefit. She knew that was his drug of choice—old-school country. It was what he played at the bar—not that she'd ever gotten to hear him play live. But they'd talked about it one day when they'd both been outside in their yards. He'd rattled off a few names of his favorite singers and bands, and she'd only heard of one or two.

Afterward, she'd gone to her computer and Googled him, finding a few YouTube videos of performances, most of them old footage, a few recent. Apparently, he'd been a bit of a big deal when he was younger—a guy on the brink of breaking out. But he'd disappeared from the scene for some unknown reason. She'd played those videos, transfixed, watching them more than once in true stalker style. He had a singing voice so deep, she'd wanted to roll around in it. Even when he sang songs about things she had no personal connection to—growing up in a small town, falling in love with a girl, and stirring up trouble—the music had resonated with her in a way no other kind had because of the way Colby had sung the lyrics. Honesty bled into his performances, and he had a voice that could make the most frigid chick go liquid. She'd become quite a fan. But, of course, he had no idea. Just as he had no idea about her other stalker-like activities . . .

She sighed. With him gone, her mind kicked into gear again, dimming some of the heady high of the kiss. She was in Colby's living room. And had kissed him. The reality was hard to believe. On her list of small steps she hoped to move through to get herself healthy for the trial, she'd just jumped from number two to like number six hundred. She glanced out the side window to find her house staring back at her like a sentinel awaiting her return. That was the extent of her whole world sitting next door. Sure, she managed to go out once a week and get her groceries and take care of necessities, but it was always a white-knuckle day made possible by her medication. That house was the only place she could exist without the crushing anxiety. Both a sanctuary and a prison.

But here she was, finally sitting outside it. Exhilarated. Terrified. Leesha was going to shoot a confetti gun when she found out. Georgia clasped her hands in her lap, her thumb rubbing her palm in a slow, methodical motion—up and down, up and down—an unconscious habit that soothed her. As long as she didn't think about this too hard, she wouldn't lose it. Colby had been right about that part. As soon as he'd started giving her instructions, she'd been able to focus on simply following and shutting down the racing part of her brain. She'd never thought she'd be able to hear commands from a man without thinking of Phillip, but with Colby it felt different—less of an affront to her free will and more an act of caring direction. It'd been a little like the yoga she did some mornings. Shut the mind down and listen to the teacher on the video tell you how to breathe and move.

Except yoga didn't involve a big, sexy man and a kiss that'd been hotter than sin on Sunday.

Colby returned to the living room a few minutes later and handed her a Heineken before sitting next to her on the couch. "All right, dinner's in the oven. Thanks for putting that together. It was going to be a PB&J night."

"No problem. I like to cook." Well, she'd *learned* to like it. Back in Chicago, it had been all about eating out. The food was to die for in the city, and she'd taken full advantage of it. But now she didn't have that option. After moving here, she'd missed going out to restaurants and had gotten tired of microwave meals and delivery, so she'd decided if she couldn't manage to go out anymore, she'd learn how to make her favorites at home via her friend the Food Network.

Colby shifted on the couch so that he was facing her and leaning back on the arm of it. "So what did you want to talk to me about?"

Hell. Talking. That was what she'd come over here for. But she certainly wasn't ready to tell him her secret now. Not after that kiss. It'd ruin it all. She scrambled for a different subject and took a long sip of her beer. Then she toed off her shoes so she wouldn't be tempted to bolt. "Is Keats still here?"

He cocked a thumb toward the hallway behind him. "Yeah, in the guest bedroom. I think he took the nighttime allergy medicine instead of the regular. He's been out for a few hours."

"I'm glad he's still around. That's what I wanted to talk to you about."

"You want to talk about Keats?" he asked, brows dipping in confusion.

"I do. And I know I'm being nosy," Georgia said rolling the bottle between her palms and keeping her voice low in case Keats woke up. "But how bad is his situation?"

Colby considered her, looking way too tempting with his still-damp hair and that snug T-shirt, but he seemed to be pondering the question. "I'm not a hundred percent sure, but I'm guessing not good. I found him busking in a park last night. He said he needed money to make rent."

"How long is he staying with you?"

Colby frowned and glanced toward the hallway, then took a draw of his beer. "He wants me to drive him back tonight. I'm giving him some money. He said it'll cover him for a while."

"You don't seem too thrilled about that."

"I'm not." Colby leaned back and laid his arm across the back of the couch, looking weary all of a sudden. "But the guy's too prideful for handouts. I offered to let him stay with me for a while, but he sees it as charity. Plus, he comes from a world where nothing is given for free. Even with one night, I could tell he was trying to figure out my angle, like there's more to it than me wanting to help out."

She picked at the label on her beer. "Is there?"

"No, he's a kid I used to know who needed help. I helped. I still want to help."

"He's not a kid anymore, Colby," she said, peeking up at him. "I'm sure you've noticed."

He raised a brow at her. "Well, apparently, you have."

"Come on," she said, barely resisting the urge to roll her eyes. "You know neither of you is hard to look at."

"Is that right? Neither of us, huh?" He grinned and pointed the neck of his beer toward her. "Does this mean I need to challenge Keats to a duel for your primary affections?"

She sniffed. "Only if you plan on taking your shirts off and doing hand-to-hand combat. Possibly while the sprinklers are running."

A bark of laughter spilled out of him, echoing through the room. "Dirty mind, Georgia. I like this side of you."

She smiled, feeling lighter than she had in a very long time. She liked this side of her, too—even though she suspected it was partly due to the residual effects of that kiss and might not last long. "I have my moments."

"Oh, I have no doubt," he said, the shift in his voice like a stroke against her skin.

She chewed her lip, the simple statement bringing to mind her nights at that window, the things she'd seen take place in the room down the hall. But she couldn't let her thoughts wander there. Already she could feel her body prickling with awareness. She grabbed a throw pillow and hugged it against her chest in defense. "Do you think Keats would consider staying if I could offer him a job?"

His forehead scrunched. "What do you mean?"

"I need an assistant. Simple stuff—errands, emails, mailing things for me. I have an extra laptop. He could do it from here—or my place, if I can handle that. It'd only be part time, but it'd be steady work, and he could look for something full time or take classes or whatever he needs to do in between."

"I thought you were looking for a virtual assistant."

She shrugged, though her attempt at casual felt stiff. This was a big, major deal for her. "I was. But he needs it more than some college kid. And . . . I think it'd be good for me, you know, to invite some people into my life."

He stared at her for a long moment. "You're kind of amazing for making that offer. But why him?"

She set her beer on the coffee table. "Because he seems like a good guy who's had some bad luck. And I don't know, when he helped me today, there was just something about him. I feel comfortable around him—which, believe me, in my world, is like finding a unicorn."

Colby's mouth curved upward. "I'm sure Keats would be thrilled to know you called him a unicorn. Very badass image. You sure this isn't just a sinister plan to live out some boss/subordinate fantasy? Because you've already admitted he's not hard to look at, and I have a feeling Keats would have no problem volunteering for that game. I mean, you already got him naked after only knowing him for a few minutes."

She grinned and tossed the pillow at him, even though the images he painted were oh-so-tempting ones. "Don't be ridiculous."

He held his beer out of the way and batted down the pillow, mischief dancing in his eyes. "Oh, come on, the thought didn't cross your mind even once? *Yes, Ms. Delaune, should I type this letter with my shirt off or maybe without pants?*"

She pressed her lips together, trying not to laugh, but it didn't work. "You're terrible."

"And right," he said, pointing the neck of his beer bottle at her.

She shook her head, a little amazed that he'd picked up on her attraction to Keats and that they were openly discussing another man. "You know, you're not like other guys."

"Of course I'm not, but what makes you say that?"

"Well, we just kissed and you're teasing me about another guy like it's no big deal if I think he's hot."

Colby shrugged. "I kissed you. I like you. But I don't own you. I don't have any right or desire to control who you find attractive. And I'd rather have your honesty than anything else."

Georgia tried not to wince. Honesty. Yeah, she was doing a stellar job at that one. Fake last name. Shady background. Not to mention that whole illegal-peeping thing. Just slap a big fat F on her report card for that one. Her conscience wagged its finger at her, bringing the guilt down heavy. Her thumb started rubbing at her palm again. She watched the back-and-forth motion. Maybe she should leave. Kissing Colby had been fantastic, but how could she pursue anything with him? All her issues. The fact that he was dominant. Everything was so complicated in her life right now. "It's getting late . . ."

"Come on, baby," he said softly. "Don't chicken out on me now."

She looked up, finding those hazel eyes studying her, flickering gold in the lamplight. "What?"

"Tell me what you really came here to tell me."

It took a second for the request to register, but when it did, it squeezed around her throat in a death grip. "What do you mean?"

"Georgia . . ."

The awareness in his eyes was like a guillotine slicing through her last shreds of hope.

Oh. Shit.

"You saw the binoculars."

TEN

Colby's expression didn't change, but he set down his beer. "I did."

She stared at the couch cushion between them, humiliation bleeding through her. This wasn't happening. "I'm so sorry, I—"

But her words trailed off when he shifted toward her on the couch. He put his fingers beneath her chin. "Hey, look at me."

That was the last thing she wanted to do, but she forced her focus upward. She'd done the crime, now it was time to pay the price for it. But when she tilted her face to him, she didn't see any censure or judgment in his.

"You must think—" she started again, but he hushed her with a shake of the head.

"I already knew," he admitted. "So I'm as much to blame as you are."

"What?" She blinked, her thoughts scattering like frantic mice. Maybe she was hearing things. "But—"

"I saw your curtains move and a flash one night when I had friends over. The moonlight must've glinted off the lens of your binoculars."

"Oh my God." She put her hands to her face, officially mortified. "Why didn't you shut your curtains?"

He chuckled and reached for her wrists, easing her arms down to her lap. "I'm guessing you can probably figure out the answer to that yourself."

She swallowed hard, the realization staring her in the face. "You liked me watching."

His dimpled smile was downright devious. "Hello, Ms. Voyeur, meet Mr. Exhibitionist."

She closed her eyes and shook her head. "God, that makes me sound like such a pervert."

He released her wrists and leaned back against the arm of the couch again. "Come on, now. You've watched me long enough to know I could beat you on the pervert scale a few thousand times over. No need to feel any shame about it. You wanted to watch. I let you—and enjoyed it."

She couldn't process this. All the times she'd watched him flipped through her mind like a dirty movie on fast-forward and repeat. All those nights, he'd known she was there. Then another thought hit her. "So last night . . ."

"Last night was probably out of line," he admitted. "All the other times, I knew you were watching, but I didn't change my behavior because of it. Last night, I did."

Her heart was moving too fast again, but for a different reason than panic. "Why?"

He considered her for a moment, then released a breath. "Because I was selfish. I needed to know if you watched my window because you just enjoy seeing other people be intimate and do kinky things or if you watched because of *me*."

Oh, hell. She bit the inside of her lip.

"Because some people like watching no matter who it is. And that's cool. I can get into that sometimes, too. But if that's all it was, I wanted to know so that I didn't go traipsing where I'm not wanted."

Her brows met. "What do you mean?"

"You've seen what kind of lifestyle I live, how I am with lovers?"

"Yes," she said, almost too low for her own ears to register the sound.

"And what do you know about me, Georgia?"

She wet her lips. "You're bisexual."

"I am."

"And you like threesomes."

Amusement lit his eyes. "True, what's not to like?"

"And you're a dominant and a sadist."

His mouth lifted at the corner. "Yes. You know the language. I have to admit that surprises me a little. Google?"

"I look that innocent?" she asked, deadpan. "I think I'm insulted."

Okay, so it was totally Google. But no way she was admitting that.

He laughed, the sound coming from deep in that wide chest of his. "I'm not trying to tease you."

"Uh-huh."

He took her hand again, his expression going more serious. "I'm only trying to figure you out—and need to make sure you know exactly who I am because that list of things would probably scare off ninety percent of the population. And if you watch me simply because I'm so out there that you find it interesting, that's fine. If we kissed because there's attraction but you're not really into the other stuff, I'll understand. Tell me that and nothing has to change. You can continue to watch and I'll let you." His thumb traced the delicate bones of her wrist, the heat of his touch burning through her. "But if you watch because you think you might crave some of those same things, if you find yourself wondering what it'd be like to be there with me instead of behind the glass, then tell me that, too. Because, Georgia, all you have to do is ask and next time I won't stop unless you tell me to."

Everything in her sparked like live wires hitting water—Colby's words overriding any residual effect from the small dose of anxiety medicine or a beer could provide. *Just ask.* She'd imagined that proposition so many times in the quiet of her guest room. Yes, the things he did were out there. Some of them scared her, in theory, but she knew real fear and she'd never felt that when thinking of Colby. She didn't feel it now. And the thought of experiencing that even once with him, having his hands on her, that big body pressing against her . . .

She leaned back, needing some breathing space and some solid ground. "I don't know what to say."

"Say what's on your mind. There are no wrong answers here."

She sighed and looked up at him. "I'm not going to sit here and lie that I haven't thought about what it'd be like with you . . . like that, submissive. I can't stop watching . . . and thinking. But it's scary. The thought of putting myself out there like that."

He watched her intently, as if considering every one of her words, then nodded. "Well, know there's no pressure here. You don't have to answer now or ever. But I'm telling you all this because I'm not one to bullshit or play games. I like you. I *want* you. But I also am the way I am, and that's not for everyone."

No lies or games—what a novel concept. Most days she felt her whole life was balancing on intricately weaved, wispy-thin threads of deceit. Something free of all that was so goddamned tempting. *Colby* was so damn tempting. But this was anything but simple. This was no longer some fantasy scenario she was watching from a safe distance. It would be *her* tied to that big bed of his.

She rubbed her lips together and peered over at him. "I don't know if I'm capable of being submissive."

"You say that." The shadow of his dimple appeared. "But you like watching me and imagining you're there with me? In those scenarios, do you picture being in charge of me?"

She held his gaze for a long while, but the truth sat full on her lips. "No. I can't really imagine you like that. It doesn't make sense."

"And when you think of being on your knees for me, does that make sense?"

She swallowed past the dryness in her throat. "Sometimes. In the fantasy world."

"That fantasy world is where a lot of truth hides. We could test what's true for you."

"What do you mean?"

"Here, let's try something." He settled back against the arm of the couch. "Turn around."

"Why?"

He cocked an eyebrow.

With a huff, she complied. "You use that eyebrow thing on your students?"

"Yes, it's very effective. Now, put your back to me. I promise I won't touch you anywhere that I couldn't in public."

She had no idea what he was up to, and the thought of letting him touch her in any way made her belly do flips. What if she panicked? But every instinct in her told her Colby was okay. Even so, it was hard to trust her intuition. It had let her down so spectacularly with Phillip. But looking back, she knew she had ignored signs early on. She wouldn't make that mistake again.

But right now, she needed to take this risk, give her gut a test run, trust that Colby wasn't a dangerous guy. He'd never done anything to make her think otherwise. And even if something went wrong, she had enough self-defense moves to get out of this position if she needed to. She'd trained hard to make sure she never got caught defenseless again. She turned around fully, and he put his hands on her waist to drag her back against him.

He situated her against his chest, wrapping his arms around her and letting her head rest on his shoulder. Lord, he was big. She braced herself for the inevitable anxiety she expected to rush forward. But instead, after giving herself a moment to take a breath, she realized she felt just fine. Better than fine. She was deliciously cocooned in Colby's warmth and the clean scent of freshly showered man. It was pretty damn nice, actually.

"There," he said, settling into the position. "Now I want you to close your eyes and keep them closed while we try this. You're a writer, so I'm sure you have a vivid imagination. I need you to use it."

"But—"

"Hush," he said softly. "Just relax and listen. I think this may help." His fingertips traced along her arms, and the music from the TV drifted around them. He took his time, caressing her and letting her adjust to being held by him, and then he started to speak low against her ear. "I want you to picture standing in the doorway to my room. I've turned the lights down and lit candles. The shadows are dancing along the walls. It takes a minute for your eyes to adjust, but when they do, all you can see is the outline of me sitting in the armchair in the corner. I'm still in my work clothes but I've loosened my tie. I'm waiting for you."

Georgia's skin warmed and tingled where he touched, the scene appearing in her mind, colors filling in with fine brushstrokes as Colby shared more details. She could see him sitting there, legs spread wide, the posture of a confident king holding court—sexy and intimidating. Her heartbeat kicked a little harder against her ribs.

"Can you see me?"

"Yes," she whispered.

"I tell you to come in. You've worn a red dress and look beautiful, but that's not what I need tonight. I want nothing between us. I order you to undress for me. Slowly."

His breath brushed against the shell of her ear with every word, and a hot shiver worked its way down her body. She pictured herself standing there in the middle of his room, the window she'd so often spied through bearing silent witness. She could almost hear the zipper dragging down as she imagined reaching behind her and tugging it to slip out of the dress.

"You're wearing a lacy bra and panties, and I can see just enough beneath to drive me crazy. I love your body, those curves, the gorgeous glow of your skin. It reminds me of warm cocoa." He pressed his lips against the curve of her neck and grazed her with the tip of his tongue. "And I know it will taste just as sweet."

Holy Moses. The tiny touch sent every muscle tightening, and a moan built in the back of her throat.

"I tell you to come closer to stand between my knees. You do so without saying a word. I haven't given you permission to speak. I don't touch you yet. You haven't earned it. But your nipples are dark shadows beneath the lacy material, the little points begging for my mouth, and your panties are clinging to you." His voice dipped even lower. "You're so wet for me already, I can taste your scent in the air."

Her thighs pressed together, the imaginary arousal becoming all too real.

"I can barely stand to stay patient. My cock is pressing against the fly of my pants, aching for you. But I like riding that edge, taking my time. And I owe you a punishment."

"Why?" she asked, her voice barely audible.

"Because you were seven minutes late for our date." His fingertips trailed along the tops of her thighs, lighting up nerve endings in their wake even through the material of her jeans. "I tell you to lose the bra and to kneel down next to me. You're being a good girl and you follow my instructions. The bra falls to the floor and those full breasts are there on display for me. I lay you across my lap and capture your arms behind you." His fingers circled both her wrists and applied pressure. "You're all mine now."

Mine, her mind repeated, the word sounding sexier than she'd ever heard it. Phillip had used that word like an angry child—*mine!*—a threat. But the way Colby said it was like he was cherishing the privilege of having her.

"I tug your panties down to your knees, exposing that heart-shaped ass to me. I can't wait to make it sting. But I can't resist dipping my fingers between your legs first, sliding them inside." A little rumbling sound went through his chest, and a very prominent bulge pressed against her backside. "You're so hot and wet for me, Georgia. Perfect. Your body clamps around my fingers, and you start to beg a little. You're close to coming already. But there's punishment before pleasure. Then one will blend into the other."

She shifted against him, her internal heat building to an almost unbearable level. The seam of her jeans rubbed against her panties, putting just enough pressure against her clitoris to remind her there was nothing she could do about the ache.

"I slide my fingers out and suck your sweetness off them. You taste so good," he said, reverence in his voice. "Then I raise my hand . . ."

Georgia's eyes were pinched shut, and she was holding her breath. The whole scene was so clear in her head—her sprawled across his lap, that big hand of his perched above her bare ass, her arousal slick between her legs. A begging word played on her lips.

"Then *whack!*"

She startled as if she'd really been hit.

"My hand comes down across your flesh, and the sting radiates through your body. You cry out because I'm not in the mood to be gentle—I rarely am—but I know that soon the sting will turn to a burn and then into something much, much better. I spank you again. And again. Seven times for the seven minutes you were late. You can barely stay still. I hold your wrists tight to keep you in place. But soon you're begging me for some relief. *Please let me come. Please.*

"I'm feeling generous now because you've taken your punishment with sexy grace, but I'm not ready to fuck you quite yet. I have a lot more planned for you. But you've earned your first one. I slide you off my lap and make you sit on the floor with your legs spread."

Georgia curled her fingers into her palms, lost in the fantasy he was conjuring.

"You're so aroused and ready. I've never seen such an irresistible sight. I unzip my pants and take my cock in my hand. Your gaze goes to it. I love that you want it. That you want me. But all in good time. Right now I want to sit back and enjoy the show. I tell you to touch yourself. *Come for me, Georgia.*"

Georgia clamped her thighs together.

"I can tell you're nervous, but you need to come, so that's making you bolder, less self-conscious, more motivated to please me. You let your hand slip between your legs. Your eyes close and I know you won't be long. My beautiful girl is going to come for me. Then when she's done, she's going to kneel for me and make me come, too, because there's nothing she loves more than taking my cock in her mouth and making me go over."

God. Georgia couldn't speak. The scene was so vivid and illicit. Her on the floor at his feet, spread wide and pleasuring herself. It wasn't something she would've imagined herself doing for a man. She'd never been a prude, but she'd also stuck to the basics in the bedroom. Now she felt like she'd explode at the thought of being in that position for Colby.

Colby's lips pressed against her ear. "Still with me, gorgeous?"

Her mouth was dry as she shifted on his lap, his erection a teasing presence beneath her. "Yes."

"Are you wet?"

She bit her lip. This wasn't the fantasy anymore. He was really asking her. He had to know the answer already. "Yes."

He made a pleased sound under his breath and kissed her neck again. "Would you like to come?"

Blood was rushing in her ears now. She should probably think about this. Things were moving lightning fast. But her body had shoved her logical self out of the driver's seat a few long minutes ago. "Yes."

"Keep your eyes closed and unzip your jeans," he said in that tone that could've talked the habit off a nun.

"I can't," she whispered, but there was no conviction behind it.

"You can and you will." The words fell hot on her. "Imagine it's my fingers slipping inside, my tongue tasting you."

She sighed at the images. And without thinking too hard on it, she unfastened her jeans and pulled down the zipper.

"Good girl," he said, the low assurance moving through her like a full-body caress. "You've waited a long time for this. You've been watching, learning, wondering what it'd be like over here with me. You've left me wondering, too, Georgia. I've thought about you more than I probably should. Show me how bad you've craved it. Touch yourself and come for me."

She let out a soft gasp.

This was crazy. Fucking nuts. She'd just tried to bring over a damn casserole and now here she was like some desperate, needy thing. This was too intimate an act to show someone she hardly knew.

But no, that was a sorry excuse and she knew it. Last night she'd watched in glorious detail as he'd stroked himself to orgasm. He'd known she was watching, giving her a show. Now it was her turn. And if she needed any additional encouragement, that visual was enough to push her over the ledge. That big tan fist wrapped around his cock, sliding up and down with slow, sensual glides. She let her hand slip inside her panties. If he could be that brazen, so could she.

The wet heat that greeted her wasn't a surprise, but the instant electricity that raced over her nerve endings was. She shuddered hard. She was right there already, a rubber band stretched to its limit by this man's hot words and poised to snap.

"That's it, baby," Colby said, his voice going sandpaper rough as he laid warm kisses along her neck. "Show me how sexy you are when you come. I've imagined it so many times. Have thought about it when I knew you were watching me, wondering what you looked like when you touched yourself. That's what I was thinking about last night when I stroked my cock. That's what I'll think about tonight."

The talk and her quick fingers were enough to send her careening into orgasm. Her back arched and she cried out, everything pulsing beneath her fingers and sensation rippling outward. Colby kept her in place, whispering dirty, sexy things to her, but she couldn't understand them anymore. The release was so much bigger than her typical ones, like breaking out of a dark cave and feeling sun against her skin. And that felt *good*. Damn, did it feel good.

She gasped her way through the last few pulses of pleasure and then sank against Colby, all the tension evaporating from her body. She moved her hand from beneath her panties and let her arm fall to the side.

But Colby had other ideas. He took her hand and brought it to his mouth. He sucked her two fingers and then ran his tongue along the seam of them in a savoring glide, making her shiver all over. "That was beautiful, baby."

"Mmm," she said, still drifting in the afterglow. Maybe she could stay right here for the rest of the night. Maybe she—

"Well, hell," another voice said from behind them. "How long was I sleeping?"

ELEVEN

Georgia flew into a sitting position and spun around, making Colby grunt as her ass rubbed against his straining erection. Colby turned his head. Keats was standing in the doorway with a plate of enchiladas in his hand.

"What the hell?" Colby ground out, while Georgia tried to button her jeans.

Keats flinched at Colby's tone. "Sorry."

Goddammit. Colby had gotten caught up in the moment and had completely forgotten about his houseguest—a consequence of too many years living alone and being accustomed to doing what he wanted where he wanted. Colby glanced at Georgia to make sure she wasn't freaking out, then looked back to Keats. "Ever heard of privacy?"

"I'm really sorry," Keats said again, and hitched a thumb toward the kitchen. "But I woke up and smelled something burning. I didn't realize y'all were uh, *occupado*, until, you know, I heard you talking."

Fantastic. Who knew how long Keats had been listening. This was just what Colby needed. He adjusted the front of his jeans, his erection barely registering the turn of events.

Keats's gaze glided over where Colby's hands were, but then he shifted his attention to Georgia. There was no missing the flare of want in his eyes. There was also no missing the outline of Keats's obvious interest in his pants. Someone had been listening long enough to get a hard-on.

Colby's cock flexed against his zipper, and he had to swallow back the groan. His dick was on board with anyone in the room right now. Preferably both. Right now.

He swung his legs to the floor. "Dammit, Keats. You could've said something to let us know you were here."

Keats shook his head and leaned against the door frame. "Nuh-uh, no way was I interrupting that train. I've lived with enough roommates to know that if you walk in on something, you don't do anything but keep your mouth shut and walk away." He looked to Georgia. "I'm really sorry for invading, but I would've ruined it for you if I said something sooner. And I didn't, you know, see anything."

Just heard. That was the part he wasn't saying.

"I think I should go," Georgia said.

Colby turned. "What? No."

"Yeah, seriously, please don't leave because of me," Keats said, turning all *aww shucks* Texas boy. "I didn't mean to mess up anything or embarrass you. I'll go eat in the kitchen and you won't see me for the rest of the night. Swear."

"No, it's fine," she said, putting on her shoes and not looking at either of them. "It's getting late anyway. And this is . . . awkward."

"Wait," Keats said, stepping into the living room and setting his plate down on an end table. "Don't feel awkward. I mean, dead honest? Yeah, I shouldn't have listened to what I did. The second I realized what was going on, I should've turned and left. This is my fault. But goddamn, I couldn't make myself move. Y'all were, well, y'all were fucking hot together."

"Keats," Colby warned.

"It's okay," Georgia said, finally looking up. She sent Colby a droll smile, no doubt deciding she wouldn't throw stones at a fellow Peeping Tom. "I get it. As long as you didn't take any videos or pictures, I won't have to kill you."

Keats laughed, looking relieved. "Damn. Video. I should've thought of that. Next time I'll come prepared. Imagine the money, I could—"

Colby grabbed an ink pen from the side table and launched it at Keats. It pinged him in the chest, shutting him up. "Keats, go eat your enchiladas."

He smirked and gave a salute. "Right away, Teach. Poof! Consider me gone."

But right as he turned to leave, Georgia called after him. "Hey, Keats, are you going to be around tomorrow?"

He peered back over his shoulder, his affable expression faltering a bit. "Didn't plan on it. I, uh, have to take care of some things that can't wait."

"Will you come back after you're done?" she asked, that irresistible feminine lilt drifting into her voice. "I have something to talk to you about, but now isn't the right time."

He stood there for a long moment but then managed to muster up that disarming smile of his. "All right. I'll see what I can do."

She smiled back at him, pleased. "Good night, Keats."

"'Night."

He disappeared back into the kitchen, and Georgia turned those pretty dark eyes on Colby. "Well, that isn't exactly how I wanted to start things off with my potential new employee."

Colby grabbed her by the waist and lifted her onto his lap to straddle him, settling her right against where he wanted her most. "Yeah, but you'll probably get a really dedicated worker. I think he's half in love with you already."

She smirked. "Half-hard for sure. Like someone else I know."

He laughed and pushed her hair away from her face. "Can't blame him. We *are* hot together. I would've stopped and eavesdropped, too, if I were him. But I'm real sorry if he made you uncomfortable."

She looked down, hiding the secret smile that had touched her lips.

The move was so endearingly sexy that he had to fight his instinct to pick her up and carry her to his bedroom. "Wait, *were* you uncomfortable?"

"I don't know." She shrugged. "Is it weird that it wasn't *that* uncomfortable?"

He tilted his head, the question spiking his curiosity. "Meaning?"

"Meaning, it was a shock and I reacted, but now . . . I don't know. Now I kind of don't care that he saw us."

Interesting. He filed that away. "And how about that he's probably in the kitchen right now replaying it in his head and still sporting that hard-on?"

Her lips twitched into that smile again, but she quickly rolled them inward and shrugged. "Not sure."

Uh-huh. Right. "Or that probably later tonight, when he's alone, he'll call up those sounds you made and use the memory to get himself off?"

"*Colby,*" she said, keeping her voice low and giving him a scandalized look. "Stop. Keep going and I'll never be able to look at him straight, much less hire him."

He gave her a wicked grin. What an undeserved gift. His neighbor was so much dirtier than he'd hoped. Not just a voyeur but an exhibitionist streak hiding in there, too. Apparently, he just had to get past that outer layer of anxiety to see that side of her. Right now she was still riding the buzz from her orgasm, and it was letting him see beneath that hard shell she always wore. "Hey, there's no shame in it. You like knowing you've gotten more than one guy hot and bothered, enjoy feeling that kind of sexual energy directed at you. Believe me, I get that. That kind of power can be heady."

"That's what it is, isn't it?" she said, glancing toward the kitchen, probably to make sure Keats wasn't there listening. "Power."

"Quite the aphrodisiac—both having it and having it taken away," he said, his fingertips playing along the base of her spine. "Even in the submissive role, there's power. The submissive knows how mesmerizing his or her surrender is, how deeply the dominant craves it. Both sides are necessary for the other to be satisfied. Very powerful."

She pulled in a breath and nodded. "I'm starting to understand that."

"I can show you, Georgia," he said, not wanting to push or pressure her but unable to let her walk out without at least posing the offer. "For real. You only have to ask. I promise you'll be safe with me."

"You didn't touch me during the fantasy," she said, her voice soft. "You know I would've let you."

"I told you I wouldn't. I keep my promises."

She traced the collar of his T-shirt with her fingertip, keeping her gaze down, a thoughtful crease in her brow. "I like that."

"It's what you deserve. You trust me with your submission, and I make sure I'm worthy of it by never breaking my word."

"My submission," she repeated, as if trying out the words.

"Yes," he said, putting his knuckle beneath her chin and making her look at him. "That's what it would be. When we're in that mode, the control would be mine."

"That idea is still scary for me. I—my life is about control."

"A little fear can be good. I'd be worried if you entered this without any. But something drew you to your window all those nights. Some curious part that made you crave the view."

"Yes, but watching you take control of someone else is like peeking in on some erotic wonderland—a fantasy. A safe, distant one."

"Yeah." He gently shifted her on his lap. "But visiting wonderland is so much better than spying on it. Not just fun things to look at but things to touch, taste, feel . . . Tickets are now available. And just for you, on deep discount."

She laughed, bracing her hands on his chest. "Even if I'm willing to . . . try. I'm your neighbor. I don't want this to get weird or awkward."

"It won't if we're honest and up-front with each other," he said, sliding his hands to her hips.

Her muscles tensed beneath his fingers for a second, a strange look tightening her features, but then it seemed to slide off like it hadn't been there at all. "How so?"

"What are you wanting from this?"

She seemed surprised by his straightforward question. "Nothing serious. I mean, I've watched you long enough to know you're not exactly a relationship guy."

He cringed. "Georgia—"

She shook her head. "No. Honestly, you don't have to say anything to defend it. That's part of your appeal, actually."

"Part of the appeal?" What he was going to say died on his lips. He'd been ready to tell her that he was completely open to seeing where things went. For years, he'd been fine with bringing home the occasional play partner from The Ranch for a one-night thing—mutual fun, no strings or expectations. But seeing all his friends fall into serious relationships had him craving more—a connection not just inside the bedroom but outside it. Someone he could actually date. But if Georgia wasn't looking for that, he wasn't going to push her. He knew it had taken a massive amount of guts for her to even get this far.

"Being here in Texas isn't a permanent situation for me. I'm supposed to go back to Chicago in a few months," she said, a little frown line nestling between her brows. "If I can get there. You saw what I'm dealing with this morning. So, really, if we do this, you should know what you're getting into as well. Things are complicated for me right now."

The fact that she was planning to go back to Chicago wasn't welcome news, but he wasn't ready to walk away from her for that. And he was already well aware that she was dealing with an anxiety disorder. "I'm not afraid of complicated."

She smiled. "I am. What I need most right now is fun. Like the real, lose-yourself-in-it kind. I haven't had that in so long. And tonight, well, it's been nice to get a glimpse of it again. I want to have that kind of fun with you."

His heart broke a little at the earnestness in her words, that keen need for escape. He wanted to ask what had happened to her, because clearly the life she led now wasn't how things had always been. But he could tell she wasn't ready to open up about personal stuff. So if she wanted fun, a break from everyday life, he could give her that. "We can make this as casual as you're comfortable with."

"Yeah?" she said, interest in her voice.

"Sure. Just list my number in your cell phone under *For a Good Time Call.*"

She laughed. "I'd dial that number right now."

"So is that a yes?" he asked. "To this, to us?"

"I've wanted you for a long time, Colby," she said, sliding her hands from his chest to his shoulders, the slightest tremor in her fingers. "I don't know if I can play this power game. But I'm tired of sitting on the sidelines too scared to try."

He couldn't hide his smile. He spread his fingers over her flared hips, loving the soft warmth of her. "You're going to be amazing at it. I have no doubt."

She pressed a whisper-soft kiss to his mouth. "I might freak out."

He ran his hands along her sides, enjoying the freedom to finally touch her. "And I'll be there for you if you do to take care of you and talk you down. Plus, you'll have a safe word to pull the plug anytime you need to. And I will always honor the word *stop* no matter what."

She lifted her head, and the last flicker of worry in her eyes seemed to fade as her gaze warmed. She touched his face, her fingertips scoring over his beard like she was learning the feel of it. "I can't believe I'm going to do this. But I used to be the girl who wouldn't have been afraid to have a fling with my unfairly hot neighbor. I want to find that girl again."

"Unfairly hot, huh?" he asked, teasing.

"Don't get cocky, country boy." She adjusted herself on his lap, and her heat pressed against him. All desire to joke fell away.

"Tell me what you want," Colby said, his voice gruff and his arousal firing anew. "I want to hear you ask for it."

She dragged her body across his hardening erection. "Corrupt my boring, vanilla world, Colby Wilkes."

He groaned at the words and the feel of her against him. "You're a liar, gorgeous."

She lifted her eyebrows.

"There isn't anything vanilla about you." He leaned forward and pressed an openmouthed kiss to the curve of her neck.

She tilted her head back, giving him access. "If that's a black joke, I'm going to kick your ass."

He chuckled against her skin. "Ooh, you get feisty when you're turned on. I like it." He moved his palms down from her hips to cup her backside. "So how daring are you feeling tonight, neighbor?"

He could tell she was losing the thread of conversation, that his touches and kisses were distracting her because it took her a second to answer. "What do you mean?"

"No time like the present to start your corruption."

Her gaze drifted toward the hallway where Keats had gone, her expression transparent—unsure but tempted by the unknown.

"I told you I wouldn't touch you earlier, and I didn't. But now I'm going to give you a choice. We can stop this, and you can go home and watch me from your window." He nestled his erection against her. "And I'll gladly give you a show—all while not allowing *you* to come until next time you see me. Or you can stay right where you are."

Her voice was breathless when she spoke again. "What happens if I stay?"

"I fuck you right here where Keats will absolutely hear everything from the kitchen." He nuzzled his teeth against her collarbone and bit gently.

She gasped softly.

"Tell me to stop, Georgia. And I'll let you go."

The word was a perfectly easy one to say. It was right there on her lips. *Stop.* She wouldn't even have to take in a breath to say it. But with him kissing her neck like that and the feel of his erection rubbing exactly where she needed it, she couldn't find it in herself to say it. *Keats will hear.* That was a guarantee. She could hear him fiddling around in the kitchen, probably eating his dinner.

The thought only made the ache between her thighs burn hotter. Colby sucked her earlobe between his lips and teased it. *"God."*

"That doesn't sound like *stop*," Colby mused.

"We could go in your room."

"Not an option I gave you," he said, that tone coming into his voice. The one he'd used in the fantasy. The one she'd imagined when she couldn't hear what was being said on his side of the window. "Take off your jeans."

"Colby . . ."

"Is that *stop*?"

"No," she whispered.

"I know you're still wet for me," he said against her ear. He cupped her through her jeans. "I can feel the heat of you. And I should be patient. I promised myself I wouldn't rush anything. But I'm also not a liar. I want you. Right now. Here. I want to fuck you hard and fast, and I don't care who hears it."

Jesus. If she ever had any doubt about if she could appreciate dirty talk, she had her answer. Phillip had always gone for the sweet and romantic words, the flattering ones. Once upon a time, she'd thought that was what she should want. A gentleman who told her loving things. But right now, filth was working like wildfire. Her whole body burned with the need to be touched, her nipples beading against her bra and her panties clinging to her.

Her body was taking over her brain, saying, *Fuck it all.* The nerves. The worry. The concern about who could and couldn't hear them. None of it mattered right now. She scooted off him, stood, and tugged off her jeans.

He watched her every move, his gaze hooded, hungry. When she'd shucked the jeans, he touched the edge of her black panties. She'd worn one of the few sexy pairs she still owned. Even if she hadn't planned on it, her subconscious must have been hoping for this when she'd gotten dressed to come over here. "Keep these on."

"Okay."

He reached behind him, opened the end table drawer, and pulled out a foil wrapper. She wondered if he had condoms stored in every drawer around the house. With the kinds of parties she'd seen over here, probably. He shifted on the couch and unbuttoned his jeans, pushing them down along with his underwear just enough. His cock sprang free—hard and ruddy and already glistening at the tip.

Her belly clenched low and tight. She'd seen him naked from afar, but in person, he was even more impressive. The man was big all over. She wanted to wrap her hand around that proud erection, lick it . . . freaking worship it. The urge took her aback. Never before had she had such a primal desire to get to her knees for the sole purpose of making a man feel good.

Colby's gaze flared with dark need. "I like the way you're looking at me, gorgeous. One day soon, I'll let you do exactly what your eyes are promising. But right now, I need to be inside you. Straddle me."

She shivered at the command and climbed on top. She had no idea why she still had her panties on, but after he rolled on the condom, she wasn't left wondering for long.

He tugged the crotch of her underwear aside and ran his fingers along her slick folds. "If a certain someone walks in, you'll be able to cover up quickly if you want."

If she wanted . . . like it was a decision. But the more she pictured the possibility, the more she realized maybe it was her choice. Maybe he truly didn't care if they screwed out in the open. The guy had let her watch him for months. "You're a filthy, filthy man."

He gave her a solemn nod and teased her clit with a maddening stroke. "I am. Still want me?"

"Hell, yes."

He held her panties aside, positioned himself at her entrance, and started to ease inside. *Oh, Jesus.* Her nails dug into his shoulders, and she hummed as the sweet sting of the breach skipped along her nerve endings. It had been so long since she'd been with anyone, and though she had toys at home, none were Colby's size. Her body seemed to fight and beg all at once.

"Easy, now," Colby said in that low, cajoling voice, his fingers tucked between them, working her clit. "There's no rush. Relax and take me in slowly. You feel so good, baby, but I don't want to hurt you."

She pressed her forehead to his and concentrated on softening the tension in her body, on letting his beautiful, hard heat inside her. She was slick for him, so her nerves were the only thing fighting her. She was getting too in her head.

He gripped her hip, kneading the curve. "You know how fucking sexy you look right now. These panties shoved to the side like you were so in a hurry to get fucked, you couldn't even bother to take them off. And you're so wet against me. Look down and see us."

She glanced down along the scant space between their bodies, and he moved his hand away so she could see their connection—that perfect carnal joining. The tightness in her muscles melted, and she took him the rest of the way ever so slowly, finally seating him deep.

He groaned and tipped his head back. "Fuck, yes."

She was making her own sounds, lost in the feeling of being filled and stretched. By Colby. She was with *Colby*. Part of her wondered if she'd really fallen into some erotic dream and she'd wake up in her house in a few minutes—cold and alone.

Colby found her hot button again, and she bit her lip to keep from crying out. The noise in the kitchen had stopped. Keats either had bailed or was listening. She should probably be as discreet as possible. But when Colby began to pump into her, she couldn't stay quiet.

"That's it," Colby said. "Ride me. Take what you've been wanting when you watched. Did you think about what my cock would feel like inside you?"

"Yes," she said on a pant.

"Good. Because I sure as hell thought about how you would feel," he said, his deep voice going gravelly. "How you would taste. What you would sound like when you beg. How this perfect ass is going to feel under my hand when I take you over my knee."

She moaned, already close again.

"I can't wait to see you surrender," he said, a little breathless because now there was no more slow and easy. The couch springs protested beneath them. He was fucking her hard and deep and fast, gripping her hip and guiding her pace, each thrust punctuating his words. All the pent-up months of watching and being watched careening together in one desperate act between them.

"Yes. *God*." She shuddered, barely holding back her orgasm, as he circled her clit with a rough fingertip.

He smiled against her sweaty neck. "No need to call me God. *Sir* or Colby will do."

She would've snorted had she not been so far gone. But there was nothing that was going to derail her now. The slap of her skin against his filled her ears, and their mingled scents—sex and sweat and soap—were invading her senses like a drug. "Colby . . ."

"Come for me, gorgeous. Let it go and let me feel you come around my cock."

That was all it took. Sexy, beastly man plus dirty words equaled an impossible mix to resist. Her hands went to his head, gripping his hair in her fists, and she came with a sharp, shaking cry. He followed right with her, apparently a master of control in all aspects, and held her tight as he pumped deep through his release.

The gruff, grunting noises he made were quite possibly the sexiest damn things she'd ever heard in her life. *Goddamn*.

This was so much better on this side of the glass.

And it was probably going to be a mistake. She already knew that. He and his proclivities were probably going to be more than she could handle once they really slipped into the dominant and submissive roles. But there was no way she was turning back now.

She'd seen his version of wonderland and now she wanted a season pass.

TWELVE

Keats was chewing his thumbnail to a ragged edge at the kitchen table. His enchiladas sat cold and uneaten in front of him.

They'd fucked in the goddamned living room, *knowing* he could hear. Were they trying to kill him? Or maybe they didn't care that he'd basically been forced to listen. Maybe he was so insignificant that it didn't even matter that he was right here. He should've been pissed. Instead, his body had only gotten hotter. When he'd heard Georgia's breathy cries and Colby's hot-as-fuck groans, he'd gotten so hard, he'd almost taken his dick in his hand right there in the kitchen. Fucking torture, that was what it was.

To distract himself from what he was hearing and his body's unrelenting reaction to it, he'd grabbed his phone from his bag to check messages. He didn't leave it on most of the time since it was one of those prepaid deals, and he didn't want to waste minutes on bullshit. But when he'd powered it up, he had multiple messages from Aaron, the manager of the Texas Star, saying that if he didn't bring money over by midnight, he was throwing Keats's shit out and giving the room to someone else.

Keats didn't have a lot, but what he did have was important to him. He couldn't afford to have it tossed in the Dumpster. Plus, he'd left his beat-up but well-loved motorcycle in one of the parking spots, and he had no doubt Aaron would have that towed when he realized it belonged to Keats.

Goddammit. He needed to get over there—and out of *here*. He checked the time on the microwave clock. Things got quiet out in the living room for a while and then he heard a door shut. Colby strolled in, looking tousled and a little smug. The back of Keats's neck burned hot, but he tried his best to look nonchalant.

"She's gone?" Keats asked, his knee bouncing beneath the table.

Colby turned his back to him to open the oven and grab the casserole dish Keats had left on warm. "Yeah, I walked her back to her place."

"She can still walk?" he asked, trying to play off how damn affected he was.

Colby's smile was wry. "Can you?"

Keats frowned and adjusted his jeans, unsure how to handle this version of Colby. He was used to the stoic, always-in-control version. The teacher. Mr. Responsible. But besides his accidental spying last night, he'd never been privy to this private side of Colby—the sexual side. The man.

Getting a peek behind the curtain felt like a secret privilege. He'd wanted Colby to stop treating him like some innocent kid, and Colby had definitely listened. But the shift was damn disconcerting. Because though Keats's brain didn't know how to process all the new information, his body certainly had ideas on how to respond.

Keats cleared his throat. "That was a dick move, man."

Colby sniffed. "Kind of like eavesdropping on me and a woman in my own house?"

"Dude, I said I was sorry. You could've just told me off or kicked my ass for walking in on you and Georgia. You didn't need to torture me with ringside seats to the show."

"You could've gone to your room. You wouldn't have had to listen to a thing."

Keats blinked. That option had never occurred to him. Hell, who was he kidding? A herd of charging elephants wouldn't have been able to drive him out of that kitchen.

Colby spooned a serving of enchiladas onto his plate and turned around with a knowing look. "For what it's worth, I didn't do it to torment you. I let you listen because it turned her on."

That sent Keats's thoughts careening in an entirely different direction—straight toward Georgia. He leaned forward on his elbows. "Seriously?"

Colby gave him a shrug that seemed to say, *Hey, my girl is a kinky sex goddess. What can I do?*

"Fuck. Me." If Keats had a spark for Georgia before, it was now a full-fledged crush. "Well, if my torture did it for her, then I guess I don't mind a little suffering on her behalf."

Colby cocked his head, studying him for a second. "Quite self-sacrificing there, Keats."

He shrugged and pushed his food around on his plate. "When it comes to a beautiful woman enjoying herself, there's not much I wouldn't be willing to do."

Colby took a bite of enchiladas, watching him with analytical eyes. "That must make you popular."

"I do all right," he said, unable to hold Colby's gaze. Sometimes it felt like the guy was looking right inside him, seeing all the crossed wires and short circuits. He went back to not eating his food. After a few quiet minutes of rearranging his plate, Keats pushed the enchiladas away. "I need you to drive me back home tonight."

Colby set down his plate. "You just promised Georgia you'd be here tomorrow."

Keats rubbed his palms on his thighs, guilt nipping at him. The last thing he wanted to do was disappoint Georgia, but what was there to gain by hanging around here longer? Disappointment, that's what. Colby and Georgia had lives that existed in another realm from his—and they were obviously starting a relationship. No matter how much Keats pretended, this wasn't his place. Sure, Colby would let him stay for a few weeks, but it wasn't like his life was magically going to change because he had a nicer roof over his head. Before long, Colby would grow tired of having a guest. He'd want to fuck his hot girlfriend on the couch without worrying about someone barging in and gawking.

Tonight, when Keats had first walked in on them, he'd been knocked over with the desire to go over there and be a part of something that erotic and intense. Georgia had looked goddamned beautiful stretched out and sighing into the fantasy. And Colby's words, the pictures he'd painted . . . Keats's blood had rushed straight south, those images of bondage and roughness making him flushed and instantly hard. He'd closed his eyes to see it all. And for a few seconds, his mind had fooled him into thinking that maybe he belonged there with them. Like the moment was a shared one. But, of course, it'd been a ridiculous thought. If he'd learned anything in his life so far, it was that he'd always be the outsider. That conclusion had been confirmed when Colby and Georgia had kicked him out and had gone on to have sex while he was there in the kitchen. He'd been a prop at best, an intruder at worst.

No, he didn't belong here. This wasn't his life.

"I'll try to come by. But I have to get back tonight or they're going to toss my stuff out. I need to give them the rent."

"You don't need to give them anything. You don't have to stay there at all. I told you there's a room here you can use."

"And I told you I don't want a handout."

"This isn't charity. It's a friend helping a friend."

Keats scoffed and pushed back from the table to stand. "Friends? Come on, Colby, that's not what we are. You see me as some debt that needs to be paid off to erase a mark on your conscience. A mistake to fix."

Colby closed his eyes and rubbed the spot between his eyebrows. Keats had seen him do that so many times in the classroom, especially when Keats kept screwing up his chords sophomore year, but that seemed like a lifetime ago now. Two different people. "Keats."

"Look, man." He stepped in front of him, but Colby didn't open his eyes. "Stop putting that shit on yourself. You were the best teacher I had and the only person who gave a damn about me back then. When I left that note for my dad and stole his gun from him that night, I fully planned on ending things." Colby looked up at that, flinching. "But I couldn't help going to you first. And there you were, the shining example of what I could never seem to measure up to—the 'real man,' the kind every woman wanted and no dude would challenge in a fight. It was what my dad always wished I would be."

Colby made a disgusted sound, making his opinion of Keats's father quite clear.

"But when you admitted you were bi, it was like giving the ultimate finger to my father and all the people who thought like him. You didn't fit in the mold. You played music. You were creative. And you didn't give a shit if people knew you fucked guys."

"Yes, that was exceptionally appropriate to admit to one of my students," he said darkly.

"It was what I needed to hear," Keats replied. "And yeah, I took it too far when I tried something with you, but that's on me. A stupid kid making a stupid mistake. So whatever guilt you're holding on to, let it the fuck go. The reason why I didn't put a gun to my head that night was because of you. You showed me that not everyone has to fit into a certain box. That a real man is one who lives life on his own terms. And that's what I've been doing since. So stop feeling like you need to take me in like a stray pet."

Colby's jaw flexed. "It's not like that."

"Good," Keats said with a nod. "Then you should have no problem giving me a ride to my place and letting me get back to my life. Like a friend."

Colby eyed him like he wanted to grab him and shake him, but instead he let out a long breath as if steeling himself against the urge. "I'll bring you home. But you're coming back tomorrow to hear Georgia out. I won't have her disappointed. You understand?"

The tone in his voice reminded Keats of the way he'd issued commands to Georgia in the fantasy, and it made something low in his gut twist. He rolled his shoulders, trying to shake off the feeling. "You got it, Teach."

"And stop calling me that." He pushed away from the counter and grabbed his keys off a hook by the back door. "After what you witnessed tonight, I'd rather not be reminded that I used to be your teacher."

Keats shoved his hands in his pockets and tried to fight the grin. Looked like Mr. Responsible was surfacing again and regretting how much he'd allowed Keats to see tonight. But no way was Keats letting Colby hop behind that line in the sand again. "Yeah, you probably prefer *sir*, or is it *master*?"

Colby peered over his shoulder with a don't-push-it expression.

"What?" Keats asked innocently.

Colby grumbled and tucked his wallet into his back pocket. "Well, now I know how long you stood in the hallway."

Keats grabbed his bag and guitar case from the table and slung the former over his shoulder. "So do you really, you know, go there?"

"Go there?" Colby was on the move, heading toward the front of the house, obviously wanting to be done with this conversation. Keats followed him, knowing he didn't have the right to ask the questions but too damn curious not to.

"I mean, was that just a fantasy game or is that how you are with women?"

Colby looked tired when he sank onto the couch to pull on his boots. "It's how I am with anyone who's in my bed."

"Oh." Right. With men, too. At that, unbidden images leaked into his brain. "So like a dom or whatever it's called?"

He'd watched porn. He wasn't completely unaware of that sub-culture.

Colby sniffed and stood. "Let's go, Keats. It's getting late. And the only people I discuss my sex life with are those who are part of it. So unless you're making a pass at me, I suggest you stop talking and get in the damn truck."

Keats's jaw snapped together.

Colby smirked as he passed him on his way to the door. "Yeah, that's what I thought."

Fuck. Keats ignored the flush of heat that brought to his face and followed him out the door.

Yeah, forget the questions. The sooner he got out of here, the better. Being around Colby Wilkes was a fucking hazard.

——————

Colby was in a truly foul mood by the time his truck rolled to a stop in front of the Texas Star Motel—or actually the *Texas tar Motel* since the fluorescent *S* had burned out. Two overly made-up women—one with thigh-high boots and the other wearing a spandex dress three sizes too small—were smoking cigarettes under the Vacancy sign, probably taking a break in between johns. On the curb in front of the office, a homeless man was muttering to himself and plucking at his pants.

"This is where you're staying?" Colby asked, fingers tightening on the steering wheel.

Keats pushed his hair behind his ears, his face more drawn than it had been a few moments before. "It's cheap and they usually aren't dicks if I'm a day late on paying. Other places would've already purged my room."

"Fuck, Keats, you said you had a place to stay."

His expression hardened. "I do. It's here while I'm saving up for something more permanent."

"You can't—"

But Keats was already pulling the door handle and climbing out. "Thanks for everything. I'll stop by tomorrow to talk to Georgia."

"Kea—"

The door slammed.

Hardheaded bastard. Colby hadn't had a door shut in his face in a long damn time. He hit the button to roll down the window. He wanted to yell at Keats and demand he get his ass back in the truck. But he stopped himself just short. He knew how that would go. Keats was an adult and had made up his mind. The only comfort was that he believed Keats would keep his word to Georgia.

He watched Keats's retreating form until something blocked his view. One of the smoking women leaned along his open window, gave him an appraising look, and offered a sure-thing smile. "Ooh, you're a big one, aren't ya? Looking for a date, cowboy?"

He wanted to bark at her for interfering with his view, but he managed to hold his tongue. No hooker was walking the streets because she wanted to be there. The therapist in him could rewind and see the broken life behind her. So he forced his tone into an easy but clear one. "No thanks, you're not my type, darlin'."

She tilted her head then looked back over her shoulder toward where Keats had gone. She turned back and winked. "Oh, I got ya. Wish I could've seen that, cowboy. Yowza."

She gave his window a little tap and strolled back to join her friend. Keats had disappeared from view. *Motherfuck.*

Colby leaned over the steering wheel, trying to see farther into the lot, but there was no one there. The homeless man was ambling over to Colby's truck, obviously intent on preaching his crazy-speak to another. Colby wasn't in the mood. With a frustrated grunt, he put the car into gear and pulled out of the lot. This wasn't his business. *Keats* wasn't his business.

This was just residual angst about feeling responsible for the kid Keats used to be. That was all this was. He'd offered to help and it wasn't wanted. What more could he do? He pressed a button on his steering wheel, activating his phone, and called a number he'd only programmed tonight.

"Hello?" Georgia said, her voice a little sleep soft.

"Shit, I'm sorry. Did I wake you?"

"Looks like it." The sound of water sloshing filled the background. "But that's a good thing. I think I dozed off in the tub."

"The tub? Are you trying to torture me?" he asked, with visions of what he imagined Georgia's naked body would look like all wet and soapy filling his head. He'd only gotten a glimpse of her tonight.

"You called me," she reminded him. "You're trying to torture yourself."

"Right."

"Is everything okay?" More water sounds, and he could tell she was getting out of the tub.

"I dropped Keats off. He's at some shithole motel on Hines that probably has more drug dealers and hookers in it than county lockup, and I'm trying to talk myself out of turning around and dragging his ass back to my house, willing or not."

"So you're calling me to convince you not to do that?" she guessed.

"Yes."

"Turn around and go get him."

"What?" he asked. "You're supposed to be the rational one here, not repeat my own crazy ideas back to me."

"Sorry, but he's being stupid and bullheaded. Someone needs to talk some sense into him. Especially since he's likely just freaked-out because—well, staying with you would probably be hard for him."

"Hard? Why? Because I used to be his teacher?"

"No, of course not." She made an impatient sound, like the answer was obvious. "Because he's into you."

Colby glanced at the screen showing Georgia's number on it as if he could see her face and effectively give her the *what-the-fuck* look. "What are you talking about? He's straight. And he was all eyes for you today."

"I don't think it's that simple."

"What do you mean?"

She let out a heavy sigh. "Look, I probably shouldn't say anything. But last night when I was, you know, watching you, I wasn't the only one with a front-row seat. Keats walked in."

"*What?*"

"You were already on the bed and had your eyes closed, but he walked in—an accident, I think, because he looked surprised. But then he stayed. And watched."

"Fucking hell." That was why Keats had been so skittish when he'd brought him a towel last night. Everything went annoyingly hot at the thought that both Georgia and Keats were there with him last night.

"I mean, I don't know," Georgia said, and he could tell she was choosing her words carefully, "maybe I misread it. Maybe he's just into watching . . . or listening, like tonight."

"That's more likely," he said, jerking the wheel to the right and exiting the highway again. "He's made it clear he's straight. But when I was talking with him tonight, I got the sense he's kind of fascinated that I'm kinky."

"What do you mean?"

He pulled to a stoplight and tapped his head against the back of the seat. He had no idea if the vibe he'd gotten from Keats earlier was truly an untapped interest in kink or if he was projecting that onto Keats, seeing what his dirty mind wanted to see. *If my torture did it for her, then I don't mind suffering* . . . The simple statement had drawn all kinds of pictures in Colby's head. And it had made him look at the guy sitting at his table with new eyes. "Just a feeling I got."

"Would you care?"

Colby scoffed. "If he's kinky? Of course not. That'd actually make it easier, considering the things he may hear or see living with me."

"And if he's bi?" she asked gently.

He hit his turn signal with more force than necessary, almost breaking the arm off the steering column. "He's not. But it's not my business what he is or isn't."

She made some noise, but he couldn't tell whether it was assent or judgment. "Just go get him, Colby. Make sure he's safe. The rest will work itself out."

Sure, it would.

Just like last time. He could almost look back over his shoulder and see the paved path of good intentions stretched out behind him. He knew where that road led.

But he was going anyway.

THIRTEEN

Keats fished out his key card as he approached the door to his room, trying not to look back to see if Colby was still in the parking lot. It'd been an asshole move to bolt on him like that, but he needed to get out before Colby went into takeover mode again. Yes, to someone like Colby, who lived in a posh suburb, this place probably seemed like a third world country. But for Keats this was just another day, another motel. Nothing to get all twisted up about.

He slid his card into the reader and the light blinked yellow instead of green. He tried again and got the same result. "Dammit."

He glanced back toward the main office, which was on the far side of the parking lot. Aaron had probably already deactivated Keats's card. But that had happened before and the light usually went red for that. He grabbed the door handle and gave a little push. The door gave—apparently, it hadn't clicked fully into the lock.

That should've given him pause, but he was in too much of a rush to get inside. He swung the door open, set his bag and guitar case on the floor, and was greeted by a looming black mass in the dark. Keats didn't have time to make a sound before a fist came crashing into the side of his head.

The doorknob slipped from his hand as the momentum from the unexpected punch propelled him to the floor. He rolled on the dingy carpet, trying to get to his feet, but the blow had dazed him, and he couldn't get his bearings in the dark.

A sharp kick landed against his ribs. "Been waiting for you all night, pretty boy. Aaron said if you didn't show up I could have your shit. But this is so much better."

"What the fuck?" Keats groaned. He recognized the voice instantly but not the reason for Hank's visit. "You said I had until tomorrow to get you cash."

"It's almost midnight, asshole. You have my money?"

"I got it," Keats ground out. *Well, some of it.* His eyes were adjusting to the dark, and he tried to calculate how far he was from a possible weapon. The lamp would be within reach if he could get to his knees, but the motel bolted everything down, so that wouldn't work. The phone had possibilities. But if he could get his arm under the bed . . . He got on his knees and lifted his hand in a placating gesture, trying to look like he was cooperating. "Just lay the fuck off and give me a second to get it."

But Hank's dirty biker boot planted against Keats's chest and shoved him back down. The wind left Keats, and he quickly realized Hank didn't give a shit about the money. He was high or drunk off his ass and looking to beat someone for entertainment. Super.

Anger moved through Keats. All this bullshit and he hadn't even stolen anything from the guy. He gritted his teeth. This idiot had gotten the jump on him, but that wouldn't happen again. He scrambled to the left before Hank could kick him again and rolled to his feet.

"Aww, look at Mr. Tough Guy run," Hank teased. "I always told Nina you were a pussy."

The insult echoed back to what Keats's father used to call him, and all rational thought left his mind. He charged, leading with his fists.

He was going to kill this fucker.

———

Colby stalked into the dimly lit office of the Texas Star Motel. A man with a fraying Cowboys cap and cigarette hanging out of his mouth looked up with disinterest. "All booked up tonight."

"I need to know what room Adam Keats is staying in."

The man snuffed out his cigarette. "We don't give out guest information. Company policy."

Right. Colby suspected exactly what their policy was. He pulled out his wallet, plucked a twenty from it, and slapped it on the counter. "Room number."

The guy's tobacco-stained fingers snatched the bill and tucked it in his front shirt pocket. "One-thirty-two. Far left side."

"Thanks for the hospitality," Colby said, not hiding the sarcasm in his voice. He shoved open the glass door, the rickety handle nearly coming off in his hand, and strode through the parking lot.

A few guys were sitting around a dinged-up Oldsmobile, blasting a song with so much bass he could feel it vibrate his chest. The ringleader gave him a narrow-eyed look, probably sizing him up to see if the three of them could be enough to get his wallet off him. This was the part of town you only wanted to visit in the morning because the criminals were either sleeping it off or in jail. But Colby glared right back, daring them to try it. He could bench-press one of these assholes for fun.

One of the men smiled in that *ain't-no-thing* kind of way and turned back to his friends. Good. Message received.

The motel wasn't big, and Colby found Keats's room without much trouble. But when he lifted his hand to knock, he heard a crashing sound from inside and angry voices. Every part of him went on alert. He grabbed the door handle and shoved. The door hadn't clicked into the lock and it swung open easily, but what was on the other side was much worse than he expected. Keats was in a tangle, scrapping with some greasy-haired dude, fists flying. Before Colby could even process what he was seeing, the other guy broke free and shoved Keats onto the floor. The resounding thump of Keats hitting the ground snapped Colby out of his momentary shock.

Colby didn't think. He launched himself at the guy. Surprise and size were on his side, and he propelled the man into the wall. The cheap drywall rattled behind him as the guy slammed against it. The man tried to swing out at Colby, but he was too disoriented to land a punch with any accuracy.

Colby pressed his forearm against the guy's throat. Keats must've already landed a few good punches. The dude's nose was bleeding and his jaw was starting to swell. "What the fuck do you think you're doing?"

The guy struggled and spat. "This fucker stole from me. I'm here to collect."

Colby peered over his shoulder at Keats.

Keats got to his knees and wiped his bloody mouth with his forearm. "I don't owe you shit, Hank. Talk to your goddamned sister. She's the one stealing from you."

"You fucking—" Hank lurched, but Colby held fast.

"If I were you, Hank, I'd stop struggling and watch how you talk to my friend," Colby said calmly, even though he really wanted to slam this guy to the floor and beat him like Hank had been doing to Keats. "I'd hate to have to crush your windpipe."

A wild look flashed through Hank's dilated eyes and he reared back. Colby saw the head butt coming half a second before it would've connected. Colby tilted to the right to dodge the attempt. But the click of something deadly had his heart stilling.

Colby turned, finding Keats holding a gun with hands as steady as a surgeon's. His eye was already swelling and his lip was cut. "Hank, you need to get the hell out of here and drop this. I don't owe you any money. Nina's just pointing that shit at me because she's mad we broke up."

"Liar!"

"You want to argue with me right now?" Keats asked, voice cold, gun trained on Hank. "You think I have anything to lose if I pull this trigger? Look around, what do I have to fucking lose?"

Hank's Adam's apple bobbed beneath Colby's forearm.

"Listen," Colby said in a quiet voice. "You know you've got no chance against me or that gun. But this doesn't need to turn into anything. You walk out that door, leave him the fuck alone, and this is done."

Hank didn't respond at first, and Keats stepped closer. That was when Hank finally saw the light of logic. "Fine."

Colby eyed Keats and tipped his head toward him, letting him know the direction he was going. Then he eased his forearm from Hank's throat and grabbed the guy's bicep in a firm grip. "Move."

Hank seemed to grow a few brain cells because he didn't try to fight. Colby led him out the door and ushered him into the parking lot with a few more warning words. He let him go but didn't take his eyes off him. The guy was hyped up on something and could make another rash move at any moment. So Colby returned to the doorway, walking backward, and didn't move away until Hank crossed the parking lot and climbed into a beat-up black Mustang and drove off with a *fuck you* and a one-finger salute. Only when the taillights winked out of sight did Colby let his shoulders relax. The bed squeaked behind him as Keats dropped onto the mattress.

Colby shut the door and locked it, adding the chain to it for good measure, then went over to the bed. Keats was hunched over, holding his side, and cursing under his breath. The gun was on the side table. Colby went to the gun first and checked that the safety was back on.

"What are you doing here?" Keats asked, letting out a soft groan when he tried to turn to look at Colby.

"A gun, Keats?"

He flinched at Colby's tone, or maybe it was from pain. "Yeah. It's the one I stole from my father when I ran away. I've never had to fire it, but you have to protect yourself."

Colby sighed and crouched down in front of him. He grasped Keats's chin and tilted his face toward the light. The skin hadn't been broken except for the minor cut on his mouth, but he'd probably have a black eye tomorrow. "Do you need a hospital?"

Keats licked the spot of blood off his lip and gingerly pressed at his ribs. "No, I don't think anything's broken. Luckily, he wasn't wearing his steel-toed boots tonight."

Colby rubbed a hand over his face. "Fuck."

"Look, it's not a big deal, all right?" Keats said, the tightness in his voice making lies out of the words. "Just a few war wounds. I'll be all right."

"Yeah, you will. Pack your shit."

"What?"

"You're coming home with me and never coming back here." Colby stood and walked to the window to make sure Hank didn't return for a second round with his own weapon.

"Colby—"

"This isn't a negotiation," he snapped.

"But—"

He stared out the window, trying to keep the reins on his temper. "Did that guy have a reason for coming after you?"

"No, my ex is throwing me under the bus. I didn't take his stash."

He looked his way. "You do drugs, Keats? Sell them?"

Keats's movements were slow and tentative as he pushed up from the bed to a stand. "No, not anymore."

"Meaning?"

"I used to sell weed when I first got out on my own to make some quick cash. But the guys I sold for wanted me to get into the harder stuff. I wasn't up for that. I try to stay away from things that will get me arrested or dead."

"Fantastic," Colby said with exaggerated enthusiasm. He stalked to the other side of the room and opened the closet. A large duffel bag was on the ground. He grabbed it and tossed it onto the bed. "Then you should have no problem coming with me. Because right now, listening to me is what's going to keep you from getting arrested or dead."

Colby folded his arms across his chest and leaned against the wall, daring Keats to challenge him again on this. But after a brief stare-off, Keats swore under his breath and started packing.

FOURTEEN

The ride back to Colby's place was a quick and quiet one, and Keats was looking forward to crawling into bed and passing out. His head was pounding, it hurt to move, and his eye felt like it had its own heartbeat. He just wanted to sleep for a few days. But Colby had other ideas because not twenty minutes after they'd gotten back and Keats had lowered himself onto the bed, Colby was back in the guest room.

Colby leaned over the bed, frowning. "Lie still. I'm going to take a look."

"I'm fine." But Keats's fingers dug into the sheets when Colby dragged Keats's shirt up and off to inspect his back and ribs. The soreness was settling in now, and even the brush of cotton over his skin felt like too much. Colby pressed a warm palm along his side, applying the barest amount of pressure.

"Any trouble taking a full breath?"

"Not really." Keats demonstrated and managed to keep his grunt of pain to himself. "I cracked a rib in middle school. This doesn't feel like that. I'll be all right."

Colby leaned back, looking unmoved. "We'll see. I have a doctor coming over to check you out anyway."

Keats rolled onto his stomach too quickly, sending a sharp pain up his side, and his breath left him for a moment. "What?"

Colby hooked his thumbs in the pocket of his jeans. "I know a guy who's willing to make a house call and won't ask too many questions."

"You know a guy?" Keats asked, adjusting the pillow beneath his head and trying to keep the bracing pain each movement caused from showing on his face. "Did you forget to tell me you were in the mafia or something?"

Colby smirked, his dimple making him look like a mischievous kid. "Not the mafia."

A few minutes later, the doorbell rang and Colby left the room. Keats pulled the blanket over himself and let his face drop back onto the pillow. The last thing he wanted to do was see a damn doctor. He just wanted to crash and forget tonight ever happened. But Colby wasn't going to be swayed, so he'd have to grit his teeth and get through this.

Footsteps and voices sounded in the hall, and Colby returned to the room with his guest. "Keats, this is Dr. Montgomery. He's going to take a look at you. Let him."

Keats kept his face planted in the pillow. "Please tell me you come bearing fistfuls of pain pills."

The doctor sniffed. "Rough night, huh? Why don't we see what we're dealing with?"

Keats peeked out with his good eye, surprised that the doctor seemed vaguely amused. Colby leaned a shoulder against the door-jamb, obviously intending to stay for the exam, and Dr. Montgomery—who was hard to think of as a doctor with his jeans and faded Oregon Ducks T-shirt—came to the side of the bed. At least he had a stethoscope around his neck. Keats gingerly rolled onto his back and moved the blanket aside.

The doc recoiled.

"Jesus." Anger crossed his features. He sent a hard look toward Colby, accusation in his eyes. "What the hell did you do, Wilkes?"

Colby frowned deep, his gaze darting to Keats for a brief second before returning to the doc. "Seriously, Theo? You know me better than that. The guy got in a fight."

"Oh." The doc's shoulders sagged as he released a breath. "Sorry. I just—"

Colby waved it off, though he still looked annoyed. "Just make sure he's okay."

Keats peered back and forth between them, trying to figure out what was going on. Why would the doctor think that Colby had hurt him?

The exam proceeded without many words exchanged. Dr. Montgomery poked and prodded, asked a few questions about pain levels, and checked Keats's vitals. When he seemed satisfied, he stood and declared that Keats had bruised ribs and a mild allergic reaction to ant bites but was otherwise okay. Then the bastard prescribed regular ol' ibuprofen because he figured Keats "could handle a little discomfort" and prescribing pain meds outside the hospital could raise eyebrows.

Colby thanked the doctor and walked him out, leaving Keats not much better off than he had been before the doctor came. When Colby darkened the doorway again, the grim expression he'd been wearing since he'd found Keats at the motel had softened a bit— relief. So Colby really had been worried. That concern burrowed into Keats and settled into a place he didn't want to examine. He shifted on the bed. "Well, a helluva lot of good he did me. Ibuprofen and rest. I could've told him that. And where does he get off knowing what I can and can't handle? This shit hurts."

"All the tattoos and the fact that you're at my place probably gave him that idea." Colby gave him a wry smile. "He thinks you're a masochist who's used to handling pain."

"Why the fuck would he think—" Then it hit him. "Shit. He thinks I'm like—"

"Mine," Colby said, leaning against the wall and looking way too entertained by Keats's reaction. "He thinks you're my submissive. That's why he was pissed when he saw how hurt you were. He thought he was coming over to tend a few battle scars after a fun night. That's usually what he's called in for."

Keats's lips parted, the information almost too much to process. "Usually? You injure people often?"

"No. I hurt people often, but with their permission, and I know what I'm doing. I've never had to call in Theo for one of my own. But I work at a kink resort on the weekends as a trainer, and Theo's the go-to guy if something goes wrong. Accidents can happen."

"So he's like—fine with all of that?"

Colby shrugged. "He's part of all of that. Very popular with the female dommes at The Ranch. Excellently trained submissive."

Keats scooted up the headboard and raked a hand through his knotted hair while trying to picture the smug doctor kneeling at some woman's feet. "I don't get it. The guy seems like a bossy asshole. I wouldn't think he'd be the type—"

"There is no type," Colby said simply. "The man's a world-class trauma surgeon. Successful, well respected, in charge in his day-to-day world. But behind closed doors, he likes something different. What people are on the outside doesn't always match the desires hiding beneath the surface."

Keats considered that. "I guess I just had an image of what a submissive guy would be like, and I was expecting some wimpy dude who wanted someone to take care of him."

Colby rubbed a hand along his jaw, observing him in that way that made Keats want to squirm. "Submission takes more bravery than anything else—especially for a guy because of all the stereotypes out there. Putting complete trust in someone else, someone who happens to enjoy using implements of torture on you? Cowards wouldn't go near a dom. And yes, a dominant takes care of his or her submissive, but that goes both ways. Some of the worst fights I've seen in my years in the kink world are submissives going into protective mode when someone tries to mess with their dominant."

"I guess it's just hard for me to understand it."

"Is it?" Colby asked with a little head tilt. "Last night in the kitchen, you said you were fine suffering the torture of listening if it turned Georgia on. You said there wasn't much you wouldn't do to please a beautiful woman."

Keats blinked. "All I meant—"

Colby held up a hand, halting him. "So if Georgia wanted to tie your hands behind your back, put you on your knees, and demand that you make her come, that would turn you off?"

Keats groaned at the image, a twinge of heat sparking low. "Well, fuck, of course it wouldn't. But what guy wouldn't be turned on by that?"

"I wouldn't," Colby said matter-of-factly. "I had to do submissive training in order to be a trainer at The Ranch. I was terrible at it. Couldn't get hard when I wasn't in control."

Keats stiffened, embarrassment and anger mixing into one. "So what? You're saying something's wrong with me?"

"I tell you I couldn't get it up for something, and you think I'm saying something's wrong with *you*?" Humor sparked in Colby's eyes and a hint of a smile appeared. "Of course not. People who like to be tied up and forced to do things are some of my favorite people."

Keats's stomach dipped, and he hated that his body responded even when he knew Colby was purposely goading him.

"I'm only trying to help you understand that there's nothing wrong with being one or the other, or both or neither. You asked me earlier about my lifestyle. Since you're going to be staying with me a while and probably meeting some of my friends, I'm simply answering some questions."

"And you think I'm submissive," he said flatly.

Colby crossed his arms, impassive. "I don't make assumptions about anyone, especially someone who's never tried kink before. Nobody really knows until they experiment and find out what does it for them. There aren't always neat boxes. I know masochists who are dominants. Submissives who hate pain. People who switch roles depending on who they're with. It's complex. So no, I haven't slapped some label on you, Keats."

"So the people you train at that resort, they already know what they are?"

"No. Some of them are still figuring it out. I help them with that if they need it."

Keats focused on folding the edge of the blanket into small zig-zag folds. "So that's what got you this house, huh?"

"What do you mean?"

"This isn't a neighborhood for a teacher's salary."

"Counselor."

"Whatever. Bet it pays a lot less than fucking people for cash."

Colby's jaw clenched. "I'm not having sex for money. I'm a trainer. I don't fuck students."

Keats couldn't help the snort that escaped. "Yeah, I got that message the night you tossed me out of your house. Loud and clear."

Colby blew out a breath and ran a hand over his face, looking drawn and exhausted all of a sudden. "You know what, Keats? Part of me wishes I had kissed you back that night. No matter how wrong or inappropriate or illegal it would've been. Maybe that would've kept you there for the night and off the street the next day and the day after that." He met Keats's gaze, regret resting in his. "You were too good a kid to have to travel down this road. The world had bigger things waiting for you than this."

Keats's lungs felt tight, and it had nothing to do with his ribs. He didn't want to think about the *what if*s. He dropped his gaze to the comforter, memories flooding him. Memories of the boy he used to be, the dreams he used to cling to, and how his dad had finally crushed the last bit of them that night. Remembering how desperately he'd wanted to believe that if he meant something to Colby, then maybe he wasn't as worthless as he felt. "I don't even know what I would've done if you had kissed me back. It's not like I had any idea what I was doing."

"Would've never happened anyway."

Keats smirked, still staring at the comforter. "You're bad for my ego. I had no shot, huh?"

Colby made some indecipherable sound and moved toward the door. When Keats dared to look up, Colby's back was to him, his hand braced on the door frame. "No, Keats. You were a kid. I didn't think of you that way. Not back then."

With that, Colby disappeared into the dark hallway and shut

the door behind him, leaving Keats staring after him. *Not back then*. But now . . .

Below the covers, Keats's body stirred to attention.

Fan-fucking-tastic.

He planted a pillow over his face and groaned.

FIFTEEN

"So how'd it go?"

Georgia sipped her coffee and tried not to smile at the eager face staring back at her through her computer screen. "Are you asking as my therapist or my friend?"

Leesha sat up straighter in her office chair, pushed her dreads behind her shoulders, and put on her reading glasses. "Therapist first. Were you able to complete your goal?"

"Yes. I made it into his house with no panic attack."

"Anxiety level from one to ten?"

"It hit about a seven, but he talked me down, helped me to breathe through it and to distract myself from the negative thoughts."

She lifted a brow—her mildly impressed face. "Intuitive."

"He's a school counselor."

"Oh," she said, shifting into her fully impressed face. "Well, that helps."

"Yeah, he's really understanding about it. I was able to stay a while without any of the anxiety coming back."

"A while, huh? Did you tell him about the watching you've been doing?"

She set her cup down. "He already knew. Apparently, I wasn't quite as stealthy as I thought. Cancel my application to become an international spy."

"He *knew*?" Leesha's green eyes went big. "So he . . ."

"Yes, he let me. He"—Georgia's face heated, but she pushed on—"he said he liked that I was watching."

"Ho-lee shit." She took her glasses off, apparently switching out of therapist mode into BFF mode. "That is either exceptionally creepy or freaking hot."

"Hot," Georgia said with a solemn nod. "Believe me. So. Hot."

"Damn, girl." Leesha glanced to the side, probably double-checking that her office door was still shut. "So what happened after that big revelation?"

Georgia sipped her coffee again and gave a shrug. "You know, stuff."

"Oh, hell no." Leesha leaned closer to her camera. "You can't get vague on me now, woman. What happened?"

She attempted a nonchalant expression. "Oh, you know, I might've broken my dry spell."

Leesha's face lit and she smacked a hand on her desk. "Hot damn! Really? That's a huge breakthrough—huge!"

Georgia laughed. "Oh, it *definitely* was. Huge, that is."

Leesha blinked, obviously surprised to hear her make a joke. It was something old Georgia would've done. But Leesha recovered quickly and grinned wide. "Lucky bitch."

"So you're not going to lecture me on why I shouldn't sleep with a guy on the first date or how I should take things slow?"

She snorted. "This wasn't exactly a first date. If he knew you were watching, you've been somewhat intimate for months, even if it was through glass. And honestly, I think something casual and fun with a guy could help. Beyond needing face-to-face connections with the outside world, trusting someone enough to be sexual with them is a big step in repairing the damage Phillip left you with. It shows progress."

"Me screwing my hot neighbor is progress? I like your version of therapy, Dr. Richards," she teased, trying to keep the mood light. She wanted to have a fun chat with her friend. She didn't want to think about treatment plans and goals and how Colby could fit onto that list. She didn't want her sexy fling to be something to check off on a list to show that she was A-OK again.

"This isn't Dr. Richards's advice. This is advice from the girl who's known you since sixth grade and wants to see you happy and healthy again."

That took Georgia's smile down a notch. "I know, Leesh. I'm trying."

"I know you are," she said, her voice sympathetic. "This is hard work, and I'm proud that you're pushing yourself. Keep stepping outside those comfort zones, and we'll get you into that courtroom. Then you can put all this shit behind you."

Put it behind her. Like it'd just been a bad marriage or misguided career decision or something. That goal sounded like a pipe dream if ever there was one.

Some scars would never disappear no matter how much salve you put on them or how much time you let pass. But maybe she could learn to live with those marks on her. A life that didn't involve hiding inside her house like some scared, helpless thing.

Of all the things, that was what she hated the most. The helplessness. Her sister wouldn't even recognize her, looking down from wherever she was. If she were still here, she'd be giving Georgia a helluva talking-to for being such a coward.

Of course, if her sister were still here, Georgia wouldn't be in this situation in the first place. Her doctors had said the trauma of losing Raleigh and finding out the truth about how her friend Tyson had died had been what set off her breakdown. When she'd turned in evidence on Phillip to the cops, Georgia had already been dealing with the cold realization that the polished, successful man she'd dated was a sick, dangerous person.

When she'd broken up with him, it had taken only a week before the phone calls, letters, and drive-bys had started. First, it'd been the sweet, please-take-me-back approach. But when she'd ignored him, it'd turned ugly and violent quick. She'd protected herself, had taken precautions. But she hadn't thought to consider her family. And Phillip had known what would devastate her more than anything. Raleigh, her baby sister, dead. Everything had fallen apart in Georgia's world after that.

Chilled by the memory, Georgia wrapped up her conversation with Leesha and promised to check in later in the week. She had no doubt Leesha would end the call and immediately send the email update to the lawyer. What would it say?

Dear Mrs. Ramirez, Client left the house and screwed her neighbor. We are making great progress on her treatment plan and are confident she will be ready to testify in court when the time comes.

Georgia snorted to herself. Of course, Leesha wouldn't give those exact details. Beyond confidentiality rules, she would protect Georgia's privacy as a friend. But still, Georgia had the distinct feeling of being observed like a circus animal—everyone peering in and wondering if she'd be able to perform for the masses when it was time.

Her doorbell rang, startling her from her thoughts. She pushed back from her desk and headed to the front door, the familiar rush of adrenaline filling her as she crossed the bottom floor of her house. She hated that it was such a hair trigger. It was probably just a salesman or Bible pusher and already her body was going all fight-or-flight. But when she got to the door and peeked through the peephole, there was a familiar profile in view.

Nerves of a different sort crackled through her. She took a breath and unlocked the door. By the time she pulled it open, she'd mustered up some semblance of a casual smile—or at least she hoped it looked casual. She didn't feel casual. "Hey, there."

"Hey." Keats tucked his hands in his back pockets and lifted his face to her. "You wanted to talk to me?"

"Oh my God." She stepped onto the porch, and her hand went to push his hair away from his blackened eye. "Are you all right?"

"I'm fine," he said gruffly. But his gaze flared when she ran a thumb along his swollen cheekbone.

She quickly lowered her hand, realizing the move had come across more intimate than she'd intended. "What happened?"

"Had a welcoming committee when I showed up at my place last night. Kind of a long story. The other guy looks worse than I do, at least." He shrugged. "It's not a big deal. I'm a little banged up but nothing to freak out about."

"I'm guessing Colby freaked out," she said, resisting the urge to check him head to foot for injuries.

Keats smirked and glanced toward Colby's place. "Understatement. I have a feeling if I hadn't come home with him last night, he would've tied me up and tossed me in the back of his truck."

She crossed her arms. "I don't blame him. I would've done the same."

Keats's gaze hopped to hers at that, green eyes sparking. "Yeah? I might've enjoyed that. Next time, you come and get me instead."

She laughed. "There won't be a next time because you're not going back."

His playful expression clouded over. "Well, I'm not going to freeload over at Colby's forever, no matter how much he says he doesn't mind me staying with him."

"No freeloading necessary," she said, taking a step back into her house and pushing the door open wider. "Because soon you'll be able to pay Colby rent. I'm going to offer you a job, and you're going to take it."

His eyebrows arched. "I am?"

"Yes."

"O-kay," he said, doubt lingering in his voice. "You need remodeling done or something?"

"I need a lot of things but not remodeling."

"A lot of things, huh?" His attention traveled down her body and up again, not bothering to hide his perusal, and then he grinned. "What kind of job is this exactly?"

She pressed her lips together, attempting a stern look, but failed when her mouth twitched up at the corners. "Stop flirting, new hire."

He chuckled and walked past her into the house. "With you? Not possible. And I haven't said yes yet."

Georgia breathed through the shimmer of anxiety that arose from Keats entering her home. Goddamn her brain and its crossed signals. But after a few seconds of focusing on her responses, she was able to recapture the calm. Each time he came over it would get easier. That was what she had to keep reminding herself. "You will."

"Confident woman. I like it." He strolled into her living room and sank onto her couch, totally at ease. No visitor had ever sat in her living room here. But somehow his nonchalance helped her to not panic about his presence. "So what is it you need?"

She shut the door behind her, headed into the living room, and sat in the armchair facing the couch. "Office work, mostly. Easy tasks but things that can be time sucks for me. And I need help with errands. I'm not—" She was tempted to make some lame excuse about how she didn't have time to run errands, but he'd seen her panic attack yesterday. She'd be fooling no one. "I'm not good with leaving the house. It's a pain in the ass, but I can't seem to fix it. So it'd be a huge help if I had someone who could take stuff to the post office or pick up things at the store."

He shifted on the couch, his fingers rubbing along his side like it hurt, but said nothing.

"It would only be part time, but it could get you started and would give you a chance to look for something full time in the off hours. Plus, I could help you put together a résumé. I'm good at those."

"Are you making up a position for me?" he asked, his tone grim.

She shook her head. "Not at all. I was looking for a virtual assistant already for the office stuff. But I figured this could be even better because you're here and could help with physical things as well."

He smirked at *physical things*.

And she had to wonder if it had been a Freudian slip on her part. Maybe this wasn't a wise idea. She should not be having any inappropriate thoughts about her too-young, too-good-looking future employee. Especially when she'd slept with the guy's housemate last night. "You're shameless."

But she was really directing that accusation at herself.

"Agreed," he said without remorse. "But this sounds like kind of a cop-out for you."

She blinked. "What?"

He stretched an arm out over the back of the couch, taking up the space like he owned it and looking older than his years. "For your panic attacks. Instead of facing it, you'll just send me instead. Sounds like cheating."

Her spine straightened. "It's not that simple."

He frowned. "Or that complicated."

That ticked her off. "You don't know anything about what I'm going through, Keats."

"Maybe not. But I probably understand more than you think. I know what panic attacks are. When I was in junior high, my father made me join a summer football camp he was coaching. I hated it. *Hated.* All the worst of the kids who tormented me in school were part of the camp and now instead of just teasing me, they could crush me on the field in the spirit of the game. And when they did and I couldn't get up quick enough, not only would they laugh, but my dad would call me a pussy in front of everyone, take off my jersey and replace it with a pink T-shirt that said *Princess*, then make me run laps for lack of effort."

Her stomach turned.

"I'd make myself sick and have panic attacks over showing up. I researched every trick there was to making myself look like I was sick so my dad wouldn't drag me out there. Of course, with him, none of it worked. I couldn't sleep or eat, thinking about what I'd face the next day. The dread was killing me. It was ruining my whole summer—the only time I usually enjoyed. So the third week, I decided that I'd stop worrying over what could happen and make the worst happen—take the control back. I showed up to practice early in that stupid shirt and told those douchebags to make good on their threats or fuck off."

"Did they back down?"

He made a dismissive noise. "No way. They jumped me. Six on one. But I got what I wanted after all. After knocking out the ring-leader with an excellent uppercut—which was awesome—I got shoved down some bleachers and broke my ankle. Couldn't play any sports for months. I spent the rest of that summer learning how to play guitar while my dad disappeared every day to camp. Best. Summer. Ever."

"God, Keats, that's awful."

"Probably, but it taught me that being scared is usually worse than what you're scared of. Facing it sucks, but it sucks less than always worrying about the *what if*s."

She sighed. She could tell him that her fear was well founded, but it wasn't really anymore. Phillip was in another state. All that was left was the residual, nebulous terror of what could happen. "I know it probably doesn't seem like it, but I am working on it and taking small steps. The fact that you're here in the house with me is one. And last night was the first time I went into someone else's house in over a year."

She had no idea why she was admitting all this, but Keats had that way about him. He had a face you'd confess deep, dark secrets to because you could tell he'd keep them.

"So why don't I help you keep that up?"

"What do you mean?"

"I'll run errands for you, but only if you come with me."

Her chest tightened. "I don't think—"

"Think of me like your personal bodyguard. I'll look out for you and if you start to panic, I can get you out to the car before anyone knows something's wrong. And if you don't panic, I'll provide rewards."

She couldn't help but smirk at that. "Rewards?"

"Yes, I'm all about the positive reinforcement, George. Can I call you George?"

"Uh . . ."

But he didn't wait for an answer. "You know, cookies. Chocolate. Full-body massages. Rewards."

She laughed.

"What?" he asked innocently.

She rolled her eyes. "I'm not sure HR would approve of an employee giving his boss a massage."

"Are we really going to talk about HR? I was one room over last night while you and Colby screwed on the couch. I think we've jumped that shark."

She rubbed her hand over her eyes, chagrin rushing to the surface. "Right, yeah, I'm sorry things got a little . . . out of hand."

"I'm not." He leaned forward and braced his forearms on his thighs, meeting her gaze. "Last night was hot. No one forced me to listen. I could've minded my own damn business. But let's not pretend that we weren't all in on it. Y'all wanted me to hear. I wanted to hear. And honestly, if giving me this job means we're going to have to be all formal with each other, then you can keep it."

"What?"

"I like you, George. And I'm happy to work for you—thankful to be offered the chance, believe me. But I'm not good at formal and polite. I work hard, but what you see is what you get."

She wet her lips, his declaration making her feel a little off balance.

"We both already know more about each other than we should, right? So pretending we don't would be bullshit. You're sleeping with the guy I'm staying with, and he happens to be kinky, so I'm guessing last night won't be the first time I see or hear more than I should."

She leaned back in the armchair, her neck burning. "Maybe this was a bad idea. You don't have to do any work for me. I'm putting you in an awkward—"

He was off the couch in a blink. He went down on one knee in front of her and took her hands. "Hey, stop. Do I look like I'm weirded out by this or being forced to be here?"

She stared down at him. Even the black eye couldn't mar how damn beautiful he was. She had the sudden desire to push her fingers through his hair, to feel those strands against her skin. *Shit.* She pulled her hands from Keats's and tucked them in her lap. This plan was feeling more dangerous by the minute.

"Listen. I'm here to help however you need. I don't care what the job is. If it's hard labor out in the yard or licking envelopes or organizing your sock drawer, that's fine. I'm in. But can't we just leave all the crap that normally comes along with jobs aside? I'm not good at faking shit." He made a circle around his mouth with his finger. "No filter."

"Keats," she said, not sure how to respond.

He braced his hands on the arms of her chair but stayed on his knee in front of her, like some knight ready to declare his loyalty to the queen. "Look, I'm already dealing with Colby treating me like I'm still a kid half the time. Honestly, if last night hadn't happened, I don't care how mean he would've gotten at the motel, I wouldn't have come back home with him. I don't need or want another parent. But last night showed me that he's capable of seeing me as an adult. So I'm giving this a shot for a few days, even though I know he's going to slip up and treat me like I'm still sixteen at times. But I definitely don't want to leave that every morning and come over here for more eggshell walking."

She let out a long breath. Could she do this without the formal walls and lines marking the boundaries? The formality and control were what she'd hoped would get her through the anxiety of having someone in her space.

"Okay," she said finally and met his eyes. "No faking. This doesn't have to be formal. But if at any time, you feel like this isn't working or you feel awkward or uncomfortable, you tell me. No hard feelings."

His lips curved. "Deal. And if I suck as an assistant, you fire my ass. Also, for the record, I'm exceptionally hard to make uncomfortable. Just so you know."

She cocked her eyebrow at him. "Colby makes you uncomfortable."

"Colby makes me crazy. There's a difference." He stood and went back to his spot on the couch. "And it's only because we have history."

"Beyond being teacher/student?"

A little color came to his face. "Nothing like . . . inappropriate or whatever. I just—I was a fucked-up kid, and Colby was the only person I could turn to back then. The only one who gave a shit about me. When I ran away from home, I left Colby with a lot of rumors and crap to deal with. It was a dick move on my part. But somehow, Colby thinks it was all his fault. I can't seem to get that dumb idea out of his head. I think all of this right now is some self-imposed penance or something."

"Or maybe he just cares."

He sniffed. "He'd be stupid to waste that concern on me. But if me sticking around for a while makes him feel better about it, then I'll do it. I owe him more than I could ever pay back already. I let him think I was dead, and he blamed himself. I didn't realize he'd do that, but looking back, it was a fucking cruel thing to do to the one person who'd tried to help me."

Her throat tightened at the thought. She was still getting to know Colby, but even through casual, neighborly conversations, she could tell that his students were everything to him. She couldn't imagine how hard it must've been on him back then—the young teacher losing a favorite student, one he'd tried to help.

"You do owe him," she agreed. "And I have a feeling it's going to take more than hanging out at his house for a few weeks to pay off that debt." She stood and grabbed a blank notebook off the coffee table. She tossed it to Keats. "Start writing down any job experiences you've had and any relevant skills so we can get started on that résumé. The best apology you can give to Colby is to show him that you're going to accept his help and take this opportunity to get on a path that doesn't involve getting jumped in a hotel room. You know he's not going to let you move out until he thinks you're safe."

Keats's expression turned sour. "The dude has a major caretaker complex."

She laughed. "He does. But that's part of his charm."

He tilted his head. "You gonna let him take care of you?"

She grimaced and walked toward her office, which was actually the small dining area that was open to the living room. "I don't need anyone to take care of me, Keats. What Colby and I are doing is just for fun."

Keats turned around on the couch, bracing his forearms on the back of it to face her. His smile turned challenging. "You gonna let me take care of you?"

She frowned.

"Because I'm going to earn my keep, George. Tomorrow, we're going on our first errand together. Just think how badass you'll look—a bodyguard with a black eye. No one would dare fuck with you."

She rolled her eyes even as nerves knotted her stomach. But she didn't say no.

She had a feeling she wouldn't tell Keats no for much.

SIXTEEN

Georgia's muscles ached from all the writing she'd done this afternoon. Keats had stuck around for a while, helping her get organized and learning her filing system on the laptop she'd given him. She'd been worried that having him there would be a complete distraction, but he was surprisingly good at being quiet and soon they'd both zoned into their work.

But she could tell after a while that all the sitting was getting to him. Whatever injuries he had from the fight were bothering him. He'd waved her off when she'd asked him about it, but she'd seen him pop open a bottle of ibuprofen a few hours in and had sent him home to rest. He'd agreed to leave only if she promised that tomorrow she'd at least attempt to go out on an errand with him.

She wandered into the kitchen, planning to figure out what she wanted to throw together for dinner when her phone rang. She strode back into the living room and grabbed her phone off her desk, smiling when she saw the name flash across the screen: *For a Good Time Call.*

"Hello?"

"I can't seem to stop thinking about you today. But I've been trying to be good and not interrupt your workday. Still busy?"

She ran her teeth over her bottom lip. For some reason, the sound of his voice made her feel like a schoolgirl. "I was just wrapping up and deciding what to do for dinner."

"I've got dinner covered. Take-out from Barcelona awaits."

"You didn't have to—"

"Of course I didn't, but I did. You're coming over tonight, and I refuse to subject you to my cooking."

"Who said I was coming over?"

"I wasn't asking, gorgeous. I have plans for you, so you'll be here. But first, I need you to go upstairs to your guest room."

She glanced at the stairs. "Why?"

"Upstairs, Georgia. Go to the window."

"Right." She was already forgetting that this was the game she'd agreed to. Her heartbeat picked up speed as she headed up the stairs. When she pulled back the curtain at the window, she found Colby looking right back at her from his room. "Well, hello."

He lifted a hand in greeting. She couldn't tell if he was smiling without her binoculars to zoom in, but she got the sense that he was. It was a bizarre feeling to be at this window and not hiding in the dark but standing there proudly.

"Now, I know you've watched me for a long time and have seen a lot. And I know you've done your research. So I'm sure you have some idea of what you'd like to try out and experience."

"Maybe." The list was long. But she wasn't sure she had the guts to announce that list.

"Good. Now, have you ever seen that show *Let's Make a Deal*?"

"The one where people dress up in weird costumes?"

"Yep. That's what we're going to play right now. Let's see how much you've paid attention. Behind door number one"—he pointed at a closed closet door—"we have things that will help your mind shut down but require a brave soul."

She squinted at the door, trying to remember what she'd seen him get from there. That was where bigger items would probably be stored. The floggers and riding crops most likely. "Okay."

"Door number two, which is technically not a door, but a chest of drawers, holds things that will bring intense focus but require the most trust."

She rubbed her lips together. Focus. Maybe bondage equipment, maybe items for pain, too. Because she guessed pain could make your mind shut down or focus only on that. "I have a feeling these are trick options."

He gave a soft laugh. "The good news is, unlike the TV show, none of them are going to have a year's supply of hot dogs."

"How about an evening's supply of orgasms?"

"That could definitely be a possibility."

She grinned, more than a little relieved that even though they were going to try out this power-play thing, Colby was approaching it in a lighthearted way with her. She knew he didn't always, so she appreciated that he was attuned to what wouldn't scare her off. "Is there a door number three?"

"Door number three is a linen closet in the bathroom. That holds only things for pleasure, but those require the most patience."

Huh. Now that had to be the trick one because who wouldn't pick that? She pictured what could be in there. Vibrators, dildos, massage oils—all things that were great in their own right. But the more she thought about it, the more she found herself not all that excited by just that. She'd used those things, been down that road already. The reason she was so drawn to Colby was that it wasn't all about the sweet side of pleasure.

"So, gorgeous, this is the one decision you get to make tonight. I want you to write down the number somewhere on your body. When I take you to my room after dinner, I'll know your decision. Do you understand?"

"I do." So did her body. Already she felt warmer, flushed, and wound up.

"Good. Now come over for dinner. Wear a dress and nothing beneath it."

She licked her dry lips. "What about Keats?"

"He's already eaten and is in his room, said he wanted to work on his résumé. He knows you're coming over, so I think he's making an effort to give us privacy."

"Won't he still hear things?"

"Maybe. I don't think he minds. But if you're worried, I can always gag you."

"No, nothing that makes me feel like I can't breathe. It's too close to how I feel when I panic."

"Understood. And while we're talking about it. Your safe word is *red*. If you need to stop for any reason, you say that word, and I stop no matter what. And like I said last night, the word *stop* will get my attention, too. You always have the power to shut things down."

"Okay," she said, nodding even though he probably couldn't see that from all the way on the other side of the fence. The safe word really did make her feel better. She'd learned what they meant from her research and knew that it was respected above all else. She had no doubt Colby would honor it if she called her word.

"You have fifteen minutes to get dressed and over here. Then we eat. After that, you're all mine."

She shivered. "I can't wait. I've heard Barcelona has excellent food."

He laughed. "Smartass. You just earned an extra swat for that one."

"Look forward to it."

With that, she hung up, shut her curtains, and collapsed onto the guest bed with a smile so big it hurt her face.

All these months she'd been sitting in the dark, watching the erotic tableaus of Colby Wilkes through that window, wondering what it must feel like to be so free, how heady it must feel to be the center of that man's attention. Tonight, she'd finally find out.

Tonight she'd be his.

———————

Keats should put in his earbuds. The voices and laughter from the kitchen drifted through his door like a siren call. He knew Colby and Georgia were on a date. Colby hadn't told him to make himself scarce—telling him this was his place right now, too—but Keats knew it'd be a dick move to hang around and insert himself into their evening. But part of him was dying to go in there.

Something about those two drew him like a mosquito in the summer, dazed by the buzzing electric light that would zap it dead. He knew it was bad for him to even pay attention to what was going on between Georgia and Colby. He had a good thing going at the moment. Georgia had given him a job to help him get on his feet while he looked for something more permanent. Colby was giving him a place to stay where he didn't have to sleep with a damn gun under his pillow. He'd be stupid to fuck it up with dumb things like his lust for Georgia and his mixed-up feelings for Colby.

But his good sense was fighting a battle with all the things the last few days had kicked up. And before long, he found himself climbing off the bed and heading out of his room. He was thirsty. That was all. Yeah, and if he could convince himself of that, he really was as stupid as one of those mosquitoes.

He was lost in his whirling thoughts, walking with his head down, when he nearly careened right into Georgia.

"Whoa." She put her hands up to block him.

Keats tried to stop, but his momentum carried him forward, and he had to grab her arms to keep from knocking her over. "Shit."

Her hands landed against his chest, and he held her there. For a second, there was silence, both of them looking at each other, her brown eyes searching his. The overwhelming urge to kiss her hit Keats like a fist to the gut. He managed to force out a "Sorry."

She backed up a step and lowered her hands, smoothing them over her dress. "No problem. Everything all right? You look like you're in a hurry."

"I—" He shrugged, feeling all kinds of awkward now. "I was thirsty."

Her eyebrow quirked.

"Really thirsty."

Lame. So lame.

"Okay."

He couldn't keep his eyes from roaming downward. Georgia looked so different than she had a few hours ago when he was working at her house. The casual jeans and sweater had been traded in for a wine-red dress with a deep V neckline. His gaze lingered and as if on cue, her nipples hardened beneath the thin fabric. He nearly groaned aloud. No way she was wearing a bra.

He imagined crowding her against the wall and sliding his hand inside that neckline, feeling the weight and warmth of her in his palm, running his tongue along her nipple until it was ripe and wet, pressing his teeth into her flesh.

She cleared her throat, snapping him out of his own personal porn reel. "Well, come on, I was heading back to the kitchen, too. We have food left if you want anything."

Oh, there was something he wanted. But it definitely wasn't dinner.

He adjusted the front of his jeans and followed her into the kitchen, where the other object of his tormented thoughts was clearing the table. Colby looked up from his task and seemed surprised to find Georgia and Keats walking in together. "Hey."

"Hey," Keats said, wishing he'd just stayed the hell in his room. After the encounter in the hallway, his whole body felt flushed, his senses edgy. He had to be wearing his frustration like a fucking billboard. He walked over to the fridge.

"Keats was thirsty," Georgia explained.

"Ah," Colby said, reaching out a hand and tugging Georgia to him. "I thought you'd gotten lost on your way to the bathroom."

"No, she just picked up a stray." Keats grabbed a soda from the fridge.

"You're not a stray." Colby frowned at him over Georgia's head. He'd pulled her against him, back to front, and had his arms wrapped around her waist. Keats couldn't decide who he was more jealous of.

Fuck. What the hell was wrong with him?

"Maybe not. But I'm definitely a third wheel." He bumped the fridge shut. "So now that I've got supplies, you won't see me for the rest of the night."

"You don't have to go," Georgia offered. "We could all hang out for a while, watch a movie or something."

"No," Colby and Keats said simultaneously.

No way Keats was going to be some pitied hanger-on.

Georgia looked up at Colby, and he smiled down at her in a way that made Keats's body surge with want. What he wouldn't give to be the one taking Georgia to bed tonight, the one peeling her out of that dress.

Or the one getting those looks from Colby, his mind whispered. He shoved the errant thought aside.

"I've got plans for you, gorgeous. You don't get to decide what happens next. And I assure you, what happens next doesn't involve a movie." He sent Keats a pointed stare. "Plus, no more free shows for Keats."

Keats laughed, but it sounded forced to his own ears. "What? You're selling tickets now?"

Colby smirked, challenge in his eyes. "I think the price of admission is way too high for your taste, Keats. Better get to bed."

His throat went dry at that, but he did his best to appear unaffected by the comment. He gave a quick nod and headed straight back to his room, his heart pounding and his cock stiffening. Until this week, he'd thought himself pretty hard to knock off balance. He'd lived a life on the fringe and had been exposed to more than most. But around Colby, he felt like a goddamned blushing virgin sometimes. The guy could be as laid-back and good ol' boy as anyone he'd ever met. But when he flipped that dominant switch? Fuck. In those moments, Keats's body didn't seem to give a shit that Colby was a dude or that Keats was a third wheel in this scenario. It just knew that it wanted a piece of whatever Colby and Georgia had.

Fuck my life.

Keats leaned against the door, pressing his forehead against it, and tried to cool down. Long minutes passed. But before he could get his heartbeat or erection under control, he heard the first smack against skin and Georgia's answering gasp.

He slid down the door, unzipped his jeans, and wrapped his hand around himself.

Maybe sleeping with a gun under his pillow hadn't been so bad. Trying to sleep here was going to be an absolute fucking nightmare.

SEVENTEEN

Georgia watched Keats go with mixed feelings. Part of her had invited him to hang out for a while because she hated the thought of leaving anyone out, especially when she'd learned today how much of an outsider Keats had been growing up. But she knew that had only been a small part of her motivation. The other, bigger part had been purely selfish and seriously ill-advised.

Something had passed between her and Keats in the hallway. It'd been brief—a blink and she would've missed it—but there'd been a shift. He'd checked her out, which really wasn't anything new. Keats was a natural flirt. But this time the look hadn't been playful. It'd been all man—alpha and hungry. He'd wanted her.

And her body had clamored to attention and responded. She'd thought maybe it was because she'd already spent a slow, sensual dinner with Colby feeding her things from his fingers. Or maybe because she wore nothing beneath the stretchy material of her dress, so she was hyperaware and sensitive. But even with all that, she knew in her gut it was something more than those simple things. It wasn't her intense attraction to Colby bleeding over onto Keats. It was something separate and maybe just as potent.

Colby was still pressed up against her from behind, and he ran his hands over her arms. "What happened out there? You both walked in looking like you'd stolen all the cookies."

She tensed, an old reaction surfacing, defensive. "Nothing, we just bumped into each other in the hallway. Like literally. It wasn't—"

He turned her in his arms and gave her a soft smile. "Hey, I'm not accusing you of anything. I was just curious." He cupped her face in his hands. "Remember, I'm not that guy. Really."

She took a breath and nodded. He was using the words *that guy* generally, but it fit exactly. She needed to remember it. He wasn't Phillip. He wasn't going to flip his shit if she glanced at another man. "We bumped into each other and he looked at me, I don't know, like he was going to kiss me."

Colby seemed amused. "Did you want him to?"

"No," she said, probably too quickly. "He's working for me."

"But if he weren't?"

"He is."

Colby smiled at that and kissed her. "That's a very black-and-white world you're living in, Georgia. Now"—he put his mouth close to her ear—"get on your knees and let me show you what happens when you try to change our plans without my permission."

Her breath caught. "Here?"

He released her and grabbed one of the chairs from the dining room table. He spun it around and pointed next to it. "Here."

Her heartbeat turned into a wild thing, but she managed to walk the few steps over to the chair and get to her knees. The tile was cool beneath her skin, hard, but the slight discomfort grounded her, giving her something to focus on.

Colby swung open a kitchen cabinet and pulled out a crock of kitchen utensils. Wooden spoons, plastic spatulas, a whisk with a thick rubber handle. She watched him with rapt attention, gnawing the inside of her lip. He walked over and set them on the table next to the chair, then reached for her. He ran his hand over the back of her head, a sweet, tender gesture, then sat and patted his leg. "Drape yourself over my thighs and flip your dress up. You wanted Keats to be part of this? Well, I'll give you your wish. His wall shares one with the kitchen. He'll be able to hear your first spanking."

She shook her head. "No, I don't want to do that to him. It's not really fair and—"

"I don't remember asking your opinion, love. And if you're so concerned about it, then don't make any noise." Instead of patting his leg again, he gripped her arm and gently guided her up and over his lap. "Now lift up your dress."

The prone position sent her body into an instant capitulation, and any further protests seemed to fade into the loud sound of her heartbeat thumping in her ears. She reached back and dragged her dress up, exposing her naked backside. The cool air on her heated skin made goose bumps rise and the damp place between her thighs burn even hotter. Her fingertips touched the floor, and she wasn't sure if it was the head rush from the position or something else, but she felt giddy. Colby adjusted himself beneath her, strong muscular thighs pressing into all of her softest spots.

"You look fucking sinful like this, baby," Colby said, running a warm palm over her backside. "I can't wait to make this pretty ass sting."

God. Her body was throbbing already. She'd never been spanked—not in a sexual way or in a disciplinary one. But there was something about being in this position that was totally doing it for her. She had a feeling it was going to be hard to stay quiet.

He slid his hand between her thighs, finding her warm, wet secret. His thumb slid inside her and his fingers moved up to stroke her clit in tandem. "Mmm, someone's been ready for a while."

She gasped, trying to stay still, trying to stay quiet, but damn the man was good with his fingers. He gave her a few more strokes and then pulled away, wiping her arousal on the back of her thigh as if to say, *Look, how much you want this.*

It wouldn't be a lie.

She braced for the next thing, knowing a hit of some sort would come, but instead a fingertip traced around her back opening. She jolted with surprise, but he held her down easily with his other hand. "Have you ever been taken here?"

She tried to swallow the drool pooling in her mouth. The sensation was so . . . decadent, forbidden. "With a vibrator, never sex."

And only on her own, a handful of times, though she'd die if she had to admit that. She'd asked Phillip once if he wanted to try it, and he'd looked at her like she'd grown another head. That kind of thing did not fit into the princess image he'd painted in his head. So he'd laughed and taken it like she'd been joking with him.

"Did you enjoy it?" Colby asked, squeezing her buttock in a firm, almost painful grip, then releasing.

She shuddered from the sensation—tingling pain, not unpleasant. "I didn't hate it."

He chuckled, that warm low laugh of his that seemed to come from deep in that barreled chest. "Good to know."

Then he smacked her with his open palm, right over the spot he'd grabbed. One. Two. Three.

She made a choked noise, half from surprise and half from the feel of the blows.

"Pain level one to ten," he asked.

She tried to suck in a breath, get her thoughts back. Her ass was stinging but not in an unbearable way. "Five."

"Good." He reached for one of the utensils. "If we get to an eight or nine, you stop me."

"Okay."

She tried not to brace for it, knew it would make it worse, but when the spatula came down on her, she was as tense as a fist. The sting didn't spread over as big a portion as it had with his hand, but it was sharp and wicked. She bit her lip trying not to make noise. She wouldn't drag Keats into this.

But good intentions were about all she had because when Colby continued to work her ass over with swats, it felt like an avalanche of sound was building up in her throat. Everything was on fire— her ass, the backs of her thighs. The pain was crawling up to a seven and she wasn't sure she was as tough as she thought.

"Spread your legs wider," Colby said, calm as a bright blue sky in June. Damn him. How could he be so calm when he was whaling on her?

But she couldn't stop herself from obeying. She opened her thighs wider, balancing on her toes. The sound of tools banging around in the crock filled her ears, and then he gave her a soft pop right against her sex. *Whack.*

She made a grinding moan, the sound leaking out between her teeth. Good God. He popped her a few more times against that oh-so-sensitive skin, not hard, but firm enough to take note, and all that pain from before started to turn into a hot tingling burning over her skin. She squirmed, needing more pressure against her clit, but Colby shifted and hit her with what felt like the wooden spoon on the back of her thigh, sharp.

A little cry of pain slipped out.

"No coming yet, gorgeous. I give that to you when I'm ready. You still have three more tools to go."

Her head was spinning, but she didn't protest. He worked her over with the wooden spoon and then with some other kind of spatula from what she could tell. But frankly, it was all starting to run together in a haze in her mind now. The pain had left, morphing into something altogether different. Now her only discomfort was from the fact that she wanted to come and couldn't.

The swats slowed and then stopped. Colby pressed a hand to the small of her back. "Do you want to come?"

"Yes, please."

"Do you trust me not to harm you?"

"I do." And she did. In that moment, she totally did.

"Excellent." He moved his fingers against her, and she almost came from that, but he knew what he was doing and didn't give her enough stimulation to put her over the edge. Then something foreign was pushing against her. She stiffened. "This is a soft rubber handle, baby. You're wet enough to take it. Relax."

Oh, God. The whisk. He was going to fuck her with a damn kitchen implement. "Colby."

"Shh," he said, his voice more soothing now than commanding. "You're okay. I've got you."

The handle slipped in and she groaned. The handle wasn't overly large but it was grooved and textured and the feel of it inside her made her heels lift. *Jesus.*

"That's my girl," Colby said, his voice going thick, as he moved the handle in and out slowly. "You're so goddamned sexy."

The fact that he was getting so aroused only dialed up her need more. She could only imagine what she looked like to him right now, tipped over his lap in the middle of his kitchen, half naked, and being violated at his bidding. Her fingers pressed against the floor, the coiling tension in her almost at its breaking point.

He rocked her against him with each slide of the handle, rubbing her clit against the rough denim of his jeans. She wasn't going to make it much longer. Then with his free hand, he began to pinch her. The flesh of her ass, the backs of her thighs, little biting squeezes that reignited the effects of the spanking. Pinch and stroke, pinch and stroke. Rasp, rasp, rasp against his jeans. Her mind began to fuzz.

"Colby," she pleaded.

"Come for me, Georgia." He reached around with his free hand and found her clit. "Come for me and let me hear it."

That was all she needed. She launched into orgasm, her body clamping around the invasion, her hips rocking against his fingers. And despite her best effort, she couldn't keep herself quiet. She cried out loud and long—a desperate, wanton sound that had to have reverberated around the house.

But in the moment, she didn't care. Colby wanted to hear it, and she wanted to give that to him.

Right now, she'd give him just about anything.

EIGHTEEN

Georgia followed Colby to his bedroom after they'd cleaned up the kitchen. Her legs still felt like they were made of pudding after her orgasm, but she managed not to stumble as she made her way down the hall. When she passed Keats's room, she put her palm to the door for a brief second, offering a silent apology and promising herself that she would talk to him tomorrow. Maybe they needed some boundaries after all, because it seemed both of them were playing with fire without them.

But when she stepped into Colby's bedroom, finding him standing there in front of his bed, big and broad and intimidating as hell, she forgot all thoughts of tomorrow. Because finally, right now, she'd arrived at the site of so many of her fantasies. She glanced at the window.

"No one to watch us tonight, gorgeous."

"I don't need an audience." She closed the door behind her.

He smirked. "Though you like one sometimes."

"Said the pot to the kettle."

He sat down on the end of the bed, legs wide in that cowboy don't-care way, and leaned back on his hands. He nodded at the spot in front of him. "Take off your dress and show me what number you decided on."

Nerves hopped in her belly as she walked over to where he wanted. She'd left her shoes somewhere in the kitchen, so she had only one thing left to take off. She pulled the shoulders of her dress down, the stretchy fabric giving way easily, and slid the dress to her waist, exposing her chest to the cool air.

Colby's hazel eyes homed in, appraising, appreciating. This was the first time he'd seen her bared like this, and somehow he made her feel completely comfortable. She pushed the dress down her hips and stepped out of the puddle of fabric.

Colby's tongue darted out and touched his bottom lip, an unconscious gesture that made her go hot wondering what thought had crossed his mind. He cleared his throat. "Where's the number?"

She swallowed, trying to find her voice. "I didn't pick one."

His brows lowered. "Why?"

"I appreciate what you were trying to do—giving me some shred of control to cling to. But that's not what I want. I need this to be a little scary. I need my surrender to be real. I want to know I really did it."

The flare of pleasure that flickered over his expression was a reward in and of itself. He shifted forward, bracing his forearms on his thighs and pinning her with his gaze. "No bunny slope for you, huh?"

She closed her eyes briefly and shook her head. "My whole life is made of baby steps and bunny slopes right now. I need a leap. And I feel like I can do that with you."

He reached out for her, and she stepped between his spread knees. He took her hands and looked up, something she couldn't pinpoint burning in his gaze. "I'm honored that you're giving me that trust. Really. It means more than you know. I promise I won't misuse it."

For some reason, she wanted to cry, but she pressed her lips together and fought back the urge. She would not fall apart. Not before this happened.

He stood and put his hand at her waist, pulling her against him. His lips met hers with a hushed reverence at first, like they were sealing some agreement, and then the kiss turned hotter and more urgent. She could feel the muscles that had tensed from nerves loosening again and melting. His tongue stroked against hers, and as she latched onto his shirt, she could feel his erection hardening against her belly.

He groaned into the kiss and pulled away.

The quick break-off of the kiss startled her. "Everything okay?"

He gave a little laugh, sounding chagrined, and rubbed a hand over the back of his head. "I've practiced this self-control thing a long damn time. But kissing you like that makes me feel like a teenager who just wants to get inside you. Right. This. Second. If I keep kissing you like that, I'll end up pawing you like it's prom night."

She smiled and touched the band of his jeans. "I can help take the edge off. May I?"

She lowered to her knees.

"Aw, proper grammar and everything?" he said, cupping her head and rubbing a thumb over her bottom lip. "How can I resist such a polite request to suck my cock?"

Even the words had excitement pinging through her. She'd never been one to get overly enthusiastic about blow jobs, but something about Colby had had her craving that from the very start. She'd watched him get off that way from her perch at her window and had always loved how he looked when he gave himself over to the pleasure.

He reached for his belt and unfastened it, then pulled it out of the loops. "Give me your wrists."

She lifted her arms to him, and he wrapped the belt around them with surprisingly efficient motions. When he was sure it was secure, he let her lower her bound hands to her lap.

He undid his fly and tucked his hand inside. When he freed his cock, putting it on proud display right in her line of sight, her mouth actually watered.

"Only your mouth," he said gruffly. "And I control the pace."

There was something about him being fully dressed, her naked and bound at his feet that made this feel so much different than anything she'd done before. She had this deep urge to please him.

He wrapped his hand in her hair, firmly enough to make her scalp tingle but not enough to hurt, and guided her forward. The first taste of salty skin against her tongue made hot things curl inside her, as did the grunting sound he made at the contact. Her hands twisted in the bindings and she closed her eyes, savoring the flavor and feel of this sinful, sexy man.

He was big, and she wasn't skilled enough to take him all, but he didn't force her to accept more than she could handle. He kept his free hand around the base and stroked toward her with each thrust, his fingers meeting her lips in an erotic kiss. She rolled her tongue around him, sucking and teasing and mapping the feel of him.

His fingers tightened against her head. "God, baby, your mouth is going to kill me. You give head like you kiss—with everything you've got."

She *mmm*ed at the praise and doubled her efforts, wanting to know what he was like when he completely lost it. But Colby had other ideas because after a few minutes, he gently eased her away. She blinked up at him, surprised, but he grasped her chin and bent down to kiss her. "Not like this. I want you in my bed beneath me. And I want to see you wearing my rope."

"Rope?"

He released her bindings and helped her to her feet. "Door number three. One of my favorites, gives me a lot of pleasure, but it takes some patience."

She sat on the edge of the bed. "I've got all night."

"Says the girl who just had a screaming orgasm in the kitchen."

She grinned and let her eyes travel down to his very hard, very obvious erection. "You going to be okay?"

"Keep grinning, smartass," he teased. "You'll learn how dangerous it is to goad your dom."

He left for a few minutes to gather his supplies, and when he came back, she learned the threat hadn't been an idle one. He made her kneel on the bed, thighs spread, and strapped a small vibrator against her clit to keep her occupied while he worked. He dialed it to the setting that had to be called Slow Ride to Hell because it was low and slow and made her want to die with need after about ten minutes.

Meanwhile, he was wrapping soft ropes around her torso in an intricate looping pattern. He had a wrinkle in his forehead while he worked and a look in his eye that told her this was a meditative act for him. But his erection didn't flag the entire time—so not just meditative but deeply sexual. And she could understand why. The pressure of the ropes against her body and the way they gently abraded her skin had her seeing the eroticism in it.

With that new sensual experience and the torturous pace of the vibrator she was near out of her mind by the time he cinched the last knot. It was like her body had completely forgotten about the previous orgasm. Like it no longer counted. She needed his touch.

Colby pulled the vibrator away and stepped back to admire his work, giving her a look that almost sent her over the edge. Pure, unabashed lust. "You look amazing, Georgia. I can't even describe it." He opened a nearby closet door and angled the mirror inside the door her way. "Look at yourself."

The reflection stunned her for a second. She could barely comprehend that it was her image looking back at her. Colby had wound the rope into a corset, tightly coiled around her torso and two rings of rope above her breasts, leaving everything else on naked display. Her hips flared in a pleasing heart shape out from under the bottom circle of rope, and her breasts stood proud in the space between the ropes. It was utterly obscene. She loved it.

She touched the ropes over her belly, the intricate looping he'd done to get everything snug but not painful. "This is an art, Colby."

"You're the art," he said, moving to the side of the bed again and palming one of her breasts. "You're lucky I'm having a lapse in self-control tonight because the sadistic side of me kind of wants to lie back and watch you get to the brink with that vibrator over and over until you're sweating and begging for me. I could look at you all night."

He pinched her nipple between his fingertips and she gasped. "I'm already sweating and if you want me to beg, I left my pride somewhere in the kitchen, so not a problem."

His dimple appeared beneath the shadow of his beard. "I'm not looking to steal your pride, beautiful. Just a little bit of your sanity for a few minutes."

"Ha. That's already gone, so if you find it, let me know."

"Hush," he said, giving her a quick kiss and reaching between her thighs to stroke her for a few maddening seconds. "Stay on your knees and get to the middle of the bed. I'm not quite done with the rope."

All snappy comebacks faded from her thoughts as his fingers brought her right to the precipice of orgasm again before he pulled back. She wanted to grab his wrist and force his hand to stay there, but he was already out of her reach. She crawled to the middle of the bed and settled into position, her heartbeat officially relocating to the spot right behind her clit—throbbing, throbbing, throbbing.

Colby took his time wrapping her forearms in rope, leaving her with what looked like the western version of superhero cuffs, and then he drew her down onto her elbows and took the long ends of the rope to secure her to the headboard. She tugged on the restraints and they didn't give. A little flutter of panic went through her.

"Anything feel too tight?" he asked, checking the bindings at her wrist.

"What if I need to get out quickly? Like if it's an emergency?"

All of a sudden she was picturing the house catching on fire or the intense need to pee or a spider crawling onto the bed. It was all ridiculous but something about being tied to the bed had pushed her fear button.

"I've got you," he said, rubbing a thumb over her knuckles. "There's a switchblade in the bedside drawer that will slice right through this rope. You say the word and you're out in less than thirty seconds."

She nodded. "Okay."

"Hey, look at me," he said, cupping her chin and tilting her face toward him. His eyes met hers with unwavering sincerity. "Your safety is always going to be my number one priority. Always. No matter what, I'm looking out for you."

The words were spoken with utter confidence, and that confidence washed over her, filling the spaces where the fear was trying to dig roots. "Thank you."

She breathed out the rest of the nerves that had tried to crop up and closed her eyes as he moved behind her. She could hear clothes coming off, and she couldn't resist. She peeked back over her shoulder. Colby had just kicked off his jeans, and he stood there in his full naked glory.

Broad and built and big all over. He looked like a beast. Or sculpture. Or every fantasy she'd ever conjured. It almost wasn't fair.

He smiled when he caught her gawking. "I feel the same way when I look at you, Georgia. All that pretty flesh, those gorgeous curves. I want to put you on the dinner table and eat you bite by bite."

Yep. That was exactly how she felt. He was fucking edible.

"In fact," he said, climbing onto the bed behind her, "I don't think I can resist a taste right now."

He palmed her ass and angled her hips up, putting a sway in her back and exposing every private part of her for his perusal. She could feel his breath caressing her, his mouth getting closer, and then his hot tongue was on her and she lost what little calm she had left.

Colby was as talented with his mouth as he was with his hands, and soon she was yanking back on the ropes, having a hard time keeping still. He knew exactly how to keep her riding the edge, on the verge of orgasm but not reaching it. She whimpered into the sheets and banged her forehead into the mattress. Please, please, please.

"God, you taste good," he said, in between driving her out of her mind and making her want to harm him. "And you're so hot against my tongue. I can feel how close you are."

"Please, Colby," she finally said. "I can't take this much longer. I'm really begging this time. Please."

"Mmm," he said against her. "You know that just makes me want to tease you more."

"Colby . . ." Now she was whining, which she knew was a ridiculous thing for a grown woman to do, but she couldn't help herself.

A soft chuckle sent a puff of breath against her. "All right. Lucky for you I'm losing my patience, too."

He shifted behind her and wrapped firm fingers around her hips, getting into position behind her. But it took longer than she could stand because he had to get a condom on first. She swayed restlessly, trying not to beg again. Everything felt oversensitive, desperate. The ropes had their own way of caressing her, reminding her of every inch of skin that was covered, and the exposed parts felt every change in the air.

But when he finally pressed the head of his cock against her entrance and thrust forward, everything in her converged to one aching, needy point. Her body still wasn't used to his size and fought to accommodate him, but the pressure of him stretching and filling her sent her senses sailing. She pressed her face in the sheets, surrendering to him fully and without reservation.

He didn't rush, even though she would've been perfectly fine with that, but he wasn't purposely torturing her anymore. He was enjoying himself, sinking in deep and taking her with full, savoring glides. This part was about him, based on the gruff, pleased sounds he was making, and she was along for the ride. The hair-curling, sexy-as-hell ride.

"You look so fucking hot bound in my rope and spread around my cock," Colby said, his twang getting heavier the closer to release he got. He ran a finger over her back entrance as he pumped into her harder. The touch was like a bolt of lightning straight through her. "I'm going to take you here one day, too. I want every part of you, Georgia. I want to find out every button that makes you moan like that."

The words, his cock pumping into her, and him touching her there were too much. A powerful wave was building inside her, ready to take her down.

"Let go, baby," he said, reaching around with his other hand and finding her clit. "Come for me."

She would've even if he hadn't said it was okay. It was too much to hold back. She cried out as everything in her burst through like sunshine piercing a thousand tiny windows. Her neck arched and she shrieked with the rush of it all, the sheer pleasure. Colby let out a shout behind her, thrusting deep and flattening her to the bed as he found his own release.

She melted into the sheets, floating in a haze, her body still contracting with aftershocks, and closed her eyes.

It was *so* much better on this side of the window.

Too bad she wouldn't be able to stay.

NINETEEN

Colby's eyes burned from lack of sleep as he lifted his chin above the bar in his garage/workout room. Last night he'd been exhausted when he'd gotten back into bed after walking Georgia home, but he'd tossed and turned, waking up every hour on the hour. Last night had been great. Beyond great. But Georgia's leaving had left him unsettled. He understood why she needed to be back at her place. And it wasn't like it was a requirement for him. He rarely had lovers spend the night. But when he'd gotten back from Georgia's, his bed had felt damn empty.

Being with her last night had felt more right than anything had in a long time. He'd started out keeping it focused on exploring some of her boundaries, almost making it like one of his beginner training sessions. Fun and sexy but clinical in a way. That was what he was used to. But once he'd gotten her into his bedroom and had seen that she'd written no numbers down, everything had shifted. Something about Georgia made him feel more dialed in, more present. Even the mild kink they'd done had felt more intense than any of the extreme stuff he'd practiced at The Ranch lately.

Plus, those moments in the kitchen when he had her under his hand, knowing she knew Keats was listening. Well, it'd added a layer that Colby hadn't been able to ignore. He'd felt like he was getting a taste of what he'd been starving for over the last few months. And it was all temporary.

Temporary. Like his job might be. Like his whole life might be right now.

He'd finally given up hope for sleep around six this morning and had gotten up to get some things done. First, he'd called Principal Anders to check in, and she'd told him that she'd set up an appointment for him late this afternoon to speak with the powers that be to give his side. She'd also informed him that a doctor had interviewed Travis, and the kid had admitted he'd been off his meds for two months and had been lying to Dr. Guthrie about it. So even if Colby had asked him, he wouldn't have gotten an accurate answer. Anders had said she thought that boded well for getting Colby cleared and back to work.

It'd been welcome news for sure. He'd gone over that session with Travis in his head again and again. And though he wished he could've done something to prevent what had happened, in his heart, he knew he hadn't been negligent in Travis's care. But he still couldn't relax. Travis's parents weren't going to stop looking to place blame. And they had money to burn if they wanted to drag this thing out. But at least Rowan seemed to be in his corner, and he would get a chance to tell his side later today to the board. He just hoped that and the truth were enough.

Thinking about all his students being shuffled around and tossed onto Dr. Guthrie's caseload made his stomach hurt. He'd made a promise to those kids. He was supposed to be the one who was there for them when they needed it. He'd promised Katelyn Bowie that he'd teach her relaxation exercises so that she could calm down before her big algebra test. That test had now come and gone. And he'd finally gotten Jake Latham, after months of near-silent sessions, to start talking about his mother's death. Now the kid would have to start over again with Guthrie.

It was fucking brutal being stuck at home, doing goddamned nothing, when he could be working with those kids. By seven, Colby had whipped himself up into a restless, angry state just thinking about it. So he'd turned to his first method of stress relief—music. He'd locked himself in his office and had managed to bang out a chorus for a song he'd been working on.

But even after all the creative effort, he'd still felt wired and restless. He'd gone downstairs to see if Keats needed anything, but Keats had already left to run an errand for Georgia. So he'd decided to go to his surefire method of clearing his head—exorcism by exercise. Most people who saw him probably assumed he was obsessed with working out, but really, it was the only form of therapy besides music that had ever worked on him. So he'd gone for a long run and was now well into his weights routine, dripping with sweat, but finally starting to feel a little more centered.

He had to keep reminding himself that things in his life had gotten complicated quickly, and his head was screwed up from all the rapid change. In the matter of a few days, his job had blown up, his neighbor had ended up in his bed, and his former student was back from the dead and all grown up. Even someone used to rolling with the punches couldn't be expected to roll with all that.

At least not all of it was bad news.

Keats was here and safe. Sure, living with him was going to be . . . interesting. Colby's wires were all kinds of crossed when it came to Keats, but it wasn't like he couldn't handle himself around him. He'd just need to set up some clear boundaries and stop doing stupid shit that blurred it—like letting Keats listen again last night. That'd been a lust-based decision, not a responsible one. Colby usually didn't let his dick overtake his good sense. He wasn't the guy who went off the rails with passion. Discipline and self-control were a bit of a religion for him. But the way Georgia and Keats had looked at each other last night when they'd walked into the kitchen had knocked Colby completely off track. He'd wanted things he shouldn't.

Now he needed to get his bearings back. He'd set it all back to rights. He'd talk to Keats and establish some rules, apologize for last night. He'd enjoy his time with Georgia even if he knew it had an expiration date. Live for today, right? That'd always worked before.

He did a few more chin-ups, counting off, then dropped back to the ground. He grabbed a towel off the weight bench and mopped it over his face and chest, letting the fast-tempo music he'd put on beat through him. Finally, he could feel his mind settling a bit. But when he turned around, Keats was standing in the doorway, leaning against the frame.

Colby threw the towel to the side and pulled his earbuds out. "Hey."

"Sorry, didn't mean to interrupt."

"No problem." Colby set his iPod to the side. "Were you able to get what you needed for Georgia?"

Keats stepped into the garage, looking around at the equipment as he did. "Yeah, just got back. She needed some boxes to ship books. I tried to get her to come with me, but she wasn't ready."

"Give her time."

"I know. But it's tough seeing anyone cooped up like that. It must feel like prison." He tossed Colby the bottle of water he'd been holding.

"Thanks." Colby caught it and twisted the cap off. "Yeah, it's hard not to want to push."

"I imagine it's even harder for someone like you."

Colby took a long swig of water. "Meaning?"

"You're used to getting your way."

Colby sniffed.

"She wouldn't stay last night, huh?"

"Eavesdropping again?"

Keats gave him a come-on-now look. "Don't pretend y'all didn't want me to. You two were so noisy, they probably heard you across the street."

Colby grimaced. "Sorry. Honestly. I'm sure that's the last thing you needed when you're still healing up and needing rest. I'm not used to worrying about having other people in the house. I'll put on music next time." He took another gulp of water, desperately wanting to change the subject. "Did you at least get some sleep after Georgia left?"

He shrugged. "Not much."

Colby set the water aside and straddled the weight bench. "Are you in a lot of pain still?"

Keats grabbed the chin-up bar, his arms stretching out above his head. It raised the hem of his T-shirt, revealing how low-slung his jeans were and how dark the bruise on his side had gotten. Colby forced his focus upward.

"No, that's not what kept me up, just couldn't stop thinking." He swung his body forward a bit, hanging from the bar like a lazy monkey.

The position had Colby imagining what Keats would look like if Colby cuffed those wrists to the metal rod and locked a spreader bar between Keats's ankles, tugged down those jeans, leaving Keats helpless and on display. Colby's cock twitched with awareness. *Fuck*. Even after a fantastic night with Georgia, his body still wanted to hop up and pant for one Adam Keats.

This was exactly why Colby had never tried to get married. He loved women, but he could never fully turn off one switch for the other. He was that annoying guy who perpetuated the unfair assumption that bisexuals couldn't commit to one side long term.

Colby scooted backward, willing his dick to stand down so he could lie back and do a few bench presses, anything to get his eyes off Keats.

When he was sure his body was cooperating, he rolled down onto his back. Keats stepped behind the head of the bench and put his hands on the weight bar to spot Colby. He loomed over Colby now, his expression pensive. Colby lifted the bar and brought it down to his chest, trying to ignore how close Keats was. He closed his eyes and began to pump the weights. One. *Breathe*. Two. *Breathe*. Three.

"Thinking about what?" Colby asked finally. It was easier now that he wasn't looking at him.

"All the stuff you told me the other night. And all the stuff I heard last night."

"Mmm," Colby said noncommittally. Four. Five. Six.

He could hear Keats shifting behind him. Breathing a little too quickly. He smelled like the Irish Spring soap Colby kept in the guest bathroom.

"I want to know what I am," Keats said after a long pause.

The bar slipped a bit in Colby's hands, and Keats reached out to grab it and take some of the weight. Colby pressed his teeth together and pushed the weights back into the holder. He couldn't have this type of conversation on his back with a couple hundred pounds hanging over him. He slid forward and sat up to face Keats, who was managing to keep his expression entirely impassive.

"You mean the submissive thing?"

"I mean all of it."

All of it. Colby could take that a hundred different ways. He grabbed the towel again to give his hands something to do. He could feel Keats's gaze on him. "You're going to have to be more specific than that."

"The other night you said you couldn't really know until you tried it."

Colby scrubbed the towel through his damp hair. "I did."

"Are you working at that place this weekend?"

Scrub, scrub, scrub. "Haven't decided yet."

"If you do, can I go?"

Colby dropped the towel and stood. "Nope."

"What?" Keats asked, stepping around the bench. "Why the hell not?"

Colby headed toward the kitchen, the garage feeling too small all of a sudden, the air too thick, but Keats followed. "Because unless you have a dom who's a member to get you in, it's ten grand to join."

"Fuck. Ten grand? *Jesus*," he said, sounding awed. "But you're a member and an employee. Couldn't you get me in?"

Colby yanked the fridge handle so hard, he rattled all the condiments and knocked over a jar of olives. "Only if you were going in as *my* submissive."

"Oh."

"Yeah. Oh," Colby said, pulling out a carton of yogurt and setting it on the counter. He bumped the fridge shut with his hip and tugged the dishwasher open to find a clean spoon, his back to Keats. He didn't want to think about Keats like this. He didn't want to imagine what he'd look like naked or chained down or taking the sting of a flogger. And he especially didn't want to think of some stranger doing that to him. But guilt nipped at him. It'd taken balls for Keats to even bring this up. And God knows Colby had subjected him to an earful of shit over the past few days. If the guy really was curious about kink, he had the right to explore it. He sighed. "Look, if you really want to check some stuff out, there are a few local clubs that aren't as exclusive. There's a good dominatrix I know at the—"

A hand gripped Colby's shoulder, and every muscle in his body went taut. He spun around and before he could process what was happening, Keats braced his hands on the counter on each side of Colby. "Would you do it if I said you could?"

"Do what?"

"Show me what it's like. You, not some random person."

Keats was too close and though Colby still had a few inches on him in height, he was not happy being in the less dominant position. He moved Keats's arm aside and stepped around him. "No."

"Why?" A hard, determined edge was creeping into Keats's voice.

Colby groaned and raked a hand through his still-wet hair. "You don't even know what you're asking, what showing you would look like."

"You said you don't fuck your trainees."

He scoffed. "You think that's all there is to worry about? You want my hands on you, Keats? *Everywhere?* This isn't goddamned guitar lessons."

Keats was across the kitchen in three strides. Before Colby could even react, Keats grabbed Colby's wrist and brought his hand right against the crotch of his jeans. He was hard beneath Colby's palm. "I don't fucking get this." He shoved Colby's hand away and stepped back, his neck shading pink even though his eyes were full of challenge. "I like women. In fact, I like *your* woman. Dudes don't hit my radar. But when you say shit, that happens. And last night when I heard what I heard, I wanted to be part of it. The sound of you . . . hitting her turned me on. So if that's the whole submissive thing, then I want to know."

Colby blinked, startled into speechlessness for a moment.

"I hate feeling like this. Off balance. Confused. I feel like a god-damned teenager again when I'm around you. If I'm going to be staying here awhile, I don't want to live like that. I need to get"—Keats waved his hand between them—"whatever is going on here figured out."

Colby gripped the counter behind him, trying to will his body's reaction into stoicism. "And you think I'm the person to help you figure this out?"

"This is hard enough to talk about already. I definitely don't want to try shit with someone I don't know. But look, I know you've got a good thing with Georgia, and I don't want to mess that up because she's great. And I don't know, I mean, I don't even know if you're like . . . attracted to me or whatever needs to be there. I just—"

"That's not the issue."

Keats looked up. "Huh?"

"Attraction isn't the issue," he said simply.

Keats swallowed. "Oh."

"But you're young and inexperienced when it comes to kink, and you've never been with a guy. Yes, I'm a trainer. But this wouldn't be splashing around in the shallow end, Keats. Don't trick yourself into thinking this would be some sterile business arrangement. Even if I never fucked you, it'd be an inherently intimate and sexual dynamic."

"Is that always the case?" he asked. "With everyone you train?"

"No. But it would be with you. I know myself well enough to know I'm not capable of treating you like one of my paying students. And I'm not sure you're ready for what submitting to me really entails or if you're even capable of it."

Keats's throat bobbed.

"The fact that you get turned on around me may simply be you responding to dominance. Maybe that's what it always was. You said you've never been attracted to other guys. What happens when I put you on your knees and tell you to suck my cock? Or tie you down and slide a plug in your ass?"

Keats laced his hands behind his neck as a little flash of panic crossed his face, confirming Colby's fears. "I—"

Colby moved forward and put a hand on Keats's shoulder, giving it a squeeze and trying to hide the twinge of disappointment that he was right. "There are wonderful female dommes I trust who I could introduce you to. It doesn't have to be me. Maybe it's best it isn't."

Keats lifted his head, and Colby started to step away. But before he could, Keats locked a firm grip on Colby's hip and stepped into his space.

"What are—"

Keats's mouth was on his in the span between blinks. Colby froze for a second, completely unaccustomed to someone else making the first move. People didn't put their hands on him without permission. But after the initial rush of shock, his lips responded before his brain caught up.

Keats wasn't tentative or careful. The kiss was hot and hungry and the grip on Colby's bare waist, hard. If Keats was scared, he wasn't showing it. Lips parted and Keats's tongue slipped into Colby's mouth, eliciting an unintentional groan from Colby. His hand drifted from Keats's shoulder to lock around the base of his neck, taking back some control. Hard against hard met in the quiet of the kitchen, Colby's still-sweaty chest mashing against Keats's T-shirt. As the kiss deepened, Colby's cock begin to stiffen, his length pressing against the ridge in Keats's jeans.

Now it was Keats's turn to groan. His fingers dug into Colby's skin like he couldn't get close enough, like he wanted every part of them touching. Colby knew they should stop, figure out what the fuck was happening, but it all felt too good, too hot, too everything. There was such a rough hunger burning between them that if he let himself move, he worried that he might just strip Keats out of his clothes and fuck him across the countertop. For the first time in as long as he could remember, he didn't trust himself.

But before he could get himself in trouble, a sound from the other side of the kitchen distracted them both. Keats stiffened against Colby, and they both jolted back from each other as if they'd been simultaneously cattle-prodded. Colby turned toward the side door.

Through the glass, he could see Georgia standing there wide-eyed, her hand still poised for the knock she'd given the door.

"Fuck," Keats said behind him.

Georgia turned on her heel, looking like she was going to head right back to her house.

"Shit." Colby lurched forward, crossing the few steps to the door, and yanked it open. "Georgia, wait."

She kept moving, her back to him, and waved a hand. "Um, no, that's okay. I'll leave you two alone. I didn't mean to interrupt."

Damn. Damn. Damn. Colby told Keats he'd be right back, then jogged to reach Georgia. He put a hand on her shoulder. "Hey, hold up."

She stopped and turned to face him. She had her lips rolled inward and looked like a kid who'd gotten caught spying. "Really, it's fine. I was only coming over because Keats left his phone at my place when he dropped off the boxes. But clearly, he doesn't need it at the moment."

Colby rubbed a hand along the back of his neck. God, he must look like a major asshole right now. They hadn't made any exclusive arrangements, but they'd shared something special last night and today, he was . . . "Georgia, I'm sorry you had to see that, I—"

"I'm not," she said, cutting him off with a little laugh. She handed Keats's cell phone over to him. "That's an image I'll hold on to, thank you very much."

He looked up, eyebrows raised. "What?"

Those full lips curved upward as her gaze traveled over his naked chest. "All that was missing were the sprinklers."

"You're not pissed?" he asked, staring at this strange creature who didn't seem bothered he'd been locking lips with someone else. "Hurt?"

She sighed. "Look, I told you up front I didn't want this thing between us to be serious. I didn't ask for it to be exclusive. And yeah, if it had been someone I didn't know kissing you, I'd probably be hurt, but I don't know . . ." She gave a little shrug. "It's Keats. I already could tell there was something there between you two, so it's not a total shock that this could happen. And it's not like I haven't seen you with other people before, so maybe I've built up some immunity. Plus, well, you two look hot together."

He crossed his arms. "Is that right?"

She poked him. "Now don't go fishing for compliments."

"Never."

She gave him a *yeah, right* look but went on. "Look, I'm a grown woman who understands what casual means. I wasn't putting up a front on that, secretly hoping you'd commit to me. But if you and Keats are going to pursue something more than that, then you just need to tell me. I know I'm leaving soon, and if this could be something real between you two, I can step aside. I don't want to inter—"

"Wait, that's not what I'm suggesting at all."

She tucked her hands in the back pockets of her jeans, her head tilted and her halo of dark curly hair catching the sunlight. "No?"

"I mean, I'm not sure what all this is with Keats. It's . . . I don't know. Fuck." He raked a hand through his hair, all the questions rushing to the surface now that his brain was catching up with what had happened in the kitchen. "Keats is confused and trying to figure things out. He kissed me, but that doesn't mean anything. He's trying things on for size, I guess."

Georgia sniffed. "And starting with Extra Large. That looked like more than trying, Colby."

It'd felt like more, too, but he wasn't going to mark that down as truth yet. Keats could be in the house freaking the fuck out right now. "He thinks he could be submissive, so he wants me to show him some things. Training. That kiss . . . well, that just kind of happened. It's complicated. But it doesn't change how I feel about you. Last night was amazing, and there's no way I'm ready to let you slip away from me so soon."

"Wait, he thinks he's *submissive*?" Her brown eyes went a little round at that. "Wow, that's . . ."

"That's what?" he asked, catching her change in tone.

She glanced toward the house. "That just gives me really, really impure thoughts. I mean, your dominance obviously works for me.

Really works for me. But I won't pretend that the thought of Keats going all slave boy isn't ridiculously hot. Not that I'm totally stunned. He's got that way about him, you know?"

Colby gave her a slow grin, her words tamping down some of his anxiety over the situation. "That look like he'd do everything possible to blow a lover's mind?"

"God, yes, that one."

Colby chuckled. "You're a dirty girl, Ms. Delaune."

"I am. It's a new personality flaw, apparently. I think I caught it from you."

Colby slipped an arm around her waist and drew her against him. "I like it. A lot."

"Me, too."

He leaned back a little, gazing down at her. "So we're good? Please tell me we're good, because last night was fantastic."

"We're good, big man." She wrapped her arms around him. "And really, if it turns out to be more than a kiss with Keats, I'm okay with that."

He smiled. "You know? I believe you on that. But I think it's time to set up a few guidelines. Because even though we're doing casual, I want you to know I'm not interested in bed-hopping all over the place. I take this seriously."

"What kind of guidelines?" she asked, her head tipping to the side in that *oh, do tell* way that he found unbearably sexy.

"While we're seeing each other, this doesn't go beyond the three of us," he said, the plan forming in his head as he spoke. "If I decide to train Keats—and that's a big *if*, because God knows we have a lot to discuss before that's even a possibility—you have my word that no one else is in my bed besides the two of you."

"Okay," she said slowly.

"And you give me your word on the same."

"That I won't see anyone else?"

"That you won't sleep with anyone else besides me . . . or Keats."

Her brows scrunched. "Keats? But that's not—he's going to be working for me and he's twenty-three and—"

"And you're attracted to each other and might have wanted to kiss each other last night and stuff could happen," Colby finished. "I'm not saying it has to. That's up to the two of you, but I'm letting you know that it's fine if it does."

She blinked, obviously stunned into silence.

He cupped her face and kissed her. "Deal?"

"I'm not going to fool around with Keats. He's working for me."

"Your call, gorgeous," he said, not wanting to push her, but knowing that if Keats dialed up the charm, Georgia might find him hard to resist. Colby clearly wasn't doing well with that particular temptation, and Keats had been anything but charming toward him. Plus, he had a feeling that Georgia had watched Colby's threesomes with more than a passing interest.

She sighed. "You've got my head spinning, Colby Wilkes."

"Good." He tugged on one of her curls. "Come over for dinner tonight."

"Don't you think you and Keats need to talk this out? I'll be in the way."

He grimaced.

She poked him in the chest again. "Don't be such a man. The guy just had his first boy-on-boy kiss. And you made out with your former student. That stuff needs to be discussed, or he's going to end up running away again. He might be packing his bags already."

Colby looked to the sky, feeling the weight of all of it. "I'll handle it."

Though he wasn't sure what he was more afraid of finding once he got back to his house—Keats regretting the kiss and backtracking.

Or Keats not . . .

TWENTY

Keats was sitting on the living room couch with his head back and arm over his eyes when he heard Colby walk back in. He felt sick to his stomach and couldn't stop bouncing his knee. It'd taken everything he had to sit here and not to jump on his bike and bail.

"You okay?" Colby asked, his deep voice uncharacteristically quiet.

Keats didn't open his eyes. "Did I mess things up for you with Georgia?"

"No. Not at all."

He lowered his arm at that. "You're kidding, right?"

Colby leaned against the wall. He'd put on a shirt before coming in here. Maybe he'd wanted the protection since Keats had basically mauled him in the kitchen.

"She's watched me through my bedroom window for a year. Seeing me with someone else wasn't that shocking to her. And she's been very up-front that she's not looking for a serious relationship. So we're good."

Keats shook his head. "Even if she's okay with you seeing other people, she doesn't care that you're bi? Doesn't that freak women out?"

"Sure, it can freak some women out. A lot of women, actually. But Georgia already knew that about me. She thinks it's kind of hot."

Keats stared at him for a second, processing that. "Unbelievable. Where do you find women like her?"

"Next door, apparently."

Keats snorted. "Lucky you."

"Yes. Lucky. Georgia is a special woman with a very open mind. She's not judging anybody. Including you."

"Right."

Quiet crept in between them even though their gazes held, and Keats's stomach twisted again.

Colby rubbed a hand over the back of his head. "Well, if you're all right, I need to grab a shower, so—"

"I'm really sorry about, you know, everything. I don't know what I was thinking." He wiped his damp palms on his jeans. "I *wasn't* thinking."

He'd never planned to kiss Colby. He'd only wanted to ask if he could go to the resort Colby worked for to figure shit out. But when he'd realized Colby was shutting him out, trying to set him up with some stranger, he'd reacted on instinct, wanting to show Colby he wasn't scared. Keats had needed to know if the urges he was feeling were real. And unlike the last time he'd performed a sneak attack on his former teacher, this time he'd known what he was doing—at least in theory. Colby's beard and the aggressive edge to the kiss had been an altogether different sensation than kissing the soft, pliant mouth of a woman, but the way Keats's body had responded had been far too familiar.

And when he'd felt Colby get hard against his thigh, his thoughts had smashed into a ten-car pileup in his head. He'd never had the desire to touch any dick but his own until that moment. His hand had flexed, itching to slide between them and see what it'd be like to touch Colby that way. But chasing that desire was also a deep, cold fear of what was on the other side of that line. Was he really ready to go there? Kissing a guy, even touching one—those things he could probably write off as experimentation or misguided moments. But what Colby would want if Keats started something with him would leave no room for Keats to rationalize. He had no doubt who would be the one getting fucked in that scenario.

Visions of all those miserable years of torment in school flitted through his brain. The *Princess* nickname that had stuck after football camp, the rumors, the insults and digs hurled his way. The goddamned locker room. *Hey, Adam, what are you doing in here? The girls' showers are that way. Hey, Adam, what's it feel like to take it up the ass? Is that why you're in private lessons with Mr. Wilkes? Does he tell you you're pretty while you suck him off?*

"You don't have to apologize," Colby said with a sigh as he moved closer. "I know what it's like to be confused—about the things you like or don't like, about the desires that flash through your mind, about all the outside consequences that are tied to those kinds of decisions."

"Yeah, but you're so . . . together and cool with it all. I don't—"

Colby laughed and propped a hip on the arm of the love seat across from Keats. "You think being attracted to guys was a fun discovery for me? You think I've always been at peace with who I am?"

Keats shrugged, remembering Colby when he was his music teacher. The guy always seemed to be on an even keel despite living in a conservative town that was prone to judging him. "I don't know, seems like you're of the 'haters gonna hate' school of thought."

"By the time we met, things were settling into place for me. You saw the *After* shot. But it took a while to get to that point. I grew up in a more backwoods town than you did and was an all-star offensive lineman on the football team. I had a girlfriend who I cared about, who everyone thought I'd marry after graduation. So getting a boner in the group showers because the quarterback had a nice ass was not on my high school bucket list. Add in all the other stuff—the sadistic fantasies, thoughts of bondage, you name it—and I thought I was about as fucked up as they come. I didn't tell anyone how I was feeling. Not in high school and not afterward. Not even the guys in my band had a clue. Well, until the guitarist caught me in the tour bus screwing one of the roadies."

Keats frowned. He'd known Colby had left a promising music career to go into teaching, but he'd never thought to wonder why. At seventeen, he'd been too concerned about his own crap. "Is that why you left the music scene?"

"Yes and no. I left because I was on a path to nowhere good. The other band members distanced themselves from me after they found out—like I was going to rape them in their sleep or something. They would've kicked me out if my voice hadn't been what it was. Plus, I wrote most of the music. But the isolation had me drinking more and partying harder than I should. Then my dad died, my little brother got himself tossed in jail, and my mom needed me home to help out. Without another income, she was going to lose what little we had."

Keats leaned back on the couch, running his hands over his face. "Jesus. So you just walked away from your dream?"

"I should've never been out on the road chasing it anyway. My family had next to nothing, and my brother was a handful. If I had stuck around and helped out sooner, maybe my dad wouldn't have had so much stress on him. And maybe my brother wouldn't be sitting in prison right now for armed robbery because I would've kicked his ass had I known what he was getting into. It was a one-in-a-million shot that I'd actually make money doing the music thing anyway."

Keats watched Colby's face for signs of regret, but all he saw was his regret over his family stuff, not walking away from the career. That he couldn't understand. From what he knew, Colby had been closer to achieving that dream than he was letting on. He couldn't imagine giving up the chance to play music for a living. "I'm not sure I could've been trusted to be so self-sacrificing. Didn't you have a record deal?"

He gave a dismissive flick of his hand. "Yeah, with a small indie label out of Nashville. But I made the right choice for me. As much as I love music, I wasn't happy in that lifestyle. I like performing and writing my songs, but all the shit that went along with it wasn't my scene. My heart wasn't in it. At the time I didn't realize that, but when I got the job at Hickory Point, that was the first time I felt like I was where I was supposed to be. Teaching, mentoring, counseling—that's what does it for me."

"Whether it's teaching someone how to survive high school or how to snap a whip?"

Dimples peeked out from behind the beard. "Yeah, I guess so. Though I won't lie. The training I do at The Ranch has been more personal necessity than a career."

"What do you mean?"

"Just because I'm comfortable with my tastes and preferences doesn't mean it's easy. I can't exactly go about my social life like a typical guy would. So The Ranch is where I find my friends, my lovers, a place where I know I won't be looked at like an outsider."

That sank in, and the nausea welled up in Keats again. *An outsider.* What he hated being most. He scraped his hand through his hair. "God, I don't know if I could—"

"What are you more freaked-out about?" Colby asked gently. "The possibility that you're bi or that you could be submissive?"

A headache was pounding behind Keats's eyes. "All of it. One sounds as bad as the other. I can't help but think that maybe all those assholes, including my father, were right about me after all."

"What are you talking about?"

He shook his head, the past as vivid as a movie screen beneath his eyelids. "All those names they called me. Maybe I'm everything they said . . . fag, pussy, cocksu—"

"Shut your mouth with that shit, Keats," Colby said, cutting him off.

Keats opened his eyes, finding Colby leaning forward, a scowl on his face.

"Your father was a small-minded prick with a God complex." He stood and jabbed a finger his way. "And if I ever hear you use one of his words to describe yourself again, I will personally beat that notion out of you."

Keats stilled, Colby's palpable anger doing something to him.

"Are you going to call me those names?" Colby asked, holding out his arms, creating an impressive wingspan. "Because they'd apply to me, too. You think if I got on my knees right now and sucked you off, it'd make me less of a man?"

Keats swallowed hard, the image almost too intense to wrap his mind around. Though, even with his head whirling, his body registered the fantasy, blood rushing south. "No, but you don't do that."

Colby scoffed. "You think because I top I don't give head?"

Keats's neck heated. He hated being the one in the dark. He

pushed up from the couch and moved past Colby, ready to escape to his room. "Look, I guess I don't know how it all works. If I did, I wouldn't have asked to go to that damn resort."

He headed toward the hallway to put his back to Colby as quickly as possible. His cock was rebelling despite his mental protests for it to behave, and the last thing he needed was to embarrass himself even more.

"Keats, stop where you're at."

He halted, the response automatic, but he wasn't sure why he was doing it.

"I need you to hear this. What I said didn't come out right. I'm not making fun of you. Of course you don't know how it works because you've never done any of it. You don't have to be afraid to ask me any kind of question. I'll answer it." He let out a long breath. "Or . . ."

Footsteps sounded behind him. Keats stared down at the ground in front of him, his heart beating hard in his chest as Colby stopped right behind him.

"Or I'll show you. If that's what you want," Colby finished.

Keats closed his eyes, some weird combination of panic and anticipation welling in him. But he didn't dare move.

"Is it what you want?" Colby asked, his voice barely audible.

I don't know. The words hovered in Keats's head but wouldn't move past his lips. *Maybe. Yes . . .*

Long, silent seconds stretched, and when Keats didn't move away, Colby seemed to take that as an answer.

"Lace your fingers behind your head and keep them that way unless I tell you otherwise," Colby said, the undercurrent of authority that always lingered in his voice brimming to the surface. "You want this to stop, you say *red*. Do you understand?"

Keats was convinced his heart was about to jump out of his mouth and onto the floor. He managed a nod.

"No, I need to hear you say you understand."

Keats forced his tongue to work. "I understand. *Red* makes it stop."

"Put your back against the wall."

Keats felt himself going into some strange version of autopilot. He closed his eyes and turned, pressing his back against the wall across from the doorway to Colby's bedroom.

"First," Colby said, his voice close, "does this position cause any pain in your ribs?"

Mentally, Keats did a quick scan of his injuries. He was sore everywhere still, but having his hands behind his head didn't make anything hurt worse. "No."

"Good. I'm going to take a shower," he said, catching Keats off guard. "This isn't a decision to make on impulse or because your dick is hard. If you're still here in this position when I get back, I'll give you your first lesson. Do you understand?"

"Yes," Keats said, his throat trying to close.

"And Keats," Colby said, so close to Keats's ear that he startled. "Know that if you're still here when I get back, I'm not going to let you keep your eyes closed. You won't be able to get away with pretending it's some girl touching you."

"You're trying to freak me out," he said, finally managing to open his eyes.

Colby's mouth went lopsided, but there was wicked intent lingering in his eyes. "First thing to learn, Keats, what gets me off is not about fucking someone's body, though that's a nice part of it. If you want this, know that my end goal isn't to get in your pants." He pressed his fingertip to Keats's brow then tapped. "It's to get in here and fuck you from the inside out."

With that, he patted Keats's cheek and went into the bedroom, shutting the door behind him and leaving Keats standing there in the hallway.

And for the first time, Keats was truly terrified.

Giving up his body in a new way he could probably handle. It was just sex after all—gay, straight, or in between. Bodies on bodies. Physical release.

But letting someone in his head . . .

He lowered his arms to his side and did what he did best—he bailed.

TWENTY-ONE

Colby knew what he'd find when he opened his door, so he wasn't surprised to see an empty hallway. He'd scared Keats. He'd meant to. He could tell himself it was for Keats's own good because the kid wasn't ready, but Colby wasn't much for lying to himself. The move had been his own panic manifesting. He'd planned to get on his knees right there in the hallway and show Keats that even someone as dominant as him, the stereotypical "man's man" or whatever Keats saw him as, could get a guy off and take pleasure in it.

But when the moment had arrived, everything had felt too intense, too at-the-surface. Keats wasn't some submissive at The Ranch he was playing with for the night. This was Keats, and he was living here and there was . . . stuff between them. It already felt complicated, and all they'd done was kiss. He didn't know what to do with that. The thought of sleeping with someone for the first time wasn't supposed to feel that heavy. But in his gut, he knew crossing that line with Keats would feel far different than just a fun first time because of their history.

He needed to fix this. Let Keats know that it wasn't a good idea for them to step over that boundary after all. Take the possibility out of play and defuse the tension. Maybe Keats could find what he needed with someone else, maybe even with Georgia. Colby shouldn't be the one.

He headed to the kitchen to find his cell phone, but it rang before he could get to it. He grabbed it as the opening notes of "Amarillo by Morning" filled the room. "Hello?"

"Want to tell me why your houseguest is currently here, begging for me to pile some work on him?" Georgia asked, her voice low, as if she were cupping her hand over the mouthpiece.

Colby cleared his throat. "I may have scared him off. But I'm glad he's there and didn't run somewhere else."

She sighed. "What happened?"

"Nothing did. His choice. A good choice, actually."

"Mmm-hmm," Georgia said in that way that made him think she didn't buy it. "So what now? I'd let him crash on my couch, but I don't think I can handle someone sleeping in my house yet. I'm still a little jittery having someone here at all."

"That's not necessary. Tell Keats . . . well, tell him we're cool. Everything's fine. I've got a meeting at the school late this afternoon, and then I'm going to play a set at the Iron Spoke tonight, so if Keats wants to avoid me for the rest of today, it won't be hard."

"And tomorrow?"

"Tomorrow, I'm not going to let you turn me down for dinner. Even with all this, you haven't been far from my mind. Every time I close my eyes I can see how damn sexy you looked wrapped in my rope and coming for me last night. I won't wait another night to see that again. I'll command your presence if I have to."

"I doubt a command will be necessary. I've been thinking about you, too. But what about Keats?"

He released a long breath. "Tomorrow I'm going to sit down and tell him nothing's going to happen between us."

Georgia hung up the phone with a sigh. Colby had sounded . . . resigned about Keats, and she had no idea how to help. Though she didn't want to interfere and should probably be happy to have Colby all to herself, her instincts told her that Colby and Keats needed to work out whatever it was between them in a far less civilized manner than talking. Most of the female population of the world would probably think she was nuts for wanting to share Colby like that. But after being caught in the inescapable beam of Phillip's obsessive love for so long, being with someone who was interested in her but not fixated was a welcome change. It helped her breathe and not freak out about how powerful everything had felt with Colby last night.

But it didn't matter what she wanted for the two guys. It wasn't her call. Colby and Keats would have to figure things out for themselves in their own way.

She headed back into the living room to join her unexpected guest. In the few minutes she had left him alone, Keats was spread out on her couch with a stack of papers in his lap. He looked up from the one he was reading and smiled. "You told on me, George?"

She smirked. He'd taken to calling her George and for some reason, she found that she liked it. "I told him you were here so he wouldn't go on a tear to find you again."

"My bike's still in the driveway. He would've figured it out."

She eyed the papers again. "What are you doing?"

"These had a sticky note on them that said *proofread*, so I'm proofreading."

"What?"

"I've marked a few typos, but, goddamn George, this is—"

"Not ready for outside eyes," she said, annoyance seeping into her tone.

"It's awesome. And like holy shit hot," he said, a touch of awe in his voice. "This Haven woman—damn."

Her teeth clenched and she stalked over to grab the pages from him. Phillip used to dig through her manuscripts, trying to get "insight" into how her mind worked—or so he said. Which just meant he'd get jealous of whoever the hero was. His possessiveness didn't discriminate, even when the men she was spending her time with were fictional. "Don't read something unless I tell you it's ready to be read."

He gave them over to her without a fight, chagrined. "Hey, I'm sorry, I didn't realize—"

"It's fine," she said, straightening the papers unnecessarily. "You didn't know. It's just, this is my work in progress, and it's not ready for others to see."

He held up his hands. "Totally get it. I don't like people hearing my songs until they're done either. I didn't mean to invade. I just saw the note and thought I could help."

She let out a breath and sat next to him on the couch, knowing her anger wasn't really about him. "It's okay. But next time, ask before you dive into something."

"Yes, ma'am," he said, all charm and green eyes. "I promise I will not peek into your book without permission ever again. Your very *steamy* book."

"Keats." She sent him a warning look. Of course the stack of pages he'd picked up had been the tie-the-guy-to-the-bed scene. He couldn't have grabbed the gunfight instead.

He grinned. "So is that Mario guy going to get the girl or is Haven just going to tease him until his brain explodes?"

"I haven't decided."

"Evil. I like it."

"Do you?" she asked, cocking her head at him. "So is that your plan with Colby?"

He straightened, his affable expression sagging. "What?"

"Running hot and cold, teasing him." She turned on the couch to face him fully. "Because earlier you two were all over each other and now you're hiding at my house."

His face went crimson all the way to the roots of his blond hair and his jaw twitched as he looked away. "Jesus, George, you don't pull punches."

"No, I don't. But I'm not saying it to embarrass you."

"Well, it's embarrassing, all right?" He shifted his position but wouldn't look at her. "That's not how I want you to see me."

"I don't see you any differently than I did before."

"Right."

"I'm serious, Keats. You think I don't understand the urge to kiss Colby? I have a bad case of that affliction myself."

"You know it's not the same."

"No, I know it's not all that different, that you probably know as well as I do how he can make your body go hot with one of those damn looks he gives—the ones that promise he'll rock you right off your foundation if you give him an inch."

His fingers curled into his jeans. "George."

"I also bet you couldn't pull away from that kiss after it started, that once Colby takes control, you just want to say yes to him over and over again."

Keats closed his eyes, his expression strained. "Please stop."

"Hey, look at me," she said softly.

After a breath, he dragged his gaze to hers.

"I'm not one of those kids in your football camp who's looking to judge you. Being attracted to Colby doesn't make you weak or less of a man." She nudged his knee with hers. "You know what I see when I look at you?"

"A hot mess?" he suggested with a self-deprecating smirk.

"Well, hot, yes. Definitely. But not a mess. You're still figuring things out like most of us. There's nothing wrong with that. I'm still working through some stuff myself. Believe it or not, Colby isn't my typical type either."

"No?"

"I'm not exactly a fan of giving over control."

He peered up again at that, curiosity flickering there.

"But I want you to realize that even though it's fine to be confused, all the back-and-forth is hard on Colby, too. And I know we haven't made it easy on you over the last two nights. It's not fair to put you in a position where you're forced to listen to things, especially if you're having mixed-up feelings about Colby."

"I could've left."

"Still, I won't let it happen again. But regardless, maybe it would be wise to think hard about what you want before you act again."

He nodded slowly, as if taking all that in, and then his lips began to curl upward, some of that roguish light returning to his eyes. "So, you think I'm hot, huh?"

She gave him a droll look. "Of course that's what you would hear in all that."

The grin went wider. "How hot?"

"Go fishing off some other pier, Keats," she said, getting up but unable to hide her smile. "You know you're easy on the eyes. It's like one of those Hemsworth boys and an archangel had a love child."

He burst out laughing. "George!"

"I'll go grab that project I wanted you to work on. Keep your hands off those pages."

She could feel his gaze on her as she walked away. "I'm so reporting you to HR. I feel completely objectified now."

"So sorry," she said, no remorse in her voice.

"Don't be. I fucking needed that." She glanced back at him, finding him with a serious expression again. "Really, thanks. My head's all screwed up with this, and it's nice to find there are still some things I know for sure."

She crossed her arms over her chest. "What's that? That you're hot."

"No," he said, meeting her eyes. "That I can still be attracted to a beautiful woman."

"Oh." Awareness pinged through her, and her back straightened. These two men were a menace. "I'll be right back."

His lips lifted and he propped his feet on her coffee table. "Sure, George. I'll be waiting for my marching orders."

Orders. Her earlier conversation with Colby came back to her about Keats's supposed preferences, and really, really bad thoughts zipped through her mind. Colby putting Keats on his knees like he had put her last night. Both of them bringing Keats to the edge and back. She turned away from him. "Feet off the coffee table, Keats."

"Yes, ma'am," he drawled again, and everything went warm inside her.

Ah, hell. She was turning out to be the worst boss ever.

TWENTY-TWO

Keats sat at the bar on the far end, where it was dark enough that no one would notice him or his black eye. He'd paint himself invisible if he could, but he needed to be here. He nursed his second Shiner Bock and kept his eyes trained on the stage. The act wrapping up was pretty good—a chick who sounded like the country version of Janis Joplin but looked like Joss Stone in cowboy boots with the pink-streaked hair. It was a good combination. One that probably would've captured his attention a week ago. But now all he could think about was the woman whose house he'd left an hour ago and the man about to get onstage.

A tall, blond guy squeezed into the space next to Keats and tapped the bar. The bartender turned and gave the newcomer a wide grin. "Well, how you doing, stranger? Here to see the big man play?"

The guy smiled, all effortless charm. "Just lucked out on that one. Robyn, the girl up onstage, works for me at my store, and I promised I'd stop by and watch her play. Plus, Evan and Andre are at a police fund-raiser tonight."

"Poor thing. All alone tonight."

"Don't worry. There are plans for when we all get home."

"Nice." The bartender slid a glass of amber liquid in front of him. "Here's to getting lucky, then."

He raised the glass in salute. "I'll drink to that."

The bartender moved to take care of another customer, and the man settled his back to the bar in between stools to look at the stage. He glanced at Keats, as if noticing him for the first time. "She's pretty good, yeah?"

Keats took a pull off his beer. "Her guitar skills need a little work, but her voice cuts right through you—in a good way."

He smirked. "You sound like my friend Colby, the guy playing next. I swear that dude doesn't think anyone plays the guitar well."

Keats paused at the sound of Colby's name. "You're friends with Colby?"

The guy set his drink down. "I am. You know him?"

"Yeah."

"I haven't seen you around before. You work at the school or something?" He held out his hand. "I'm Jace, by the way."

"Keats." He shook the guy's hand and then reached for his beer again. "And no, not from the school."

Jace's eyebrow arched and he gave Keats a more assessing look, then smiled. Keats must've given something away in the comment because Jace looked like he'd answered some question for himself. "No wonder I haven't seen Colby around lately."

Embarrassment welled in Keats when he realized what Jace was assuming. "It's not—"

"Any of my business," Jace finished, and lifted his glass again. "Here's to both of us getting lucky tonight then, huh?"

Jace clinked his glass against Keats's beer and appeared far too amused at how uncomfortable he'd made him. Keats wanted to hightail it out of there right then, but he wasn't going to be a coward about this.

Robyn, the girl who'd been performing, wrapped up her set and then strolled out a few minutes later. She was grinning as she walked up to Jace and gave him a big hug. "You came!"

Jace released her from the hug and laughed. "That's what she said."

Robyn rolled her eyes. "Seriously, boss, you gotta give that line up."

"Never. I will cling to it with my dying breath." He moved out of the way and let her take the stool next to Keats. "You did great, kiddo. You're way too talented to be working for me."

"Whatever."

"Hey, have a drink on me. This is Keats, Colby's friend. He'll keep you company. I'll be right back."

Robyn barely glanced Keats's way at first, but then turned to take a second, slower look that said she liked what she saw. Normally, Keats would've flipped on the switch and sent a flirty smile back. The girl was pretty, talented, and closer to his age than Georgia and Colby were. But he couldn't muster up that side of himself. Plus, he was too busy being annoyed that Jace had assigned him a job. Did Colby only have friends who liked to dish out orders?

Robyn slid onto the stool, ordered a beer, and then twisted her curly hair into a loose ponytail, securing it with a rubber band. She fanned her neck. "Damn, those lights are hot up there." She leaned his way. "At least that's what I'm telling myself and not that I'm sweating like this from nerves."

Keats smiled at that. "First time I ever played at an open mic night I looked like the *Before* shot in a deodorant commercial. I learned to always have a jacket on hand."

She popped the collar of her khaki army jacket. "Already ahead of you." She took a sip from her drink. "So you're a musician, too?"

He shrugged. "When I'm not doing things that make actual money, yes."

She laughed. "I hear ya. I'd starve to death if I used this to support myself. But I have a good gig with Jace. I'm the manager of his store, and he's easy to work for, even if he insists on calling me *kiddo* no matter how old I am."

Keats smirked. "I know the feeling."

She turned to face him fully, the pink highlights and her dark hair making her green eyes stand out in the dim light of the bar. "So how come you're not playing tonight? It's open mic."

Keats shook his head. "I'm just here to see my friend. I haven't done the stage thing in a while. I'd probably bomb."

She pressed her lips together in mock consternation. "No way you could be worse than the dude who went on before me and sang about his dead dog." She put a hand to his knee and leaned forward. For all the sweating she claimed, she still smelled like some light, flowery perfume. "Come on. You can even borrow my guitar if you need one. I'd love to see you play."

Keats licked his lips. If he'd had any doubt she was flirting before, he knew for sure now. Her hand was more on his thigh than his knee. A week ago, this would've been a perfect setup. He'd always had a thing for confident girls who weren't afraid to make a move. But it didn't feel right tonight.

Big hands landed on Robyn's shoulders, and Jace gave her a little squeeze. "Fall back, kiddo. This one's nice to look at, but I think Keats belongs to someone else."

Robyn peered up at Jace and then back to Keats, sending him a slightly apologetic look as she moved her hand from his leg. "I was only trying to convince him to take a turn onstage."

"Uh-huh," Jace said, his smile sly. "Sure you were."

Keats had been rendered speechless at Jace's comment—*Keats belongs to someone else*—but now his mind snapped back into place. Irritation edged his voice when he finally spoke. "I don't belong to anyone."

And fuck it, maybe this was what he needed after all. A pretty girl who seemed more than interested in what he had to offer. But just when he was about to make a really self-serving move, the deep, rumbling voice of one Colby Wilkes filled the space around him. Keats stopped everything he was about to say, his attention drawn inexorably toward the stage. Colby was perched on a stool, one foot braced on the rung and the other leg stretched to the floor. His ball cap was low over his eyes but his hair curled around the edges, and the flash of dimples hid in the almost-smile. Even on that small stage in this small bar, wearing jeans and a simple flannel shirt, Colby looked like a fucking rock star.

Colby gave a brief greeting, thanked the crowd for coming out tonight, and then launched directly into what he said was a new song. Deep, molasses-laced notes resonated through the room, wrapping around him and infiltrating every part of Keats. And when he heard the chorus, lyrics aching with want and desire for untouchable things, feelings that Keats knew all too well, he sank back against the bar like he'd been punched.

Jace leaned over, close to his ear. "You sure about that? Because I only look at one other guy like that, and I certainly belong to him."

Keats closed his eyes and ran a hand over his face. "Fuck."

Jace gave a low chuckle. "I know how you feel, brother. That shit is never convenient. Now, come on, you two. Let's grab a table so we can see better."

As if his free will had decided to put up the white flag for the night, Keats let Jace lead him and Robyn to a table closer to the stage. It was dark enough in the bar and the lights were bright enough on Colby that Keats would still be hidden. But at least now he wouldn't have to pretend he wasn't staring.

Colby's set was only supposed to be a couple of songs, but the audience encouraged him to play a few more when he tried to say goodbye. According to Jace, Colby was a paid act and rarely came to the open mic nights anymore, so this was a special treat for the crowd. At the praise, Colby tipped the bill of his cap, the pleasure on his face warm and genuine, and asked if there were any audience requests.

The houselights went up before Keats could register what was happening. He blinked in the brightness, stars imprinting on his vision, and he immediately slunk down in his chair, trying to blend into the crowd. But when his vision cleared, Colby was looking straight at him. Colby stared, as if confused for a moment, and then his jaw tightened. No one but Keats had probably noticed, but the change had twisted Keats's gut.

A woman called out the name of a song, and Colby pulled his gaze away to address her. He gave her that smile of his, even if it didn't light his whole face like it usually did, and started the song. But suddenly Keats felt as if there were a wire of tension strung between him and Colby, the whole thing vibrating with Colby's clear annoyance.

Jace leaned over. "He didn't know you were here?"

"No," Keats said on a hard swallow.

Jace frowned. "Sorry, I wouldn't have dragged you over here. I thought—"

Keats shook his head. "It's okay. I'll live."

Jace sniffed. "Maybe. I have a feeling Colby is thinking through all three hundred million ways he knows how to torture someone right now."

Keats groaned but realized the sound wasn't born of dread. It was of need. He put his head on the table. The impossible-to-ignore reaction was like a hammer hitting that final nail. Boom. *Here lies Keats*. Buried.

He took a long, steadying breath and forced himself to straighten. He wouldn't run this time. He reached out and touched Robyn's elbow. "Does that offer for the guitar still stand?"

She gave him a conspiratorial smile. "Absolutely. Come on."

Right. So this was what jumping off a bridge felt like.

Colby was more than ready to get offstage by the time he wrapped up the last song. Usually, he left a performance feeling lighter and more energized. But he'd had a frustrating meeting at school earlier, and the stress of still not knowing where he stood with his job had already been wearing on him. Then he'd spotted Keats in the audience, and his mood had plummeted to an even darker place.

What the hell was he doing here? And how did he end up sitting with Jace? Colby knew Jace wouldn't make a pass at Keats or any-thing. The dude was off his rocker in love with his two lovers. But Jace also had a knack for saying inappropriate things and putting people on the spot, even if it was delivered with a heavy dose of charm and humor. And Keats was in no condition to be put on the spot.

Colby quickly made his way over to the table where he'd spotted Keats but found only Jace and Robyn. "Where is he?"

Jace leaned back in his chair and crossed his arms. "Oh, look at that, you're worse off than him, Wilkes. I never thought I'd see it from you."

"Shut the fuck up, Austin," Colby said, not in the mood for his friend's ribbing. "Where'd he go?"

"Turn around," Robyn offered.

Colby spun toward the front and saw Keats striding across the stage, a guitar slung over his shoulder. His black eye stood out in relief under the bright lights but so did his tattoos, giving him the ultimate bad-boy effect.

"God, why do the good ones always turn out to be gay?" Robyn huffed.

"Or bi," Jace corrected. "Don't forget us."

"He's fucking beautiful," she declared.

Colby hadn't taken his eyes from the stage and he wholeheartedly agreed. Often when Keats looked at him, he saw the vulnerability there, the insecurity. But up on the stage, that guy was gone. Keats had swagger under those lights, and when one of the women in the audience gave a little catcall, he peered over at her and graced her with a smile that could be an ad campaign for sin.

"Have a seat, Wilkes," Jace said, pushing a chair out with his foot. "I have a feeling the show's going to be worth watching."

Colby sat and Jace, being the annoying yet considerate friend that he was, ordered Colby a double shot of whiskey.

Keats adjusted the microphone and moved the stool aside so he could stay standing. He plucked a few strings and twisted the tuning pegs. "You'll have to forgive me. Robyn was kind enough to lend me her guitar since I don't have mine, so I'll have to feel my way through this a little."

"I know what he could feel his way through," muttered one of the chicks at the table next to Colby. Her friend giggled.

Colby gritted his teeth, a rare bolt of possessiveness taking hold.

Keats looked out at the audience. "I only have one song for you tonight. And to be honest, it's one song for one person. So let's hope he likes it."

Colby's breathing stopped. *He.*

Holy shit. The guy who could barely say the word *bi* had just come out *onstage*.

Jace smiled over at Colby and held up a finger, his head tilted. "And that's the sound of female hearts breaking all through the audience."

But Colby couldn't respond. Keats started strumming, and that smooth, melodic voice of his moved through Colby. He didn't recognize the notes, but once Keats opened up his mouth to sing, Colby forgot anyone else was there in the bar with him.

The country flavor in Keats's voice was different from Colby's, but warm, full, and rich. Like slow honey sliding off a spoon. Much deeper than it had been in Keats's high school days. And sexy as fuck.

Keats looked down at his guitar as his fingers moved with confidence over the strings, his words seeping into Colby's very being.

Light the match, I said.
Feed the flames, I beg.
I need your fire to snap the beams.
Consume the doubts I hear.
Ignite the truths I fear.
Burn me down, baby.
Burn me down.

Colby closed his eyes and knocked back his whiskey, the burning in his throat matching the heat Keats's song was fueling in his gut. Keats hadn't looked his way once, but he'd made it clear who he was singing to. Colby didn't know how he was going to walk away this time.

"Goddamn," Jace muttered. "This is getting me hot under the collar, and I'm not even into the kid."

"He's not a kid," Colby snapped.

Jace lifted a hand. "Sorry. Didn't mean anything by it. Honestly."

Colby felt like an asshole. He wasn't one to let his temper leak into things, especially when it was unfounded. Jace was just being Jace. But everything felt on edge at the moment, like even a breath on his skin would be too much.

"The guy can sing, though, Wilkes. He's really fucking good."

"Always has been," Colby said gruffly. "Just never had a chance to catch a break."

"That sucks. Want me to talk to Foster's friend, Pike?"

"For what?"

"Pike's doing some producing now. He could help him put together a demo. Robyn's going to do one."

Colby adjusted his cap, only half able to stay engaged in the conversation. "Yeah, do that. I'm sure Keats has some stuff ready to go."

Jace said he would do just that. But Colby's attention stayed on Keats, and he was rewarded when on the final line of "Burn Me Down," Keats's eyes locked on his, and he sang the words right to him.

That was all it took for Colby's good intentions to go up in flames. Burn me down, indeed. He shoved his chair back. "I'll see you guys later."

Jace grinned. "Happy trails, Wilkes."

TWENTY-THREE

Keats managed to return Robyn's guitar and say his good-byes, but his hands shook when he tucked them in the pockets of his jacket. He didn't regret what he'd done onstage. Like Georgia had said earlier today, the back-and-forth wasn't fair to anyone. He knew he wasn't going to be able to settle inside until he faced up to whatever this was with Colby. But now that the moment was over, his thoughts were unraveling in every direction and knotting into new worries. Colby had walked out, and Keats had no idea what that meant.

Maybe he'd fucked it all up again.

But when he headed out of the bar to get on his bike, he found himself standing in front of an empty parking spot. No bike. "What the hell?"

He spun around to scan the lot and saw Colby's truck across the way. Keats's motorcycle was in the back. Colby slammed the tailgate shut and leaned against it, crossing his arms over his chest and not saying a word.

If an outsider had been watching them, it might have looked like Colby was about to challenge Keats to a fight. Or maybe that Colby was about to star in a country music video. He pulled off the broadshouldered, boot-wearing, worn jeans look to ridiculous perfection. All he needed was a damn dog sitting at his feet.

Keats's throat tightened. No, that wasn't what Colby was expecting to be at his feet.

Colby cocked his head toward the truck. "You gonna get in, Keats? Or do I need to roll your bike back out?"

Keats barely heard him over the blood roaring through his ears. He cleared his throat, searching for his voice. "The bike can stay there."

"The song was good," he said, pushing his back off the truck and taking one step forward. Keats internally flinched. The gravel crunching beneath Colby's boot sounded loud even with the crowd noise and music filtering out from the bar. Everything was amplified in his mind right now, his senses dialed up to eleven. "You're a natural up there."

Keats breathed in the cold night air, trying to calm himself. He didn't need to act like some scared virgin. He hadn't played this game with another man, but he could hold his own with flirting. The gender shouldn't matter. "I had a good teacher."

Colby hooked his thumbs in his belt loops. "Yeah?"

"Yeah." Keats was the one to take steps this time. He crossed the parking lot and stopped just short of arm's length. "I was hoping he could show me a few more things, though."

The temperature had dropped in the last two hours, and Keats watched as their frosted breath mingled in the air between them. Colby's eyes were darker than normal in the shine of the orange streetlight, and what Keats saw there had his heart thumping faster.

Colby gave him a long, evaluating look, then a barely-there nod. "Get in the truck, Keats."

Keats's fists clenched at his side, fear trying to take hold again, but he forced his fingers open. "Okay."

"*Yes, sir* would be the proper response," Colby corrected. "I expect your full respect from this point onward tonight."

Keats wet his lips. "Yes, sir."

It should've felt strange on his lips. But, then again, it wasn't the first time he'd called Colby *sir*.

When Keats attempted to move past him, Colby turned and stepped fully into Keats's personal space. Keats leaned back against the side of the truck, both of them now covered in the shadows of the parking lot, shielded from the bar's entrance. Colby braced a hand on the truck, half-caging Keats in. "You know, I had decided this was a bad idea."

Keats couldn't look away from the hard gaze. "I know."

"I thought you weren't ready. And I thought I'd never be able to see past the kid I used to know, that it'd feel wrong to me."

"I'm not that kid anymore," he said, his voice barely loud enough for his own ears to hear it.

"No, you're not," Colby said, moving closer and bringing their belt buckles together. Denim against denim.

Keats's dick, already half awake for the party, went hard in an instant.

"My body had already figured that much out," Colby said, his lips a breath away from Keats's. "But when I saw you onstage, my head finally caught up. I saw the man. A talented, artistic, hot-as-fuck man who I'd be damn lucky to have in my bed." He slid his hand to boldly cup Keats's erection. "And under my command."

Keats's head fell back against the window of the truck as Colby gave him a stroke through his jeans. "Fuck."

Colby's lips touched his ear and whispered words full of promise. "Soon. I'm looking forward to breaking you in, boy."

The words sent electricity through his system, and Keats worried he'd shoot off in his pants like a teenager if Colby stroked him again. So he was grateful when Colby backed away and swung open the truck door. He gave a little nod, indicating that Keats needed to get in. They didn't speak the entire drive home. And though fear of the unknown was ever present, Keats stayed rock hard and aching the entire way home.

When Keats tried to adjust the front of his suddenly too-tight jeans without success, Colby noticed. And smiled. Evilly.

He really was a sadistic bastard.

They pulled into Colby's driveway a few minutes later, and

Keats glanced over at Georgia's place. He wondered what she'd think if she knew what was happening right now. Knowing her, she'd probably be cheering them on.

"What're you smiling about?" Colby asked, cutting off the ignition.

Keats hadn't even realized he was doing it. "Nothing."

Colby sniffed. "She's hard not to think about, huh?"

"She was the one who encouraged me to go watch you play tonight. I don't think she bought either of our bullshit excuses."

Colby huffed a quiet laugh. "I'm guessing you're right. Plus, that gorgeous woman has a serious boy-on-boy fetish. Maybe she's hoping we'll let her watch."

"Would you do that?"

He shifted on his seat and met Keats's gaze. "Not tonight. Tonight, you're mine and mine alone."

Somehow the words settled the jumpy feeling in his stomach. There was safety in knowing that this first time would be private and that Colby would take the lead completely. Keats had come to terms with the knowledge that he wanted this—God, how he wanted it. But if it had been up to him to make the moves or decisions, he probably would never manage to go through with it. He'd psych himself out like he had when Colby had left him standing in the hallway.

"Before we go in, we need to get a few necessary things out of the way," Colby said, all business but his gaze no less heated in the chilly cab of the truck. "I'm tested monthly as an employee of The Ranch, and I always use condoms."

Keats licked his lips quickly. "I have to get a physical and blood work every six months for the temporary agency I get the construction work through. I've always used condoms, too. And I got tested last month after I found out my ex-girlfriend was using. I haven't been with anyone since."

Colby nodded. "Do you have any things you're absolutely not okay with? Hard limits."

Keats didn't know what to do with his hands. He tucked them in his jacket pockets. "I'm not sure I know enough to even know where those limits would be yet. But I'm okay with . . . trying stuff to see how it goes."

Colby seemed to approve of that answer. "We're going to use a stoplight system. *Red* is your safe word. That stops everything immediately, no questions asked. Use *yellow* if you need me to check in with you, if something might be too much. And if I ask you how you're doing and you're completely on board, you can give me a *green*. We can find your limits together."

Keats smirked but couldn't look up. "Is it bad that you slipping into teacher mode is getting me even harder?"

Colby made some sound in the back of his throat. "Are you *trying* to fuck with my head?"

"Come on," Keats said, feeling braver now that he'd made the decision to do this. "You never had a fantasy about a teacher? I know you're not panting after your students, but what about back when you were in school?"

"I did have an English professor in college who had that hot librarian thing going on. She was so damn prim and pretentious, but I had a feeling it was all for show. I wanted to tie her to her desk and spank her with the awful book she was making us read just to see what she'd be like when she dropped the façade."

Keats shifted in the seat, the image of Colby doing that making his blood heat. He chewed his lip for a moment. "I remember I used to focus on your hands when you were teaching me guitar because anything more than that was too scary. I would wonder what you did to guys with those big hands, how they would feel."

Colby let out a gruff sound, proving that Keats wasn't the only one getting hot and bothered. "Well, at least now I know why it took you so long to get the hang of your F chord."

Keats smiled, still focusing on his lap.

Colby's fingers closed around the back of Keats's neck with firm pressure. "You ready to feel those hands, Keats? I'll gladly show you exactly what I like to do with them."

Keats inhaled a long, shuddering breath. "Yes, I'm ready."

"Good. Then go inside and to my room. Shut the curtains, take off your shirt, boots, and socks. All I want you wearing are these jeans. Lace your hands behind your head and put your back to the door. I'll come in when I'm ready."

Keats might have been shaking, but he refused to acknowledge the weakness. "Yes, sir."

Colby's fingers pressed harder into his neck. "You have ten minutes. Don't make me wait longer than that."

Keats nodded in Colby's grip and reached for the handle on the door. He didn't want to hesitate or overthink things this time. So he focused on simply moving forward and following the instructions. He was in the house, stripped, and in position in probably less than four minutes. The curtains were closed and only the lamps had been left on, so he tried to steady his nerves by counting the stripes on the curtains. He'd gotten to thirty-seven when he heard footsteps behind him.

And for the first time, Keats had no desire to run.

Colby stood in the doorway for a long minute, staring at the man in the center of his bedroom. Keats had followed the instructions to a *T*, so Colby was graced with an unparalleled view of Keats's muscular back and arms, those tattoos flexing beneath Keats's subtle, nervous shifting. Even the wicked bruising from the fight seemed to add to the beauty of the man—a sign of his bravery, a toughness that had allowed him to survive on the streets. And those worn blue jeans that had molded so nicely over Keats's erection hung low on his hips, giving Colby the tempting sight of the dimpled indentations at Keats's tailbone and the top curve of his ass. The man was finely built. Strong and masculine and proud.

The urge to conquer and bring forth that submission filtered through Colby's bloodstream like a drug. But he would be gentle tonight. Keats was injured and he was new to all this. Colby would make it good for him.

He crossed the room with slow steps, his boots clomping against the wood floor, then silencing when he stepped onto the area rug that filled the space in front of his bed. He placed his hands on Keats's hips. Keats startled but quickly reeled himself in, stilling.

"You still hard for me, Adam?" he asked, using his given name to help Keats understand things were different when they were in this mode, that he was vulnerable.

The muscles in Keats's neck worked. "Yes, sir."

Colby fitted his erection against Keats's ass. "Makes two of us."

Keats's whole-body shudder made Colby smile with satisfaction.

"You're going to learn to be still and how to be touched. You own nothing right now. Every part of you is mine. Do you understand?"

"I do."

"Close your eyes and focus on my hands. You wanted to know what they feel like. Now you get your wish."

Keats's lids fell shut, and Colby stepped in front of him. Starting at the top, he mapped the contours of Keats's brow, his cheekbones, his jawline, then traced the edge of his shiner with a gentle fingertip, trying to get Keats used to being touched. Keats was already breathing fast, but when Colby ran a thumb over Keats's lips, the guy's chest stopped moving.

Colby didn't kiss trainees, and he rarely kissed a partner during a play session. It felt too sweet and intimate for his tastes. But he'd kissed Georgia, and now he found himself unable to pull his attention away from Keats's mouth. He leaned forward and brushed his lips over Keats's and gave his bottom lip a nipping bite.

Keats rewarded him with a sharp intake of breath, and Colby went back for a second taste before moving his hands down to Keats's shoulders. "Lower your arms to your sides."

Keats obeyed and Colby indulged in running his hands over Keats's biceps and then his chest. He avoided the bruised areas on his side but paid extra attention to the flat, brown nipples. He gave a hard pinch to one, and Keats muttered an oath. But from the way he clenched his fists at his sides, Colby could tell it had been a positive response.

"These would look good pierced. Would make them easier to torture." Colby flicked the other one.

Colby let his gaze travel down Keats's abdomen and then lower. Keats's erection hadn't diminished even if he was still harboring some nerves. If anything, the jeans looked to be straining even more in the front.

"Unbutton these, pull the zipper down."

Keats complied, his fingers fumbling for only a second. When he spread open the fly, visible relief crossed his face. Colby took his fill, tracing the faint trail of hair that tracked below Keats's navel with a fingertip. Then he dipped his hand inside, palming Keats through the thin cotton of his boxer briefs.

Keats groaned when Colby gripped him, but Colby was the one whose dick flexed. The guy was long and heavy in his hand. "Fuck, Keats. Now I know why those guys used to give you shit in the locker room. Goddamned jealousy."

Keats tipped his head back as Colby gave him a stroke. "Yeah, well I'm kind of terrified of you. I've seen your shoe size."

Colby laughed low and menacing against his ear as he moved his hand away. "You should be."

He walked around Keats in a slow circle and then stopped behind him again. He slid his hand between the two layers of fabric protecting Keats's ass. Keats stiffened instantly, but Colby wasn't going to let him pretend this was something other than it was. He braced one hand on Keats's shoulder to steady him and then let his other hand dip lower. He ran two fingers around Keats's opening, rubbing the soft cotton fabric of his underwear along the sure-to-be-sensitive skin.

The choked sound Keats made wasn't a bad one.

"Ever had a woman play with you here?" Colby asked, continuing to massage him with gentle but focused pressure.

"No," he whispered.

Colby leaned forward and peered down over Keats's shoulder. The front of Keats's boxers already had a wet spot. Even if Keats's mind was still adjusting, his body was all for it. Colby pulled his hand away and went over to the chest of drawers on the side wall. He slid open the top drawer and selected a pair of leather cuffs along with a few other items. Keats would look amazing in rope, but Colby's patience wasn't at its best tonight.

He moved behind Keats again and drew his hands up behind his neck. When they were in the right position, he locked the cuffs around them. "Walk over to the closet door. Put your back to it."

Colby stepped to the side and watched as Keats opened his eyes. Keats blinked a few times, looking a bit dazed, before locating the door. The sight of Keats already zoning out had Colby's stomach coiling with need. Nothing was hotter than someone slipping into that submissive mental space, and knowing it was Keats's first time gave Colby more possessive satisfaction than it should.

"Work your jeans off and kick them to the side. I'll take care of the boxers."

Keats's gaze met his briefly, but he automatically lowered it and moved to get the jeans down and off. He really was a sight standing there bound and aroused as fuck. Colby unfastened his own jeans, room getting scarce in his as well. Keats's eyes zeroed in on Colby's hands.

He tipped his head toward Keats. "Tell me your thoughts right now. Unedited."

Keats's tongue swept over his bottom lip. "I was wondering if you keep your clothes on for everything. I've heard that's a thing."

"Sometimes," he said, but started releasing the buttons on his shirt. "But I'll let you look a little since you're being such a good sub tonight."

Colby let his shirt hang open but didn't shrug it off his shoulders and walked toward Keats. Without giving him warning, he squatted down and yanked Keats's boxers down and off. Keats let out a breath and closed his eyes again. His cock stood out proud, the head leaking fluid. Colby leaned forward and swiped his tongue over the tip, capturing the salty drops. The back of Keats's head hit the closet door with a thump and a curse.

"Spread your feet hip width apart," Colby commanded, staying in a squat and grabbing the spreader bar he'd gotten out of the drawer.

Keats complied and Colby locked Keats's ankles into the device. He set the last item he needed to the right of Keats's foot, then rolled onto the balls of his feet and stood. Keats's biceps were trembling, but Colby knew that the position was putting no real strain on his arms. It was the quiver of a man on the edge, desperate for release.

Colby crossed his arms over his bared chest, his stance wide. "Now, Adam, you can get exactly what I know you want right now. It's only going to take two simple steps."

His throat worked before he spoke. "And what's that?"

"Open your eyes and beg me."

TWENTY-FOUR

The feel of the singular swipe Colby's tongue had given his cock was still reverberating through Keats and everything inside him ached. Colby's hands had touched him everywhere but not enough. Even his ass was clenching for something it had never wanted before. The slow, torturous massage Colby had used to tease his opening had nearly driven Keats to his knees.

But he knew what Colby was offering right now, and any pride Keats might have had before this moment had disintegrated in the first touch of Colby's tongue. He opened his eyes and his gaze collided with Colby's. The man looked like a savage in that moment. Shirt opened on that impossibly broad chest, curly dark hair peppering the way down to cut abs and a trail leading into the band of his open jeans. There was no underwear beneath, just tanned skin and his cock forming an intimidating outline against the dark denim.

Keats loved women, adored their softness, the sweet scent of them, their taste. He'd spent his adult life happily worshipping the fairer sex. But in this moment, he couldn't think of anything more enticing than the raw masculinity of Colby. Keats craved those edges, the roughness he knew Colby could provide. So when he opened his mouth, he had no problem obeying Colby's command and begging.

"Please, Colby. I need . . ." he said, his voice gritty with the desire coursing through him. "Whatever you want to do to me, I'm ready."

"You want me to suck your cock, Adam?" he asked, his voice holding challenge.

A hard shudder went through Keats's muscles, and he tightened his laced fingers behind his head. "God, yes."

"Ask me, then. Nicely."

"Please, Colby. Please suck me."

Colby turned his ball cap backward, the switch transforming his look into some frat-boy version of himself, and stepped closer. He captured Keats's chin in his hand. "Eyes on me, Adam. I don't suck dick for just anyone. But when I do, I don't take shortcuts. So watch and learn. There may be a pop quiz one day soon."

Keats's mouth was too dry to form words, so he nodded in Colby's grip.

Then like some strange, erotic dream, Colby Wilkes, the teacher he'd fantasized about alone in his room in high school, the one who'd seemed larger than life, an impossibility, went down on his fucking knees and took Keats's dick into his mouth.

Keats moaned as the hot, wet suction closed around his flesh. His eyes tried to roll back, but he refused to look away from that ball-cap-covered head. Keats knew Colby had told him to keep his eyes open so that he didn't drift off and insert some woman in his mind's eye to make himself feel better. But there was no shot of that. What was making the fire burn inside Keats was the very fact that this was Colby. The scandal of it all was almost enough to put him over the edge before Colby really even got started.

Colby worked him over slowly with his mouth and tongue, knowing exactly how much pressure to give and when. When he pulled back all the way to the tip, his tongue traced the slit, sending knee-weakening sensation up Keats's nerve endings.

"Jesus," Keats murmured.

Colby hummed his response, and the decadent vibration made Keats's heels lift off the floor, the bar locked between his ankles preventing much more than that. Colby was taking his time, and Keats got the impression that Colby wasn't doing this so much to give Keats pleasure as to gain his own enjoyment from the act. For some reason, that made Keats sink even more into the moment. He didn't want to be Colby's charity case. He didn't want to be someone Colby was helping to find himself. Keats wanted Colby doing this because Colby wanted him for purely selfish reasons.

A clicking sound snapped Keats's attention downward, and he saw Colby take a small black bottle from the floor and tip it over his other hand. Clear fluid dribbled onto Colby's palm and fingers. Keats's stomach clenched, but Colby's mouth was still busy and it was hard to hold on to any worries for any amount of time.

Colby's lips slipped off with a soft popping sound and he looked up, those hazel eyes fiercer than Keats had ever seen them. "You don't have permission to come until I tap your thigh twice. Understand?"

Keats had trouble finding his voice. "Yes, sir."

"Close your eyes now. Feel everything. Get lost in it."

Keats leaned his head back against his bound hands and let his eyes fall shut. Colby's mouth closed over him again, the burning heat enveloping him, and then his warm, lubricated hand cupped Keats's balls and massaged. The muscles in Keats's thighs tried to go liquid, and he had to lean some of his weight against the closet door. It was going to take every ounce of effort he possessed to hold off coming.

Especially when it became clear that Colby had more plans. The hand on Keats's scrotum moved farther back, slick fingertips stroking the sensitive area behind it. His breath turned into sharp catches in his chest, but he didn't dare move. Colby took Keats's cock to the back of his throat, his lips pressing against his sac. Keats moaned, and the sensation was distraction enough that Keats didn't have time to panic when Colby's thick, callused fingers tracked over his back opening, coating it with the lube.

Colby pulled his mouth away for a second, but his fingers continued to circle Keats's rim with slow, coaxing pressure. "Try to relax and let me in. Remember, every part of you is mine right now. Give over to me. I won't hurt you."

Keats bit his lip at the foreign sensation, but a low, aching need was building fast—both in his cock and deep inside the forbidden place Colby was teasing. He managed a nod, and Colby must've seen it because he didn't demand a verbal response. A fingertip probed at the ring of muscle and Keats couldn't help it, he tensed. His thighs probably would've snapped together if there hadn't been a bar keeping his legs spread.

Colby gave him a sharp pinch on the thigh with his other hand. "Easy, Adam. Don't pretend you aren't curious about this. You knew what being with me would mean. I bet you've imagined me here—wondering what it'd feel like to be stretched and penetrated." He inserted the very tip of his finger. "To have me deep inside you."

Keats whimpered like a fucking wounded dog and then cringed at the pitiful sound.

"Tell me, Adam," Colby said, his voice a soothing, cajoling soundtrack to the cacophony going off in Keats's head. "Tell me you've thought about me fucking you."

Keats's eyes stayed squeezed shut, and sweat trickled down the side of his face. "Yes, I've thought about it. I always knew if I did this, you'd be the one on top."

"I've thought about it, too," he said, easing his finger a little deeper. "When you were half naked, wearing that robe in my kitchen, I could barely concentrate. I imagined tying you down across the counter and spreading you out, taking you hard."

"Fuck," he whispered, the images and the feel of Colby's finger too much to process.

Colby's finger sank all the way in and his hot mouth closed over Keats's dick again.

Keats cried out from the shocking pleasure—the two sensations intertwining and racing up his spine. Oh. *God*. Release built like a damn tsunami in his groin. His teeth ground together as he fought to hold it off.

But Colby had picked up the pace and now he was moving a second finger into Keats's opening, stretching him and causing a burning that somehow only made everything feel better. Colby pumped his fingers slowly in and out as he gave Keats the blow job of his life. Colors swirled behind Keats's eyes, and he wondered if he was going to pass out. Had he remembered to breathe in the last few minutes?

But just when he thought he would die from it all, Colby gave his thigh a swift double tap and then the fingers inside him shifted and rubbed across a place that sent stars bursting in Keats's brain. *Holy fuck.*

Orgasm rumbled through Keats, the avalanche of sensations sending him into the abyss and burying him whole. He couldn't have stopped it if he'd tried. He cried out with a gasping shout. All systems go. Colby pulled off at the last second, though he kept his adept fingers moving, and Keats's release jetted out in what seemed like the longest orgasm of his life.

He moaned through it, his mind spinning, his body lit up. All the while, Colby's low, dirty words of encouragement played soundtrack and chased away any embarrassment Keats might have felt otherwise. This was good. This was so good. He would not be ashamed of this.

When Keats finally had no more to give and his stomach was heaving with ragged breaths, Colby slipped his fingers out. With all the effort he could muster, Keats rolled his head forward to look down at Colby. And fuck was he a sight.

Semen striped Colby's chest, and his cock was hard against the fly of his jeans. But the look on his face was damn satisfied—smug, even. Keats wanted to fall to his knees in gratitude.

Colby tugged off his shirt and wiped his lubed fingers on it. "You okay?"

Keats licked his dry lips. "I'm—yeah, I'm okay. Very, very okay."

"Good." Colby stood and unhooked the cuffs binding Keats's wrists. He handed Keats his shirt. "Then clean me up, sub. You made a mess."

Keats gripped the shirt in his hand, but he was still riding high from the orgasm and feeling braver for it. He tossed the shirt to the floor, gripped Colby's waist, and then bent over to lick a trail of come off Colby's chest.

Colby made a soft, grunting sound, but it wasn't one of disapproval, so Keats kept going. Maybe when he looked back tomorrow, he'd find some shame in this, something to feel humiliated over. He was licking up his spunk off another dude. But in this moment, it felt right. In this moment, the fear was gone.

Keats stopped at a spot right above Colby's open fly, his heart thumping like a rabbit's foot, and lifted his hand.

Colby caught his wrist in a firm grip. "I told you to clean me. I didn't give you permission to touch me."

Keats licked his lips, tasting the remnants of sex and salty skin. "Can I touch you? I want to make you feel good, too."

Colby kept hold of Keats's wrist and his mouth flattened into a tense line. "You're tempting me more than you know with that hungry look you're giving me. But tonight, I'll handle things myself."

Keats's stomach dropped and he straightened. "You don't want anything from me?"

Colby smirked and laid Keats's hand over his rock-hard erection. "I want it all from you. Give me a list of sordid acts, and I've thought of every one in the last ten minutes. But things often look different in the light of day. This is your out. If you wake up tomorrow and regret any of this, you can write it off. Lots of straight guys would take a blow job from a willing mouth, regardless of who was giving it. It wouldn't make them any less straight."

Anger rose quick in Keats, and he yanked his hand out of Colby's grasp. "What the fuck, Colby? You just had your goddamned fingers in my ass, and I licked my come off you. Even my ability for denial isn't that spectacular. I get that what we're doing means I'm not exactly who I thought I was. Daylight isn't going to change that."

"I hope it doesn't. But I'm leaving that option available." He bent down and unhooked Keats's ankles.

Keats stepped out of the cuffs and stalked across the room to grab his jeans and yank them on, annoyance rolling through him. He kept his back to Colby. "Whatever. If you'd rather use your fucking hand, then I'm going to take a shower."

He didn't know why this was pissing him off so much. It wasn't like he even knew how to give a blow job. But he would've damn well tried.

"I'm going to give you one pass for talking to me that way," Colby said, warning in his voice. "I haven't released you yet."

"So sorry, *sir*," he said, bitterness edging his tone.

As swift as a breath, Colby's hand was locking around the back of Keats's neck again. He squeezed hard. "Get on the fucking floor. Nose to my boot, knees underneath you."

"What the f—" But Keats didn't get a chance to finish it because Colby dug his fingers into Keats's neck even harder and guided him down by force. Keats went to his knees, and Colby pushed his head down toward his shoes. The curved tip of Colby's cowboy boots filled his view.

"Wrap your hands around my right foot and press your forehead to the leather."

Keats could barely process what was happening, it was all going down so fast. But that take-no-prisoners tone of Colby's had his stomach flipping. Not knowing what else to do, he shut down the argument and followed the instruction.

"Now stay there until I tell you to kneel up."

Keats could hear the sound of denim moving, the squirt of the lube again, and then the distinct sound of slippery skin. Fuck. Colby was jerking off above him, and Keats wasn't even allowed to look up.

"You will learn how to show me respect. And you will accept my orders and trust that I'm doing shit for your own good. Push me and you're not going to like the consequences."

The hot-as-hell sound of fist over dick had Keats's own cock perking up again, but he didn't dare move. Not even when he could feel his still-unfastened jeans sagging down and exposing his ass again.

"Nice view, sub," Colby said, his voice changing with what Keats recognized as Colby's bedroom voice. "Kneel up now and give me something to aim at."

Keats quickly released Colby's boot and pushed himself up to a kneel, finding himself staring at the big, slick cock he'd seen only from a distance when he'd spied on Colby. Fuck, the dude was hung. Of course, lucky Keats, he'd have to get interested in an over-achiever in that department. He tried not to think about how tight those two fingers had felt inside him.

But the worries over that were soon eclipsed by the erotic sight of Colby's big fist moving over his cock. The guy wasn't gentle with himself, and Keats found himself transfixed.

"So you think you'll still want this in the morning, huh?" Colby taunted, fucking his hand with more speed now. "Guess we'll find out."

With that Colby's release jetted out and splashed against Keats in hot streams, landing on his shoulder, his chest, his jeans. He didn't look down, though, because he couldn't pull his attention away from Colby's lost-to-the-moment expression and the deep groan that escaped him. The guy looked fucking sinful when he came.

Colby stroked a few more times, milking the last of his orgasm, then let out a long breath. With economy of movement, he tucked himself back in his jeans and zipped up. His gaze tracked over Keats and the dripping mess he'd become. He nodded in his direc-tion. "Rub it into your skin, Adam. Every drop of it."

Keats blinked at the unexpected command. "What?"

"It wasn't a request."

Acting as if on autopilot, Keats moved his hand over his chest and stomach, rubbing the fluid into his skin.

"You can wash your hands but you're not allowed to shower until the morning. You don't think you'll regret tonight, and I hope that's true. But I guess we'll see when you wake up tomorrow sticky from my come and covered in my scent."

The thought sent a trail of goose bumps up Keats's back.

Colby put out a hand and tugged Keats to his feet. He grabbed the waistband of Keats's jeans, pulling him close, and gave him a quick, openmouthed kiss. "Thanks for the song, kid."

Keats's gaze dropped to the floor, a strange lightness filling him. He smiled to himself. "Anytime, Teach."

TWENTY-FIVE

Georgia had slept like the dead for what seemed like the first time in a year. Usually she woke up multiple times a night, plagued with nightmares or hearing phantom sounds in the house. But last night, she'd fallen asleep with comforting thoughts of the new turn in her life. Finally, she felt like she was finding her way through the dark cave and seeing thin shafts of light. She'd had two fantastic nights with Colby and had managed not to panic, even when she'd been tied up and fully under his control. And now her long days in her empty house would be filled with Keats's teasing and laughter. Signs of life were leaking back into her existence.

She'd made that happen. She'd let these two men in her life and doors were opening inside her again, doors she'd long left locked and forgotten. Things were going to get better. She wasn't broken forever. Leesha had been telling her that from the beginning, but now Georgia was finally allowing herself to believe it.

She shuffled into the kitchen in pursuit of industrial-strength caffeine, feeling a bit drunk and bleary-eyed from a night of such deep sleep. She'd set the coffeepot on a timer, and the smell alone was enough to perk her up. She needed all the help she could get because Keats had told her he'd be on a mission today to get her out and about with him. The guy wasn't going to let her be a chicken for much longer. Especially after Keats had taken on his own fear last night and told her he was headed out to see Colby play at the bar so he could talk to him. She couldn't wait to hear how that had turned out.

She smiled to herself and reached for an upper cabinet to pull out her favorite mug, while simultaneously opening the fridge to get the milk. But multitasking had been a bad idea. The heavy fridge door shut on her hand and when she yanked backward, she lost her grip on her mug with her other. The ceramic crashed to the floor. And in that shred of a second, all the bubbly happiness that had been coursing through her drained away, and everything inside her seemed to plummet at that chillingly familiar sound. *No, no, no . . .*

She gripped the edge of the counter, trying to hold on, but her eyes squeezed shut and she sank to her knees, the rush of memories and panic overwhelming her. The familiar movie reel from hell rolled behind her eyelids.

Georgia moved through her best friend's kitchen, straightening this and that, unable to stay still as she waited for the electric kettle to come to a boil. Once she heard the steam starting to eke out, she grabbed a canister of the new chai tea blend she'd picked up a few weeks ago at a cute shop in downtown Chicago and spooned the loose leaves into her infuser. This blend was decaf, so she hoped it wouldn't key up her nerves like coffee had lately.

But as she poured the hot water over the leaves, she knew it was hopeful thinking to blame it on the coffee. She hadn't had a drop of caffeine yet this morning and already that unsettled, on-edge feeling was humming through her. These days it was like she was always plugged into a faulty outlet—electricity getting pumped into her system in large, uneven doses, her adrenaline always primed for the next time Phillip popped up unexpectedly.

Up until a few days ago, she'd convinced herself it was mostly harmless. Phillip had fixated on her after their breakup, and this was his way of getting over it—even if it was a little nuts. When she'd notified the cops of his stalker-like behavior, they'd assured her that as long as she didn't engage him or encourage the behavior, Phillip would eventually move on. And with him doing nothing particularly threatening beyond calling her too much to profess his love, sending her bouquets of flowers, and showing up in places she happened to be, the cops couldn't really help her anyway except tell her to change her phone number and take out a restraining order if she felt threatened.

But then Antonio, the new guy she'd started casually seeing, had called her two days ago to tell her his house had been broken into while he was out of town. His bed had been slashed up along with all his clothes. And when he'd gone into his garage, he'd noticed a faint smell and fluid stains beneath his car. If he hadn't left the car sitting closed up in the garage for a week, he probably would've never noticed. But thank God he had because his brake lines had been punctured.

When he'd told her the story, Georgia had gone cold all over. Failed brakes had been what the police suspected had gone wrong on her good friend Tyson's car when he'd crashed one late night driving home from work. He'd been killed on impact, and with not much left to examine after the car fire beyond the lack of skid marks, the cops had ruled it an accident most likely due to mechanical failure or driver intoxication. But it'd never felt right to Georgia. Tyson's BMW had been only a year old, and Georgia had never known Tyson to drink on work nights.

But Phillip, Tyson's friend and co-worker at the time, had stepped in to comfort her after the loss, and he'd confided that Tyson had started to drink when he worked late, that his caseload had been crushing him. Georgia had felt even more bereft after that. Not only had she lost a man she cared about, she'd failed him as a friend by not seeing that he was under too much stress and needed help.

But after the incident at Antonio's, the pieces had started shifting into a new pattern, and she'd had the bone-chilling realization that Phillip might've been lying the whole time. That maybe he wasn't lovesick, but truly sick. She'd rewound back to when she was happy and casually dating Tyson. Phillip had been around a lot—a good friend to Tyson. But looking back, Georgia could now see that maybe Phillip had made himself too available, too present. He'd subtly crept his way into her life by always volunteering to run errands or do favors. He'd become a go-to guy for both of them. From the outside, he'd seemed to just be an all-around nice guy. But now she had a feeling it had all been carefully calculated.

Phillip was a brilliant man and once they'd started dating, she'd never known him to go out of his way to do favors for others. Only for her. Had he developed an unhealthy obsession with her from the very beginning? All of her instincts were now pointing in that direction. And if that was the case, had he taken it upon himself to remove the only obstacle from having her? Tyson.

Her gut clenched at the thought. If Tyson had been killed because of her . . . God, she couldn't even think about it. Sweet, sexy Tyson. They'd only dated casually, more friends with benefits than anything else, but he'd been a good man and a stand-up guy.

Yesterday, she'd taken her suspicions to the police. The detective she'd talked to had been skeptical, but that was his job. He'd asked a lot of questions and had assured her he'd look into it. She'd also gone ahead and filed that restraining order. So now all she could do was wait and worry. She was probably overreacting and coming up with far-fetched theories, but she wasn't going to take any chances. She'd called her friend Leesha last night and had made arrangements to stay with her for a while so she wouldn't be alone at her house if Phillip decided to show up.

But now that Leesha had left for work, Georgia couldn't help but be unnerved by the creeping silence in the unfamiliar house. She wrapped her hands around her mug of tea and blew across the top, trying to bring her mind to a settled state. But before she could turn to head toward the living room, a hand grabbed the back of her hair, jerking her backward. The mug slipped from her grip and shattered on the floor, the spray of hot tea burning the tops of her bare feet.

A scream tried to escape, but a hand clamped over her mouth before she could make much of a sound.

"Don't you dare," the menacing voice uttered in her ear. "Don't you think you've already caused enough trouble?"

Georgia couldn't see who was behind her, but she'd know that voice anywhere. She screamed behind his hand again and tried to writhe out of his grip. But he was far bigger and stronger than she was.

"I've tried and tried to make you understand, sweetheart," Phillip said, switching to a soothing tone. "I've sent you flowers and letters. I've given you everything you could want. I love you and am not going to give up on us. Can't you see that? We're meant to be together. Do you know how hurt I was when I heard about the restraining order? Why would you do that to me?"

She whimpered behind his hand.

"You know, I think you're just working too hard. The stress is messing with your head. You're not thinking straight. Maybe you should see someone or take a break. We could go away together."

She stretched forward, trying to reach the kettle, but it was just out of her reach.

"Now, now, none of that," he said, his voice soft but his grip tight. "I want to work this out. I don't want to fight. But you're going to have to calm down and get your head together. Then you're going to go to the cops and tell them you were mistaken. You were just hurt that I broke up with you."

She made a sound of strangled disbelief.

"I won't let you embarrass me, Georgia. What if my clients found out about the order?" He pulled her tighter against his body, the smell of his designer cologne burning her nostrils. "You don't want to make me angry, sweetheart. I've tolerated your behavior these last few weeks because I know all couples go through rough patches. But I'm losing my patience. Don't make me prove how far I'm willing to go for you."

Tears leaked out of her eyes.

"Are you going to make this right and take back what you said to the police?"

She nodded, willing to do just about anything to get him away. Right. Now.

He pressed his nose to the curve of her neck and inhaled deeply. "Mmm, that's my smart girl. I knew we could talk this out."

She closed her eyes, fighting the urge to recoil. He needed to think she was calm and in agreement if she had any shot of him letting her go.

"What time is that bitch Leesha getting back?" he asked, still nuzzling her neck. "Because now that we're back on the same page, I want to show you how much I've missed you."

His erection pushed against her backside and a wave of nausea slammed into her. She shook her head.

"Come on, I know you've missed me, too. That limp-dick Mexican can't be doing much for you."

He tilted her head to the side and pressed his mouth to her neck, his tongue touching her skin. Georgia began to shake, her gaze darting around the kitchen to see what she could use against him. The knife block was a good possibility, but she'd have to break free for a few seconds to make the two steps to reach it.

She raised her elbow, ready to jab, but a sound from the front of the house made her pause. A door clicked shut. "Georgia, you still home?"

Georgia had never been happier to hear another human being.

Phillip swore and pressed his mouth against her ear. "Say a word about this to anyone and you'll regret it. Don't test me, Georgia."

With that, he released his hold on her and hustled out the back door, leaving her in a sobbing heap on the floor.

Leesha had found her there, and they'd gone straight to the police. Georgia had told the cops everything but had no hard evidence to back it up. She couldn't prove he'd been the one who'd attacked her at Leesha's. He had an alibi and she'd admitted she hadn't seen the intruder's face. They had put Phillip in jail for a few nights, but they were no match for his legal maneuvering. They didn't have enough to hold him.

And soon after he'd gotten out, he'd made good on his threats.

Two weeks later, she'd been standing at her sister's grave site. Suicide.

Sure, it was.

Georgia's eyes snapped open, clothes clinging to her and her heart pounding in her throat. Sunlight streamed through her kitchen window, but the shadowed corners from her flashback were still assaulting her. She pressed her hands to the floor and took a few big gulps of air, trying to push away the memory of that day in Leesha's kitchen. She could still feel Phillip's hands on her, the threat and intention in his voice. That had been the day she'd gone from worried to terrified. The breaking point. Nothing had been safe or good since.

After a few moments, she lifted her hands and realized her left hand had been braced on a broken piece of the mug. She watched her bloodied hand tremble in front of her. Goddammit. She rose to her feet and grabbed a dish towel to press to her palm and paced, trying to purge all the adrenaline coursing through her, but it was no use. Her entire system felt zapped.

She reached for her cell phone, which she'd left charging on the counter. Keats was due to come over for work in half an hour, and she needed to call him off. She wasn't in the right headspace to handle much of anything right now, much less other people. She felt strung out and . . . off. Flashbacks were rare, but she knew what that meant for the day. That overwhelming wallop of adrenaline and anxiety short-circuited her for hours. Her panic attacks would come more easily, and any little thing would set her off. She'd have to take an extra pill just to get through.

Maybe she'd gotten too cocky about her progress. Maybe she'd been kidding herself.

These were the days she didn't just feel frustrated; she felt crazy.

She typed a text to Keats.

Change of plans. Take the day off. Not up to working today.

Then she sent another to Colby because he'd called and left a message first thing this morning about getting together for lunch.

Today's not good. Let's talk later.

With that taken care of, she forced herself upstairs and into the shower. Maybe she could wash off the bad memories, watch them swirl down the drain and disappear. Ha. If only.

After her shower, she bandaged the small cut on her hand and went downstairs to make some toast so that she could take her meds. She also needed to clean up the mess she'd left behind. But before the toast popped up, there was a knock at her door. She groaned, knowing all too well who it probably was.

She could ignore it, but regardless of which neighbor it was, she knew neither Colby nor Keats would walk away that easily. With a sigh, she headed to the front of the house and checked the peephole. Fantastic. Double-teamed. She swung the door open. "Yes?"

"We got your texts," Colby said, his gaze sweeping over her.

"And thought we should stop by," Keats declared.

"Was I not clear that I wanted to be alone today?" she asked, knowing it sounded bitchy but unable to wrangle in her emotions. She didn't want them to see her like this. Fractured. Weak. And the only way she knew to hide that was by lifting up the don't-fuck-with-me drawbridge until she got herself back together.

"What's going on, Georgia?" Colby asked, concern lacing his tone.

The house phone rang behind her and she startled, complete with a little yelp.

"Shit." She put her shaking hand to the door frame. "Sorry."

Keats frowned and reached out to touch her elbow. "Hey, you okay? Want me to get that?"

She shook her head, embarrassed. "No, it's fine, just let it go to voice mail."

Colby stepped forward but honored the invisible barrier of her doorway. "Tell us what's going on, Georgia. Maybe we can help. Are you sick? Did something happen? You look spooked."

"It's nothing. I just . . . I had a nightmare, old memories, and sometimes that throws me off for the day. I'll be fine. Maybe we can talk tomorrow."

"Or maybe you can not be alone today," Keats said, a mule

digging in its heels. "The last thing you need after a nightmare is sitting by yourself to stew in it all day."

"Keats—" she warned.

"No, he's right. Sometimes distraction is the best medicine," Colby said. "We could help with that, you know. We'll even wrestle in the yard for you." He peeked over his shoulder. "Where do you keep your sprinklers again?"

She stared at him for a moment, the joke not registering in her tweaked-out brain, but then she let out a breath and smiled. "Right. Wrestling. So I guess you two guys worked things out, then?"

Keats's gaze slid toward Colby, the look telling her everything. "You could say that."

"Good. I'm really happy for you both." The knowledge buoyed her spirits a little, but it also made her feel intensely *other* all of a sudden. Here these two guys were in the midst of that excitement at the start of a new relationship and she could barely get one foot in front of the other today. She'd been delusional to think she was ready for anything with either of these two. She wasn't in a stable enough state to inhabit that sunshiny space blooming between Keats and Colby. They didn't need her baggage and dark clouds pressing down on them. They'd be fine on their own.

"Can't we keep you company today?" Keats asked.

She blew out a breath and reached for their hands. They each took one of hers, Colby frowning deeper when he saw her bandaged one. "I appreciate the offer, really. You two are amazing. But I think you should spend the day with each other. I'm . . . I'm a disaster."

When Keats opened his mouth to refute her, she shook her head and squeezed his hand.

"I can fake that I'm not sometimes, but then I get hit with a day like this, and get a big fat reminder. I'm not—I can't . . . do this. With either of you." She looked to Colby, her heart breaking a little. "I think I should've stuck to watching. And Keats, any work I need done you can do remotely from Colby's. I don't need to bring the crazy into your lives, too."

"No, I know what crazy looks like," Colby replied, his gaze holding hers. "You're not crazy. You're scared and going through something. But whatever it is, I guarantee that the only way out of it is forward. Don't close the door and get stuck again. Please. Don't shut us out."

She let their hands drop from hers, tears burning her eyes. "I'm sorry."

"Give us one chance," Colby said, bracing his hand on the door frame. "Give us today. Remember what happened when you let me take over, when you trusted me to take care of you? Let's try that again. Turn your day over to me and if by the end of it, you still want to be alone, we won't knock on your door again."

She looked down, her emotions rioting through her—the urge to run, the urge to say yes, the fear of what could happen if she did, and if she didn't. "Colby—"

"It's just one day, George," Keats said softly. "What's the worst that could happen?"

She shook her head. "I could completely lose it in front of you, embarrass myself, possibly inspire you to check me into a mental institution."

Colby reached out for her hand again, taking her hurt one between both of his. "I swear no men in white coats will be called no matter what happens today. As for the other two things, so the fuck what? Lose it and we'll help you get it back together like we did the day with the ants. You're dealing with a disorder. There's no embarrassment in that. All I see is a brave woman fighting tooth and nail to get free of it."

"I can't get free," she said, tears escaping now. "Not until he's locked up. Every time I think I'm making progress, I'm knocked backward again. The past never goes away. It doesn't matter that he's hundreds of miles away. He's in my goddamned head."

"Who?" Keats asked, not bothering with boundaries and stepping forward to put his arm around her. "Who's in your head, George?"

The embrace undid her, shattering the barrier she was frantically trying to hold in place, and she couldn't do anything but sag into him. The brave face. The grip on her secrets. All of it faltered in the warmth of the simple hug. All the energy was used up. Tears turned into sobbing.

"Dammit, Georgia." Colby crossed the threshold and wrapped an arm around her waist, closing ranks on the other side of her. "You don't have to do this all on your own. Let us in."

She loathed the tears, hated that her body was rebelling against her yet again. *Look at the poor, weepy girl leaning on the big, strong men.* Pathetic. But she couldn't do anything about it. Her body was in a state of emotional expectoration, spilling all the white-knuckled emotions and fear out in a flood.

Colby and Keats didn't say anything more, just held her tight, one of their hands rubbing her back. The cocooned state between the two of them was more soothing than she wanted to admit to herself. She didn't want to have to depend on anyone for anything, especially these two. They were supposed to be her lighthearted fun, not more people hoping to fix her. She had enough of those. Her issues were hers to deal with and no one else's.

But she was so damn tired of being alone. And not trusting anyone. And being scared. So. Damn. Tired.

So when she shut the door behind the three of them, it wasn't about flings or sex or even romantic notions—none of the things she'd entertained about either of these men before. Right now, she needed their friendship.

She needed to surrender to that. To let them be there.

Even if it was for just one day.

TWENTY-SIX

Colby sat on a chair in Georgia's living room, listening to her story and fighting the urge to scoop her up and hold her in his lap while she told it—buffer her somehow from the memories. She wasn't crying anymore. After letting him and Keats inside and getting through a wash of tears, Georgia had left them briefly to wash her face and get some water. When she'd returned, she'd been composed again except for the telltale puffiness around her eyes. Emotions tucked back under the bed.

Colby understood why Georgia felt the need to wear that kind of armor, but he wished she felt safe enough to be vulnerable in front of him. No one was here to judge her on how tough she was. But despite her current stoicism, he knew it was a huge leap of trust that she was telling them her story.

She tucked her hands in her lap, her thumb rubbing the center of her palm. "I dated Phillip for a year. He seemed like a great guy. There for me after my friend Tyson's death, understanding, supportive. Our connection felt comfortable and familiar. He was smart and successful, good-looking. He seemed to almost worship me like I was on some pedestal. Doted on me. Spoiled me. Always bringing me little gifts and going out of his way to do nice things for me. I loved that. I know that probably sounds self-centered and stupid."

"Not at all," Colby said, keeping his voice quiet so as not to startle her out of sharing this with them. "No one is going to fault anyone for wanting to feel cherished."

"Looking back, I realize now that he knew exactly what buttons needed pushing for me. I was getting older. My friends were getting married and starting families. I hadn't dated anyone seriously for a while, and I was getting that itch for something more long-term, getting those white-picket-fence fantasies. Tyson hadn't been up for that, and really, we were better suited as friends, anyway. But once he was gone, Phillip could step in and fill that need I had by lavishing me with all the romance, courting me with gifts, trips, giving me all of his free time, talking about our future like it was an inevitable conclusion. It was hard not to fall into. But it was an acquisitions game for him, and I was simply the target. He wasn't going to settle for anything less than complete possession."

Colby's neck prickled. He had a feeling this guy's ideas of possession had no relation to the sexy kind in his world.

"At first, it was heady to be at the center of all that attention. That's what women are supposed to want, right? The guy who only has eyes for you. But then he started to do things that weren't so romantic, like make negative comments about my close friends or plan things so that it made it hard for me to spend time with them. His jealousy went from sweet and amusing to irrational over the course of the year we dated. By the end, pretty much any guy I came in contact with became a suspect in his mind. He'd swear he trusted me but not them. I'd had friends in abusive relationships and saw the signs heading that way, so I broke it off."

"I'm guessing he didn't take that well," Keats said, his tone gentle but his eyes flickering with barely banked anger.

Colby knew the feeling. The thought of anyone hurting Georgia, of making her this fearful, sent murderous thoughts running through his head.

Georgia rubbed her lips together and shook her head. "No, he became obsessed, relentless. A creepy stalker right out of one of my novels. I hoped it would pass. I talked to the police, ignored the behavior, didn't encourage him. All the things everyone had advised me to do. I started dating again, hoping that would send a clear message that I wasn't coming back. But then . . ." She paused to take a shaky breath. "That just sent him over the cliff."

Colby couldn't stop himself this time. He moved from the chair to sit next to Georgia on the couch. He didn't try to touch her but stretched his arm over the back of the couch. To his surprise, she scooted closer to him and leaned in. His arm went around her. "If this is too hard . . ."

"No," she said with a little head shake. "Maybe it's good I get it all out."

Keats leaned forward and put a hand on her knee. "Go ahead, George. We're listening."

She didn't speak for a few seconds but then seemed to gather her strength again. And when she told them the rest of the story—Tyson's car accident, her almost-rape, her sister's murder—Colby went cold all over, rage like an icy river running through him.

"He didn't want to kill me because in his twisted mind, we were still meant to be together. But he wasn't above hurting everyone around me to get to me. He took everything from me. And didn't leave a bit of evidence behind."

"Jesus," Keats breathed. "George, I can't even—please tell us he's locked up."

She lifted her gaze to him. "He's out on bail in Chicago but can't leave the state. No one except the legal team and my therapist knows where I am. I'm supposed to testify in January. I'm the key witness since I'm the one who saw his erratic behavior up close. And I'm the one who talked to my sister every day and can vouch that she was in no way depressed or suicidal. I'm the one who can tell them about that day in the kitchen and the threats he made. Without my testimony, they don't think they have enough to get a murder conviction. And here I am, the girl who can't even cross the street without panicking."

Colby rubbed her chilled arm. "Baby . . ."

She sat up, her shoulders stiffening, before he could say any more. "God, it sounds so pathetic when I say it out loud."

Keats frowned. "Of course it doesn't. You had a murderer after you. You lost people you loved. No one would blame you for being scared."

But there was a fierceness morphing Georgia's expression as Keats spoke. She stood. "Don't give me an out, Keats."

Keats's eyebrows raised. "I was just—"

"Raleigh fucking died. Tyson died. *Because of me.* And here I am like some damn mouse hiding in the basement." She paced across the floor, then turned to face both of them. "This isn't what my sister would've done. She would be on the steps of the court-house, shouting into the microphones and demanding justice. She would be fighting."

"You *are* fighting," Colby said. "Every damn day. Sometimes our bodies and brains don't cooperate like we want, but I don't see a woman giving up."

She shook her head, her eyes wet again, but not in defeat—in frustration and anger. "No. I'm not fighting. I'm only surviving. That's not good enough. I broke a mug in my kitchen today and freaked out. *That*—something as stupid and simple as that—should not control me."

She stalked over to the coffee table and lifted the glass of water she'd been drinking.

"George—"

But her arm was already in motion. She tossed the glass against the wall, where it shattered into glittering wet shards. She bent over, hands to her knees, breathing hard.

Colby went to her side, and Keats jumped up from the couch. Keats disappeared into the kitchen, probably to get something to clean up the mess, and Colby wrapped his arms around her.

"Ready to call the men in white coats yet?" she quipped.

The comment brought a little smile with it, and relief coursed through him. She was upset but not panicking.

Keats was back in a flash, but instead of a rag, he had a tray full of coffee cups. "Come on, George. Let's not do this halfway."

She lifted her head. "What?"

He set down the tray and handed her two mugs. "Fuck these mugs. They're nothing but colored sand. They don't mean anything. They can't hurt you."

Colby stared at Keats as Keats lifted one of the mugs and launched it against the same wall Georgia had used for target practice. It hit with a thud, then broke when it hit the wood floor.

Georgia blinked, glanced between the two of them.

"See?" Keats said. "Nothing. Take that sound back. Breaking glass isn't about the past. It's about right now when you and your insane, but devastatingly handsome, neighbors completely demolished your coffee cup collection for shits and giggles."

"You're nuts," she said, but there was light in her eyes.

"Yeah, he is," Colby agreed, taking a cup from Keats. "And a genius." Colby sent a cup flying. It shattered on impact, the simple act of destruction sending an odd zing of satisfaction through him. "Ahh, that's definitely what I wanted to do when the principal put me on leave."

Keats threw another. "And that's what I wanted to do to Hank when he broke into my place."

Georgia tossed one of her cups with more strength than Colby would've suspected she had in her. "And that's for every time this damn fear has kept me in the house."

Keats cheered and handed her another. Before long, they'd gone through most of Georgia's set, Georgia doing most of the tosses. And she wasn't crying anymore; she was laughing. They all were.

As Georgia launched the last mug, Colby reached out and grabbed the back of Keats's neck, giving it a squeeze. He looked over at Colby, his gaze questioning. Colby leaned close to his ear. "Good job, Adam."

Keats's eyes warmed in a way that Colby knew he'd never get tired of. Hell, he'd still been shocked to wake up this morning and find that the former straight guy he'd sent to bed sticky and used had woken up without regrets. Keats had shuffled into the kitchen, looking fucking edible with his mussed hair and loose pajama bottoms, and had walked straight up to Colby and said, "I woke up smelling like you."

"And?" Colby had asked, expecting the ax to come down.

"And it took everything I had not to jerk off." Then Keats had kissed him.

Colby's chest had filled with some feeling he couldn't pin down, and he hadn't been able to stanch his need to touch Keats again. He'd pushed Keats's pants down and off, then used them to bind his wrists to the handle of the fridge. He'd then sat down and eaten his breakfast while he watched Keats stand there naked and hard. After Colby had eaten his last bite, he'd stripped, grabbed a bottle of olive oil, and jerked them both off, cock against cock. They'd both been weak-kneed and recovering when the texts had come through from Georgia.

Colby had read them aloud, and Keats had switched from obedient, willing submissive to man on a mission in two seconds flat. He'd pulled off the bindings and yanked up his pants. "Get in the shower and be quick. We're going over there."

Colby hadn't corrected him on the sudden order. He'd wanted to get to Georgia as soon as possible, too. So they'd jumped in their respective showers and gotten ready in record time. Colby had at first insisted he go over alone so that they didn't overwhelm her. But Keats had refused outright. Now Colby was glad he hadn't wasted any time fighting that battle. Because Georgia had needed them. *Both* of them.

Colby knew he was good at being a calming force. With hysterical teenagers. With subs bottoming out. With his not-always-stable family. He'd learned how to be a steady and soothing presence amongst chaos. And Georgia had needed some of that this morning. But that hadn't been all she needed. She'd also needed a little wildness, a way to fight the bad crazy with good crazy. To find her own fire again. And Keats knew how to jump outside the lines and act on pure emotion. He knew how to light matches.

So seeing Georgia laughing and visibly relieved as she walked over to the pile of broken glass felt like a victory for all of them.

"Looks like you're going to need to send your slacker assistant to Bed Bath and Beyond," Colby said. "Or give up coffee."

Georgia turned around, her brown eyes full of emotion as she stared back at them. "What am I going to do with the two of you?"

"Would you like a list?" Keats asked. "Because I have some suggestions."

Georgia laughed. "Most inappropriate employee ever."

Keats shrugged, unrepentant. "Want to fire me?"

Georgia glanced at Colby, smiled, then walked over to Keats, put her hands on his cheeks, and planted a full smacking kiss right on his mouth. "Yep. You're canned."

Keats blinked, clearly astonished. But when Georgia moved to step away, Keats hooked the collar of her shirt and brought her back in for more than a peck. Colby could hear Georgia's gasp at the contact and he watched, riveted, as Keats parted Georgia's lips and gave her the full devastating power of his mouth. Colby knew firsthand what that felt like and how impossible it was to resist. And sure enough, though Georgia had stiffened when Keats had pulled her back to him, now she melted in his grasp and kissed him back, sliding her fingers into Keats's hair.

Colby had to swallow back the groan. So. Fucking. Hot. Both of them. His lovers.

No, not quite. Not *his*. Not really.

Not yet.

The last thought punched him right in the chest. The driving intention seeming to come from outside himself.

No, that wasn't what this was. This was supposed to be casual, messing around. A little fling with Georgia. A little training with Keats. Maybe a threesome thrown into the mix if the two of them were open to it. That was what they were doing. That was what he'd agreed to.

But watching Georgia and Keats together, he knew he was lying to himself. If they all three ended up in bed together, he couldn't imagine he'd be able to simply move on like he did every other time. Have some fun, do some kink, on to the next adventure. No way. He was in too deep already with both of them separately. Put them all together, and he didn't have a fucking shot at staying cool and devil-may-care about it.

Because as he stood there he found himself wondering what it would be like to have more. To have it all. To have them both. What if they were truly his?

But he had to shake himself out of those fantasies. What he was imagining was a pipe dream. There were three of them. And two of the three weren't looking for a relationship. Plus, even if they were out for more, this wasn't a simple boy-meets-girl or boy-meets-boy arrangement. This shit would be more than a little complicated. And yes, his friend Jace had somehow managed to maintain a triad relationship, so Colby knew it could be done. But he'd also watched many others at The Ranch try nontraditional arrangements like that and fail miserably. Hell, his own record with all types of romantic relationships was damn dismal. Just because he'd started to want a committed relationship didn't mean he'd necessarily be good at it.

He just needed to get his head together and enjoy this for what it was—friendship and a hot time with two kinky people.

Colby brought his focus back to the two people in front of him. Keats was in control of the kiss and pulled back after a few hot seconds. He smiled broadly at a stunned Georgia and touched the tip of his finger to her wet lips. "Now that one was worth getting fired for."

Georgia's wide-eyed gaze slid to Colby, her eyelashes fluttering as she apparently tried to get her bearings. "Uh . . ."

Colby smiled. "Keats, I don't remember giving you permission to kiss my girl."

Keats glanced over his shoulder at him. "Punish me later, Teach. Whatever the consequences are, they will have been well worth it."

"Mmm," Colby said noncommittally. "Or maybe I'll just let her do it."

Keats coughed, or maybe it was a choke, but he looked more turned on at the thought than worried. Colby would've called him a slut if he didn't think Keats would perceive it as an insult.

Georgia put a hand to her forehead and shook her head. "Well, you two said you came over here to distract me. Mission accomplished."

Colby walked over to her and tugged her into his arms. She came willingly, bringing her body up against his and peering up at him. He pushed a hair away from her cheek. "So what do you want to do next, Ms. Delaune? Sprinklers? Ordering Keats to take off his shirt and clean up the mess he made with the dishes?"

She smirked but there was a resolute look to her gaze. "It's Lawrence, not Delaune. And no, I don't want to do any of that. I want the two of you to take me out of here to get some new cups and maybe to lunch. And then wherever else you want to go. I don't want you to let me back in my house until it's time to go to sleep."

Colby tightened his hold on her, hope building in him. "You sure?"

"Yes." She looked to Keats, then back to Colby. "And if I panic and embarrass you while we're out, I'm giving you permission to leave me be and pretend you don't know me."

Colby grabbed her chin. "Shut your mouth, Georgia Lawrence. You think I give a shit what anyone else thinks? You panic, we've got you covered."

"Damn straight," Keats said, stepping closer to them. "You're safe with us, George."

She smiled at the two of them, her gaze softening. "I know. I feel that. Thank you."

Colby's heart felt as if it had inflated in his chest. Trust. Coming from someone like Georgia, it was like pure gold being dropped in his hands. He wanted to lift her up, kiss her, tell her he was honored to have it because he knew how valuable a commodity it was for her. But he held himself in check. He needed to play it cool.

Even if he felt anything but on the inside.

Damn, he was fucked.

TWENTY-SEVEN

Georgia's heart was beating so fast, she was surprised the pendant around her neck wasn't vibrating from it, but so far, she hadn't gone into full panic. Colby had arranged for them to eat in the private dining room at Sawgrass, one of his best friend Kade's restaurants. They'd had to walk through the busy restaurant to get to the private space, and that had sent her brain firing with worries as she scanned the faces in the crowd. But having Colby's arm around her had helped. Beyond being a reassuring emotional presence, his sheer size provided a feeling of safety on some elemental, cavewoman level. If someone wanted to hurt her, not many people would mess with a guy as big and intimidating-looking as Colby. And though Keats wasn't as massive as Colby, she had a feeling he could be as vicious and tough as a junkyard dog when provoked.

So sitting between the two of them had her more settled than she'd been in over a year in any public place. She could breathe a little. And the air smelled damn sweet.

She still couldn't get over all the events of today. The morning had started off so awful and bleak. And when Colby and Keats had shown up, she'd been more than annoyed that they'd ignored her orders to stay away. She'd wanted to lock herself in the darkness.

But then so much had changed so quickly when she hadn't been able to scare them off. Just saying her story out loud to someone who wasn't Leesha or a lawyer had felt liberating. Her secrets were like bars on a cage, keeping everyone at a distance while simultaneously holding her hostage. With secrets, she was only a character playing a role, a fake. So throwing back the curtain and putting it all out there had taken some of the power out of the memories and had brought her closer to the two men she'd confided in.

Then there'd been dishes breaking. And strange relief. And Keats had kissed her. *Really* kissed her. The dynamics had shifted to sandy terrain again, leaving her unsure where exactly this was going. Colby hadn't seemed to mind the kiss. In fact, he'd looked like he'd enjoyed the show. Kinky bastard. And God knows her mind had been whirling on the drive over here, wondering what exactly had transpired between the two men. That speculating had painted some very vivid pictures in her head. But she knew this could be dangerous territory.

Keats and Colby had something new between them, and she got the sense there was more than just a hot hookup brewing there. There were feelings. And though she was attracted to them both and more than tempted by the thought of falling into bed with them, she didn't want to screw up what they had going on. She was in no position to get involved in anything serious when she hoped to move back to Chicago in January. Plus, she didn't want to muddle things for them.

Georgia tried to shake off the worries and focus on the conversation the two men were having.

"So they still haven't given you any idea how long you're going to be on leave?" she asked.

Colby's expression had darkened considerably in the last few minutes at the shift in topic. "No. My boss says it's mostly posturing by the board. They want to look like they're doing everything they can so that the parents don't sue. But when I talked to the powers that be yesterday, it was like I was on trial. I'm worried they're going to cover their ass by throwing mine under the bus."

"That's bullshit," Keats said, his jaw twitching. "Why doesn't the kid step up and tell everybody it had nothing to do with you?"

Colby sighed. "The kid's parents didn't listen to him before. They're not going to now. He's tried to tell them what happened."

"You shouldn't have to take the fall for a messed-up kid with messed-up parents making a dumb decision," Keats said. "Not again."

Colby sent Keats a tired look. "Last time I earned some of that fall."

"No. You didn't." He smirked after a few seconds. "But damn, you'd be hanged in the town square if they saw us now. Nobody would believe nothing happened back then."

Colby shook his head and scrubbed a hand over his face. "God, I don't want to even think about that."

Georgia smiled. "You two would be quite the scandal, huh?"

"You have no idea," Keats said in between bites of food. "They'd probably think that we ran away together back then and have been hiding out in secret since—my innocent straight mind brainwashed by the big, bad bisexual teacher."

Colby sent him a wry smile—one laced with affection. And in that moment, Georgia felt the two's shared history like a fourth member at the table. She believed them when they said that nothing inappropriate had happened between them back then, but she also could tell their bond had started way before this recent reunion.

Maybe she should step back and get out of their way.

"She's thinking too hard again," Keats observed as he twirled some pasta on his fork.

"What's got that wrinkle in your brow, gorgeous?"

"Nothing, really." She smoothed the edge of the tablecloth. "I guess I'm just processing everything. It's been a crazy few days."

Colby held out a bite of his steak. "Stop analyzing everything and give yourself a break. We have good food, good wine, and good company. Sit back and enjoy."

She took the bite, chewed, then took a sip of her wine. "You're right. If I overthink this one, my brain will explode."

Colby leaned back in his chair, fingering his wineglass and considering her. "You mean thinking about being out of the house?"

"Sure, but also being here with you two." She adjusted the napkin in her lap. "I have to be honest. I keep bouncing from feeling like I'm with friends to feeling like we're all on a date to feeling like an interloper between you two. It's scrambling my brain a little."

"If you're an interloper, then I am, too," Keats said with a shrug. "You two were together first."

Colby sipped his wine, then set it down. "I think there are a lot of blurred lines at this table, and trying to label them right now is a pointless exercise. God knows every time I try to draw a line with this one"—he tipped his head toward Keats—"the guy bounds right over it."

Keats smirked. "Boing, boing."

"But know"—he reached out and gave Georgia's hand a squeeze—"there are no expectations. We're here because we wanted to spend the day together. There's no pressure for anything beyond that."

She let her hand curl into his.

"He's right," Keats said, his amused expression sobering. "I know I was out of line kissing you like that this morning. I acted first, thought second. Kind of a bad habit of mine. But I don't want you to feel like I'm trying to horn my way in on what you two have going on. Just because Colby's a total manwhore who's fooling around with both of us—"

"Hey now, watch it, smartass," Colby said, narrowing his gaze.

Georgia bit her lip, trying not to smile.

"All I'm saying," Keats continued, "is that I'm not going to interfere if you and Colby want to do your own thing."

"I appreciate that," she said, not exactly in a place to figure out how she felt about the whole thing, much less Keats individually. But she couldn't deny that the kiss had made it hard to focus on the reasons why she shouldn't want Keats. "Same goes for me. Last thing I want to do is get in the way with you two."

Colby looked between the two of them, a sly smile touching his lips. "Eat, both of you. We've got the whole afternoon ahead of us."

Keats lifted his glass. "Here's to George's first day out of prison! May she make this day her bitch."

Georgia laughed and lifted her wine. "Hear, hear."

They all clinked their glasses together, and Georgia closed her eyes, tasting the freedom in the moment.

Maybe she could win this battle after all.

TWENTY-EIGHT

Colby and Georgia had been in his bedroom way too long. Colby had said they were going in there to find a movie for all of them to watch, but that'd been half an hour ago. Keats tried not to feel left out as he sat sprawled on the couch, strumming his guitar. Their day out had been more successful than he'd expected after everything that had happened this morning. He'd been worried that it would be too much for Georgia, that the outing would overwhelm her. But she'd been determined to fight today and she'd kicked ass.

They'd kept it low-key. After Sawgrass, they'd gone to a quiet suburban shopping area and picked out new coffee cups to replace the ones they'd demolished. Georgia had had one rocky moment in one of the shops when a dark-haired man in a suit had brushed by her. She'd seized up and her fingernails had dug into Keats's arm. Apparently, the guy had resembled Phillip. But Colby had swooped in and steered her out into the fresh air, leading her through some breathing exercise all the while, and calmed her before her anxiety took her off the rails.

Keats had been fascinated watching Colby slip into therapist mode, seeing that uncanny ability to morph his hard-edged dominance into this gentle but firmly reassuring presence. Georgia had responded to it instantly, and Keats had been glad it had been so effective. But while watching the two of them huddled together, he'd also felt his age and inexperience acutely for the first time. He could make women laugh, he could turn them on, but he wasn't sure he'd ever be able to be such a steady rock for someone, like Colby was. Colby was solid—the kind of guy built for marriage and fatherhood and all the hard stuff. The stuff someone like Georgia would eventually want. The stuff Keats wasn't sure he was capable of.

So right then and there, Keats knew that even if something happened between all three of them, Keats would eventually become the bonus prize at the bottom of the cereal box—a fun thing to have around but not the stuff that nourished you. He was the expendable one in this equation. And he needed to keep that in the front of his mind going forward. He couldn't lose himself to it. He'd already left himself too open by singing to Colby last night and letting some feelings show. That shit needed to stop. This was temporary fun, and he needed to enjoy it for that. Otherwise, he was going to get himself crushed.

After the day out, they'd come back to Colby's. They'd ordered pizza and Georgia had managed to make it through the rest of the evening without any panic attacks. During dinner, they'd all shared a few beers, and Keats had finally been able to relax a little and find some peace in his role. They'd laughed and told stories about this and that. It'd felt warm and laid-back and like they all had been hanging out forever. And for a little while, Keats had felt a part of something instead of sitting outside the borders. But then Georgia and Colby had gone off to Colby's room, reminding Keats of his place in this group, and the chill had settled in again.

Keats released a long breath and focused on strumming the notes for the song he was tinkering with. If nothing else, the last few days had provided a crap-ton of fodder for new songs. Nothing like your entire world and what you thought of yourself rearranging beneath you to inspire new material. Though the song he was fooling around with right now would get his ass beat down in most of the honky-tonks around town since it was clearly about a dude. Maybe he could go to open mic nights in gay bars.

Gay bars.

He shook his head at the thought. He'd have no fucking clue how to navigate those waters. When this all ended with Colby, would those be the kinds of places he would go? Now that he'd ventured down that road, would he crave men in the same way he craved women? All he could picture was one of the gay clubs down-town that looked like it was trying to revive Studio 54. So not his scene. Or what if he found that he couldn't do without the kink? Where the hell would he seek that out? He sure as shit couldn't afford the place Colby belonged to.

Suddenly, he had new understanding for how tough it must've been for Colby growing up in the middle of backwoods Texas and not just bi but deeply dominant and craving kink. What a fucking nightmare.

His fingers played over the strings with no real direction now, and he shifted on the couch, considering getting up and going to his room. He'd spent last night and this morning with Colby; he should let Georgia and Colby have some real time alone. But right when he set his guitar aside, the two of them walked back into the living room. Colby had his arm around Georgia's waist and his button-down flannel shirt looked wrinkled. Georgia's halo of hair was even more wild than usual. Almost fucked. That was the look. She wore it well.

Heat pooled low, Keats's body waking at the sight of the two of them. *Hell.*

"Found what you were looking for?" Keats asked, trying to sound nonchalant.

Colby held up a DVD of some zombie flick. "Yep. Turns out Georgia is a horror fan."

"Only the supernatural stuff," she clarified. "Nothing that could really happen. I save that for my books."

Keats schooled his expression into a serious one. "Zombies could totally happen."

Colby put his hands out to his sides. "Right? That's what I'm saying. But she wanted this one anyway."

Colby headed over to the DVD player and squatted down in front of the big screen on the wall. Georgia glanced at Keats's guitar. "You sure you still want to watch with us? I don't want to interrupt if you want to play."

Keats didn't know if she was being nice or if she really wanted him to be here. "I can leave you two alone. I don't want to bother—"

"Scoot over and make room, Keats," Colby said, his back still to them. "You're not ditching movie night."

A command, not a request. Dominant fucker. He shifted over and Georgia sat down next to him. God, she smelled good. Like some sort of spice—cinnamon, cloves, and something else he couldn't quite place—probably *eau de Colby*. He tried not to notice how well-kissed her lips looked—glossy and a little puffy. Or maybe she'd been sucking Colby off. Keats's stomach tightened, and he was unsure what turned him on more, the thought of Georgia wrapping her pretty mouth around *him* or the thought of being on his knees for Colby. He let his head fall back against the couch. He was a disaster. A horny disaster.

Georgia reached out and gave his hand a squeeze. "Hey, everything okay? I noticed you were moving a little slower this afternoon. Are you still sore?"

Yes, right between my goddamned legs. Can you make it better, please? He lifted his head and caught Georgia's concerned gaze. He mustered up a small smile for her. "I'm all right. The injuries aren't as bad as they look. It's just been a long couple of days."

She sent a sidelong glance toward Colby before looking back to him and lowering her voice to a near-whisper. "Do you want me to leave? I mean, if you need some time with Colby."

He reached out and tugged one of her tight corkscrew curls, liking the way it sprang back when he released it. "No, George. I want you right here." He looped his arms around her shoulder and then turned his head toward Colby. "Teach, I'm hijacking your woman for the movie. She's warm and smells good."

Colby peered back over his shoulder at the two of them. "That's up to Georgia."

Georgia's gaze moved between the two of them. "Fine by me." She settled her back against his side. "And Keats, let's not pretend that you aren't trying to hug up on me because you're the one freaked-out by zombies."

"Yes, you're right. The undead aren't to be messed with. I apologize early if I end up burying my face in your hair or something."

"Or something," she repeated under her breath.

Whoa. Okay. He'd only been messing around. Over-the-top flirting was his defense mechanism when he was nervous around a woman. But he definitely was down for staying like this if Georgia was into playing the game right back. The night had just gotten infinitely more interesting.

Colby snorted at the exchange, but there was a wicked glint in his eyes. He hit Play on the movie and turned the lights off, then sank onto the couch on the other side of Georgia. Without asking, he lifted Georgia's legs and laid them across his lap, which meant Georgia had been turned farther sideways and was now half-lying against Keats's chest.

He adjusted his arm fully around her and glanced down, inadvertently getting a view straight down her V-neck sweater. A lacy blue bra cupped round, full breasts. His free hand curled into his thigh, the temptation to touch her almost too much to bear. Now he was definitely thinking of much more fun places to bury his face than in her hair.

He forced his eyes upward and collided with Colby's gaze. He'd caught Keats looking. Keats opened his mouth, not sure what he was going to say—*Sorry?*

Colby lifted an eyebrow in warning and mouthed, *No. Touching.* But then a smirk curled his mouth and he added, *Yet.*

Colby turned back to watch the movie like there'd been no exchange at all.

All Keats's blood rushed downward.

Well, fuck. This was going to be the longest movie ever.

⸻

Georgia absolutely could not concentrate on the stupid movie. Her heartbeat was going to make a dent in her ribs it was pounding so hard. Colby hadn't sent her into this blind. They'd talked in his room before the movie. Well, talked and touched and made out. She'd been on a high from surviving the day mostly unscathed. But when they'd managed to come up for air, he'd told her that tonight could be whatever she wanted it to be. A simple movie night with friends. A one-on-one night in his bed. Or she could have Keats, too, if Keats was game for that.

It had been the obvious question hovering over them all day. Would they cross those fuzzy lines? Colby had left the decision firmly in her hands. And that'd made it harder. In the end, she wanted to watch the movie and decide later. She didn't want the pressure of a plan.

But when Keats had asked to cuddle with her on the couch, it'd felt natural to say yes. So she was going with that. She'd been all too aware of the both of them at dinner. The sexual tension zipping through the room had been palpable—all three were having normal conversation with each other but in the undercurrent, they also were acutely aware of the secrets they knew about each other—how Colby looked when he jerked off, how Georgia sounded when she came, how Keats had been in Colby's bed last night. Even watching the two guys throw verbal jabs at each other had gotten her warm because she could so easily sense the electricity between them.

But now she was freaking nervous. Yes, she was doing some kinky things with Colby. But a threesome was a whole other level on the Richter scale for her. These two really, really beautiful guys could easily overwhelm her. Colby alone was almost too much to handle. If she did this, she'd be jumping from a state of deep freeze into boiling lava, no pit stops in between.

She needed to breathe and calm down. Maybe she wasn't ready for this quite yet. She just needed to watch the movie and enjoy the company. Though it wasn't helping her state of mind that Colby had moved her long, flowy skirt to her knees and was idly stroking her calves as they watched the movie. And Keats had shifted behind her to where she was now basically lying against his chest. His knees were spread wide in that relaxed guy pose, and his cargo pants were situated in a way that had her imagination drawing pictures, especially when he'd discreetly adjusted himself a few minutes ago.

Dammit.

She forced her attention back to the movie, finding that the film was at the mandatory sex break in between the zombie attacks. The heroine and her boyfriend were locked inside a house and all was quiet for now. So, as per B-horror-movie protocol, clothes had come off. The woman was presently naked and astride the guy, rolling her hips and tipping her head back, making the oh-right-there face. Of course, they were showing none of the rather good-looking guy except his hands and face. A little grumble escaped her.

"Everything all right?" Colby asked, sending her a look of amusement.

"It's annoying that all they ever show in movies is the girl. I mean, sure, she's pretty and has a nice body. But would it kill them to throw the female viewing audience a little man ass or something? That guy has a good one. Boy parts shouldn't be off-limits."

Keats's chest bounced gently beneath her as he laughed, and Colby's dimples appeared.

"It's unfair," she concluded.

"Agreed. Horribly sexist," Colby said, trying to look serious. "I do have Internet access on this TV. I could pull up some gay zombie porn for you. There will be man ass and boy parts galore."

She sent him a sidelong glance. "Please, God, tell me that doesn't exist."

"When it comes to porn, *everything* exists," Keats assured her.

She turned her head to look up at him and gave him a poke in the arm. "Speaking from experience?"

He gave her an *oh-please* look. "You do realize I'm male and grew up in the age of the Internet, right?"

"Wait, are you even old enough to watch porn?" she asked, blinking innocently.

Colby barked a laugh.

Keats pinched her side, and she yelped before falling into her own laughter.

"Low blow, George," he said, but his smile was warm.

"Ha!" Colby said from the other side of the couch.

Georgia turned to face him.

He pointed the remote at the TV and announced triumphantly, "Would you prefer *The Sucking Dead* or *28 Dicks Later*?"

Georgia was already a little giggly from a night of nervous tension and the beer, so at the sight of the two movie posters displayed on the screen, especially the one with the very shapely green male behind, she lost it. She slipped out of Keats's hold as she bent forward, her shoulders shaking with laughter.

"Only nine ninety-nine. Yeah, we're totally getting this," Colby said, lifting the remote. "And I'm opening up the account in your name. Georgia Lawrence, lover of gay zombie ass."

"Don't you dare!" She went for the remote, launching herself at Colby. He lifted the remote out of her reach, and she landed half across his lap. He locked an arm around her waist, dragging her against him and giving her a flash of teeth. "Hey, I'm giving you what you asked for."

"All I wanted was male nudity, not zombie ass," she said, still stretching for the remote, but he tossed it over her head to Keats.

"Hit Buy, Keats," Colby called on a laugh.

"Oh my God, the zombie fucks people back to life and that turns them into zombies," Keats said, apparently reading the description. "Do you think he walks around saying 'Asssss' instead of 'Braaaains'? Because if that's the case, we need to watch this. I mean, how could we not? It's like an obligation."

She sent Keats a look of mock betrayal. "You are not siding with him. All I asked for was a little equal-opportunity nudity. Is that too much to ask?"

"Hey, I'm fond of nudity of all types," he said with a grin, and reached behind him. He tugged his shirt over his head with one quick motion and tossed it aside. "There, it's evened out now. Topless girl in the movie, topless guy for your viewing pleasure."

But she was slipping out of Colby's hold as soon as the shirt hit the floor and moving to Keats's side, the purple bruises draining all the humor from her. "Oh my God, Keats. You didn't say it was this bad."

She laid her palm against the purple blotches, concern flooding her, but anger building as well. How could someone do this to him?

Keats sucked in a breath at her touch, but he put his hand over hers. "Aw, now don't get yourself worked up over it, George," he said gently. "It looks a lot worse than it feels. You've been lying on me all night and I was fine."

She glanced up. "I've been—why didn't you tell me? I would've never—"

"You were pressed up against me. It was worth any discomfort."

The words were so honestly delivered that it tugged at that thing inside her she couldn't resist. "Now you're just not playing fair. I can handle cocky. But I can't handle sweet."

The corners of his eyes crinkled, though his gaze stayed serious. "You can tell me to stop and I will. Seriously. Just say the word. I'll leave you two alone."

"You want this?" she asked, knowing Keats was well aware of what was on the line here. "I mean, truly, both of us?"

He brought her hand to his mouth and kissed her knuckles. "Of course I do, George. You two are driving me a little crazy, actually. I have no goddamned idea what happened in the movie. But seriously, there's no pressure."

She traced gentle fingers over his injuries, her desire having a knock-down, drag-out fight with her good sense. "You scare me."

He let out a little laugh at that. "*Me?* I would never hurt a hair on your head."

"It's not that. It's just—you're going through some big-deal discoveries about yourself, and I don't want to be the girl you're using to reassure yourself that you're still into women. I don't want to play buffer or get in the way."

He shifted at that, sitting up straighter and taking her hands in his. "Look, George, I get the concern, and I may be a confused son of a bitch sometimes, but let me tell you what I know for sure. One—I'm into women. Really into women. I haven't been faking it my whole life. So, sure, discovering I'm attracted to a guy is new and a lot to deal with, but it's *in addition to*, not *in replacement of*, women. And two, I'm into *you*. This isn't about finding the nearest girl and hooking up. If this were about proving my manhood or whatever, I could've gone to a bar tonight and gone home with a random girl.

"But instead I stayed here. Not just to hang out with Colby but to be near you, the woman who I haven't been able to get out of my mind since I heard the two of you on the couch. I'm used to forward women. Or girls who know how to use their assets to get my attention. But it's all flashy advertising. Once you get in bed with them, the confident act disappears as quick as the push-up bra and what seems like a daring night is really just . . ."

"Vanilla," Colby offered from behind them.

"Yeah," Keats agreed.

Georgia couldn't help but smile. "Well, to their defense, you're dating young women. At twenty, most of us don't know what we want or how to ask for it. And the guys are usually thrilled enough if you know how to give a good blow job, so there isn't a lot of motivation to explore further."

"Exactly. And I enjoyed that kind of thing as much as the next guy, but when I heard you and Colby together, I realized I was missing out. The way you two own your dirty side is something I haven't been able to stop thinking about. You're both these professional, put-together people on the outside, but you have kinky streaks a mile wide that you aren't afraid to embrace." Keats's green eyes were dark in the low light as they met Georgia's, and she lost her breath for a second. Naked desire sat there, any shield he'd been keeping up falling away. "And it's so. Fucking. Hot."

Georgia closed her eyes, her heartbeat speeding to that rampaging pace again. Colby's hands slid onto her shoulders and gave them a squeeze, a show of support for whatever happened next.

"If you don't want me here with you two, I'll leave you alone," Keats said, his voice quiet. "But if you want me to stay, I'm all yours. For whatever either of you want from me, I'm in."

Nerves were trying to seize her. Having Colby behind her and Keats only inches away, offering himself whole, was almost too overwhelming to process. But there was no denying the deep, hot ache building within her nonetheless. She wanted Keats. She wanted Colby. Plain and simple.

She'd spent so long in a locked-down, smothering relationship and then trapped alone in fear. This was everything the past two years wasn't. A fantasy, sure. But more than that, this was part of her old self clawing to the surface and gasping for air, looking for the light.

"What do you say, gorgeous?" Colby asked, his whisper tickling over her ear.

She slid her hand down to Keats's hip and lowered her head. Keeping her eyes closed, she pressed a kiss to his bruised ribs, then slowly moved her hand to the hardening ridge between his thighs and curved her fingers around it.

Keats breathed out a curse and Colby's grip left her shoulders.

She lifted her head and brought her face close to Keats. "I think we're done with movie night."

"Yeah?" Keats asked, his voice strained.

"Yeah." She stroked him gently through his pants and put her mouth to his, letting the pent-up desire she'd been feeling for him from the very start pour into a slow, rolling kiss.

Colby's mouth touched the back of her neck, his hands sliding over her waist, and it was done. The three of them.

No more lines in the sand. No more pretending.

They were all tumbling into the churning ocean together.

Not a life raft in sight.

TWENTY-NINE

Georgia felt a hand in her hair and one cupping her breast, but she wasn't sure if it was Colby or Keats touching her. Or both. *Both.* God, she was actually doing this.

She was still kissing Keats, but things were happening around her. Buttons were unfastened and her skirt ended up on the floor somehow. All the while mouths and hands were moving, exploring—her own, theirs. She kissed her way along a line of song lyrics curling over Keats's bicep, and Colby unhooked her bra, sliding it off her shoulders. Her nipples grazed Keats's chest and he groaned against her ear as his palm found her breasts. "So goddamned beautiful."

His hands were warm and rough-skinned against her, the gentle friction sending sensation straight to the burning spot between her thighs.

"Straddle him, baby," Colby commanded. "Spread your legs and let him feel how wet you are. How wet you've been for us during the whole movie."

Keats's green eyes met hers as she hooked her leg over his lap and got in position. His gaze ate her up with pure lustful hunger before his fingers dipped beneath the waistband of her panties and slid along her slick folds. "Fuck, George, you're so ready for us."

He stroked along her clit with deft, callused fingertips, and her nails dug into his shoulders. "God, that feels good."

"Don't let her come yet," Colby said. "Keep her riding her edge. Same goes for you."

Keats continued to tease her but eased some of the delicious pressure. "I have a feeling Colby's going to be beating the shit out of me later for disobeying because I'm feeling anything but submissive at the moment. I want to see you come for me, George. I want to hear my name on your lips."

She groaned at the shift in attitude in the man beneath her. Keats might be submissive under the intense dominance of Colby, but she was seeing anything but that in him right now. He looked like a man on a mission to fuck her into oblivion. And she felt like a woman ready for exactly that.

"Please, Colby," she said, sending him an appeal as she rode Keats's fingers. "I'll never last unless I get the first one out of the way. I've been wound up for hours."

Colby's ominous eyebrow lifted. "How bad do you want it?"

Keats's fingers curled inside her, surprising her by rubbing slowly along the perfect spot. Goddamn, she had to give the guy credit. When she was twenty-three she hadn't even known how to find her own G-spot. And here he was pressing all the right buttons. "Pretty damn bad."

"I play fair. You're two grown adults. You want to fuck before we get started. Do it. But there'll be a price to pay afterward."

"What price?" Keats asked.

"That you don't get to know until afterward. And Keats, she has permission to come. You do not."

His jaw clenched, but Georgia could see the flare of lust in his eyes at the command. There was that submissive side. Nice. "I can wait."

"I don't care if you can, you will." Colby ran a hand over the back of Georgia's head. "You two have twenty minutes in his bedroom alone. Then you meet me in mine."

"You're not coming with us?" Georgia asked.

"Your first time with someone shouldn't be with an audience," he said. "Plus, I have a few things to get ready. Better make that twenty minutes good, though, because after that you two are all mine."

Colby leaned over and gave her a deep kiss full of promise, all while Keats's fingers continued to stroke her. Colby pulled away, leaving her a little breathless, and then he turned his head and kissed Keats as well. Seeing their lips and tongues clash up close had Georgia almost coming on the spot.

Oh. My. God. They were sexy together.

Keats yanked his head back with a grunt. "Damn, she just clamped down on my fingers hard." He looked to Georgia, a little amazed. "It really does turn you on, doesn't it? Seeing us kiss?"

Colby grinned. "Told you she had a fetish. Bet she already owns *28 Dicks Later.*"

She laughed and pushed off Keats, letting his fingers slip out of her panties with a delicious, clenching glide. "Shut up. I'm a woman on the verge here and you're teasing me."

Keats climbed off the couch, his erection providing a prominent outline against his shorts, and wrapped his arms around her. "Come on, George. You're all mine for twenty minutes, and I'm definitely not going to waste a second of it."

Then he was lifting her up and draping her over his shoulder.

She yelped in surprise. "Keats! No, your ribs."

He delivered a swift smack to her ass, surprising the hell out of her. "Hush. Indulge my caveman impulses right now because I have a feeling once Colby gets hold of us, he's going to make me get on all fours and bark like a dog or something."

"The dog thing isn't my kink. But all fours has definite possibilities," Colby said as Keats carried her down the hall.

She didn't miss the ripple that went through Keats's muscles at the comment. Was that fear? She wondered exactly how far Colby and Keats had gotten last night.

But she wasn't able to let her mind wander for long because in the next few seconds, Keats was shutting the door to his room behind them. He lowered her to her feet and clicked off the overhead light, leaving only a bedside lamp on, then shucked his pants and boxer briefs. Keats's gaze met hers, hungry anticipation there, as he closed the scant distance between them. If he was nervous at all about being with her for the first time, he didn't show it. He might be submissive in certain circumstances, but confidence in the bedroom wasn't something he lacked. She could feel the heat rolling off him and seeping into her skin.

It took everything she had not to reach out and explore, tracing those muscles and tattoos with fingertips and lips. He was art and sex and sharp, beautiful edges. But she got the sense he was leading the show right now.

"Can I touch you?" she asked.

His mouth canted up at the corner. "I'm not him, George. You never need permission from me."

"Do you want me to take charge?" she asked, wanting to give him what he needed if that was what he craved. "I mean, I've never done it formally, but I'm not afraid to try."

He cupped her face and brushed his lips over hers, silencing her. "Actually I'm fighting hard not to jump on you and devour you whole. Seems you bring out my aggressive side. So if it's all the same to you, I don't need any labels or roles right now. I just want you naked, in my bed, and coming as hard as you can."

She wet her lips, her body tightening in the best possible way at his words. She could see all the barely penned-in desire skating across his features. He was holding back with her, trying not to overwhelm her. "You don't need to be easy and romantic with me, you know? I'm not those girls you've been with. If you want to be rough, be rough. I won't break."

His jaw twitched and he took a deep breath. "I would never hurt you."

She slid her hands along his hips and aligned her body with his, her own confidence building. "I know that. So stop holding back and take what you want from me. Let go with me."

He growled, his hands sliding into her hair gripping tight, and kissed her hard. "You're a fucking fantasy, George. I'm going to wake up and be back in that shitty hotel."

He didn't give her a chance to respond but instead kissed her more deeply and tugged at her panties. She helped them along down her legs and stepped out of them. His hands moved down her back and he gripped her ass in his palms, seating her against his erection and digging his short fingernails into her skin. The sting of pain only made her feel wilder, more desperate for release. She tangled his hair in her fingers and moaned his name.

He pushed her down on the bed. "I love that sound—my name in your mouth. Say it again."

"Keats," she whispered against his lips.

"Tell me what you want me to do to you."

"I want to feel you inside me. I want you to fuck me, Keats."

His green eyes went almost black in the lamplight. "Patience, beautiful. First, I need a taste."

He crawled down the bed and braced his hands on the back of her thighs, pushing them open. Then he bent down and did what she could only describe as outright worship. Lips and tongue and even the graze of teeth moved over her with unbridled enthusiasm and surprising skill.

Her fingers dug into the sheets. Jesus, she was never going to last like this. The sounds of his mouth on her alone were careening her toward orgasm. The men she'd been with in the past had been . . . neat when it came to oral sex. Precise. Which she would've figured was the best way to go. But Keats's mouth, nose, and tongue were everywhere. Her inner thighs, the crease where pelvis met leg, stroking her clit. Sloppy and wet in the best way possible. And all the while, he had two fingers moving inside her, leaving her no doubt that this man loved every moment of this. He wasn't simply trying to get her off. *He* was getting off on it.

And nothing was hotter than that.

"Keats," she begged, trying to warn him that she was going to go over.

But he obviously had no intention of stopping. He curved his fingers inside her and sucked her clit between his lips and hummed.

That did her in. Her fingers gripped his head hard as orgasm slammed into her with a force that had her arching off the bed. She cried out, heels digging into the mattress, and Keats rode the wave with her until she collapsed back onto the bed with panted breaths.

"Scoot up the bed, George," he said, kissing the inside of her knee. "I'm not nearly done with you."

"I'm not sure I can," she said, still trying to catch her breath but knowing she didn't want to leave this room without feeling Keats deep inside her.

Keats was all male satisfaction when he smiled down at her. "You look good all wild-haired and sweaty. I'm thinking of making this a daily goal to get you looking this way."

He bent down and kissed her, his lips tasting of her arousal, and despite the rocking orgasm, a steady, unfulfilled throbbing between her legs remained.

"Your mouth is a lethal weapon," she said.

He gave her a smug smile as he pulled a condom out of a bag on the floor. "I'm inexperienced in kink. That doesn't mean I don't know how to treat a woman in bed."

"Amen to that."

After rolling on the condom, he gave her thigh a quick smack. "Move up the bed and put your legs over my shoulders, George. I want to hear you come again."

She did as she was told and draped her knees over his shoulders. Thank God for yoga. But she wasn't sure she could come again so soon. "I don't think I—"

But before she could finish the sentence, he was pushing into her and making her eat her words. He wasn't as thick as Colby but he was long and curved in a way that let her feel every inch as he entered her. Her sensitive tissues gripped him and tightened with desperate need.

He released a long breath when he seated deep, his hold on her thighs tightening. "Why the fuck did I promise not to come? You feel amazing."

"Tread carefully. He'll punish you. I don't think I'm supposed to come again either."

He pulled back and thrust deep again, tension tightening his features. "Whatever it is would probably be worth it."

His motions gained momentum, and she could tell he was getting lost to the moment. Unfortunately, she was, too. Just seeing him above her, all blond hair and bad boy, was almost enough to send her over. "I can take it if you can."

"Thank God," he said, draping himself over her and reaching between them to rub her clit as he pumped into her with more force. "This is worth suffering some torture."

Her eyelids fluttered shut, her resistance faltering, and she gave herself over to the moment. Colby had known they wouldn't keep their word. She'd studied Colby long enough to know that he was an attentive lover but also an unrepentant sadist. Punishing them would get him off. And right now, she was happy to provide him the opportunity. Because the guy she'd worried was too young and inexperienced for her was currently rocking her goddamn world.

Keats's thrusts turned earnest and rough, knocking the headboard against the wall with a steady rhythm. His hair tickled her face with each movement, the sensation a simple but intensely erotic one. And when he came, he didn't even try to be quiet. The sounds, the feel of his hair on her, and his fingers against her clit sent her over the edge with him. She reached up, wrapped her arms around his neck, and held on, taking everything he gave her.

When he'd finished, he eased her down to the bed and lay atop her, sweaty naked skin fusing together. He pressed his face into the curve of her neck. "So worth it."

"You might want to withhold judgment on that one for a while, Adam," a deep voice said from behind them.

They both startled, and Georgia turned her head to find Colby leaning against the doorjamb with crossed arms. "You're four minutes late. And you broke the rules."

Georgia's throat went tight but she managed a feeble, "Sorry 'bout that."

Colby's smile was slow, sexy, and malevolent. "No, you're not. But you will be."

THIRTY

Colby schooled his face into impassivity as he led Keats and Georgia to his bedroom, but underneath the surface, he was running hot, every button firmly pressed. When he'd opened the door on the two of them at the twenty-minute mark, he'd been captivated by how fucking perfect they had looked together. Keats's muscles straining with every thrust, Georgia clawing at Keats's back and making those soft sounds of hers. Everything about the scene, including him standing there watching, had felt right in a way he wasn't sure he'd ever experienced.

Most men would've probably had a meltdown standing there—pissed and jealous that their girl was being handily fucked into oblivion by some other guy. He knew that by society's standards, that was how he was supposed to react. But his wiring had never been what anyone would call typical. And he was okay with that. Through his eyes, all he'd seen were two beautiful people finding pleasure—and breaking Colby's rules, which only meant more fun for him. Reward for making it through the night so far with monk-level patience.

During the movie, he'd been so keyed up, he'd barely been able to sit still. Even if the two of them had been unaware of the cues they were giving each other, Colby hadn't missed it. Keats had adjusted his pants every few minutes, obviously fighting a hard-on each time Georgia shifted against him. And Georgia had gotten goose bumps when she'd glanced back and forth between Keats and Colby. Colby had known exactly what was on her mind. His sexy girl and her dirty thoughts.

And Keats, *damn*. He'd had him under his command twice in the last twenty-four hours, but it hadn't been enough. Seeing him with Georgia had only heightened the need. He wanted to see Keats pleasing Georgia, that eager desire to make her lose it. And he wanted to see Georgia's adventurous side come out and play. His solo encounters with each of them had been off the charts. But knowing they were going to all three be sharing everything tonight was adding an element of heat and an inner restlessness that Colby could hardly contain. They were both his tonight. That notion did something to him on a primal level.

They all walked into the bedroom together. The lights were low and the curtains were closed. He didn't need any audience tonight. This was his private show and only two others were invited. Keats stopped in front of him, and Colby set his hands on Keats's shoulders. Keats stilled beneath the touch but didn't move away.

Colby pressed his front to Keats's back, letting him feel how aroused he was and allowing Keats to relish the vulnerability of being one of the lucky ones under his control tonight. "You like fucking my woman, Adam?"

"Yes."

"*Yes, sir,*" he reminded him.

"Yes, sir," he whispered so goddamned sincerely that Colby's cock flexed against his zipper at the sound of it.

"You have no self-control, do you?"

"Not when it comes to her."

"I don't blame you." He squeezed Keats's neck. "But that doesn't mean I won't punish you. Both of you."

Keats's cock was already half-hard again. Colby smirked to himself. There were some benefits to having a twenty-something-year-old guy around. What Colby could offer in experience and staying power, Keats could match in recovery time and eagerness.

"Spread your feet wide, hands clasped behind your neck," he

said to Keats as he pulled something from his pocket. Keats moved into position, and Colby caught Georgia watching the two of them with unblinking focus. "Georgia, bring me that black bottle from the side table."

It took her a second, but she snapped out of her haze and grabbed what he needed.

"Next time, you won't be able to come so fast," Colby said, crouching down in front of Keats and squirting a little lube on the black silicone device in his palm.

Keats's gaze turned wary. "What is that?"

"A cock ring."

"For what?" Keats stared at the ring like it'd bite him.

"It'll keep you hard longer," Georgia said, her eyes fixed on what Colby was doing.

"Give the pretty lady a teddy bear. She's been busy on Google." Colby stretched the top ring and leaned forward to swipe his tongue over the head of Keats's cock, then slid the ring to the root of the shaft, lube easing the way but the fit a snug one. Keats was tense as a bow but didn't move until Colby stretched the bottom ring and fitted it around the base of Keats's testicles, making them bulge in a pleasantly obscene way.

Keats groaned and his hands fisted. "Oh, fuck."

"That will only get more intense the more turned on you get. But tell me if it becomes pain instead of pressure. This part is not supposed to hurt. Understand?"

"Yes, sir."

"Good, on your knees." Keats lowered to the floor with a darting glance toward Georgia to gauge her reaction. "Now . . ." Colby strolled over to grab his favorite flogger from his closet and ran his fingers through the tails of buttery-soft elk hide. "You both broke the rules, but I can't very well beat a man with bruised ribs. Not even I'm that cruel. So Georgia will have to take the flogging for you both."

"What?" Keats said, distress filling his voice. "No way. I can take it. Don't make her—"

"I can handle it," Georgia said, her gaze meeting Colby's without fear.

Colby smiled. His tough, sexy girl. She wasn't being self-sacrificing—though Keats would probably see it that way. No, Georgia wanted this. She'd done beautifully with the spanking the other night, reacting just how he'd hoped. And he suspected she'd secretly craved this part for a long time even if it'd scared her. All those nights she'd watched him from her window, touching herself. How many times had she wished it were her taking those stinging blows? God knows he'd imagined her there stretched out and vulnerable, waiting for the kiss of pain he could give her.

"Stand in front of Keats, right under that silver ring in the ceiling. I want you close enough that he can see your face when you take your punishment."

Keats still looked more than a little concerned for Georgia, but Georgia was following directions like a pro. She positioned herself under the O-ring Colby had installed in a roof beam. He brought a long length of soft hemp rope and strung it through the ring.

"Arms over your head."

Georgia complied, looking like a goddess as she stretched out with that mass of hair and glowing brown skin. Colby took his sweet time wrapping rope around her wrists, enjoying the ritual of binding her in a way that would keep her secure but wouldn't injure or chafe. For his own pleasure, he bound her forearms, wrapping her to the elbows again. Adornment, not function. The two of them painted a stunning picture, one he knew would stay burned in his memory: Georgia bound in rope and Keats at her feet, cock and balls in the grip of the rings.

He was the luckiest bastard on the planet tonight.

He checked Georgia's bindings one last time, making sure they'd support her if her knees got weak during the flogging. "Anything hurt or too tight?"

"No, Colby," she said, her voice breathier than normal, her eyes already getting that far-off look.

Oh, very nice. Someone responded well to bondage. "You look perfect strung up for me, baby. Beautiful."

"Thank you."

"Tell me your safe word."

"Red," she said after a moment.

"Good girl. You've earned eight minutes under my flogger because you both went four minutes past my deadline. Each stroke will get more intense. Last for all of it, and I may be generous enough to give you two rule-breakers another chance to come tonight."

She nodded and spread her feet a little wider while lowering her head—preparing for him. He stepped a good swinging distance behind her and readied.

"Georgia, you don't have to—" Keats began, but Colby let the first stroke fly diagonally across her back, the resounding thud against her skin cutting Keats off.

The soft exhalation of air from Georgia was like a drug to Colby's system. Nothing sweeter than the sound of a submissive taking what he gave with grace.

"You better tell your boy to stop protesting for you," Colby warned. "Every time he opens his mouth without permission, you earn another minute."

He crisscrossed another few strokes over her back in quick succession, increasing the level of sting.

"Keats, shut up," Georgia managed in a choked voice. "I've got it."

Colby felt his dominance rising fully to the surface. She's got this? Well, that sounded like a challenge if he'd ever heard one.

Georgia realized she'd been too confident. On the next hit, Colby must've put a flick in his wrist because the recoil of those tips of leather snapping against her felt like a hundred tiny licks of fire across her ass. Georgia gasped and arched in her bindings, her natural human instinct to get away from the source of pain kicking in without her conscious effort. Her heels lifted off the floor.

"Reach down and cuff her ankles with your hands, Keats," Colby said, the pleasant, nonchalant tone in direct contrast to the swats he was meting out. "I don't want her to hurt herself moving those pretty feet."

"Yes, sir." Keats scooted forward on his knees and peered up at her, his eyes holding a hint of apology, though his body looked to be responding just fine to the show. He was already fully hard again, the cock ring standing out in relief against the taut skin. He locked long fingers around her ankles and provided downward pressure, fastening her to the floor and giving her a nice view of those tattooed arms and muscular shoulders.

"No escape for you yet, gorgeous," Colby said from behind her. "You've still got six more minutes."

"*Six?*" He had to be kidding. Surely she'd been standing there an hour. Already every part of her back and ass was throbbing and tight. Not necessarily in a good way. Maybe she wasn't a masochist after all. Maybe a spanking was as much as she could handle. But she also wasn't going to back down. She'd endure.

The leather strips came down again, and she cried out with the biting sting. Keats's grip tightened on her ankles when she tried to shift forward. Goddamn, Colby wasn't going to be shy about it. She squeezed her eyes shut, trying to catch her breath.

But Colby didn't let her. No more one hit and pause. The flogger was coming down again already, a figure eight of fiery pain lighting her up. *Wham. Wham. Wham.*

Blood was rushing through her head, and a buzzing started in her ears. But Colby didn't let up. He was in a steady, focused rhythm. Her vision began to blur a bit, and vaguely she registered that she might be crying. But her mind was fuzzing around the edges.

"Put your tongue to use, Keats," Colby said, his voice terse. "I know she can take more, but she may need a little added motivation."

Before Georgia could line the words up in her head to process them, a hot mouth was sucking and laving at her pussy. *Oh, yes.* Her knees softened and a shudder of relief chased up her body. She whimpered as the next hit landed but it wasn't from the sting. No, her skin was going tingly and fever hot, her body converting the pain into something other, ethereal and erotic, as Keats lapped at her.

The two men seemed to be in sync somehow. The rougher Colby got, the more lovingly sensual Keats got. Soon, she found herself anticipating the next swing and teetering on the brink of another release. Instinctively she knew coming was not allowed right now. This was supposed to be punishment. But with the next blow, she came anyway—the rolling power of it impossible to fight.

Colby didn't even pause, and Keats just rode her orgasm with his mouth, softening his assault but still pushing her higher. Another hit came and sensation cracked wide open, spilling over her, making her near-delirious.

God, it was so . . . she couldn't even find words. She let out a choked laugh, which sounded hysterical to her ears, as she imagined her writer brain being emptied of words, letters soaking into the floor. Yep. They'd officially hijacked her mind and shipped it to another place.

Another hit came.

She let her eyes fall shut and fell into that lovely, floaty space. Time passing without a desire to mark it.

———

Keats couldn't help but gaze up and be awed at the transformation in Georgia. She wasn't flinching away from anything anymore. In fact, she'd pitched her body more toward Colby in full surrender. Keats knew what it meant to be masochistic— suspected he had a strain of that, too, since he'd been known to get hard while getting inked—but he'd never expected to see someone look downright high from it.

Colby set down the flogger and peeled off his shirt, a faint sheen of sweat marking his brow. He looked like some wicked god, standing behind Georgia and admiring his handiwork. He stepped up and pressed himself to Georgia's sure-to-be-burning back, laying a kiss on her shoulder. "Beautiful."

"Please," she murmured.

"What do you need, baby?" Colby asked. "Ready for me to get you down?"

A quick shudder went through her. "I just . . . I don't know. I need . . ."

Colby closed his eyes and inhaled against her bare shoulder like he was savoring the words. "You need a break."

She shook her head, but it was erratic, like a horse shaking off a fly.

Keats sat back on his calves when Georgia seemed to sag fully into the bindings. "Is she okay?"

Colby smiled down at him. "I like that you've got her back, that you want to watch out for her."

"I'd do the same for you."

"I know you would. You're a good man, Adam Keats."

The statement was simple but for some reason it filled Keats up in a way that made his chest ache. "Thank you."

"And yes, she's fine, but we need to get her out of these ropes and onto the bed. Stand up and put your arms around her waist to hold her up while I untie her."

"Yes, sir." Keats rocked to his feet and wrapped his arms around Georgia, careful to not cause any undue pressure on her tender back.

Her forehead sank to his shoulder. "Lethal," she murmured.

Keats smiled and kissed the top of her head. "Shh, let us get you down before you flatter me profusely about my skills in the sack."

She snorted against his shoulder.

Colby made quick work of the ropes and lifted Georgia into his arms to carry her to the bed. He settled her on her side and pulled a blanket over her. "I promise we will give you what you need, but you need to come down a little first and hydrate. Keats is going to lie here with you while I get you some water. Just rest for a minute. You did great."

She smiled softly but didn't open her eyes. Colby nodded at Keats, and Keats didn't need him to say more. He stretched out behind Georgia, propped up on his elbow, and spooned her. She made a quiet sigh of satisfaction as he stroked his fingers through her curls, then down along her arm.

"I can't even tell you how amazing you looked tied up for him, George," he said, keeping his voice low and soothing. "I know I'm still figuring out a lot of stuff, but no one will ever be able to tell me there's any shame in submission. You looked like a warrior princess up there, so tough and sexy. Thank you for letting me see that side of you."

She rolled over and snuggled into him, brushing a quick kiss over his collarbone. Her voice was low and lazy when she finally spoke. "I can't wait to see your warrior side. You're going to undo him, Keats, unravel him completely."

Keats sniffed. "I think you're still flying high, George, and got that one backward."

"Nope," she said without hesitation. "I'm the fling. You're the guy he's falling in love with."

Keats stared at her, unsure he'd heard her right, a tight, anxious feeling curling in his stomach. "You really are out of your mind right now, aren't you?"

She didn't have time to answer because the man in question strode back into the room. "She say something?"

"Nothing," Keats said. "She's not making much sense."

Colby sat down on her other side, gave her a few sips of water, then ordered her back down. He traced the back of his hand along her hip and thigh in a slow, soothing motion. Soon, Georgia's breath evened out and she was fast asleep.

Colby looked up and smiled. "Having heavy thoughts over there, Keats, or is the cock ring just cutting off your circulation?"

He smirked. "Nah, I was just thinking she's pretty spectacular when she lets go. It was like all that crap that smothers her every day just blew away for a few minutes. It was like seeing the real Georgia for the first time."

"Yeah," he said, glancing down again and looking at her with a tenderness that proved Georgia was dead wrong. Colby didn't see her as a fling at all. "That's the beautiful and dangerous part about kink. It cuts away the husk and exposes the tender center. It can show you the truth. And sometimes it's scary to see. Or feel."

"For the dom, too?"

Colby nodded, looking pensive. "Maybe even more so. We don't have subspace as an excuse."

The truth. Keats swallowed hard, Georgia's words running through his head. *You'll undo him, Keats.* Was that what she was talking about?

The thought of seeing Colby's truth, Keats's own truth, was damn terrifying. He should probably get up and walk back to his room, leave these two alone. They were all getting too deep too quick. But no one had ever accused him of being wise.

Keats lifted his gaze to Colby's, then let it slide downward, knowing his intent couldn't be mistaken. "So what now, Teach?"

Colby's easy expression darkened.

"Because it looks like everyone in the room has come except the guy we're supposed to be serving."

Colby's smile was slow and sinister. "I like your initiative, kid."

Keats got up, careful not to jostle Georgia, and walked around to the other side of the bed. He climbed between Colby's knees and reached for the button on Colby's jeans. "I'm not a kid anymore, Colby. But I've always been an excellent student."

The deep groan he heard as he closed his mouth over Colby was worth any price Keats would pay for forgetting to ask for permission.

THIRTY-ONE

Colby stared at the ceiling, watching the morning light track across it. He hadn't planned to wake up this early, but once his eyes had opened and he'd felt Georgia curled up next to him, all the memories from last night had rushed up and he hadn't been able to fall back asleep. Last night had been beyond all his expectations. When Keats had gone down on him, they'd made enough noise that Georgia had woken up a few minutes into it. Her wide-eyed surprise had switched quickly to interest as her gaze had zeroed in on the spectacle.

"I think we have an audience," he'd told Keats.

Keats had paused, fleeting panic appearing. Sucking a guy off and doing it in front of someone else were two different things. Keats had turned toward Georgia as if to measure her reaction, but there was no mistaking the desire on her face. That had settled Keats. *See, we're all okay here.* Colby had gripped his hair and guided him back down. Keats had found that submissive headspace again and had given himself over to it.

"You don't have to just watch," Colby had told Georgia, reaching out for her and cupping her cheek.

She'd nuzzled his hand. "But it's such a pretty view."

"Always the voyeur, huh? Come 'ere."

He'd drawn her over to him and kissed her. She'd sunk into the kiss immediately and had reached out to stroke Keats while he worked Colby over. Then they'd all gotten into a tangle, switching positions and rotating who was pleasuring whom. Somehow they'd found a rhythm where no one was left out. Everything had felt organic, natural. In the moments that followed, Colby had lost track of time passing. They'd each ridden their edges as long as they could, drawing out the pleasure.

Georgia had declared that she could last in this game way longer than they could, so both of them had taken that as a challenge and gone after her simultaneously. She'd shrieked and had tried to run away. But Keats had caught her by the waist, dragging her down to the carpet. Colby and Keats had attacked Georgia with mouths and tongues and roving hands. She'd given them a fight, playfully swatting at them and crawling away, swearing she didn't have another go in her. But she'd been fun to capture.

She'd tipped over into a laughing, shrieking orgasm in record time. And she'd kindly returned the favor, taking both his and Keats's cocks in her hands and stroking them against each other. They'd all collapsed into a sticky, sweaty heap at the end, and when Keats had declared the throw rug a complete loss, they had all started laughing again—overtired, overstimulated, and overwhelmed.

It'd been nothing like Colby had ever experienced before.

He'd had more than his fair share of threesomes but never like that. Never had he ended up belly laughing with a partner. Or experienced that contented, all-is-right-with-the-world warmth going through him when he looked at his lovers, that unshakable need to see these two people wake up next to him the next day. And when Georgia had agreed to try to stay—to spend her first night outside her house in over a year—the feeling had turned into a twisting ache in his gut.

He was so deep in the shit it wasn't even funny.

If his friends could see him now, they'd be laughing their asses off. Colby Wilkes, the dom no sub could pin down for more than one or two sessions, was having the *feelings*. God help them all.

His cell phone buzzed on the bedside table. He rolled over and grabbed for it before the noise woke his bedmates. His boss's phone number flashed on the screen. On a Saturday? This couldn't be good. He quickly rolled out of bed and hit Talk. "Hi, Rowan. Can you hold on one sec?"

"Sure, I'm at your front door. I can wait," Principal Anders said.

"What?" *Shit*. "Okay, be there in two minutes." Colby hit End on his phone and grabbed a pair of sweats and a T-shirt from a drawer. He tugged them on as quickly as possible and quietly made his way out of the bedroom, shutting the door behind him. There was no time to do anything else but scrub a hand through his hair to make sure it wasn't standing up on end. What in God's name was his boss doing at his house at seven in the damn morning on a weekend?

He pulled open the door to find her wearing her serious face. "Hey."

Rowan gave him a quick head-to-toe perusal. "I'm really sorry to pop in on you like this on a weekend, but I wanted to talk to you . . . not at work. And you've said you're an early riser." She glanced at his driveway, where Keats's bike was parked. "I was going to knock, but I was afraid you might have company."

"I do, but that's okay. We can talk in the kitchen."

He led her inside, an unsettled feeling moving through him. Whatever this was, it wasn't good news. No need to make a house call for that.

"Coffee?"

"I'll never turn that down," she said with a little smile.

"So what's going on?" he asked, getting the coffee started. "Is Travis okay?"

She sighed and slid onto the stool at the island. "Yes, he's okay. He's in an inpatient facility for a few more days while they get his medications right. But his parents are getting more and more determined to find someone to point the finger at. That's what I'm here to talk to you about."

Colby set two mugs on the counter and turned around. "Lay it on me."

She frowned and met his eyes. "Their lawyer dug up information on you from Hickory Point. I guess he Googled the old news stories or whatever about Adam Keats's disappearance."

Colby's stomach flipped over.

"So they're chasing that trail. And even though you were never accused of anything, it's enough of a flag that their lawyer can make himself feel useful."

"Jesus," he said, rubbing the back of his head. "What the hell good is it going to do to ruin my career? Their kid needs them dialed into him, not distracted by some wild-goose chase."

Empathy crossed her face. "I know. But they don't know how to deal with Travis, so they're doing this instead. But I wanted to come and tell you what was going on. I know how hard that whole thing was on you. I remember you telling me about it when you first came to Graham. They plan to interview teachers you worked with and talk to the family of the kid who ran away. The father lives in Burleson now, so they'll probably go out there to see him on Monday or Tuesday."

Colby had been reaching for the coffeepot, but his whole body went cold at that. He lowered his hand to his side. "They're going to talk to his family?"

"Do you think anyone is going to say anything that would reflect badly on you?"

Colby just stared at her. "Adam Keats's father *hated* me. He thought something was going on. So yeah, he'll give them all the nasty accusations they could want."

"And nothing was going on," she said, making it sound like a statement, but he knew it was a question.

"Of course not."

She nodded and rubbed the spot between her eyes. "I'm sorry. I had to ask, even though I've never seen you be anything but professional, and I know you're great with the kids. I'm beyond frustrated that this is going so far. I need you back at school. Dr. Guthrie has his strengths, but there are too many kids to be seen, and many of them connect better with you. I don't like witch hunts. It's hard enough to find counselors who want to work with this population of kids. But the school board doesn't like scandal, so I'm afraid that if this keeps getting bigger, it's going to cause problems for you."

Colby set her coffee in front of her and took a long draw off his, trying to stay calm. "What can I do to help?"

"Be cooperative. The school board wants you to give a written statement and to do another interview. Be prepared to answer questions about that day with Travis but also about Adam Keats."

"Dude, what the hell are you doing up so damn—" Keats froze in the doorway to the kitchen, hand on the waistband of the boxers he'd probably just pulled on. "Uh . . ."

Rowan's eyes went round. "Oh."

Alarm bells blared in Colby's head, but he forced himself to not outwardly react. He didn't give a shit if Rowan knew he slept with men, but if Keats introduced himself . . .

He strode over to Keats and put a hand on his shoulder, hoping he was conveying the don't-say-a-damn-word warning with his eyes. "Hey, can you give us a minute? This is my boss, Principal Anders. She stopped by to talk about some stuff going on at school."

Awareness flashed over Keats's expression. "Yeah, sure, sorry. Didn't mean to interrupt."

Keats sent Rowan an apologetic smile and slipped back down the hallway. Colby thought his heart was going to pound right out of his chest. He could see trying to explain how the kid who went missing all those years ago was now standing in his kitchen half naked.

When Colby turned back to Rowan, there were patches of pink high on her cheeks. "I'm so sorry. I shouldn't have stopped by like this. I should've called and asked if it was okay and—"

He held up a hand. "It's fine. Really. No big deal."

Her hands fluttered around her coffee cup before grabbing and taking a sip. Awkward silence ensued.

He sipped his coffee, watching her. "You can say whatever you're thinking, Rowan. We're off the clock, and I'm not going to be offended."

A little puff of breath escaped her. "I just never would've, I mean, it's fine, but—good Lord, if you heard what some of the teachers say about you. They'd be crushed to know they were barking up the wrong tree."

He chuckled, back on comfortable ground. "I date both men and women, so equal opportunity. But I keep my private life private."

"Of course," she said, waving a dismissive hand. "Which is why I feel like a jerk for barging in on you like this. I just didn't want to have this conversation at school. That lawyer would've liked to keep you in the dark, but there's no way I'm letting you walk into that interview to get blindsided."

"I really appreciate that," he said, setting his cup down. "I'll answer whatever questions they have. I want to do whatever it takes to get past this so I can get back to my students."

"You and me both," she said, getting up from the stool. "And now I've taken enough of your time. I'll let you get back to, well, whatever."

He smiled, enjoying seeing his usually unflappable boss blushing her face off. He had a feeling she was still picturing Keats in his very well-fitting underwear. "Any idea when they're going to want to talk to me?"

"This Friday. They need to do the Hickory Point interviews first. I'll call you with a time," she said, grabbing her purse from the counter.

"I'll be there whenever they need me."

He walked Rowan to the door and exchanged good-byes, keeping his nothing-bothers-me face in place. But when he shut the door, he leaned back and tapped his head against it. "Fuck me."

"Everything all right?" Keats asked, coming into the living room. He'd thrown on a T-shirt and a pair of gym shorts.

"Not so much."

He leaned against the back of the couch. "What's wrong?"

"You know how I told you that kid's parents hired a lawyer?"

"Yeah."

"Well, turns out he's a nosy one. He's digging into my background and talking to people from Hickory Point."

"*What?*"

Colby laced his hands behind his neck and sighed. "They're going to look into your disappearance, Keats. And they're going to talk to your father. He lives in Burleson now, so the lawyer is driving down there early this week to see him."

Keats paled.

"Does he know?" Colby asked. "Did you ever go back to tell him you were okay?"

"No. He would've killed me." He stared down at his hands. "I couldn't go back."

"How did you manage to get a license? Or identification to work?"

Keats looked like he might get sick. "When I turned eighteen, I went to the local police station to tell them who I was. I was tired of only being able to take jobs that paid under the table. I told them I didn't want my family to be notified because my dad was abusive. They said they couldn't make any promises, but nothing ever came of it, so I guess they just quietly closed the case."

Christ. Colby rubbed a hand over his face. "Okay."

"Is this going to mess things up for you? Like, are they going to hold what happened with me against you?"

Colby pushed away from the door. "I didn't do anything wrong back then, so no, it shouldn't be held against me."

"But if they talk to my dad, who knows what kind of lies he'll say about you? He could make you look really bad."

"I'll figure it out. I'm a big believer that the truth usually prevails. It'll work out." He headed back toward the kitchen, needing more coffee for this kind of morning.

Keats followed. "I could tell them who I am. My side of the story."

Colby pressed his palms against the counter, keeping his back to Keats. "Then I have to explain to my boss why the student I had no inappropriate relationship with was in my kitchen in his underwear."

Keats groaned. "What we're doing now has nothing to do with back then."

"You know people wouldn't see it that way. Best to lay low. I'll handle it."

But Colby had a bad feeling that this wasn't going to go well. Keats's father had been a self-serving, cruel bastard from the get-go, and Colby had no doubt the guy had only gotten worse with age. Given the chance to screw with some "fag" teacher's life, that guy would take it.

But there was no way he was going to ask Keats to face that man. He could see that buried little-boy fear flash over Keats's face at the thought that his father was less than an hour's drive away. He wouldn't put him through that.

Colby walked over to Keats, who still looked to be freaking out a little at the news, and put a hand on the back of his neck, giving it a squeeze. "Come on, let's start today over and leave this be for now. We have a naked woman sprawled in our bed who would probably appreciate a creative wake-up call. You game?"

The wrinkle was still parked between Keats's brows, but he gave a nod. "I'm always game."

THIRTY-TWO

"Well, look who's up and smiling a cat-that-ate-the-canary smile so early in the morning," Leesha said as she adjusted the angle of her monitor for the video call.

Georgia shrugged. "Always happy to talk to my infinitely wise therapist."

"Bullshit," Leesha said, leaning back in her chair. "That is a morning-after smile if I've ever seen one. You've had that same smile every time I've talked to you lately. I guess things are still going well with the neighbor?"

Georgia tried to swipe the goofy smile from her face. She could see it staring back at her in the little video chat box in the corner, but she couldn't seem to keep it down long. Since last Saturday, when she'd stayed overnight at Colby's for the first time, each day had been another step forward, another victory—not to mention another hot night. "Things are going really well."

Complicated. But well.

"He's a great guy. I'm having a good time with him." And Keats. But she wasn't going to tell Leesha that part. Her best friend wasn't one to judge, but Leesha would flip the shrink switch and analyze it to death. She'd probably tell Georgia she was acting out or rebelling or something.

Hell, maybe she was. But right now, for the first time in over a year, she felt like there was sun shining on her face. Things were looking up.

"Uh-oh," Leesha said. "He's a great guy? You're not getting serious about him, are you?"

Georgia rubbed her lips together, smoothing the balm she'd swiped on before running over from Colby's house to her own to make it in time for this call. "Would that be so awful?"

Leesha grimaced. "Babe, I'm glad you have that capacity in you still. But now's not the time to be starting something serious. It's only a few weeks before we need you to move back here. I don't want to see you get attached to a guy and be heartbroken when you have to break it off."

Georgia knew Leesha was speaking the truth, but she didn't want to hear it this morning. Not after the amazing two weeks she'd had with the guys. The past few days had been the best of all. Waking up in the morning surrounded by their warmth and affection had felt more right than she wanted to admit to herself. And even though she knew it was temporary, she didn't want to think about the end when it felt like so much was just beginning. "I could come back here after the trial."

Sympathy crossed Leesha's face—the *oh-honey* look. "The trial could take months. He'd have to wait on you. And what if . . ."

Georgia raised her palm, her happy mood plummeting. "Don't. I know what you're going to say."

What if Phillip is acquitted? That was what Leesha was going to say. Georgia didn't want to consider that possibility, but of course, she had, over and over again. It kept her awake at night.

Leesha sighed and opened a drawer in her desk. She pulled out a stack of envelopes and set them on top of her day planner. "I wasn't going to mention it because I didn't want to add to your plate, but the lawyer said that you have the right to make the decision on it since technically it's your mail."

Georgia leaned forward, wanting to reach through the screen and pick up the stack. "What are they?"

"Letters from Phillip," Leesha said, her frown lines marring her flawless mocha complexion.

Georgia's skin chilled. "I thought those had stopped when I moved away."

"No, he only adjusted where he sent them. He's sent one every couple of days to my office since the last restraining order expired, but they're addressed to you. I'm sure I broke some law, opening them without your permission, but I needed to make sure they weren't threats or anything we could use against him in court."

"He's too smart for that."

"Yes, he is. But you should know they're long love notes. He says he wants to forgive you. He asks for you to take your accusations back. He wants to be together no matter what, blah blah blah."

Georgia closed her eyes and rubbed them. "He's so goddamned sick."

"And obsessed, Georgia. If he walks out of that courtroom, he's not going to give up on you. You need to be prepared for that, have a plan."

And that was when what Leesha was really trying to tell her settled in. Phillip wouldn't stop. If he went free, he would focus everything he had on finding Georgia. And when he did, everyone she cared about would be at risk again. Maybe he wouldn't "hurt" her because he *loved* her. But if he showed up and saw she was in a relationship, he would go mad with rage again. Both Colby and Keats would be in the line of fire.

Phillip had tried to kill a man she had seen only a handful of times. He certainly wouldn't hesitate to go after the two men Georgia was sharing a bed with every night.

She would never be free if Phillip walked. She'd never be able to care about someone without wondering if Phillip was watching and waiting for the perfect opportunity to quietly take that person out.

She sat her elbows on her desk, put her face in her hands, and screamed in frustration.

"I know, sweetie," Leesha said. "I can't imagine how impossible this feels right now. But we still have a good shot at getting him locked up. And if that doesn't happen, we'll figure out something for you so that you can feel safe. Renew the restraining orders, register things in a different name."

"I don't want to be some goddamned sitting duck the rest of my life, Leesh," she said, getting more pissed than scared now. "I can't take it. I'll kill the motherfucker first. I'd rather be in jail than running away my whole life."

Leesha frowned. "Let's not go with that plan. Though I don't blame you for considering it. Even when I know he's too smart to do anything to me because it'd be too obvious right now, he's got me looking over my shoulder everywhere I go. I check under my car for brake fluid every morning. I can only imagine what things have been like for you."

"There's got to be something we can do, something more than we're doing already."

"The best thing you can do is get yourself strong enough to come back home and face him in the trial. Your testimony is the best shot we've got."

"Oh, I'm going to be there," Georgia said, not putting up bravado but really, truly believing it for the first time. "This bastard is not going to win. I don't care if I need to ask one of the guys to sedate me and carry me into my plane seat. I'm going to get there."

Leesha's expression turned puzzled. "One of the guys?"

Shit. "Nothing. Long story."

Leesha still looked confused, but she didn't push. "I know you can do this—and without sedation involved. You've been making leaps lately, just don't let up now. Train like you're going to be climbing Mount Everest. Every day push yourself a little more. We need you here, babe."

"I know," she said, nodding and making plans in her head. "I promise. I'm not going to let anything . . . or anyone get in the way."

Keats stared at the screen on the laptop, the letters starting to merge together after a while. He tilted his head back and closed his eyes.

"How's the résumé coming?" Georgia asked from her spot on

the couch. She'd had her head buried in a stack of edits all morning and hadn't said much to him at all. When he'd asked her if everything was okay, she'd assured him she was just busy. But he didn't believe that work was what was bothering her. He'd sensed something was wrong when he'd first walked in today. She'd been distracted and jumpy. But obviously she wasn't ready to talk about it.

Keats stretched his neck and closed out of the window he'd been staring at—which had not been his résumé. He'd finished that on Wednesday and had already emailed a few out to job listings. "Okay. I think it's pretty much ready to go. But I'm having trouble concentrating today."

She marked her place in the stack of pages. "Worried about Colby?"

"He's been up at the school for hours. That can't be a good sign, right?"

"I'm sure he'll be fine. He has nothing to hide."

"But they talked to my father. That's bad, George. He probably made Colby sound like some pedophile."

"Did Colby say that?"

Keats shook his head. "All he would tell me was that they met with my father on Tuesday. But I heard him talking with his boss last night on the phone before you came over. I couldn't decipher most of the conversation, but he was angry and called someone a backwoods bigot. I'll give you one guess who he was talking about."

Georgia frowned. "He seemed okay this morning."

"He puts on the all-is-well face because he doesn't want us to worry about him. He's good at helping people with their problems, but he sucks at sharing his own." Keats shifted in his chair. The thought that Colby was taking any flack for what happened back then made him want to jump out of his skin. "I just hate that he has to deal with this."

"It's awful," she agreed, concern on her face. "But I'm not sure there's anything we can do to help except be there for him if he wants to vent."

Fuck that. He clicked the laptop closed, the address on the screen imprinted on his mind, and set it on the coffee table. He had to do something. He couldn't just sit on his hands and hope for the best. George and Colby might be optimists, but he'd learned not to make that mistake in life. You couldn't trust that things would turn out okay, because so many times they absolutely didn't. Even if it wasn't right. Even if it wasn't fair.

He rubbed his palms on his jeans, nervous energy making his hands tremble.

Georgia must've picked up on his agitation because she set aside her papers. "Hey, you okay?"

He wet his lips. "You up for an outing this afternoon?"

Her forehead scrunched. "We already did all the errands I needed this morning. What'd you have in mind?"

"You want to keep practicing, right?" That was what she'd told him when he'd walked in this morning. She'd been raring to go, ready to run those errands, a new resolve in her whole demeanor.

"Sure. I mean, every little bit helps."

He nodded. If he tried to do this for himself, he'd chicken out. But if he could convince himself that he was getting in the car to help Georgia and going where he needed to go to help Colby, maybe he wouldn't freak the fuck out.

"It's a little bit of a drive. And I'm not going to promise that I won't turn around halfway there. But if you're willing to come with me, I might be able to do it."

Her face was the picture of concern now. She leaned forward. "Where are we going, Keats?"

"I need to see my father."

THIRTY-THREE

Keats couldn't get out of the car. They'd driven the forty-five minutes, found the address Keats had memorized from the computer, and parked across the street. But the walk from Georgia's car to the tired-looking house a few yards away seemed to stretch for miles in Keats's mind.

There was an older-model Ford truck sitting in the driveway with a Dallas Cowboys bumper sticker. Keats had no doubt it belonged to his father. The truck was an updated version of the one Keats had grown up with. His dad had simply switched colors when he traded in the other.

But Keats couldn't quite grab hold of the fact that the man who had tormented his memories for so long was in there, living some quiet life in small-town Texas. So many questions filled his mind. Had his dad grieved him? And what had his father told Keats's older brother when he'd come back from overseas? Keats had always felt bad about leaving his brother behind without a word. They'd been close when they were kids, even though Justin was five years older. But when Justin had hit his teen years and become a star football player and then gone into the Marines, fulfilling all that their father wanted him to be, Keats had spent a lot of time resenting his golden boy of a brother. That hadn't been Justin's fault. Their father had created those bad feelings by always comparing the two of them—Keats always coming out on the short end.

But the biggest question of all that plagued Keats as he sat there was how would his father react to seeing him now?

Keats pressed his forehead to the steering wheel, a wave of nausea overtaking him.

Georgia took his hand. "You don't have to go in, you know? No one is making you do this."

Keats clasped her hand and tried to take a deep breath. She'd been intensely calm the whole ride down here, a solid support there next to him. He wouldn't have been able to make it this far without her there. If she of all people could put her anxiety aside and be calm on his behalf, he could be brave enough to face this. "I need to see him."

"Want me to go in with you?"

He leaned back in his seat and turned to look at her. "George, I can't ask you to do that. My dad can be ugly and angry and mean. I've already asked you to do too much by dragging you so far from home."

She peered at the house, then turned back to him. "I want to go with you. You and Colby have backed me up when I've had to face difficult things. Let me back you up for this. I'll be more worried sitting out here."

He blew out a breath. Part of him wanted to tell her no, to handle it on his own because God knows he didn't want Georgia to see the version of himself that his dad brought out in him. But the other part was damn relieved to not be facing it alone. Because he didn't get scared of much. He'd taken on much bigger guys in fights and hadn't flinched. But there was something about facing his father that made him feel helpless and small again.

He brought her hand to his mouth and kissed the top of it. "Thank you, George."

"Anytime," she said, that warm smile giving him the last burst of confidence he needed.

"Okay, let's do this."

They climbed out of the car and made their way to the door. The grass needed to be cut. His dad would've never let him get away with letting it go this long. *Get your ass out there and clean that yard up. Can't you do anything useful?* Keats had a moment of panic right at the last second, hearing that familiar angry voice rattle through his head, but managed to lift his hand and knock. Seconds passed, and Keats began to wonder if they'd gotten the wrong house or if maybe his dad was at work. But right when he was about to turn away, he heard heavy footsteps on wood floors. Keats's spine went stiff.

The door swung open and all the breath rushed out of him.

The man on the other side was still broad and intimidating in size, but his blond hair had grayed at the temples and there were more lines in his face than Keats remembered. His dark eyes met Keats's, and Keats couldn't move. His father blinked rapidly a few times, his attention shifting between Keats and Georgia. But when his gaze settled back on his son, Keats knew that his dad recognized him.

Keats's throat felt like a fist was closing around it. "Hi, Dad."

His father coughed, though it sounded more like a horse chuffing, and glanced back over his shoulder like he was considering shutting the door and walking away. Finally, he looked back to Keats. "What are you doing here?"

The question didn't sting as much as it probably should've. Keats hadn't exactly expected a warm reunion. "There's something I wanted to talk to you about."

He made a sour face, looking fully put-upon by their presence. "Do you need money? Because it's not like I have—"

"Excuse me," Georgia said primly, stepping forward from where she'd been hovering behind Keats. "Did you ask him if he's here for *money?* You just found out your son is okay and alive and that's your first question?"

"George," Keats said, reaching out to touch her elbow. "It's fine."

"No, excuse *me*," his father said, narrowing his eyes at Georgia. "But I don't know you and you're on *my* porch. I can ask damn well what I want. And if my son didn't bother to find me for the last however many years it's been, then why should I think he's looking me up for any good reason now?"

Nice. His father didn't even know how many years it'd been since Keats had left. Glad he was so concerned.

"Well, most people would be happy to know their kid is alive," Keats offered in Georgia's defense.

His father's lip curled. "I knew you were alive. They told me when you went to the cops."

"What?" That punched the starch out of Keats. "They told you?"

"Yeah, I told them you owed me my best gun and the money you stole from me, but they didn't do a damn thing about it."

The news that his father hadn't bothered to come look for him shouldn't have surprised Keats. Alan Keats wasn't the kind of man who chased. He would've been waiting for Keats to crawl back and admit he couldn't make it on his own.

That was probably what he thought this was. Keats coming back to admit defeat and ask for help.

"Can we come in?" Keats asked, holding his ground.

"Why?" his father groused.

Georgia made a little noise of disbelief, and Keats almost smiled. She was kind of cute when she was pissed on his behalf.

"We need to talk. It's not about money. It'll only take a few minutes."

His dad didn't look pleased at all. "And who is this, anyway? I don't let strangers in my house."

"This is Georgia, my—"

"His girlfriend," Georgia said, taking Keats's hand and surprising the hell out of him.

His father's heavy eyebrows shot up. "You into women now?"

Keats knew that Georgia was posing as his girlfriend to help him out, to let his dad see he was wrong about Keats's preferences. But Keats found that he no longer gave a shit what his father did or didn't think. "I date both."

His father's face twisted in disgust. But he opened the door and let them in, muttering to himself the whole way.

The house was simple on the inside, utilitarian. His father had never had much of an eye for nice things. It was as if he wanted to live his life like he was still in the Marines—neat corners and neutral colors.

They all sat in the living room, his dad in a worn brown recliner and he and Georgia on the couch. The room had a stale smell, like microwaved soup and faded Pine-Sol. Keats had the intense desire to be anywhere but there.

But the urge to leave wasn't about fear anymore. As Keats watched the man sitting across from them, he no longer saw the larger-than-life football coach who could make him cower with his booming voice and intimidating presence. Instead, he saw an aging man with a toxic personality in a lifeless house. A man who didn't know how to love anyone.

Maybe his father had been different once upon a time. Keats's mom had died when he was three, so he didn't really know if his dad had loved her. But whatever the case, this man was a bitter and miserable person now and would die that way. So Keats could only muster up one emotion for his father now—pity.

"So what is it you want?" his father said finally. "I don't have all day."

Keats's anger flared at that, all that resentment bubbling to the surface. "I want you to shut your mouth and stop lying to lawyers about Colby Wilkes."

"Now, wait just a minute," his father said, leaning forward. "If you think you can walk in here and talk to me like that—"

But Keats wasn't going to stop. He'd shut up at his father's request too many times. "No, you need to hear this. You have no business stirring up shit for Colby. That lawyer is grasping at straws and you know it. Colby Wilkes never did anything wrong to me."

"Right. 'Cause two gays hanging out after school every day was all about the guitar lessons. That school needs to own up to its negligence."

Keats's fists balled against his thighs. "Are you serious? Is that what this is about? You're trying to get a court case going for yourself?"

"They put that man in charge of children and look what happened."

Un-fucking-believable. This was about *money*? Keats had read in the news stories after he went missing that his father had threatened to bring a suit against the school, but there hadn't been enough there for him to go through with it. Now the guy was looking for a new angle. "Colby Wilkes was the only decent adult I knew back then. I sure as hell couldn't count on you."

"He put those disgusting ideas in your head."

Keats scoffed. "You think he turned me *bisexual*? Come on, Dad. Even you can't be that dumb."

"I've heard enough. I won't be insulted in my own home." His dad's voice was going into that megaphone zone again.

Keats quickly glanced at Georgia to make sure she was okay and not getting panicky. But he shouldn't have worried. Her jaw was set, her eyes blazing with anger. She looked ready to take down his father on her own.

"I'm not leaving until you promise to drop the thing with the lawyer. Tell him that I came to talk to you and that if he has any questions about what happened, he can call *me*. I'll tell him the truth. I had a crush on Colby. But he never crossed a line. And when I tried, he turned me away."

His father stood. "You have some nerve coming here and ordering me to do anything. Get out of my house, Adam. And don't bother me with this shit—"

"*Adam?*"

The voice came from somewhere behind Keats, and he swung around. Georgia turned with him. The shocked face that greeted Keats made him lose all his gumption. "Justin."

Keats's brother stood frozen in the doorway, leaning on crutches. Keats's gaze traveled down to the spot where Justin's right leg used to be. His pant leg was neatly folded up at the knee joint. There was nothing below it anymore. *Jesus.*

"Adam," Justin repeated, his eyes going glossy with tears. "It's really you?"

Keats stood, not sure what to do with his big brother's tears. He couldn't remember ever seeing him cry. "Yeah, it's me."

"He was just leaving," Keats's father bit out.

Justin's attention snapped to his father. "What the hell is wrong with you? It's *Adam*, Dad."

"I know damn well who he is."

His brother swung himself on his crutches with what looked to be practiced ease toward Keats and pulled him into a crushing one-armed hug. Keats didn't know what to do but hug back. "Hey, big brother."

The embrace only got tighter and Justin's chest bounced with silent sobs. "You're okay. I can't believe you're okay."

That was when Keats realized Justin hadn't known. His dad hadn't bothered to inform him that Keats was alive. For Justin, his little brother had just come back to life.

And he cared. His badass Marine big brother was sobbing.

Emotion welled in Keats as he hugged Justin back in a fierce embrace. And before long, his face was wet, too. Because he was happy to see his brother. But also because he realized how much pain he must've put him through when he'd run away. He'd wanted to hurt his dad. But he'd never intended to hurt Justin, too.

Justin finally leaned back, eyes red, and smiled. "I'm trying to convince myself that I'm not having some weird medication reaction or something."

Keats laughed and swiped at his eyes.

"I'm so freaking happy to see you," Justin said, shaking his head. "I never believed what they'd said about you. You had too much fight in you. But after all these years passed, I started to lose hope."

"I'm so sorry," Keats said, the guilt weighing heavy on him now. "I never wanted to put you through that."

Justin grabbed Keats's shoulder, his grip strong. "I know why you left. I don't blame you."

They both looked toward the empty recliner.

During their hug, Keats had heard the front door slam shut and the rumble of an engine. Keats glanced down at Georgia, who was watching him and Justin with shiny eyes. "So he left."

She folded her hands in her lap. "I'm sorry."

"I'm not," Keats said, putting his arm around Justin, careful not to knock his crutches. "Now we can relax and catch up. Georgia, I'd like to introduce you to my brother."

She smiled and stood, putting her hand out. "So nice to meet you."

Justin took her hand to shake it.

"Justin, this is my girl."

And even though Keats knew that wasn't exactly true, right then he wanted nothing more than to make it so.

THIRTY-FOUR

Georgia hadn't made it two steps into Colby's house before Keats's hands and mouth were on her. He'd seemed wrung out by the time they'd wrapped up visiting with his brother, and she'd figured the emotional day had taken its toll. But as soon as the front door had clicked shut, his whole demeanor had shifted.

Her back hit the wall of the living room, and Keats pressed his body against her as he kissed her hard. She grappled for a hold and latched onto the back of his shirt, loving the feel of him taking what he needed. He was usually her kinder, gentler lover. But she liked seeing this side of him, too.

She gasped when he slipped his hand beneath her shirt and cupped her breast. "God, George, I need you right now. Tell me this is okay."

"It's definitely okay," she said, letting her head fall back against the wall. Whatever he needed, whatever demons he was exorcising, she was on board. After the day they'd both had, she craved that oblivion, too. "I'm all yours."

"Thank God." He tugged her shirt up and over her head and unhooked her bra, leaving her bare from the waist up. He tapped the waistband of her jeans. "Lose these."

She almost said, *Yes, sir*, but then caught herself. She worked at the button on her pants, and Keats lowered his head to suck and tease her nipples. Kiss. Suck. Kiss. Bite. Good Lord, he was going to undo her before they even made it to the bedroom.

She kicked off her shoes and shimmied out of her jeans and underwear, pieces of clothing landing in a haphazard pattern around them. Late-afternoon sunlight slanted over them from the front window, and Keats's blond hair was painted in pinks and oranges as he got to his knees and spread her open with his thumbs. His mouth was sweet fire against her, licking and nibbling every tender, aching part. She moaned his name and slid her fingers into his hair. He hadn't tied it back today, and she loved how cool and silky it felt around her fingers.

Keats looked up at her, eyes making promises she knew he'd keep, and breached her with two fingers—stroking, stroking, stroking. "I never get tired of this, George, hearing those sounds you make, my name on your lips."

"I can't help it," she said. "You and Colby make me lose my mind."

If I'm not careful, you're going to make me lose my heart.

His thumb found her clit, sending a dart of swift pleasure up her spine and chasing the worry from her mind. "Best job ever. Making a beautiful woman mindless."

"Or man," a voice behind them said.

Georgia lifted her head, finding Colby leaning against the entryway from the kitchen with a lazy smile and predatory gaze.

"Welcome home," Georgia said, half gasping, as Keats went back to pleasuring her with slow, torturous glides of his tongue.

"I can't say there's any better sight to come home to after a hard day than my favorite woman naked and spread out for my favorite guy. If I had known this was waiting for me, I would've driven faster." He headed to where they were and leaned over Keats to kiss Georgia. His hand found her breast and teased as he deepened the kiss.

She moaned into the kiss. The combination of Colby's rough fingers against her nipple and Keats's talented tongue against her clit had her ready to go over already.

Colby pulled back from the kiss and ran a thumb over her mouth. "Make her come, Keats. Looks like she needs one now."

"Gladly," Keats said, his gaze meeting hers as he angled his fingers inside her. "Want to join me?"

Colby grinned at Georgia, somehow playful and threatening at the same time. "Turn around and plant your hands against the wall."

Georgia did as she was told, her feet squeaking against the wood floor and her heart pounding.

Colby's hands spanned her waist. "Now slide your hands down and bend over, legs spread."

"Goddamn," Keats said from behind her as she got into position. "I'm starting to see the appeal in Colby wanting to restrain us. I wish we could cuff you to the wall just like this. You should see how fucking hot you look."

Georgia felt flush all over and her knees wobbled. She wasn't sure she'd ever felt quite so exposed.

Colby ran a hand over the back of her thigh. "Don't lock your knees, baby. Relax and let us make you feel good."

She loosened her limbs a little and planted her feet, almost bracing for a hit of some kind. But that wasn't the mood Colby was in. Because before long, she felt hair brush against her leg. She peered down to find Keats slipping into the space she'd created between her and the wall. He gripped her outer thighs and situated his mouth against her, then resumed the languid, luscious circles he'd been making with his tongue before. She let out a soft moan, her head dropping forward.

At the same time, big, warm hands coasted over her backside. Colby's touch was light but confident as he teased her. And she could hear him shifting into position behind her. He was going to the floor. *Oh, God*. Even though she suspected what was coming, when a finger buried inside her channel and hot, wet kisses landed right along the curves of her ass, the arches of her feet lifted off the floor.

She groaned a groan that came from someplace deep and forced her eyes open, needing to see the two men working in tandem on her. But she couldn't keep her eyes open for long. Because Colby was spreading her for more than kisses. The hot wet tip of his tongue teased close to her back entrance and he bit one of her cheeks. *Oh, God.* It was all so much. The feel of two mouths burning hot along her most private, sensitive spots had her fingers pressing so hard into the drywall, she worried she was going to push right through.

Colby's fingers dug into her ass cheeks, adding a snap of pain to the already overwhelming sensations, and spread her wider for him. She braced herself for it, but there was no preparing. His tongue traced a path around her rim, slow and sexy, the scruff of his beard tickling her tender skin, and she nearly lost it. She'd never had anyone put their mouth to that forbidden place before, but hell if it didn't feel like the most sinfully erotic thing ever. Knowing that he wasn't afraid, that nothing was off-limits for him when it came to her body, did something to her. Like full-out acceptance. *I am turned on by all of you. Every bit is mine to explore and pleasure.*

Keats added a finger inside her, his now sharing space with Colby's, and her hands curled against the wall as the two men stretched and stimulated her. Their fingers moved in easy rhythm inside her, one sliding downward while the other sank deep, their knuckles grazing each other on the exchange. The image was enough to nearly do her in. They were both inside her, both mouths sucking and laving at her with sexy, wet sounds. Her body clenched around their invasion, everything so slick and alive with sensation that she wasn't sure she'd be able to stand much longer.

"I'm not going to last," she whispered.

Colby spoke against her skin. "We didn't say you had to. Take what you need, baby. Come for us."

And with that, they both increased the speed and enthusiasm of their oral assault. She couldn't tell who was where when. It felt like a hundred tongues and hands touching and devouring her at once. Her teeth clenched, the wired tension inside her coiling tight, tight, tighter.

Colby's blunt nails dug into her flesh, and his tongue pressed against her right as Keats swirled his tongue around her clit. She lost it. Sparking energy raced over her skin, and she cried out, her neck arching and her heels lifting. Colby shifted his hold quickly, grabbing her hips and keeping her in place as they continued to kiss and taste her everywhere.

She gasped through the orgasm, harsh sounds coming out of her, and finally her knees really did give way. Both men backed off, guiding her downward until she was on her knees in front of Keats, Colby's arms wrapped around her waist to keep her from tipping over.

She let her forehead rest on Keats's shoulder as she breathed her way down from her intense release.

"You okay, George?" Keats asked softly as he ran a hand over her head.

"Definitely okay," she said, repeating her words from earlier and smiling against his shoulder.

"Good," Colby said, "because we're not done with you." He slid his hands up to her breasts, caressing. "Because I know when you watched from your window and imagined what having two men would be like, your mind went to where we're about to take you."

Oh, God. She bit her lip, knowing what he was suggesting.

"I bet that's when you played with your other vibrator, testing out how it would feel to be oh-so-full and helpless."

Keats groaned along with her. And Colby was absolutely right. She'd imagined it then. But she'd imagined it a lot more lately. "I don't even know if I can . . ."

Colby turned her around, his eyes catching her gaze. Despite the dirty talk and the commanding tone in his voice, his hazel eyes were tender when he looked at her. "We want you, Georgia. All of you. But know that we would never hurt you. You know how to stop things."

She inhaled deeply and reached out to trail her fingers along his beard. "I don't want to stop."

He smiled and leaned forward as if to kiss her, but then stopped himself short, always respecting her boundaries if they hadn't discussed some act yet. He touched his forehead to hers instead. "Go in my room and wait for us on the bed. We'll be just a minute."

"Okay."

She let him help her up, and he gave her a pat on her ass before she headed toward the bedroom. "There's a blindfold in the top drawer of my dresser. Take it out and tie it over your eyes once you're kneeling on the bed."

A little shiver went through her and she nodded. A few minutes later, she was arranged how he asked—kneeling on the bed with a red sash tied over her eyes. Every nerve in her body seemed to be standing at attention, and she had to take a few deep breaths to center herself. She wasn't scared. She had no doubt that Colby and Keats would take care of her and would stop if anything was too much. They'd proven that each time they were together. If she needed to slow down, they did. If she had questions, they were answered. And they were always so tender with her after an intense night—bathing her, soothing any aches or pains with salve, tucking her into bed. Colby had even given her the option of not doing anything that would leave a lingering mark. But she'd declined the offer. She'd never admit it out loud to anyone, but the faint bruises and rope burns she'd gotten from their nights together gave her some strange sense of pride. Those marks said she was brave and daring. They were proof she was taking chances again. Signs of her old self. So right now, she was ready to give them whatever they wanted.

For so long, she'd felt so unbelievably scared and vulnerable, questioning everyone and everything around her, always on guard. Every time she went out, she still had to fight the urge. But here with Colby and Keats she could let all of that go. She could tear away the defenses and literally leave herself naked and at their mercy without fear. Somehow she felt more free in this moment than she had in a year, even though she was giving over complete control. This was her get-out-of-jail-free card.

Footsteps sounded somewhere off to her right, and she knew she was no longer alone. She licked her lips, trying to stay still. A hand touched her shoulder and she jumped.

"Easy, there," Colby said. "We're here with you now."

She nodded. The bed dipped and more hands touched her waist—

Keats had climbed behind her. "We're going to make you feel so good, George."

Hands and mouths coasted over her and she tilted her head back. The guys were being gentle, warming her skin again, sampling every inch of her, kissing away any nerves that might've lingered.

Colby's fingers glided over her sex, and she nearly sagged into him to hold herself up. "Look how wet you are for us. So gorgeous. Blindfolded, nipples hard and damp from our mouths, pussy lips swollen and shiny."

"You have a dirty mouth, Colby Wilkes," she said softly.

"Mmm," he said, a smile in his voice. "Good thing you like that kind of filth."

"You're a bad influence."

"I hope so." He teased her entrance with the tip of his finger and she made a needy sound.

"What's wrong?" Keats asked as he wrapped his hands around her breasts from behind and kneaded them in his palms.

She panted through the surge of desire. Usually, she was all for a long night of foreplay, but her body was demanding the full show.

"I think we're torturing her with our patience," Colby said, though he sounded none too apologetic about it. "How about we give her something to focus on? Keats, lie back on the bed so I can tie you down."

Georgia groaned, wishing all of a sudden she didn't have the blindfold on. The men moved around her, and she could only imagine what it looked like. Keats splayed out on the bed, Colby tying him to the headboard. Another surge of need went straight downward.

The wait seemed endless, and it was a good ten minutes before Colby's hands were on her shoulders again. But thankfully, he was in the mood to give her a reward. He guided her to turn around on the bed, then tugged the blindfold off. When her eyes adjusted to the lamplight, she found six feet of blond, built, aroused man spread out in front of her.

"Good God," she said, genuinely awed at the sight.

Colby had looped rope around Keats from elbows to wrists and then tied each hand to the headboard. Keats also had a length of rope looped around his chest. His cock stood long and proud, and his gaze was solely on her.

"He's only here for your pleasure tonight, Georgia," Colby said, massaging her shoulders. "You can use him however you want. Right, Keats?"

"Yes, sir. I'm gladly providing my services." He sent Georgia a shameless grin.

"He doesn't get to come until you and I do. Understand?"

"Yes," Georgia said, her voice sounding breathy and light to her own ears. "I can do what I want with him."

"Yes, you can," Colby said. "But if he's here for your pleasure, you're here for mine."

Goose bumps chased across her skin.

"The question is, what would you like to do to him first?"

She let her gaze track over all that smooth tattooed skin and then let it linger on the glistening tip of his cock. "I'd like to taste him."

Keats groaned.

"Keats, you're a lucky man. Go ahead."

Georgia situated herself between Keats's knees and lowered her head to wrap her lips over the crown of his cock. She didn't go any farther but rolled her tongue around the head and then teased the slit. He made a soft grunt, and she smiled to herself. Torturing him could be kind of fun. She let her hands slide up his legs, rubbing circles on his inner thighs with her thumbs, and then got oh-so-close to his testicles before dragging her hands down again.

"Ah, fuck," Keats said, arching a bit. "She's taking sadist lessons."

"I like watching you two play," Colby said, stretching out next to them and taking in the view. He was still in his shirt and tie from his meeting, but his erection was a prominent outline against his slacks, and he stroked it almost idly with that big hand of his. Him being fully clothed while she and Keats didn't have a stitch on made

Georgia even hotter. "I could get used to this. Spread your legs, Georgia, and touch yourself while you suck him."

She hummed as a new wave of arousal went through her, and Keats made a pained sound again. She took Keats farther into her mouth and lowered her hand between her legs. Even the light touch had her wanting to go over. But she was learning the art of patience and kept her strokes slow.

"That's it," Colby said. "Tease yourself while you tease him."

Colby unzipped his pants slowly and slipped his cock free. His size was still overwhelming each time she saw it, but knowing what he had planned tonight had a new anxious flutter going through her. She had no idea if she could take him that way. But God knows she was willing to try.

"I like how you're looking at me," he said, giving himself a long stroke. "Are you imagining what it's going to feel like when we're both inside you? Because I know that's what I'm imagining. How tight and hot you're going to feel around me. How it's going to feel to have two cocks rubbing against each other inside you."

"Fuck," Keats said, his hands fisting as he arched in the bindings.

She seconded that emotion and had to move her hand away from herself for a moment so that she wouldn't take it too far. Colby smiled, like he knew exactly how he was affecting her.

She went on, sucking Keats and dropping lower to lick his balls and nuzzle him. She took her time and brought him to the brink a few times. All while teasing herself and riding the edge along with him. Colby watched them with heated interest. She knew then that she was definitely more than a voyeur. There was a whole other level of intensity when someone was watching—especially when it was Colby. Because when he looked at her, it was like the devil planning his list of temptations and sins. She couldn't wait to check off the list.

Finally, when Keats started panting, Colby reached out and gripped the back of Georgia's neck. "Enough. Get off the bed and stand beside it."

She scooted off the bed and followed the instruction. When Colby moved to stand in front of her, he pulled something from his pocket—a small vibrator with elastic straps.

"Step into this. Keats can't use his hands, and I want you flying high for this. It will be easier for you."

She swallowed hard and stepped into the straps. The elastic positioned the little silicone vibrator against her clit. Colby hit a button and she gasped as the low-level vibration moved against her already sensitive flesh.

"Now, climb on top of Keats and get his condom on."

He handed her a condom, and she made her way back onto the bed and over Keats's body. Keats's gaze had gone hooded, and he was watching her like he wanted to eat her bite by bite. A beautiful, wicked man spread out for her enjoyment. She'd heard of being house poor. Right now she was man rich.

Colby stepped to the front of the bed and reached for the black-and-white cityscape hanging above it. He lifted it off the hook and took it away from the wall. A mirror hung behind it. Colby moved a latch and the whole thing angled forward, giving them a perfect shot of the bed. Georgia found herself staring at her wanton reflection.

"Might as well enjoy the view, right?" Colby said, those lips curling up at one corner. "I know I will."

For a second, she couldn't take her eyes off the scene in the mirror. Her naked, aroused body. Keats spread out beneath her. It was like some erotic painting. Her gaze stayed fixed on the scene as she rolled the condom on Keats, and Colby positioned himself behind her, his big body radiating heat.

"Pretty, isn't it?" Colby asked, his eyes meeting hers in the mirror.

"It's amazing. And you really are a deviant. Who has a hidden mirror?"

Colby smiled and laced his fingers in her hair, then turned her head to the side so he could lean in and kiss her. The kiss was deep and full, and he didn't try to hide the need in it. She gave herself over to it, to him. Her whole body dialed up to eleven. In this moment, she'd probably give this man anything.

When he pulled away, the look he gave her nearly undid her. "I'm ready for you, gorgeous. You ready for us?"

The question seemed to hold more weight—like he wasn't just asking if she was physically ready. Like there was more to ask. And what those hazel eyes held scared her.

But she managed to whisper, "I'm ready."

He released her hair and moved his hands to her waist. The vibrator hummed steadily against her—enough to torture but not send her over. "We're going to take good care of you, baby. Just listen to what I say and you'll be fine."

"I know," she said, meaning it.

"Good girl." He kissed her shoulder. "You're going to need to let Keats in first."

"Excellent plan," Keats said with a drunk-on-lust grin. She had to smile back. She loved that they could still be playful in bed. She'd worried that with Colby's dominance, it would be formal. But both men liked to laugh and have fun along with everything else.

She lowered herself, taking Keats in slowly, the stretching of her body jostling the vibrator against her clit and making her eyes want to roll back. God. Keats was gifted in his own right, and she felt full with only him in there. She seated him deep, and Keats's eyes fell closed.

Colby's tie brushed against the top curve of her ass, and then his hand was on her. Their gazes met in the mirror as he slid two slick fingers between her cheeks, finding her back entrance. Those warm fingers made a slow circle around her opening, massaging the lubricant over it, and she had trouble keeping the groan to herself. His mouth moved close to her ear. "Fuck him, Georgia. But don't you dare come."

That would be a miracle if she could manage that. She lifted her hips, drawing Keats almost all the way out, and then dipped down again. Up and down, up and down. Her focus moved fully to Keats, who was watching them both with rapt interest—his belly rising and falling with strained breaths. "I could die right now and be happy," he said, his voice like sandpaper.

"We'll try not to kill you," she said as Colby's fingers continued to move over her, getting her slick and aching. "But no promises."

"Lie over him, baby," Colby said after another few minutes.

She draped her body over Keats and rocked forward, letting him slide out almost all the way and then sinking against him again. That movement enlightened her on why Colby had wrapped the rope around Keats's chest. With every thrust, her nipples were now rubbing against the soft hemp. Evil, evil man.

Colby's finger moved against her ass again. "Relax and let me in, baby. Push out and it will make it easier."

She'd been riding the edge so long now that relaxing her muscles actually came easy. She wanted him in. She needed to feel him. One finger slid in and then another. The sensation was like a rocket booster to her arousal. She made a guttural sound and pressed her forehead against Keats's shoulder.

"That's it. So good," Colby said, his pleasure clear. "You're doing so good."

His fingers moved inside her, scissoring gently and stretching her, as she continued to fuck Keats slowly. Everything in her wanted to come right this very minute, but she fought hard to keep it at bay.

"I'm not sure how much longer I can last," she said.

"I don't want to rush you or hurt you, baby," Colby said, his slow thrusting continuing.

Another spark of arousal went through her and her fingers gripped the sheets. "Can we try? I'm hanging by a thread. And I want to try—"

"Anything hurts, you tell me to stop," he said, command in his voice.

"I promise."

"Stay still for a second then," he said, shifting behind her.

She glanced up, the angle of the mirror affording her part of a view of Colby behind her. He hadn't taken his clothes off, but his fly was undone and he was pouring lube into his hand. He rubbed it over his cock until it was shiny and glistening. She was mesmerized by the sight of it.

Then he was getting into position behind her. He pushed fingers into her again, separating them inside her and opening her, preparing her. Keats was trembling beneath her. She imagined it was taking a lot of work on his part to stay so still. He had to be close to coming, too. But the look on his face was pure rapture. He was being denied, but he was into this one hundred percent.

Colby's fingers slipped out of her and something much bigger nudged her backside. A bolt of panic moved through her. He felt impossibly big. Maybe she'd misjudged what she could take.

"Colby, I—"

"It's okay," he said, squeezing her hip. "You can take me. You just have to relax and let me in. I'll go slow."

Her gaze went to Keats and he smiled softly. "We've got you, George. He's going to make you feel good. Trust him."

"Says you who hasn't done this yet."

He laughed. "Show me how it's done, then. I'll take notes."

For some reason, that eased her tension. She gave a little nod and put all her concentration on loosening her muscles and relaxing. She shifted back a bit and the head of Colby's cock breached her.

The burning sensation was intense and she lost her breath for a second—regretting everything in that instant, but he kept moving forward and once the thick head moved past the ring of muscle, the rest slid forward more easily. An overwhelming flood of sharp need moved through her.

Colby made a deep, rumbly sound behind her. "God, baby, you feel amazing. You okay?"

"I'm good. I just—" She felt impossibly full and didn't dare move. She might never be able to move again.

"Just hold on. You don't have to do anything else but feel from this point on," Colby said, easing more of himself inside her. "You can come whenever you need to."

Thank God for that because she felt on the verge of exploding already.

The two guys must've talked about this at some point because somehow, they knew how to move one at a time in a kind of rhythm. It was slow and steady and impossibly sensual as they rocked into her in turn, stimulating every inch of her flesh along the way. The vibrator buzzed steadily against her, and with each move from Colby, her nipples rubbed along the rope on Keats's chest.

Then Keats was lifting his head to kiss her, parting her lips and pouring all the passion that must be rumbling through him into it—frantic, hungry, a little crazed. She felt dizzy with the power of it all. She was going to lose it. Colby's hands gripped her hips hard, his cock sinking even deeper, and there were so many sensations at once that it felt like there were a hundred hands on her, a crowd of men taking her.

Everything detonated inside her. Her nails dug into Keats's shoulders, earning a lust-filled grunt from him as he pulled away from the kiss, and her back arched. Both men buried fully inside her, their cocks pressing against each other through the thin wall in her body, and she thought she would die from the feel of being so fully taken.

"I can't—" she panted.

Colby must've used that as his cue to hit the button on the remote for the vibrator. Because the soft purr turned into an urgent buzz and she cried out. The moorings broke free. She shook with the force of the orgasm as it overtook her, and the noises she made stopped sounding human.

Colby and Keats started moving again and all she could do was hold on for the gasping, shrieking ride. Soon, Colby's grip turned bruising and he groaned behind her, his own release sending him over the precipice.

Keats, ever patient, pressed his teeth against Georgia's shoulder, biting hard enough to sting but not enough to break the skin until it was clear Colby was coming. Then Keats let loose, too, bucking beneath her and calling her name as he thrust upward, his arms yanking at his bindings.

It was all so much. Too much probably. But when her gaze caught their reflection in the mirror, all of them lost to passion, she had a feeling that for her . . . it was just right.

These two men were right.

Too bad she couldn't keep them.

THIRTY-FIVE

Colby shifted in the chair in Principal Anders's office, dread sitting heavy in his stomach. She'd called him in for a last-minute meeting, and after the interviews he'd been through last week, he didn't have a lot of hope. Keats's father had apparently painted quite the picture of an irresponsible, devious Colby Wilkes, and the board had treated Colby in a way that let him know they were giving Alan Keats's claims some credence. They'd even asked him if he thought his "homosexual status" made the male students reluctant to open up to him. He'd wanted to break things.

And walking through the busy hallways to get here this after-noon, seeing the kids stream past him, some waving and happy to see him—it had physically hurt. These few weeks away felt like years. He'd enjoyed spending his off time with Georgia and Keats, but he missed his job more than he could say.

Rowan breezed in, a stack of folders in her hands and her hair tucked neatly into a low ponytail. "Thanks for getting here so quickly. Sorry I'm running a few minutes late."

Colby leaned forward in his chair, forearms braced on his thighs, as she slid behind her desk. "Not a problem. What's going on?"

She looked up after putting the folders aside and met his gaze. "Well, Adam Keats is going on."

Colby's stomach dropped to his feet. Oh. Shit. She knew. She'd figured out who the half-naked guy in his kitchen had been. "What do you mean?"

Principal Anders spread her fingers wide across the papers fanned out on her desktop. "He came forward and spoke with the lawyer and a school board official a few days ago."

"He did *what*?" Colby's jaw went slack.

"He defended you, Colby, taking full responsibility for what happened back then. He stated that you tried to help him and he ran away because of his father."

Colby's brain scrambled. Keats had come forward? Had Rowan seen him? "I don't know what to say."

She lifted an eyebrow. "You didn't know he was going to do that?"

Well, that answered one of his questions. He swallowed hard. "You know who he is."

She nodded. "He requested a private meeting with no school staff there, but I saw him walking out afterward. I pulled him aside to talk to him."

Colby rubbed a hand over his face. He was so fucking fired.

"It took some convincing to get him to talk to me, but when I told him your job was on the line, he told me the story. He promised me nothing had happened between you two back then." She smirked. "And he told me to hook him up to a lie detector test if I didn't believe him. There may have been a few expletives involved in that last part."

Colby blew out a breath. "I know it looks bad, Rowan, but he's telling the truth."

She tapped a finger on her desk. "I know."

He looked up, surprised.

She gave him a small smile. "I've been in this position long enough to have a pretty good bullshit meter. If I had believed anything bad had happened back then, I would've never hired you in the first place. Plus, I met Adam Keats's father the other day and don't trust him as far as I could throw him."

"The guy's scum."

"Yeah, I got that."

Colby scrubbed a hand through his hair. "So what happens now? Are you going to tell the board what you know?"

She shook her head. "In my opinion, that has no bearing on the current case. They've interviewed who they need to and have the pertinent information. Two teachers from Hickory Point vouched for you. Adam Keats vouched for you. And Travis told his doctors at the inpatient facility that he hid his plans from you and left too fast for you to get any real information out of him. The only person who had anything negative to say was Adam's father. Travis's parents don't have any evidence to really back up a court case at this point. What happened to their son was unfortunate but not anyone's fault. Their lawyer has advised them not to pursue a case."

All the starch drained out of him. "They're going to drop it?"

She gave him a full smile now. "Yes. And if the board had any notions about continuing to investigate you anyway, I told them that you could sue their pants off for discrimination for the homosexual comment they made. I almost threw something at Martin Davis when he asked you that question."

Colby stared at her, afraid to believe what she was saying. "So . . ."

"You're cleared, Colby," she declared, triumph in her voice. "You can come back to school after the Thanksgiving break."

Colby sagged in his seat, relief flooding him. "Holy shit, Rowan. I can't even tell you how happy I am to hear that."

"And"—she leaned forward like she was going to tell him a secret—"if you're still open to it, I'd like to move you to full time after the first of the year."

"Seriously?"

"A principal never kids," she said, pulling a stern face.

"I could kiss you right now."

She laughed. "How about you save that for the good-looking guy you have at home."

He grinned. "I definitely will."

She stood and put her hand out. "I'm glad to have you back on the team, Colby. The kids have missed you. We all have."

He took her hand and shook it as he stood. "I've missed them, too. I can't wait to get back to it."

Colby left the school feeling so good he couldn't stop himself from whistling a tune on the way out. He couldn't wait to get home and share his news. And tell his two sneaky lovers what they were going to get for keeping this secret from him. Because he had no doubt Georgia knew exactly what Keats had done.

Hiding things was a no-no.

But it was going to be oh-so-fun delivering the consequences.

Colby leaned against the doorway to Keats's bedroom, watching as Keats's fingers moved over his guitar. He had a look of full concentration—tongue sticking out the corner of his mouth, brows drawn—as he tried out a few different combinations of chords for whatever song he was working on. There might as well have been a sign around his neck that said Creative Genius at Work.

Colby took his time soaking in the view, knowing that Keats was so involved he hadn't noticed him standing there yet. Colby didn't think he'd ever been more drawn to a guy. The shy teenager had grown into a man who was so quietly amazing, Colby couldn't get his head around it. This kid, who'd had no fucking shot growing up with that scum of a father, had survived on his own on the streets without any help. He'd kept his shit together enough to not end up in jail or hooked on drugs. He hadn't taken the easy way out for anything. And though he was still getting on his feet now, he'd somehow managed to become a man with so much heart and loyalty that Colby was damn humbled. He hadn't been half the man Keats was when he was twenty-three.

"I had a meeting at school today," Colby said quietly.

Keats looked up from his guitar, his fingers pausing midstrum. He pushed his hair behind his ear. "Yeah?"

"Yeah. Principal Anders informed me that the long-dead Adam Keats magically appeared to make a statement to the school board officials a few days ago. A miracle. Runaway kid all grown up just strolling in to set everything right."

"Imagine that. Must be a full moon. I've heard that's when people come back from the dead."

"Keats," he said, stepping into the room. "You didn't have to do that."

He shrugged like it was no big thing. "You're a good teacher and shouldn't be getting dicked around for something that wasn't your fault. Plus, I wasn't going to let my father fuck things up for you. I knew he wasn't going to take back what he'd said about you, so I did what I needed to do."

"Thank you." He sat on the edge of the bed. "Though saying thank you doesn't seem like enough. You went to see your dad first, didn't you?"

He blew out a breath and set the guitar aside. "It was time."

The idea of Keats having to face that man again made Colby sick to his stomach. "You shouldn't have gone alone."

"I didn't. George went with me."

"Oh, well, I'm glad." It was probably good Colby hadn't been there anyway. All those years ago, Colby had held back his opinion because he was a teacher, and Alan Keats was a parent of one of his students. But if that man said one cross word to Keats now, Colby probably would've knocked the bastard off his feet.

"I'm sure you'll be shocked to find out that he's still a heartless asshole," Keats said dryly. "Apparently, he knew all along I was in Dallas but didn't bother to look me up."

"God, Keats."

Keats leaned against the headboard and pulled a knee up. "But I got to see my older brother, so it was worth dealing with my dad for a few minutes. And hopefully it helped you out, too."

"Helped me out? They gave me my job back. I don't even know what to say to you right now."

His face broke into a broad smile. "You got it back?"

"They're even going to make me full time after the Christmas break."

"Holy shit, that's great. I mean, I hoped I could help, but I didn't know how much damage my father had already done."

"Your father did more than enough. You sure you're okay after seeing him?"

He rubbed a hand over his jaw. "I'm all right. He was my dad. I'm used to that. But you should've seen how pissed George got. She looked ready to take a swing at him."

Colby smirked. "I have a feeling Georgia would have no problem going to the mat for the people she cares about."

Keats's smile was wry. "It was kind of hot, her going into badass mode."

"Yeah? Maybe one day we can convince her to try out the domme role on you for real. I know a good trainer who could show her a few things."

He shifted on the bed. "I'm not sure I'd survive both of you topping me, but I'd sure be willing to try."

"Such a martyr, Keats."

He laughed. "Yep, a really horny martyr."

Colby moved Keats's guitar to the floor and scooted up the bed to sit next to him. "Not getting tired of us old folks yet?"

"Shut the fuck up with that crap," Keats groused. "You act like you're hobbling around on a cane."

"I do own a cane."

Keats sniffed. "I'm not talking about the kind you torture people with."

"There's another kind?" Colby asked innocently.

Keats shoved him, but Colby captured Keats's wrist before he could take his hand back. He dragged Keats closer, bringing their faces inches apart. "No one's ever put themselves out there for me like you did. I can't tell you how much that means to me, Keats. But you know that you don't owe me anything, right?"

The light in Keats's eyes darkened, and his jaw clenched. "You think I did it because I owed you?"

"You're a guy who doesn't like to leave a debt."

"No, I'm the guy who has your back. You needed my help. I

gave it to you. Maybe you should learn how to accept help as much as you like to dish it out."

The comment landed square. "You know, sometimes you're smarter than you look."

"Fuck you," he said, his smile returning.

"Funny, that's exactly what I had in mind."

Keats gave him an up-and-down look. "Yeah?"

"Yeah, Georgia's cooking dinner over at her place to celebrate with us. What do you say I bring my toy bag, and we give her a go with a little control tonight?"

"I say I'll be the happiest fucker in the neighborhood."

Colby closed the last sliver of space between them and kissed him, letting his appreciation for all that Keats had done for him spill into it. This guy was turning out to be so much more than a fun time or a training relationship. Colby knew it before today, but now he couldn't pretend to deny it. This was getting serious. *He* was getting serious—about a twenty-three-year-old kid who would soon realize he still had oats to sow and a woman who was going to move away in a few weeks.

He'd waited this long to let his heart get involved with someone, and he'd picked the two people with the highest flight risk.

Way to go, Wilkes.

THIRTY-SIX

The package waiting on her doorstep Thursday morning made Georgia's insides twist. She recognized Leesha's familiar scrawl and knew what the innocuous-looking box contained. She'd asked for it. Now she wasn't sure she wanted it. But when she heard heavy footsteps on the stairs, she bent over and grabbed the box.

Colby stepped up behind her and wrapped his arms around her waist, kissing her neck. "Mornin', gorgeous."

She leaned back into him and managed a smile as she nudged the front door shut with her foot. "Morning. You lazy boys finally decided to get up?"

"Hey, you wore us out last night, George," Keats said as he made his way down the last few steps and joined them. "We need our beauty rest to keep up with you."

Colby set his chin on her shoulder. "Got anything good?"

"Huh?" she said, completely distracted by the thing in her hands.

"The package."

"Oh, right." She tossed the box onto the table by the front door like it was on fire. "Just some legal stuff from Leesha."

"Sounds like loads of fun." Colby spun her around in his arms and smiled down at her all sleep-mussed and sexy. He gave her a soft kiss. "Want to grab a late breakfast with us? I know a good pancake place."

"Mmm, pancakes." Keats sidled up behind her and nipped at her neck. "Or maybe we can just pour some syrup on you."

She closed her eyes and sighed into their touch. Being between them felt so good, so *right*. Last night they'd celebrated Colby getting his job back. They'd all been on such a high. Everything had seemed so bright and hopeful. But now with the arrival of the letters, it felt like a storm cloud had moved over her. Real life was knocking at her door. She slipped out of their hold.

"I'd love to, but I can't today, guys. I'm behind on work and need a day in a quiet house to catch up. Y'all should go without me."

Colby's gaze caught hers, evaluating, but she must've hidden her feelings well enough because he gave her a quick nod and a smile. "Got it. You need a break."

"It's not—"

Keats put his fingers against her mouth. "Say no more, George. It's been a busy few days, and we've kept you from work a lot. I actually need to get some things done, too. I got a message this morning from Colby's friend Pike. He's going to help me cut a demo."

She gave a genuine smile at that. "That's fantastic."

"Yep. But that means I need to get my shit together, decide which songs I want to record, and polish them up."

"And I need to drive out to The Ranch later to talk to Grant about my trainer schedule. Once I go full time at school, I'm not going to be able to do much out there."

Georgia nodded. "Then I guess I don't need to feel guilty for skipping out if we all have big to-do lists."

Colby tugged one of her curls. "Never feel guilty for that, beautiful. There are three of us in this relationship. That can be intense. None of us should feel bad when we need to do our own thing or be alone."

"Thanks." But the words fell heavy on her. *Relationship. Us.* The ache in her chest spread wide. Part of her so wanted those words to be real. But she couldn't let herself forget that this was temporary. Next week was Thanksgiving. She only had a little more than a month left before she was supposed to head back to

Chicago. She gave the two guys a weak smile. "Now get out of here, both of you. I'm a busy, important woman."

Colby and Keats laughed, and each leaned in for a quick kiss before they grabbed their things to head out. It all felt so domestic and comfortable.

But she couldn't let herself latch onto that feeling, that comfort. This was not her life. This was her temporary fantasy.

She peered over at the box of letters and inhaled a long breath. Time to remember why she was here in the first place.

After pouring herself a cup of coffee, Georgia sat on the floor in her living room, letters fanned out around her as she went through the pile Leesha had reluctantly sent her. Her skin chilled as she read each line of the sick love notes Phillip had penned. On the surface, they sounded sweet and romantic—words from a man deeply in love. But Georgia could read the threats tucked between the lines.

No one else can ever love you like I do.
Fate wants us to be together.
I don't go an hour without thinking of your face.
I won't let what's happened get in the way of our love.

She wanted to claw at the words, rip them into shreds, and toss them into the fireplace. But she forced herself to go through each one, trying to find something she could use in court. Surely, people would see that a sane man wouldn't write a woman a letter every two days when she wasn't returning them, right? But maybe some would see it as wildly romantic instead of wildly aggressive—a Valentine's Day movie in the making.

Blech.

She'd learned that she liked her men without all that gloss on them. Colby and Keats didn't need to write her letters or send her flowers. They didn't need any flash. Every day they showed her they cared just by being themselves—the little kindnesses, the teasing jokes, and the way they made her feel when she curled up between them.

Being with both of them was . . . overwhelming and intense and sexy and perfect. But the day they'd come back from Keats's father's house, something had changed. Instead of just thinking about what fun they were having, she'd found herself entertaining what it would be like if this were something real, if she came back after the trial and tried to live this life with the two of them.

She'd fallen for them hard and fast.

And it had to stop. She couldn't let herself continue like this.

She'd sensed things moving too quickly from early on. Even Leesha had picked up on it. But now Georgia knew beyond a doubt that it was more than a crush or a fling. Keats and Colby looked at her in a way that made her physically hurt. They looked at her like she mattered. Like this was so much more than sex. Like they wanted her to stay.

But she couldn't.

She had to go back to Chicago for as long as it took. It wasn't fair to ask the guys to wait around for her or put their lives on hold. Beyond the fact that there was no guarantee a relationship with the three of them would work long term anyway, her fate was in the hands of the court. If Phillip went free, she wouldn't be able to come back, and she definitely wouldn't be able to date anyone.

These letters confirmed exactly how dangerous that would be. *No one else can ever love you like I do.* Translation: *I will kill every bastard who tries.*

No. Phillip needed to be out of her life for good before she could let someone else in.

She knew what she needed to do. And part of that meant ending this relationship with Colby and Keats when she left. They could enjoy their remaining time together, but she couldn't string them along with no definite outcome, and she wouldn't do that to herself either. Her heart was already breaking, thinking about walking away from them, and that wasn't where her head needed to be. She needed to put all her focus on Phillip. On beating this man who had hijacked her life and taken her sister away.

Until he was locked away, there was no space in her life for anything else. Love had gotten her in trouble the first time, but she wouldn't let it derail her again.

She didn't get to fall in love right now.

The guys would be fine without her.

Even if she might not be fine without them.

THIRTY-SEVEN

Keats popped a chunk of bell pepper in his mouth as he chopped the rest of the vegetables for the stir-fry he was making and sang along with the Keith Urban song playing on the radio. The door opened behind him, and he glanced over his shoulder to find Georgia hauling in a bag of groceries.

He set down the knife and went over to take it from her. "What's all this? I've already gotten everything for Thursday."

She handed over the bag and set her purse on the counter. "I didn't see any sweets in your stash, so I bought stuff to make dessert. It's Thanksgiving, we need pie."

"Pumpkin?" he said, trying not to make a face. He wasn't a fan. That was all he remembered about Thanksgivings with his dad and Justin—going to the crappy diner in town and eating instant mashed potatoes, mushy turkey, and wet pumpkin pie.

"Nope, pecan. Plus, cranberry vanilla cheesecake. Got the recipe from my good friend Giada."

"So Food Network?" he teased. He'd learned over the past few weeks that Georgia had a bit of an addiction to cooking shows.

She touched her finger to her nose and pointed at him in the universal *you guessed it* gesture, but her smile seemed distant, distracted. "It will probably be a complete disaster. I've never made it before, and I had to buy a special pan and everything. Is your brother still coming?"

"Yeah, he's bringing the liquor, which is good. He may need it when he finds out that I'm also dating a guy and that the guy is Colby."

"You think he's going to freak out?"

"Probably. But I think he'll be fine once he gets over the initial shock. I went to lunch with him the other day and told him I'm bi. He was totally okay with it. He said my dad's views were never his and that after almost dying from that roadside bomb in Afghanistan, he's learned how important it is to grab happiness wherever you can find it."

Something flickered through Georgia's eyes, but whatever it was disappeared before Keats could pinpoint it. "I'm really glad things are working out for you two. It's good to have family around."

"Yeah, it is. I didn't realize how much I missed having that in my life." He peered into the bag. "Did you go out and get all of this on your own?"

She tilted her chin up. "Yep. Second solo trip this week and no panic attacks. I even strolled through a bookstore before I got the groceries. They have my newest book on one of the front tables."

He set aside the groceries and swept her into his arms. "Score."

Since that day they'd gone to see his dad, she hadn't let herself go more than two days without leaving the house. She'd put herself on a training schedule like a marathon runner. Each time she went out, she stayed out for longer, pushing herself to her limit. He and Colby had taken to humming the *Rocky* theme music to her every time they got in the car, which always made her roll her eyes. And late last week, she'd decided she was ready to try it without him or Colby accompanying her.

And really, since that first shopping trip they'd all taken together, she'd had only two occasions where the panic had gotten the better of her. Once when an overzealous fan of her books had recognized her in a store and had hugged Georgia without warning. And another this past weekend when they'd gone to the bar to listen to Colby play and a drunk guy had crowded her in the hallway, trying to come on to her. Keats had been a few yards away and had hurried over when he saw what was happening, ready to kick the guy's ass if he put his hands on Georgia. But before Keats had reached her, Georgia had put out her palms and shoved the guy back, shouting, "Back off, asshole."

The guy, unsteady on his feet already, had hit the wall and said something nasty to her. She'd stepped up to him, poked a finger into his chest, and told him something Keats hadn't been able to hear. The guy's eyes had gone wide and he'd raised his palms in surrender.

When she'd stalked back Keats's way, she'd grabbed his arm and dragged him with her out to the parking lot. "Get me to the truck so I can get this damn panic attack out of the way."

She'd been shaking but clear-eyed. He'd hustled her into the cab of the truck, and she'd leaned her head back and breathed through it. Afterward, she'd insisted they go back into the bar to hear Colby's set. She'd ordered a drink and had been fine for the rest of the evening. When Keats had asked her later what she'd said to the redneck, she'd smiled sweetly. "He told me to suck his dick. So I told him exactly what I would do with that appendage if he put it anywhere near me. It involved rusty knives and profuse bleeding."

Keats smiled at the memory and looked down at Georgia. "Well, two solo trips in a row. That's definitely something to celebrate."

She shook her head. "No way. Tonight we're celebrating you. I can't believe you walk in to find out about a demo tape and land yourself a job."

He gave her another squeeze and let her go. "I have a feeling a certain Mr. Fix-It pulled some strings, which normally would piss me off. But I'm not going to complain this time because it's too good a gig. Entry-level, errand-running kind of stuff but at a recording studio, so I can't ask for a better shot than that. And I really liked Pike, the guy who owns the place. You'd dig him. He has this bleached blond spiked hair and that whole rocker thing going on— more ink than me. And his band is a pretty big deal, so I kind of expected him to have that I'm-a-badass attitude. Because, really, I've heard their music. He *is* a badass. But he was so laid-back. And he's totally into this pet project of having his own studio and producing start-up acts, so I think it's going to be fun."

"Is he interested in your music?"

He shrugged and went back to the cutting board. "He really liked the song I played and said he'll try to bring in one of his friends to hear my stuff, a guy who has more experience with country music."

"That's awesome, Keats," she said, sliding onto a stool at the island. "Maybe one day I'll be able to say I knew you when."

He frowned. "I don't want that word to ever be in the past tense with you—*knew*. Fuck that, George."

Her gaze flicked up to his, strain there. "I leave in a few weeks. You know that."

"Doesn't mean you can't come back afterward."

She looked down the counter, her posture stiff. "The trial could take months."

"So."

"My life is there, Keats. My friends, the house I own. My lease is up on the house next door in January. You know this was never meant to be permanent. It was an unexpected detour."

He put his back to her and turned the dial on the stove, a foul mood seeping in. "And me and Colby? We're just a detour, too, then?"

"Come on, don't be like that."

He put oil in the pan, the dismissive comment stinging more than it probably should. He knew he was too attached already, that he shouldn't be feeling like this after only a month, especially when Georgia had made her intentions clear all along. But some part of him had been harboring hope that this happy turn in his life wasn't just an interlude before everything went to shit again. That'd been his cycle so far in life. Like those games at the fair where you throw a ring around the bottle and get a big stuffed animal. It seems so easy. *Ooh, look, you're going to get to have this really cool thing! Look, look how awesome it is. Here we go! Then,* clunk, *the rings fall back into the pit. Ha, ha, just kidding. Hand over another dollar, kid.*

He could hear Georgia's heavy sigh behind him and then she was against his back, wrapping her arms around his waist. She set her chin on his shoulder. "Believe me, it's going to be hard on me, too. But you know even if I were staying here, this isn't realistic."

"Colby's friend Jace has that kind of relationship. From what I understand, they do all right."

Her breath coasted along his neck. "Is that what you really want, Keats? I've loved being with you two, and part of me wishes the three of us could make it work because I care for you both so much. But it's complicated. And you're twenty-three. I'm almost thirty-one and at a different stage in my life. I'm in a place where I want to settle down. One day sooner rather than later I want to start a family."

His stomach knotted. "And you assume I don't want those things, too? That Colby doesn't?"

"Maybe Colby does. And I'm sure you do, too. One day. But at your age, you're—"

"Immature, barely employed, incapable of taking care of you or kids." He stepped out of her embrace and went over to the cutting board again. "It's fine, George, I get it."

"Keats, that's not what I meant."

But it was. They both knew it. If he wasn't in the picture and it was just Colby, would she be saying the same stuff? With Colby she could have all those things she wanted—traditional marriage, a family, a guy who could win Dad of the Year awards. But no, here he was, in the way. And she was too nice to kick him out of the picture.

Colby got home from running errands a few minutes later and the conversation was dropped. They spent the evening eating together, talking about Keats's new job and how Colby couldn't wait to get back to school. It'd been relaxed and domestic. Comfortable. Happy.

It'd been that stupid game from the fair, waving the pretty stuffed animal in Keats's face.

But he'd sat back and really watched Colby and Georgia together and could paint their future in his head. Things would be so much easier for them both without him photobombing the picture. Colby wouldn't have to hide the fact that he was dating a former student. Georgia could have the kind of life she wanted without having to answer questions about her lifestyle. God knows what people would call her around here if they found out she was in a relationship with two guys. That kind of thing raised eyebrows anywhere, but here in Texas, it'd be a social death sentence. And he couldn't even imagine what that could turn into if kids were ever part of the picture.

Maybe he *had* been immature to think something like this could work long term. He'd lived his adult life on the fringes of society, where people looked the other way and minded their business about things. The street had its own code of *don't ask, don't tell.* But that wasn't the real world. That wasn't the world Colby and Georgia lived in.

And so, as he lay in bed that night, watching Colby and Georgia curled up in sleep next to him, he knew what he needed to do.

Tomorrow, he'd get up and look for an apartment. Because he'd finally figured out how he could repay Colby for all that he'd done for him.

Keats would give him the girl he loved.

And get the fuck out of the way.

Georgia rolled over in bed, expecting to run into another warm body, but only cool sheets pressed against her back. She opened her eyes in the gray morning light. Colby was next to her, sleeping soundly. Keats was gone. She wasn't surprised, but melancholy rolled through her like winter fog.

Yesterday she'd been honest with Keats, but it had come out all wrong. She'd told him their relationship was temporary; he'd heard *disposable.* She'd told him he was young; he'd heard *immature.* The words had cut him. She'd seen it on his face, how he'd instantly shut down. That sweet, open soul had scrambled back under its hardened shell, and the bitter mask he'd honed on the streets had slid back into place. Never before had she felt like such a selfish bitch. In that moment, she'd realized that no matter how genuine her feelings were for both of them, she'd used them.

She'd always known she would have to leave, but she hadn't kept the boundaries clear. Yes, she'd told them the situation was short-term from the start, but her actions had sent a completely different message. She'd led them on, letting hope linger and bloom—maybe because she'd latched onto a little bit of it herself. Then she'd gotten those letters, and reality had slammed back into her.

She'd been stupid and reckless with two men who had been nothing but thoughtful and loving with her. And now her continued presence was only driving the knife deeper for them all. She'd felt it last night throughout dinner and their evening together. She'd wanted to talk to Keats one-on-one since they'd never finished their conversation from the kitchen. But he'd actively avoided being alone with her all night.

So when they'd finally reached the bedroom late last night and Colby had stepped out to get something from the bathroom, she'd broached the topic. But Keats had shaken his head. "It's okay, George. We don't need to talk about it. I'm fine."

"You're not. I'm sorry. I didn't mean it the way—"

Keats had pressed his fingers over her mouth, a tender, sad smile on his lips. "Don't. Please. I get it. Let's not ruin tonight over it. I'm going to be fine. I just want to be with you tonight and leave the rest of the stuff outside the door."

She'd nodded and he'd cupped her face and kissed her. Kissed her like he wanted her. Kissed her like he loved her. Kissed her like it was good-bye.

And when all three of them had made love, she'd wondered if Colby had somehow sensed the cracks appearing in the foundation as well, because he'd left the kink to the side. They'd taken their time and had indulged in the freedom of touching and making each other feel good. It had been sweet and sexy. It had felt amazing. It had broken her heart.

Because in those moments, looking at the faces of the two men as she took them inside her body, she'd known that she couldn't keep doing this—to them or to herself. They'd all broken the rules. They'd gotten attached.

And there was only one way to fix it.

It was time.

Georgia reached out and ran the backs of her fingers along Colby's bearded jaw. He inhaled deeply and his eyelids fluttered open, dark lashes blinking over sleepy hazel eyes. He turned his face toward her and smiled a lazy smile. "Mmm, good morning, gorgeous."

She drew her hand lower and let it linger on his chest, feeling his heart beating steadily beneath her fingertips. God, how she'd enjoyed waking up next to him these last few weeks. "Morning."

He tucked an arm behind his head, his gaze tracing over her and becoming more focused. "Everything okay?"

She rubbed her lips together, hoping her voice wouldn't shake. "I just wanted to let you know I was heading out."

He turned his head to glance at the clock. "This early?"

"Yeah. I'm behind on everything. I need to . . . do stuff." It sounded lame to her own ears, so she could only imagine how it sounded to his.

His brows knitted, and he reached out to take her hand. "You sure that's all it is? You're wearing your serious face."

She tried to muster up a neutral expression even though her heart felt as heavy as an anvil in her chest. "I just need some time."

Something flickered in his eyes—the ever-vigilant counselor not one to miss much. His voice was soft when he spoke again. "What kind of time, Georgia?"

Her lungs squeezed tight, and she let her hand curl into his. What could she say to this beautiful, wonderful man who'd turned her world inside out, who'd helped her find herself again? She couldn't get the words out, couldn't face the finality. She was such a fucking coward. She forced a facsimile of a smile. "Don't worry. I'll be back for Thanksgiving dinner. I would never deny you cheesecake."

He didn't smile back, but he didn't push. He gave a little nod. "Whatever you need, Georgia."

"Thanks." She leaned down to give him a quick kiss, but when she moved to sit up again, he grabbed the back of her neck and tugged her down.

"We can do better than that." He kissed her long and slow until she was breathless and on the verge of tears. Everything poured into the kiss—the need, the sweetness, the heat, the sadness. When he finally released her, her insides felt like they were folding in on themselves.

She swallowed back the tears that were trying to break free and climbed out of bed, a painful smile frozen on her face. She grabbed her jeans and sweater off a chair and tugged them on, her hands trembling so much that she struggled to get her button fastened. "Well, I better get going."

He propped himself up on his elbow, the sheet sinking low on his hips, and gave her a long look. She took a snapshot in her mind, never wanting to forget the sight of him like this.

What they'd had was short.

But what they'd had was beautiful.

"See ya, Georgia," he said, his eyes never leaving hers.

Good-bye, Colby.

"See ya."

THIRTY-EIGHT

december

Colby sat in his living room, staring at one of the *Die Hard* movies on television. He hadn't paid enough attention to know what the hell was going on, but the booming sound of things blowing up certainly fit his mood.

He flipped over his cell phone. No calls. Neither Keats nor Georgia had bothered to respond to his invitation to grab dinner together. That seemed to be the case a lot lately. They always had good excuses, but he wasn't dumb. Everything had changed.

He wasn't sure exactly how it had happened or what had triggered it, but he'd felt the shift as sure as the cold front that had rolled through overnight. One day, it'd been the three of them, having a good time, falling into this exciting, oddly comfortable relationship. Things were turning around for them all. Colby had his job back. Georgia had made massive progress with her anxiety. And Keats had landed a gig that excited him.

Colby could've taken a photo and labeled it perfect. But the moment had been as fleeting as the click of the camera. Because after that, he'd felt the tug of the inevitable, the unraveling. Georgia, who'd been so open and up for what they were doing, had pulled away—spending more time at her place in the name of making a writing deadline. She was still pushing herself to get out of the house, but she wasn't asking him and Keats to come along anymore. And Colby's bed had been cold since before Thanksgiving.

Then if the writing hadn't been all over the wall already, Keats had come home one day with apartment brochures. That had really punched Colby right in the gut. He'd known that Keats couldn't stay here forever. They'd done their relationship backward, moving in together first. And that had made things more intense and intimate for the start of something. Keats was a young guy who was just discovering a big piece of his sexuality. Of course he'd want some freedom and independence. He wouldn't want to shack up with a guy in his thirties and play house indefinitely. But Colby had to admit, part of him had imagined that scenario. And he'd imagined Georgia in that mix, too.

The days he'd walked into his place and had both Keats and Georgia hanging out there, waiting for him, happy to see him, had been some of the best of his life. He loved the way being around them dialed him up to rattle-and-hum mode. It was like everything was sweeter when he had those two to share it with. And though he'd tried to convince himself it was just the amazing sex that was making him feel so damn good, he knew that was bullshit. Because some of the best nights he'd had with them had involved no kink or sex at all.

He liked being with them. Period.

No, he loved being with them. He loved *them*. Both of them.

And now he suspected he was losing both for good.

The sound of a key in the door drew his attention away from the TV. Keats hurried through the front door in a gust of frigid air and dry leaves. He shut the door with a bang. "Goddamn, it's cold out there. Did someone forget this is Texas?"

Colby lowered the volume on the TV. "They said we could get snow."

Keats slipped out of his coat and hooked it on a peg by the door. "I have no idea why George is so anxious to get back to Chicago. If it's this cold here, I can't imagine what it must be like there."

"Picture this thirty degrees colder with wind that will make your bones hurt."

"Fuck that." He plopped down in the armchair across from Colby, looking windblown, red-cheeked, and damn fine in his dark green sweater. "You should use that in your argument to get her to come back here after the trial."

He frowned. "I don't think weather's going to convince her."

"You want her to stay, though, right?"

Colby sighed. "I do."

"Have you asked her to?"

"No. She told me where she stood up front. It was her hard limit— no pressure, nothing serious. I'm not going to break my word on that."

He blew out a breath. "I asked her. Right before Thanksgiving."

Colby's brows lifted. So that was what had happened. "I'm guessing she said no."

"She said no to me. Not to you."

"Saying no to you is as good as saying no to me, Keats. All three of us are in this together. Or *were* in this together. She's got to want to be here on her own. And this is still so new to all of us. It's a lot to ask her to give up her life in Chicago for that. It'd be a huge leap of faith."

"And what if I weren't involved?"

Colby frowned. "What do you mean?"

"George told me what she wants. She wants to get married, have kids one day, do the family thing."

Colby sat forward. "She told you that?"

"Yeah. The day I asked her to stay. And I'm guessing that's what you want, too. I mean, I know you've done this bachelor gig for a long time, but I've seen how you are with kids. And I see how you look at Georgia. You could offer her what she wants if she comes back and gives your relationship a shot. You'd make a great husband and dad, Colby. You know you would."

Colby wasn't going to deny that a big part of him wanted those things in his life. He hadn't always, but at his core, he knew there was no going back to the way he lived his life before. He'd already put in his resignation for his position at The Ranch. Those impersonal hookups held no appeal anymore. But he also knew a triad relationship didn't exclude the possibility of having a family. And he didn't like where this was going. Keats had that look in his eye. "Why are you even saying all this?"

Keats pulled something out of his back pocket and set it on the coffee table. A key. "I got my own place today. I can move in right after Christmas. You can tell Georgia before she leaves how you feel about her. And that you just want to be with her. That will make her come back to you when she's done with the trial. I know it will."

Colby stared at the key, trying to process Keats's words and logic, cold moving through him. "So you're just going to walk away?"

"Yeah." He shrugged, though he wouldn't meet Colby's eyes. "I mean, it was going to have to happen eventually, right? Three's fun, but it's not real life. Someone was going to have to step back at some point. You two can have what you want together."

"That simple, huh?"

Keats plucked a piece of sweater fuzz off his jeans. "Yep."

Colby's teeth clenched, and he reached out and thumped Keats on the thigh. "Look at me."

Keats, ever the good submissive, lifted his gaze. Something heavy sat there in those green eyes.

"So you're ending things with me?" Colby clarified.

"It's not like that. It's just . . . you two are great together. Y'all don't need me in the way." He pushed his hair behind his ears. "Me being involved complicates things for no reason."

Colby fought the urge to find his riding crop and snap some sense into Keats. "Is that right?"

Keats shrugged again—like it was no big thing, like it was a foregone conclusion.

Colby leaned forward, pinning Keats with a hard stare. "Keats, you listen to me because obviously you need to hear this. If you're walking away from me because it's gotten too serious too fast or because you want to explore this new side of yourself with other people or because you're not ready for a relationship, then by all means, take that key and go start your new life. I wish you well. Truly.

"But if you're doing this because you think you owe me something or because you think you're in the fucking way, then pay attention to what I'm saying."

Keats's jaw flexed.

"I'm falling for Georgia, yes. If I could get her to come back and be in a relationship, I could see myself marrying her one day and having kids who have those pretty dark eyes and curls of hers."

Keats closed his eyes like it made him ache to picture that.

"But outside of how I feel about her, stupid me has already fallen in love *with you*. The twenty-three-year-old kid who I should be pushing out the door because he doesn't need to be stuck with some guy in his thirties who's ready to settle down."

Keats lifted his gaze and stared at him, expression going slack.

"So if you walk out on this, do it because you want to be free, because you're not ready for a commitment, or because you don't want to be with me. But don't you dare do it because you think you're doing me some solid. Because all it's going to do is rip my fucking guts out."

———

Keats couldn't get his brain to kick in or his mouth to work. All he could do was gape dumbly at the man across from him. The man who'd just admitted he was in love with him. *In love.* Colby Wilkes loved him.

A thousand thoughts raced through Keats's mind at once. What Colby wanted—commitment, long term, settling down. Those were words that should scare the ever-living fuck out of Keats. But somehow he couldn't grasp onto the fear. After that afternoon in the kitchen with Georgia, he'd made an effort to separate himself from the situation, to find his own way. He'd started going out to clubs and bars here and there after work. Straight ones, gay ones. He hadn't gone out to hook up with anyone, but he'd done it trying to wean himself off the intense feelings he was having about Colby and Georgia, to get a taste for what the single life would be like for him now. And to give Colby and Georgia some alone time.

But though he'd danced with beautiful girls and hot guys and had been flirted with, propositioned, and even kissed by one dude, he hadn't been able to muster up any real interest. As he watched people play the mating game, he'd wanted nothing more than to go home and curl up in bed with Colby and Georgia. He didn't crave variety. He craved *them*. They felt like home. Maybe more than anything had in his life.

And Colby wanted him here. He wanted *him*. For real. Not because this was part of some fun threesome. Not because Colby was training him. And not because he was doing Keats a favor. Colby loved him.

Keats pushed to his feet, feeling as if he were filled with helium. All the heavy shit that had been weighing him down for weeks seemed to fall away. He grabbed the key he'd plunked down and walked around the coffee table. His pulse pounded at his temples, so many emotions running through him at once, but he managed to take Colby's hand, unfurl his fingers, and place the key in his palm. Colby's hand closed around it. Then Keats lowered himself to his knees.

All felt right in the moment. The restless energy that had been plaguing Keats quieted as soon as he was there at Colby's feet. He lifted his head and met Colby's gaze. "I don't want to be free."

Colby's throat worked. "No?"

"No. I love you, too. So goddamned much." The steel fingers that had gripped his chest for the last few weeks loosened, letting him finally take a full breath. "I'm starting to think I always did."

Colby smiled a smile that threatened to crack open Keats completely. The guy could break someone with that smile. "So you'll stay?"

"Looks like you're stuck with your stray now. You should've never fed me."

Colby shook his head and cupped Keats's chin. "You were never a stray. You've always been a guy who needed to make his own way. I'm just lucky that you found your way to me." He lifted Keats's chin higher. "But maybe it's time I get you a collar so that you never doubt again where you belong and who you belong to."

Keats closed his eyes and breathed that in. His heart felt like it was trying to climb out his throat so it could hand itself to Colby. Goddamn, he was turning into a sap. But he knew what a collar meant in Colby's world. No, not Colby's world. *Their* world. "I would love that. I want to belong to you."

And to Georgia. But Keats knew you couldn't always get everything you wanted. He and Colby could be happy together. He would do everything he could to make sure of it.

Colby leaned forward, drawing Keats up to him, and kissed him slow and deep. The kiss said everything words couldn't. And something inside Keats that had been out of alignment maybe all his life clicked into place.

Colby pulled back, meeting Keats's gaze. "I think it's time for bed."

"I'm all yours, sir."

Colby nodded, that steely dominance coming into his eyes—a look that made Keats's bones liquefy. "Good. Because I'm taking everything tonight."

Keats shuddered at the promise of what that meant, but it was pure anticipation at this point, no fear. Up until now, Colby hadn't pushed Keats to move to that final step in the bedroom. He'd told Keats he wouldn't fuck him until he knew Keats was ready. They'd touched, they'd played, Colby had used toys on him. At points, Keats had been so turned on, he'd begged Colby to take him. But at the root of it, he hadn't been ready, and Colby had picked up on that.

Now, he had no doubts. He wanted to give Colby everything. He wanted to surrender it all.

They made their way to the bedroom, Colby's hand on the back of Keats's neck, and Colby ordered him to get undressed. Keats got to work as Colby disappeared into the closet. Keats's eyes lingered on the closed curtains for a moment, wondering what Georgia was doing. He wished he could open them and see her standing in that window, looking down at them. She'd probably love this kind of show. Keats smiled to himself. Dirty, dirty George. Damn, he missed that woman.

He shook free of the wistful feeling and unbuttoned his pants. He couldn't worry about *what ifs* tonight. *What is* was far too good to let anything spoil the mood. He finished undressing and set his folded clothes on a chair by the door. He'd learned the hard way that Colby didn't like his submissive's clothes thrown around the floor.

When Colby stepped out from the closet, he was rolling a riding crop between his fingertips. "I think we'll keep it simple tonight, which isn't to say it won't involve some suffering on your part."

Goose bumps pricked Keats's skin. This was the part he might like best. Before this, he would've never thought of himself as a masochist, even though he'd always enjoyed getting his tattoos. But he couldn't deny what a dose of pain did to him now. And Colby had gotten increasingly more aggressive in dishing it out with him. Keats knew Colby went a little easier on Georgia because, though she was generally up for anything, she didn't seem to be a dyed-in-the-wool masochist. She liked the shifting power dynamics and the adventure of it all. She'd even had fun taking a little control herself. Somehow, Colby seemed to instinctively know what each of them responded to best and set it up to provide maximum enjoyment for them all. He wasn't a one-size-fits-all dominant.

And from the look on Colby's face right now, Keats knew that Colby had decided that tonight, Keats needed some sting.

Colby walked over until he was right in front of Keats and leveled him with a look. He tapped Keats's cheek, which was a sign to open his mouth. When he did, Colby put the riding crop between Keats's teeth. "Bite down."

Keats obeyed, the unyielding handle of the crop pressing against his teeth.

"Now go over to the bed and bend over, forehead to the mattress, hands behind your back. Let go of the crop and you'll regret it. Nod if you understand."

Keats nodded, sweat already gathering on the back of his neck.

He walked over to the bed, keeping his back straight, and then bent over to get into position. He clasped his hands behind his back. Despite the cool air in the bedroom, his cock went hard almost instantly.

"If you need to safe out, you drop the crop and say your word or lift an arm." Colby ran a warm hand down the length of Keats's spine, and Keats had to fight to stay still.

He had no idea if Colby was just going to go for it. Was this the moment? A blanket of nerves fell over him.

"Widen your feet," Colby said, his tone militant. "And relax. If you want to take me, you're going to have to learn to let me in."

Keats sucked in a deep breath through his nose, careful to hold on to the crop, and released it, trying to let go of the tension as well. He did it three more times.

"Very good, Adam. I like that you can follow instructions." Colby ran his hand along Keats's inner thigh and then cupped Keats's testicles in his hand with a firm grip. He gave them a little tug.

Keats groaned, the snap of discomfort mixing in with the pleasure of being handled.

"You should see how fucking sinful you look right now. That gorgeous body, all that ink, this hard cock and spread ass. One day I'm going to tie you down like this and enjoy the view while you beg me to touch you."

Fuck. Keats almost lost his grip on the crop.

"But I'm not feeling patient tonight. I'm ready to mark what's mine." His fingers trailed along Keats's crack and found his opening. He teased around it for a second and then pulled away.

Keats made a sound of protest in the back of his throat, but then he heard the sound of the lube squirting into Colby's hand. Soon, the fingers were back, painting Keats's most forbidden spot with the slick fluid. Colby pushed a finger inside, and Keats thought he might die from the wave of need it sent through him.

"You're going to take this plug for me," Colby said, adding another finger to the stimulation. "It's not quite my size but it will get you ready for me."

"Yes, sir," Keats mumbled around the crop.

Colby took his fingers away and then something colder and more pliable pressed against his opening. Keats forced himself to relax, taking a few deep breaths again, and then the tip of the plug breached him. The pressure felt good, but Keats had seen what the plugs looked like. They got wider at the base, so he tried not to brace for what was to come. Colby twisted the toy, the ripples in the silicone stimulating Keats's sensitive flesh, and then he pushed it deeper. The stretching feeling was almost too much to take for a second—some weird combination of pain and pleasure intersecting. Keats desperately wished he could reach down and stroke his cock, tip the scales more to the pleasure side, but he kept his hands clasped tight behind his back.

Finally, the plug seated deep, and Keats's body melted around it, the flared base holding it in place. Colby gave it another twist and Keats fought to keep from begging.

"You're good?" Colby asked.

"Yes, sir," he said again from between clenched teeth.

"Perfect. Then you won't mind this."

The plug hummed to life, vibrating a place that had never been vibrated in Keats's life. He dropped the crop. "Shit."

"Oh, well, would you look at that," Colby said, the Texas twang getting heavy in Colby's voice. Keats had found the more turned on Colby was, the more country came out. "Looks like you couldn't follow the rule."

"Sorry, sir," Keats said, fighting the urge to move his hips and rub his cock along the bed. The vibration was going to drive him to the brink.

"I'm not. More fun for me. Get up, Adam, and stand beneath the hook."

Keats released his hands and pushed himself off the bed. The plug made him feel full in the most erotic way, but he managed to get his legs moving so he could go to the spot where Colby wanted him.

Colby went over to his drawer and pulled out his favorite—rope. Then he took his goddamned time, tying Keats's arms to the hook in the ceiling. Keats felt his thoughts hazing around the edges already, the high of submission kicking in.

Colby made sure Keats was secure and then grabbed the riding crop off the bed. He stood in front of Keats. "Look at me, Adam."

Keats lifted his head, finding Colby looming big and powerful in his jeans and dark blue sweater—the teacher transformed into the all-powerful master.

Colby stepped into Keats's space and reached down to give Keats's cock a squeeze. "Ready to fly for me?"

Keats swallowed hard. "I'm ready to do anything for you."

"Good answer." He pulled a strip of black satin out from his pocket and tied it around Keats's eyes. "See you on the other side."

The blindfold was the last thing Keats needed to settle in fully. He felt himself slipping into the happy place where all he had to do was give himself over to whatever Colby was going to do to him. Freedom.

And what Colby did was more than he'd ever given Keats before. The riding crop, which he'd seen Colby use in such a playful way with Georgia, was a wicked bitch when yielded with force. And Colby wasn't holding back tonight. The sharp snap of the leather marked a path against every part of Keats's back, ass, and thighs. *Snap, snap, snap.* The rhythm brutal and unrelenting. It echoed through the room without any words being spoken to interrupt. Every part of Keats's backside burned and tingled. That, paired with the vibrations going on inside him, had his knees going weak within minutes.

"Stand tall," Colby said, snapping the crop right against the base of the plug.

Keats's spine went straight and stiff.

"Better. I'm only halfway done, and I know you're tougher than that."

"Yes, sir," Keats said, breathless, sweating.

The sound of Colby's footfalls moved off to Keats's left and then another lighter blow hit his nipple. Oh, shit. Colby had moved in front of him.

Colby hit the other nipple with a little more sting added, and Keats grunted.

"Still with me?" Colby asked, pushing the leather of the crop beneath Keats's chin. "Looks like your cock certainly is."

"Still here. Both of us."

Colby gave a low chuckle. "And still a smartass."

He traced the tip of the crop down Keats's neck and over his chest—lower, lower, lower. Keats felt everything in him cinching tight, knowing what his deviant lover had planned.

But even though he'd known it was coming, when Colby flicked the crop against Keats's balls, Keats almost lost hold of what little composure he had. It hadn't been a hard hit. But even so, knowing he was that vulnerable, that his most delicate parts were at the mercy of Colby's whims, dialed into something elemental in Keats. In that moment, he felt his body surrender fully. Without conscious thought, his stance widened.

"Mmm," Colby said, his voice rougher than it had been a moment before, like his own arousal was overtaking him. "You like that."

Keats didn't think Colby was expecting an answer on this one, so he simply lowered his head.

Colby took that as assent. He tapped the underside of Keats's cock, then his inner thighs and balls again, marking a path that quickly morphed into erotic stimulation instead of pain. Every part of Keats's body felt like it was humming with electricity, all of it alive and awake, his cock leaking with the intense arousal. And he couldn't find a shred of shame in any of it.

This was who he was. And this man was who Keats could be all versions of himself with—no judgment. This was what love felt like. He wouldn't apologize for that.

Soon, hands were cradling Keats's face, and Colby's mouth was on his. As their tongues stroked against each other, Keats found himself sinking into that state where he was all feeling and sensation.

Colby pulled back, cupping the back of Keats's neck. "I'm going to get my knife and cut the ropes. I don't want to waste time untying everything. But I need you to stay still. Can you do that for me?"

Keats nodded and let himself drift on the sensations of his tingling skin and the vibrator working its magic. Colby moved quickly and got Keats out of the ropes. He rubbed Keats's arms and hands, bringing the blood rushing back to them. Then he tugged off the blindfold.

Colby had stripped out of his clothes, and Keats let himself take in the view with hungry eyes. Because Colby sometimes stayed dressed in the bedroom, it always felt like a special privilege to see him completely stripped down.

Colby nodded at Keats. "Get on the bed, lie on your back."

Keats licked his dry lips. "My back, sir?"

Colby stepped closer, using the few inches in height he had on Keats to his full advantage. "Yes, Keats. Tonight I need to fuck you face-to-face. I want to watch you as I make you mine."

Keats's stomach flipped over. He couldn't imagine anything better.

Getting onto his back on the bed reignited some of the sting the crop had caused, but he welcomed it. It brought him back into the moment, centering him again. He liked the buzzing feeling from the pain, but he didn't want to miss a second of this. He scooted up the bed.

Colby grabbed supplies from the bedside table and then climbed onto the bed between Keats's legs, looming over him. "Put your palm out." Keats lifted his hand to Colby, and Colby drizzled lube onto Keats's palm. "Stroke yourself while we do this. It will make it easier for you. But you don't get to come until I do. So you slow down if you feel yourself getting close."

"Yes, sir."

Keats wrapped his hand around his cock and gave it a welcome stroke. But the lazy pleasure didn't last long because Colby chose that moment to tug on the plug. "Easy now."

The plug slid free but not without almost sending Keats into orgasm as it glided over that sweet spot inside him. Colby set the plug aside and replaced it with his generously lubed fingers. He peered down at Keats as he moved from one to three fingers, stretching him and readying him. It had to be one of the most erotic moments of Keats's life. Colby gazing down at him with lust and love in his eyes, his fingers working him like he owned him.

Colby moved his hand away and shifted position, and then he was rolling on the condom and lubing up his own cock, turning it glossy in his grip. Keats gave his own dick a squeeze, warning his body not to jump the gun yet.

But luckily, Colby wasn't going to make him wait any longer. Colby put his hands on the backs of Keats's thighs and pushed his legs upward, opening him fully to Colby. Their eye contact didn't break as Colby positioned himself at Keats's entrance.

"Ready for me?" Colby asked.

"Yes. Please."

Colby pushed forward slowly. The head of Colby's cock felt so much bigger than the plug. An impossible amount of pressure. And Keats had a brief moment of panic that they wouldn't be able to do this, that his body wouldn't be able to accommodate Colby. But he breathed through it and stroked his own cock, focusing on relaxing and accepting the pleasure. The tight ring of muscle stretched and burned as Colby eased forward and before Keats could drag in another breath, his body gave way, taking Colby inside.

The taut, full feeling almost sent Keats into orgasm before Colby slid deep, but Keats squeezed the base of his cock and locked onto Colby's gaze, determined to hold off for him.

Colby's eyes closed, and the veins in his neck bulged as he seated himself fully inside Keats. It was the hottest damn thing Keats had ever seen—Colby overtaken with need. And he got the sense that he wouldn't be the only one fighting back a too-quick orgasm.

"Fuck," Colby groaned.

"That's the idea." Keats smiled.

Colby opened his eyes, his gaze holding playful warning.

"Sorry, sir."

"Don't be. If you can make jokes, then I must not be hurting you too much, which means I don't have to hold back as much as I'm trying to."

Keats shook his head. "Don't hold back. I want everything, Colby. I know what my safe word is. Trust that I'll use it if I need to."

Something broke over Colby's expression and he gave a nod. "I do trust you."

And with that, there was no turning back. Colby rocked back

and then sank deep again, continuing with long, slow thrusts that had Keats feeling as if every cell in his body were ready to split in half and re-form into something new.

Colby's eyes never moved away from Keats's face. Keats held on to that connection as his hand moved over his own cock in the same rhythm, and he welcomed Colby into every corner of himself.

Time seemed to stretch and lengthen, the room fading around them. It was just him and Colby and this intensity brewing between them. This was so much more than Keats had ever expected. And he knew without a doubt that he was where he was supposed to be. Everyone else be damned. Nothing wrong could feel this right.

Soon, sweat glazed them both, and slow and steady fell by the wayside. Keats's hand was moving faster and faster and Colby was pistoning into him with tense need on his face, his damp hair curling at his temples. "You ready to come for me, Adam?"

"God, yes."

"Then come." Colby pushed on Keats's thighs, opening him even wider, and sank impossibly deep, rubbing over that sensitive spot over and over again as he pulled back each time.

Every drop of blood in Keats seemed to race downward, and he exploded. His release jetted out over his hand, splashing his belly and chest as he groaned and grunted like a crazed animal.

Then Colby went over, his face contorting in pleasure and his cock pulsing inside Keats as another wave of sensation moved through Keats.

Colby had promised to send Keats flying, but he'd launched him into the fucking stratosphere instead.

When they both quieted, Keats reached out and wrapped his arms around Colby and pulled them both into a heap in the sheets. They were a mess. They were spent. It was perfect.

Keats glanced at the window. Well, almost.

After their night together and a long, hot shower, they both should've been exhausted. But Colby's mind was whirling as he lay in the bed, Keats stretched out on his back next to him. And from Keats's constant shifting of position, he could tell Keats was struggling to settle down, too.

"What are you worrying about over there?" Colby asked, keeping his eyes closed. "I can hear you thinking."

Keats was quiet for a long minute. "Do you miss it being the three of us?"

Ah, *that* question. It could be a sticky one, but he wasn't going to lie to Keats. "Are you asking if you're enough?"

"No," Keats said, moving onto his side to look at Colby. "It's not about that—honestly. I was just wondering if you miss her."

Did he miss Georgia? He missed both of them when they weren't around. "I do."

Keats's eyes looked gray in the moonlight, pensive. "Do you think she's doing what I was trying to do?"

Colby glanced toward the window, trying to picture what Georgia was up to right now—probably curled up and sleeping. Alone. "What do you mean?"

"She told me you were falling for me on that first night we were all together. She saw what was happening between us but couldn't see that she was part of it. Do you think she pulled away from us to give us room to be together?"

Colby grimaced. "Y'all are a bunch of misguided self-sacrificing fuckers if that's the case. But no, even if that's in the back of her head, I don't think that's the main reason. I think she cares about us. And I know we could make her happy. But she can't see past the trial. She's protecting herself. And us. There's a big possibility that sicko could walk. If he does, she won't come back here."

Keats's jaw clenched. "If he goes free, that would be the end for her. She'd never feel safe again."

"No, she wouldn't, and this guy has murdered people who are close to her. That's his M.O. So guess who'd be first on the list if she stayed in a relationship with us?"

"I'm not afraid of that shitbag. I wish he'd try to come after us. That'd give me a chance to take him out of her life for good."

Colby rubbed a hand over his face, the urge to tear Phillip apart a recurring one. "Look, I'm with you. But Georgia's not going to risk anyone she cares about. If he's acquitted, she's going to disappear again and not let anyone near her."

Thinking of Georgia all alone, always hiding, locked in some house somewhere again, made Colby ill. And angry. And fucking helpless.

"God. We can't let that happen," Keats said, stricken.

Colby sighed. "I know. And it's hard putting faith in our justice system—especially when it comes to a sociopath who has a lot of money and legal knowledge."

"That's like putting faith in fucking roulette," Keats complained. "Maybe we should just go to Chicago and hunt that bastard down ourselves. Accidentally run him over with your truck. Oops, sorry, motherfucker, good luck in hell."

Colby snorted. But then got quiet. Thinking . . .

Keats nudged him in the side. "Okay, you know I wasn't serious, right?"

Colby tapped his fingers along his sternum, thinking, thinking, thinking. How hard would it be to make a trip to Chicago and draw Phillip out? If the guy was so fixated on Georgia, knowing she was seeing someone else could drive him to the brink again. If Colby could get him to try something, set him up, maybe he could get the guy caught in the act.

But before he could open his mouth to share his thoughts with Keats, there was a loud banging at the door.

"What the fuck?" Colby said, pushing up on his elbows and peering at the time. Past midnight.

"Want me to go?" Keats asked, sitting up.

"Nah, I got it." Colby swung his legs to the side of the bed and reached down for his discarded pants and shirt. He stood and tugged both on. The banging came again. "Goddammit. I'm coming."

He headed into the hallway and strode toward the front door, his body prickling with worry. Midnight house calls were never a good thing. The last one he'd gotten was when he'd been notified his

brother had been arrested. He didn't turn on any lights to alert anyone he was home. If the face on the other side of the door wasn't a
cop, a firefighter, or a friend, the door wasn't getting opened.

But when he peered through the peephole, he went for the lock
instantly. He swung the door open. "Georgia?"

She shook her head and tears leaked out her eyes.

"Baby, what's wrong?"

But before she could answer, he heard the gun cock. A man
stepped out of the shadows from behind her. "Better let us in, *baby*."

THIRTY-NINE

Georgia couldn't stop shaking as she crossed the threshold into Colby's house, Phillip's gun at her back. Her panic was pounding at the doors, trying to break through, but she forced her breathing to stay steady. She couldn't risk passing out right now. No way was she leaving Phillip alone with the guys. She'd done everything she could to persuade him not to come over here. But he'd been watching and waiting. As always, he'd done his homework.

At some point in the last month, he'd broken into Leesha's office and had gotten Georgia's information. And he'd sent a private investigator down to Texas to see what Georgia was up to. Georgia could imagine exactly how Phillip had reacted when he saw a photo of her with another man. He wouldn't have been able to get it out of his mind. And clearly, he hadn't been able to resist the need to come down here and take care of it.

Because he knew how to take care of these things.

He was going to make her watch while he killed the two men she loved.

Colby backed up, hands out to his sides but his eyes trained on the man behind her. "Let her go, Phillip. I know you don't want to hurt her."

Colby's voice was strong and forceful, and she knew he was trying to alert Keats, who had to be somewhere in the house. His bike was outside. But Keats stepped out from the hallway a moment later, unaware of what he was walking into.

"Stop right there, asshole," Phillip called to Keats, shifting to Georgia's side and aiming the gun at Colby. "I'd hate to accidentally pull the trigger."

Keats lifted his hands, his shocked gaze flicking to Georgia's.

Phillip gripped the back of her neck. It was a place Colby often held her, and she hated Phillip touching her like he owned her. He squeezed tight. "Don't you see what's going on?"

"Please let us go," she pleaded. "You don't need to do this. Please."

"No!" he roared, shaking Georgia like a dog shaking a rag toy. "I need you to *see*. Open your eyes and look at what's going on here, sweetheart." He said the last word with a cloying, whiny tone. "This scum you're giving yourself to cares about you so much that when you're not around, he's sticking his dick in whatever hole he can find."

Georgia's teeth rattled in her head from the shake. But she'd registered enough of what Phillip had said to realize he hadn't put it together that Georgia had been seeing both Colby and Keats. Phillip thought he was uncovering her cheating boyfriend. So his hatred was going to be directed at one person. Colby would be his target.

"I didn't know," she whispered, scrambling to get him calm. "You were right. I should've never dated someone else."

"You let him disrespect you, Georgia," he said, seething. "All that I've done for you. All that I was willing to give you, and you let some redneck cocksucker in your bed. What is wrong with you?"

She could see what it was doing to Colby and Keats, to see her treated this way, but she prayed they wouldn't do anything stupid. If they made one move, Phillip wouldn't hesitate to kill them.

"I'm sorry, Phil," she said in her most placating voice. "I needed to take a break. I needed to get some perspective. I wasn't ready for a commitment yet. You deserved more than I could give you." The words made bile rise in the back of her throat, but she pushed past it and kept talking, frantic. "But if you hurt them, you'll go to jail for good. There'll be no way to hide it. And we'll never be together.

I know what you did before was just to show me how much you wanted to protect me. But you don't need to protect me from these guys. It was just a fling. I was using Colby. We can leave and go back home now. I won't testify in the case, and we can be together. No one has to know you came down here."

Phillip's hold on her neck softened ever so slightly, and he gave her a narrow-eyed look. "How do I know you mean any of that? You've lied to me before."

She blinked rapidly, searching for something, anything that would keep his focus on her. "I can show you."

His gun arm wavered a bit. "How?"

"Colby has . . . restraints. We can tie these two up and then go to the bedroom." She fought hard to keep her voice from shaking. "It's been so long since you've touched me. Let me show you that I mean it."

The flare of interest in his eyes was hard to miss. "Now you're talking some sense, sweetheart." He ran a knuckle over her cheek with his free hand. "And won't it be fun to let these two watch while I show them how a real man takes care of his woman?"

Colby made some low noise deep in his chest, but she forced herself not to look his way. She wet her lips in what she hoped was a provocative way. "I'll help you tie them up."

Phillip released her neck, his eyes on her but his gun still aimed at Colby. "Take off your clothes, sweetheart. I want to trust you, but I also want to make sure you don't try to do something stupid like run."

Panic welled up in her gut, but she wouldn't let it take hold. If she gave in to that now, she had no shot. "Of course. Whatever you want."

She moved slowly so as not to startle the dude with the gun and tugged her T-shirt and sleep shorts off.

"Panties, too," Phillip said, his voice dropping lower.

Working hard to keep her hands from shaking, she pushed her panties down and off. She knew when she looked up again that this was her best chance. Phillip was getting aroused. And an aroused man was a distracted one. She gave him her best come-hither smile. "Let's go to the bedroom."

"Lead the way, love." He waved the gun at Colby and his voice hardened. "Follow her. Try anything or touch her and it's a bullet in the back."

Georgia could tell it was taking everything each man had for Keats and Colby to obey Phillip, but she sent them both pleading looks that she hoped conveyed that she needed them to play along.

They all filed into the bedroom, and it was clear that Colby and Keats had definitely had a fun night. Cut rope was on the floor and a riding crop was on the top of the dresser. The sheets were in a tangle. A pang of sadness went through her that she hadn't been part of it. That she'd shut them out.

"Jesus Christ," Phillip said, taking in the scene. He waved the gun at Colby and Keats. "On your knees, hands where I can see them."

The men obeyed but not without shooting Phillip death glares. *Please, please don't try to be a hero.* That was the plea she tried to channel their way over and over again. Phillip was expecting the guys to try something. He probably wanted them to try just to make it more fun to kill them. The guys had to play along or they were all done.

If there was any chance at getting out of this, it was up to her. She was the only one Phillip had a hair of trust in. She went to Colby's chest of drawers and pulled out handcuffs. "These should work, right?"

"Are there two sets?"

"Yes."

"Cuff them with their arms behind their backs."

Revulsion filled her at the sound of Phillip giving her orders. Revulsion and resolve. He didn't have that privilege. For the last year, her whole life had been a daily fight, trying to fix the things Phillip had broken in her. And right when she was getting her feet under her and her confidence back, he was going to waltz in here and act like he had a right to her, had a right to hurt the people she cared about? Fuck. Him. She wasn't going to let him do this to her again.

By the time she made her way over to Colby and Keats, her hands were steady. She kneeled down next to them. "Give me your hands."

Both followed her directions but Colby peered back over his shoulder, whispering. "Don't do this. These don't have a release. We can't get out without the key."

She gave a slight shake of her head. *Don't talk.*

The cuffs snapped in place, securing both of them.

Phillip stalked over and gave the chains a tug. "The real police issue stuff, huh? Sick fuckers. Give me that rope. I want to make sure these two don't try anything."

Georgia stood, and she schooled her expression into one of cool calm, despite the frantic, careening thoughts in her head. She pictured herself that first night she'd walked over to Colby's house. *I am in control of my body.* She headed over to the discarded rope. It'd been sliced open—like Colby had been in a rush to get Keats untied—but there was enough length to make it work for Phillip's needs. She rubbed her thumb over the frayed edges of the cut ends before handing it over to Phillip.

"While you're doing that, why don't I get the bed cleared off?" she suggested.

He flicked the barrel of the gun her way. "Strip it to the mattress."

Phillip tucked the gun in his waistband and went to work tying the men's ankles and looping rope through the cuffs. This would be her only chance.

She put her back to them, busying one hand with tugging off the sheets. With the other, she opened Colby's bedside drawer, praying she hadn't misheard him that first night they'd spent in his room. And praying Colby hadn't left it somewhere else tonight.

"Something wrong, sweetheart?" Phillip said, his voice too close.

She jumped, balling her hands in the sheets. "Fine."

He stepped closer and peered over her shoulder into the open drawer, which contained a TV remote, a novel, and condoms. Phillip gave a low laugh. "We won't be needing those."

"I'm not on the pill anymore," she lied.

He kissed the side of her neck. "Good. I'd love to have my baby growing inside you."

The shudder that went through her couldn't be stopped, but Phillip must've read it as anticipation instead of abject terror. Fucking sociopath.

He trailed kisses down along her shoulder and she felt the gun, still tucked in his pants, press against her spine with cold certainty. His hands wrapped around her and cupped her breasts. She gritted her teeth and tried to shut her body off from connecting to her brain. This wasn't happening to her. Phillip wasn't touching her. That wasn't what she needed to focus on.

She took a deep breath. "Kiss me."

He made a pleased sound behind her. "You don't know how long I've waited to hear you say that. Turn around, sweetheart."

She spun around slowly, still gripping the sheets in her hands, and he pulled the gun out of his waistband. He set it in the drawer behind her and closed it. "We don't need to worry about that ugliness for now. Come here."

He gathered her to him and his dry lips met hers. She waited until he closed his eyes, which seemed to be the longest second of her life, and then she dropped the sheets and wound her arms around his waist. His tongue parted her lips, and he took her face in his hands. He tasted of cinnamon gum. He'd always tasted of cinnamon gum.

She remembered his breath on her that day in the kitchen. Remembered what happened afterward. Remembered giving the eulogy at her sister's funeral. She ground her hips against him, making soft, sexy sounds, and hit the button on the switchblade.

Phillip's body stiffened for a fraction of a second before she drew her hand back and jabbed with every bit of strength she had. The blade went into his lower back clean. And the scream that came out of him landed half on her lips.

"You fucking bitch!" he shouted, reaching for the point of entry with a crazed swipe of his arm.

She shoved him hard, getting some space between them, and

lunged for the drawer. The knife had stayed lodged in his back when he'd jerked away from her, but there was something more effective she was after. The gun wasn't like the one she practiced with at the range in Chicago. It was heavier, bigger, and had some silencer thing screwed on the end. But she turned around, channeling everything she'd been through, everyone she'd lost, and aimed it right at Phillip.

His fingers were covered with blood, and he had the knife in his hands. He stumbled toward her, cold rage in his eyes.

It was the thing of her nightmares. The vision that had spawned so many panic attacks she'd lost count. Phillip was going to finally kill her. He would win.

He took another step.

She squeezed the trigger.

The gun didn't make a sound, but the body hitting the floor certainly did.

She crumpled to her knees and finally allowed the panic attack to roll over her.

FORTY

Leesha buzzed around Georgia's house with a notepad in her hands and a look of consternation on her face. "Is this TV stand yours?"

"No, it was here when I moved in," Georgia said from her spot on the couch.

Leesha checked off something on her notepad and then pulled a roll of stickers from her pocket. She tagged the TV stand with a blue dot, which Georgia assumed meant *do not pack* for the movers.

"If you give me that roll of stickers, I can help, you know."

"I've got it."

Georgia sighed in frustration. Leesha had insisted that Georgia relax, that she'd take care of everything, but it was driving Georgia a little crazy to be forced into sitting still.

A week had gone by since she'd shot Phillip in Colby's bedroom. The scene still played over in her head every night when she tried to go to sleep. But she tried to chase away the nightmares by reminding herself that Phillip couldn't hurt her or anyone else anymore. She was free. Finally.

But she'd killed a man to get there. Part of that stained her conscience, even though she knew he was a murderer and would've killed her or one of the guys without a bit of remorse. She didn't think any normal person could take someone else's life and not be affected by that. And it seemed people were giving her space or treating her with kid gloves because of it. Leesha, her parents when they flew in to see Georgia the day after, and the boys across the way.

She'd spent a long night in the police station with Colby and Keats after everything had happened. They'd gone through endless interviews while the cops tried to put together exactly what had happened. She'd never been offered coffee so much in her life. It was as if that were all anyone could come up with to do for her. *More coffee, hon?*

All the while the cops were offering it to her, though, she knew they were trying to determine if she'd killed Phillip in cold blood, especially when they'd realized she, Colby, and Keats were all in some sort of relationship. She could already see the headlines in her head: *In an erotic-crazed night, three people took out a scorned lover in an elaborate plan.*

But when the local cops talked to the police in Chicago, the focus had shifted. Phillip hadn't been so careful on his way out of town since he hadn't planned to return. He'd purchased the gun illegally from a police informant. And yesterday, he'd emptied out his savings and had bought a used car with cash.

When the locals searched Phillip's vehicle, things became even clearer. He had a notebook detailing all of Georgia's activity from back when she was in Chicago through now. The most recent entries had stopped using her name and referred to her as *the whore* or *the ungrateful bitch.* Colby was labeled as *the cocksucker.* And beneath the liner of the car's trunk was a bag of cash and two fake passports—one with Georgia's picture on it. All evidence pointed in one direction. Phillip had come down to kidnap Georgia and escape across the border. The police concluded that it was enough to show that Georgia had acted in self-defense. Plus, based on Keats's and Colby's separate statements, it was clear Phillip had forced his way into Colby's home, which in Texas gave the occupants the right to use deadly force.

They'd released all three of them around lunchtime the next day.

She'd been numb and shell-shocked still. And the guys had seemed to sense that she didn't want to talk about it. When they'd gotten into the back of the cop car for the ride home, Colby had put his arm gingerly around her, offering support if she wanted it, and he'd whispered, "You saved all of our lives. I've never seen anyone be so brave."

Keats had taken her other hand and laced his fingers with hers. "I'm sorry we let you down and didn't protect you like we promised."

She'd shaken her head, wanting to tell them that they hadn't let her down, that the very reason she hadn't collapsed into a panic when Phillip had surprised her in her garage when she'd gotten home from running errands was that they'd helped her find her strength again. But she couldn't get the words out.

"He's gone now, George," Keats said softly. "You're free of him."

She'd finally cried then, sagging into Colby's shoulder and squeezing Keats's hand tight.

When they'd arrived at her house, she'd asked them to come in with her. She hadn't wanted them facing the crime scene at Colby's house and . . . she'd needed them there with her. Maybe they'd all needed each other. They'd gone quietly upstairs, showered until the hot water ran cold, and crawled into bed, simply holding each other until sleep finally overtook them.

But the following day had been chaos. The cops had wanted to talk to everyone again to fill in details. Leesha had called to say she was flying in with Georgia's parents. And all the wheels had started turning without Georgia.

Colby and Keats had left with the promise that they would all talk soon. But with everyone visiting and so much happening, they hadn't gotten the chance to do more than check in by phone.

But she'd seen carpets being pulled out and furniture being removed and replaced over at Colby's. She didn't blame him for not wasting any time removing memories of what had happened there. But part of her had seen it as erasing it all. The bedroom that she'd looked in so many times would be different now. And the people on the other side of the window had been changed in ways that could never be undone. She didn't know where she fit anymore—if she fit at all.

Leesha certainly had her own ideas. She'd gone into get-Georgia-back-to-Chicago mode as soon as she'd arrived. And Georgia hadn't protested. Phillip was gone. Her old life was waiting there for her in Chicago. Her house. Her friends. All the things that had once been so familiar and comfortable. But she couldn't find it in herself to get excited about it.

"I was thinking maybe we should do Christmas dinner at a restaurant this year," Leesha said, breaking Georgia from her ruminating. "I talked to your mom, and we're all so excited to get you back home. But no one wants the stress of cooking this year. Not with all that's going on. I've heard that restaurant in the Trump Hotel has a great Christmas menu."

"That's fine," Georgia said, picking a loose thread off the couch.

Leesha paused what she was doing and turned around, hand on her hip, dip in her brow. "What's wrong? You sound like I suggested a meal of cat eyeballs."

"Sorry. It's just hard for me to think about Christmas . . . it's hard for me to think about Chicago."

Leesha stared at her for a moment longer, then sighed. She tossed her notepad onto the coffee table and sat in the chair across from Georgia. "Is this about the neighbors?"

Georgia didn't feel like having this conversation right now.

Leesha shook her head. "Oh, honey, you got attached, didn't you?"

"Please don't patronize me," she said, irritated at her friend's *I-told-you-so* tone.

Leesha flicked her dreads away from her face, a dead giveaway that she was trying to hold on to her patience. "I'm not patronizing you, Georgia. I've met the guys you got involved with. I get it. They're good-looking and seem like nice enough men. But you can't think to really stay here and be in a relationship with two people. I mean, I'm not one to judge what people like to do for fun. And I can see how with everything you've been through you needed a wild escape. But I *know* you." She leaned forward in the chair. "Before everything went wrong with Phillip, when you dated men, you dated with the purpose of finding a partner—a husband. We both date with that in mind. We're planners. You want to get married, have a family, do all those milestones we pin on that timeline in our heads. And neither of us is getting any younger. Hopping in bed with two guys is fine when you're in your twenties and experimenting, but we're grown-ups now. Come on, you know some three-way isn't a sustainable relationship. Staying here longer is just going to mean wasting more time and getting your heart broken anyway. You've had enough heartbreak, honey. I don't want to see you go through more."

Georgia released a long breath, letting go of the retort that had jumped to her lips. She knew that Leesha had nothing but Georgia's best interests at heart. And her friend wasn't saying things that were untrue. Georgia *had* always wanted that neatly planned-out life. She liked the idea of having a relationship like her parents—a long-lasting love and close family. She'd felt safe and loved growing up, and she wanted to create that in her own life. But now when she tried to picture going about finding that, she couldn't stop thinking about the two men next door.

"Maybe I just need some time to clear my head," she said lamely.

Leesha's face brightened with a smile. "Exactly. That's the best medicine. We'll get you back home and on your feet, and you'll see how everything falls back into place." She stood and came over to hug her. "God, I've missed you, girl."

Georgia swallowed past the knot in her throat and hugged her friend back. She'd missed Leesha, too. But Georgia had a feeling when she got back to Chicago she'd miss something else much more.

Georgia's phone buzzed from its spot on the coffee table. Leesha straightened and smiled. "Back to work for me."

Georgia reached for the phone and hit the button to read the text message. One word appeared on the screen: Window?

Her heart leapt. She bit her lip and glanced over at Leesha, but her friend was already back to tagging and marking furniture. Georgia typed back OK and excused herself on the pretense of getting something from her bedroom. Her mind was still whirling about what to do, and she dreaded having to say good-bye to Colby and Keats in a few days, but she couldn't hide from facing them any longer.

When Georgia walked into the guest bedroom, it was a little like stepping back in time. But like all the times before, her heart was pounding and her palms were damp. She didn't know what she wanted to see on the other side of that curtain. Her head was spinning with so much right now. But she knew, if nothing else, she couldn't walk away from this invitation.

She moved over to the window and pulled back the curtain. The sun was almost down, and the lights in Colby's bedroom were glowing. On the other side of the glass, two men stood, waiting for her. They seemed so far away now.

She lifted her phone, expecting it to ring. But instead Colby bent down and came back up with what looked to be big squares of poster board. Keats took the one from the top and held it against the glass.

TOP 10 REASONS CHICAGO SUCKS

Keats dropped the sign and put up another one. Georgia leaned closer to the window, her lips curling upward.

10. IT'S FUCKING COLD
9. PUTTING TOMATOES ON HOT DOGS IS <u>WRONG</u>

She laughed, and Colby handed Keats another sign.

8. NO ONE SAYS "Y'ALL" OR CALLS YOU SUGAR
7. TWO BASEBALL TEAMS—HOW TO DECIDE???
6. THEY DON'T DEEP-FRY EVERYTHING—A TRAGEDY

Georgia smiled wider. Leave it to those two to try to make her laugh right now when she needed it most. Another sign went up.

5. WE WANT YOU TO BE HAPPY
4. AND WE WON'T PRESSURE YOU

She held her breath. Keats dropped the sign, and Colby stepped next to him. They both lifted their white poster boards and pressed them against the glass.

3. BUT THE TWO MEN
2. WHO LOVE YOU
1. ARE HERE.

She stared at the big block lettering, the words blurring when her eyes filled with tears. She pressed her hand to the glass. They did the same.

And for the first time in a week, she didn't feel numb at all.

She looked at their splayed hands, imagined those fingers linked, hands piled on top of each other. Bodies tangled in bed. Mornings full of laughter and teasing, stolen kisses, and naughty comments. Nights filled with warmth.

All along, she'd never really let herself think past getting back to Chicago. She wouldn't allow her mind to go there. Any time she'd felt those feelings developing for these two men, she'd drawn it back in—like a border collie herding escapee sheep back into their pen. Don't get attached, don't get attached. It had become her mantra. But thinking about the two of them now—Colby with his kind eyes and solid presence, Keats with his cocky humor and giving heart—she knew she hadn't kept it in check. Those sheep were hopping around in the wild with giddy feelings—hope, affection . . . love. Especially when the guys looked at her like they did. Like they'd love her forever if she'd let them.

They'd become so much more than the silly *For a Good Time Call* label she'd put in her phone. The thought of leaving them had been tearing her up for weeks. But she still hadn't let herself consider the possibility of staying. Phillip had been such a looming threat overshadowing every thought of the future.

And beyond that, all this time she'd been looking at returning to her life in Chicago like the brass ring. The sign that she was A-OK again, fixed. But now it felt like an empty victory. When she imagined going back, she didn't get excited about that fast-paced city life she used to lead. She felt . . . nothing.

So what would happen if she stayed here?

The question had been knocking around in her head the last few days like a Ping-Pong ball gaining momentum.

Was Leesha wrong? Could Georgia build a long-term relationship with Colby and Keats? Let this wonderfully strange, just-for-fun arrangement become something else? Become real and lasting?

The practical part of her brain always said no. How would three people even go about that? But another part of her rebelled against that. And when Leesha had outlined all the reasons why it wasn't a good idea, Georgia had wanted to go into full debate mode. Who cared if the relationship wouldn't fit into the mold of what everyone expected her to do? Her mother, who had taught women's studies at Northwestern since Georgia was a kid, had always raised her to not give in to gender expectations, to make her own way. She could still remember the talks her mother had given her through her teen years. *If you don't want to get married, don't. A woman doesn't need a man to have a life. If you want kids, have them. If you don't, don't let anyone make you feel guilty about it. You find your own road to happiness, my girl. No one else can tell you what's right for you.*

Back then, Georgia had kind of rolled her eyes at her mother's rah-rah, you-are-a-strong-independent-woman speeches. Mainly because despite her mother's opinions, Georgia had always been a traditionalist at heart. She'd wanted the perfect fairy-tale life— Prince Charming in the castle on the hill. But now her mother's words washed through her, raining water on the seeds Keats and Colby had planted. If she wanted to stay here, she could. She could have whatever kind of life she wanted.

She didn't need some dusty fairy tale. She could make her own new, shiny one.

She didn't need to be scared anymore.

She lifted her phone and hit *For a Good Time Call.*

FORTY-ONE

Colby wasn't sure what to expect when he opened the door to Georgia a few minutes later. He and Keats had done what they could. They'd bared their feelings. Put it all out there. But even if Georgia loved them back, they were still asking a lot.

Even so, when he opened the door and saw her face, saw that brightness in her eyes, a weight that had been pressing down on him since he'd left her the day after the attack lightened a bit. He'd worried that when everything set in, she might be overwhelmed by it. That old fears would resurface. Or worse, new ones would come up. But he should've known better. He'd seen firsthand how unshakable and brave she'd been that night with Phillip. She hadn't flinched. Their girl was softness built on steel.

Well, not *their* girl. Not yet.

Keats sidled up next to him, and Colby could feel the nerves vibrating off him. So much for being tough guys. They were goners when it came to this woman. She could knock them down in one swoop.

"Hey, neighbor," Colby said, keeping his tone neutral in case she was coming over here to give them the big send-off.

"Hey," she said, and glanced down at her feet like a nervous teenager.

He shifted his stance. "How's the packing going?"

She smirked. "Leesha has tackled it like a sergeant implementing a military operation. I am a mere soldier in her plan."

"You can hide over here for a while," Keats offered. "We promise we won't tell."

She smiled then. "I am kind of sneaking over here. She doesn't approve of you two hoodlums who are trying to persuade her friend not to go home."

"We are, indeed, selfish, selfish hoodlums," Colby agreed. "But we couldn't let you go without telling you how we feel. Even if you're still going to Chicago, we needed you to hear the truth."

Georgia wet her lips. "Well, at least now I know your feelings on hot dog toppings. Tomatoes on hot dogs are awesome, by the way."

Colby laughed, the unexpected comment breaking some of the tension.

"Sorry, George, I have to take a stand on that one. No tomatoes. Or that electric green stuff they put on there."

She looked to Keats. "Ever tried it?"

"Don't need to. I know I wouldn't like it."

She gave him a sly smile. "I bet I can convince you otherwise."

Colby tucked his hands in his pockets, fighting the urge to reach out and drag her against him. "Coming over here to cook Chicago dogs for us, then?"

"No," she stepped inside. "I was hoping I could buy you the real thing."

Colby's brows went up.

"How does Christmas in Chicago sound?" she asked, her tone tentative.

"What do you mean?" Keats asked. Colby was wondering the same thing. Was she inviting them up there for an extended good-bye?

She took a deep breath and released it. "You guys stepped out on a limb for me, and I know that wasn't easy. So I came over here to tell you both the truth as well."

Colby braced himself.

"I love Chicago. The city. The culture. The food. I love being close to my family. And I have friends there I miss."

Colby's heart was pounding, pounding, pounding. Oh, shit. Maybe she *had* come over to let them down easy.

She reached out to take both of their hands. "But it's got one glaring negative that I can't seem to get past."

"Yeah?" Colby asked hopefully. "What's that?"

"The two people I've fallen in love with won't be there with me."

"George," Keats said, his voice catching.

"I need to go home to see my family for Christmas. I miss them. And with my sister gone, I think we all need to spend the holidays with each other even more. But I'm going to tell them while I'm there that I've met someone . . . some*ones*. I'm going to tell them that I'm in love and that Texas is where I need to be. And I want them to meet you two."

Colby felt like he was going to break open, the flood of joy and relief like a force of nature moving through him.

"You're going to tell your *parents*?" Keats asked, not hiding the shock from his voice.

Georgia smiled his way. "My parents want nothing more than for me to be happy. And you two make me happy. I've wanted to tell you that for so long. You both totally broke the rules of the fling—making me care about you and shit."

Colby chuckled. "Neither of us has ever been very good with rules."

She squeezed their hands. "I won't try to predict where this is going. And I know people are going to say we're crazy. And maybe we are. Maybe that's okay."

"It *is* okay. We can be crazy together," Colby said, pulling her against him, everything loosening inside him at once.

She gazed up at him, the love in those big brown eyes taking his breath away. "I can't stand having the windowpanes between us. I wouldn't survive a thousand miles."

Keats moved behind her and slid his hands to her waist, pressing his forehead to her shoulder. "God, George, we've missed you so much."

She smiled up at Colby and looped her hand around Keats's neck. "I'm all yours. No expiration date this time."

The words soaked into Colby's soul and lit him up inside. The two people he loved were his now. For good. "We're all yours right back, gorgeous."

His hands moved to her face, and he did the thing he'd been wanting to do for so long. He kissed her with everything he had, finally not having to worry that he would scare her away or that she'd slip through his fingers.

This time he had the real thing. Georgia. Keats.

Love.

He didn't need to take a snapshot. There'd be albums of happy moments to come. Starting now.

He shut the door behind them and locked the world out.

He had everything he needed right here.

EPILOGUE

spring

Georgia adjusted her position in the booth and Colby put his arm over her shoulders, pulling her closer, as they watched Keats practice his song onstage. The small club was empty except for a few employees milling around since the doors didn't open for another hour or so, and she and Colby were tucked away in the corner, trying not to make Keats even more nervous by being front and center.

Pike, Keats's new boss and self-designated mentor, was climbing onstage to give Keats some advice. Keats had been right. That Pike guy bled rock star when you looked at him—bleached hair, eyes that seemed to always be laughing at some private joke, and a smile that promised he could show you things that could turn you inside out. But he also seemed supremely down to earth and laid-back. A live-and-let-live kind of guy.

Georgia watched as Pike put his hands on Keats and adjusted his stance at the mic. The words *own it* drifted her and Colby's way.

"Poor Keats looks like he's going to puke," Colby mused. "I remember the first time I played for record execs. I'd had the flu for a week and almost passed out onstage. Not pretty."

"I wish there were something we could do to help him. He knows he's good, knows Pike wouldn't put his name on the line if he didn't think Keats was worth it."

Colby smirked. "I'm not sure if the nerves are all about tonight.

I think Pike kind of freaks him out. The guy can be intense when he's focused on getting something right."

Georgia glanced up at Colby and poked him in the side. "I think Keats deals with intense guys just fine."

"Who, me?" he asked innocently. "I'm just a big teddy bear."

"Uh-huh. Until the bedroom door shuts." She stretched up to kiss him. "But that's one reason why we love you."

He grinned down at her and gave her a look that made her wish they weren't just in a dark corner but a place with a door to close. She pulled her gaze away and peered toward the stage again. Pike was behind Keats, hands on Keats's shoulders, as he coached him. Keats looked to be taking in every word, a serious expression on his face.

"Damn," she said, considering the beautiful man onstage with a touch of awe. "Look at him. You realize that if he's successful with this music thing, women—and men—will be throwing themselves at him. We're going to have to fight them off with sticks. Even Pike can't keep his hands off him."

Colby leaned back, amused. "Well, don't worry about Pike. He's straight. He's just one of those people who thinks personal space is optional. But yeah, that's the beauty and curse of being in a relationship, especially one like ours."

"What's that?"

"We all have to be willing to fight for it."

She turned in his hold, taking in the way he looked at her, her gorgeous, big-hearted man. Some days she still couldn't believe all she had. She looped her arms around his neck. "I'll always be willing to fight for you two."

"Glad to hear it"—he pushed her hair away from her face—"because we aren't going to let you go either. You're stuck with us."

She leaned into him and pressed her face against his neck, breathing him in. A few months ago that kind of declaration would've sent her running. Guys who didn't want to let her go—no thank you. But now she couldn't imagine wanting anything more. She'd found her space in the world where she fit just right—and it happened to be between these two men.

A few minutes later, Keats wrapped up his practice onstage and headed to the back. She slid out of Colby's hold, watching Keats's retreating form. Everything about his stance said he was nervous as all get-out. She nodded her head toward him. "So I thought of a way we could help him out."

Colby lifted a brow. "Yeah?"

"It's a devious plan."

"Well, then I'm obviously in."

She grabbed his hand. "Come on."

———

"So he's actually here?" Keats asked, anxiety tightening his stomach as he paced back and forth in the dressing room of the club. "Harlen Biggs, the exec from Nashville?"

Colby set his guitar case down and gave Keats's shoulder a squeeze. "Yes. But don't get all twisted up about it. He's a nice guy, really laid-back. He introduced himself to me and Georgia a few minutes ago. Remember, he's already heard your demo tape. He liked you enough to stop in tonight while he was in town."

"I might throw up on my shoes."

Georgia gave him a sympathetic look.

But Colby chuckled and headed over to the counter on the far wall to set the rest of his things down. "You'll be fine. And I'll be up there with you for a few songs at the end, so you'll have some backup."

"Good, you can hold my hair back for me when I puke on the front row."

Georgia stepped over and slid her arms around Keats from behind. She set her chin on his shoulder. "You're going to do great. And I will totally hold your hair back if needed."

Keats turned around in Georgia's embrace and touched his forehead to hers. "You say the sexiest things to me, George."

She gave him a wry smile. "I try. And really, I can't wait to hear you both perform. I've never seen either of you play for this big of a crowd. Well, except for the stuff I saw of Colby on YouTube from back in the day."

Colby turned to her, surprise on his face. "You watched old footage of me?"

She stepped back from Keats and shrugged. "Before we got together, I'd see you leave with your guitar and was curious, so I Googled you."

"See, all this time I thought you were dating me for me. Now I know you're after me for my former dive bar fame," he said with a sigh. "I feel so used."

She strolled over to him and patted his chest. "Oh, babe, don't worry. That's not what it's about at all. I'm using you for your killer body and your hot boyfriend."

He laughed and hooked an arm around her waist. "I can live with that. He *is* pretty hot."

They both turned and peered Keats's way. And it was *that* look. He backed up and picked up his guitar case, using it to block. "Oh, hell, no. There are all kinds of people outside that door. And we don't have time. And I need to focus. I'm too worried to—"

Georgia's eyebrow arched. "Sounds like someone needs to relax."

Colby's smile was slow as he walked over to the dressing room door and locked it. "I think you're right. Good thing I know a few tricks."

Ah, shit. Keats knew then resistance was futile. When either of them looked at him like that—like he was the only thing they wanted in the world—he couldn't think straight. "I'm on in fifteen minutes."

"Unbutton your jeans, Keats," Colby said, looming large against the door.

Keats's dick jumped to attention like it'd never been touched in its life and this was its one and only chance ever to get off.

Fuck, fuck, fuck. Now he definitely couldn't walk out onstage. He set aside his guitar and his fingers fumbled with his fly.

"Pull your jeans down and brace your hands on the edge of that counter," Colby said, nodding toward the far wall.

Keats strode over to the counter with the long mirrored wall, his nerves about the performance morphing into something much, much more pleasant. He shoved his pants and boxers to his ankles, freeing his erection, and locked his fingers around the edge of the counter. The counter was low, so he had to bend over a bit, which he knew was Colby's intention. The guy couldn't resist putting Keats in a vulnerable position. And Keats couldn't stop himself from loving the way it felt to be at his mercy. At both their mercies. Georgia had taken to switching roles back and forth pretty easily. Keats lifted his head, finding his own reflection. He almost didn't recognize himself—flushed-faced, determined, and in full surrender.

Georgia walked over to him, meeting his gaze in the mirror. She smiled and dipped beneath his arm until she was right in front of him. She took his face in her hands and kissed him softly, the slow twining of their tongues unwinding more of his nerves. She pulled back and touched a finger to his lips. "Let's take care of those jitters."

She slid down his body as she lowered herself to the floor, and when she got to her knees, Keats decided he didn't need to die to go to heaven. He'd somehow found it in the mortal world with these two amazing people. He had no idea how he'd gotten so lucky, but he wasn't in the mood to question it. He groaned deep when Georgia wrapped her lips around him and took his cock inside her mouth.

Colby stepped up behind him and dangled a red bandanna in front of his face. "Open up. That door's thin and no one needs to know what your pre-performance ritual is."

Keats opened his mouth, and Colby created a makeshift gag.

"If you need to safe out, spit out the gag or use your hand to take it out."

Safe out? What exactly was Colby planning? It wasn't like he had a flogger lying around. But Keats should've known not to doubt him. Because when Colby stepped back, Keats could see him holding a towel in one of his hands.

Keats might've mustered up the energy to be worried, but right at that moment, Georgia ran her tongue around the tip of his cock, and Keats suddenly didn't care about anything at all.

Colby flicked the towel with sound-barrier-breaking speed, and the wet corner of the terry cloth snapped against Keats's ass with a surprisingly potent sting. He bit into the gag, muffling the *oomph* sound that tried to escape, and a fiery burn bloomed over the spot that had taken the brunt of the impact. *Holy shit.*

Keats had been snapped with towels in locker rooms before. It had never been a pleasant experience. But when Colby flicked again, the loud *crack* reverberating in the small room, and hit the back of Keats's thigh, Keats had to grip the edge of the counter to keep his knees from sagging. Colby continued to pepper Keats's ass and thighs with lightning-fast pops from the towel, and Georgia continued her slow, sensual assault one lick at a time. The combination was deadly good.

Keats broke the rules, reaching for Georgia with one hand and threading his fingers in her hair as she moved. Up until this point in his life, he'd never believed girls really liked giving head. They did it to be nice or to impress a guy. But with Georgia, he believed that she really did take pleasure in giving pleasure. She never rushed things and seemed to relish the experience. He could relate. He went into the same headspace when he went down on her or Colby. Maybe it was the submissive thing. He wasn't sure. But he'd never had any woman make him feel so comfortable, so free to enjoy the moment.

And the combination of that mind-bending pleasure mixing with the relentless blows of Colby's evil towel had Keats on the verge in mere minutes. His entire backside was on fire in the best way possible, and he'd no doubt feel that burning all through his performance. The thought turned him on even more. No one in the audience would know that as he stood there he was wearing Colby's marks on his ass and Georgia's lipstick on his dick.

"Open your eyes, Adam," Colby said, close to Keats's ear.

Keats hadn't even realized Colby had stopped the beating, his brain buzzing too much. But his eyes popped open immediately at the command. Colby pressed against Keats's back and met his eyes in the mirror.

"Watch what we do to you," Colby said quietly. "What you do to us."

Colby slid his hand over Keats's ass, rubbing the marks and tracking lower. He cupped Keats's balls and ran his fingers along the base of his dick. Georgia's mouth enveloped both Keats's cock and Colby's fingers, getting everything slick. Then Colby traced backward with wet fingers. He found Keats's rim and put pressure there with his fingertips.

Keats groaned behind the gag. Spit didn't work quite as well as lube so Colby was careful with him, but when a fingertip breached the ring of muscle, Keats rocked forward on his toes.

Georgia made an *mmm* sound and increased her pace and pressure. Keats tried to hold on to the image in the mirror—Georgia's curly-haired head bobbing at his waist and Colby watching every moment, his attention bouncing between Georgia and Keats's face as he slowly pumped one finger inside Keats—but there was no hope for Keats to keep his eyes open.

The need to come was blasting through him, pounding against his resistance. He put everything he had into holding on. But when Georgia took him to the back of her throat and Colby found Keats's sweet spot, everything fell apart. Keats's teeth ground into the bandanna and his release jetted out with so much force, his thighs shook. Georgia held on to him, taking everything he had to give, and Colby didn't ease his finger out until Keats was gasping for air.

Georgia ducked out from her position, and Keats collapsed onto his elbows, panting hard. He spit out the gag. "Jesus Christ."

Colby tugged Keats's underwear and pants back up and patted him on the ass none too gently, right over a spot where Keats knew welts were probably rising. Fucker.

"Five minutes until you're on, kid," Colby said cheerfully as he went over to the sink and washed his hands.

Keats shook his head and smiled. "Well, I don't want to throw up anymore. But now I'm not sure I can remember my name much less any songs."

Georgia laughed. "Just know that your number one fan is out there in the audience. And I don't care if you forget the words."

Keats turned to her and cradled her face in his hands as he gave her a good, long kiss. He could taste himself on her tongue, and suddenly he was regretting that he had to leave her behind and not return the favor. "You are the best girlfriend ever. In case I haven't told you today."

She smiled. "If anything goes wrong, I'll take one for the team and flirt with this record guy to make sure he gives you a second chance. Or with Pike since he can pull strings for you."

"Oh, hell, no. No flirting, George. I'd rather not get the shot than have to compete with some rock-star drummer."

She smirked and gave him another quick kiss. "There's no competition. I don't need some rich guy or a rock star. I make my own money. And I already have my two badass country singers. That's all I need."

The way she said it made warmth bloom deep in Keats's chest because he knew she truly meant it. Like some dude who women literally fell over themselves to get to had no chance at turning her attention away from Colby and Keats. "I love you, George."

She gave him another quick kiss. "I love you, too. Now go out there and show them how amazing you are."

Georgia was buzzing with the energy from the night as the three of them made their way up the driveway. The neighborhood was quiet and still around them, making it feel like they were the only ones in the universe right now. Just them and the stars.

Keats came up behind her, lifting her off her feet and spinning her around. "I feel like I could run a marathon right now."

She laughed, trying to keep her voice down and failing. "I know what you mean."

Keats had killed it up there onstage. The guy who'd been nervous and stiff during practice had disappeared and the performer had emerged. He'd had the club in the palm of his hand—especially the female segment of the audience. And the record executive had been enthusiastic after the performance, wanting to talk to Keats more and even interested in some duet material from the songs Colby and Keats had performed together. Nothing was inked yet, but it was a great start.

Keats set her down, and Colby wrapped his arms around her from behind, moving them into the shadow by the garage. "I don't feel like running a marathon, but I can think of some other things we could do to burn off energy."

"Charades?" Keats suggested.

Georgia turned her head. "Monopoly?"

Colby grunted and his hand slipped under the hem of her shirt, tracking over her belly. "Smartasses."

Keats's eyes followed the movement of Colby's hand, and his teasing expression melted into something more base. "Well, there are some other games we could play."

"Agreed," Colby said next to her ear as he let his hand dip just a little below her waistband. "I'm thinking that How Many Times Can We Make Our Girl Lose Her Mind in One Night could work."

Keats closed the space between them and pressed his body up against hers, his hips bumping the hand Colby had against her. "Best game ever."

Colby kissed the back of her neck, and Keats leaned forward to take her mouth. She closed her eyes, falling into the sensations of being caught between the two of them. They could overwhelm her in an instant and she loved it, loved losing herself to the moments where it was all roaming hands and warm bodies and whispered words.

Both men were growing hard against her as they stood there, making out in the dark corner of the driveway. Her insides turned molten. She wasn't sure she could ever get enough of these two. Every time they touched her, it was like her body was starved all over again, like she'd never been touched before.

Colby kissed the spot behind her ear, sending goose bumps down her neck. "Maybe we should take this inside."

"Good idea," Keats said, pulling back and smiling. "Wouldn't want to disturb the neighbors. They may want to join in."

Georgia laughed, but when they took her by the hand, and she turned to look back at the house that had been her prison for so long, she saw a shaft of light fall over a face in the window. Her old hiding place.

Her breath caught for a moment, but then their new neighbor, an older lady who'd moved into the house after Georgia had vacated it, lifted her hand in a little wave as if to say, "Don't mind me. Go on and do what makes you happy."

And Georgia couldn't help but smile and give a wave back.

Because she was.

Finally, she was the scene on the other side of the glass. She was one of the happy ones.

She was theirs.

Dear Reader,

First, thanks so much for reading Nothing Between Us! *I hope you had fun watching Colby finally get his happily ever after. But don't close the book yet because* wait, there's more! *(said in my best infomercial voice). I have a special bonus Loving on the Edge story for you.*

"I Surrender" is a story I've been hoping to write for a long time. For those of you who've read Caught Up in You, *you might remember Hawk, Kelsey's football player client who was hiding his submissive side from his girlfriend, Christina.*

Hawk and Christina popped into that story and had their own subplot—something I'd never intended originally. But Hawk was such an interesting guy—alpha male but harboring a submissive side, sweet but tough, and totally in love with his girlfriend but ashamed—that I knew when I finished Caught *I had to find out more about how he and Christina worked through things.*

"I Surrender" is their story. I hope you enjoy reading their journey as much as I enjoyed writing it. Also, find a sneak peek at Pike's book, Call on Me, *at the end.*

Happy reading!

Roni

ONE

Christina

"Hawk! Hawk! Hawk!"

The male chanting comes from across the room, and I try to ignore it. But I can't look away from my boyfriend downing his God-knows-what-number beer in front of the cheering group of his fellow football players. Hawk's throat works as he tips back the bottle—*glug, glug, glug.* Ugh. Most of the time I think he's one of the sexiest guys I've ever laid eyes on. Right now? Not so much.

He chugs the beer in one go and then roars with victory. All the guys chest-bump him and exchange high fives. Jesus. I feel like I've stepped out of my life and entered some Judd Apatow bro movie. I want to go over and smack Hawk in the back of the head. I sip my Coke instead.

My best friend, Amaya, shakes her head and sends the group of guys an annoyed look. "I don't know how you put up with that crap. Give me a geek any day over the meatheads. I don't care how hot their bodies are."

I frown, still watching the antics. "Hawk's only like this when he's around them and drinks too much."

Which seems to be every weekend lately.

Amaya purses her lips, which still have bright pink lipstick on them despite the long night of celebrating the end of the football season with half the campus. "Chris, you sound like some girl who says, 'He only beats me when he's wasted.' Please don't be that girl."

Ha. A sound escapes the back of my throat. If she only knew. "Hawk would never hit me."

No, my dear boyfriend prefers to be the one taking the hits, not dishing them out. Not that anyone would ever guess that by looking at him in all his broad-shouldered, football-star glory.

Amaya blows her bangs out of her eyes. "You know what I mean. I know you love him and I've seen him be sweet with you, but he's barely talked to you tonight. He's the one who wanted you to come to this party, and then he bails on you to be the chug-a-lug king. Fuck that."

I sigh, unable to refute her observation, but not wanting to agree with it either because talking bad about Hawk makes my chest feel tight. I know he isn't normally like this. I know he's having a rough time lately, and we're trying to figure things out together. But I also know that since we've made changes in our relationship, things haven't been going as smoothly as I hoped.

I thought when I discovered that my sweet, loving boyfriend was into kink and happened to be a submissive that I could roll with it. We love each other, so we should be able to tackle anything together, right? But even though I've been training to be his domme and have learned a lot of things, something's not quite clicking. Hawk is all gentle and sexy and willing when we're alone. But when he's with friends, he's acting like Mr. Macho Asshole, which doesn't make any sense. Before I discovered his secret, he'd had no problem being sweet to me in public, doting on me even. But now it's like because I have control behind closed doors, he wants to strut around like he's the man with a capital *M* when we're other places.

And it's not as if I need or want him to be submissive to me in public. I know he's a tough guy and an alpha male. I get that. I like that. It's part of what drew me to him in the first place. But I'm also getting really tired of being ignored like this and then being responsible for dragging his drunk ass home afterward. This shit has to stop.

Hawk runs a hand through his disheveled blond hair and one of his friends hands him a shot of Jack Daniel's. *Oh, hell no.* I hand my drink to Amaya. "Hold this for me."

She takes my cup and gives me a nod. "Go get 'em, girl."

I push to my feet, smooth my dress, and stalk over to the other side of the room. Dustin, one of Hawk's friends, catches sight of me first and his *oh-shit* expression appears. I must look as pissed as I feel because Dustin nudges Hawk before Hawk can lift the shot to his lips. Hawk turns my way, and his eyes widen.

I know I'm wearing my mistress face. *Yeah, be afraid, sweetheart. Be very afraid.*

I stop at the edge of the group, ignoring the juvenile *ooh, someone's in trouble* quips from the other guys. "Hawk, I'm ready to leave."

Hawk stares at me for a moment, and then his mouth curls into a drunk, lopsided smile, those stormy blue eyes of his hooded. "Aw, baby, come on, it's early. Why don't you have a drink and relax? We've got a lot to celebrate."

"Yeah, *baby*," one of the guys says, and puts his arm around my shoulders, his beer-and-Doritos breath hitting me with full force. "Chill."

I glare at the guy and shrug from beneath his arm, making his cup of beer slosh in his other hand. "Get off me."

"Damn, dude," the jerk says, backing up and scowling at the beer that spilled onto his jeans. "You need to get your chick under control."

"Do what?" I say, and look to Hawk, who usually doesn't let anyone get away with being rude to me.

"Come on, Chris, calm down. You don't need to be such a bitch about it," Hawk says, his words slurring as he moves closer.

I straighten, my skin going cold. *Bitch.* Hawk can be a Neanderthal when he's drinking. He can act stupid. But never in our relationship has he ever called me a bitch. It was my father's favorite word to throw at my mom when he was trying to make her feel like shit, and Hawk knows how much I hate it. This is so not going to work.

I move into his space before he takes another step and jab my finger to his chest. I have to look up because my five-five is no match for his six-two, but I know you don't need size to intimidate. Lady K at The Ranch taught me that. "Call me that again, Hawk, and see what happens. See me walk right out that goddamn door alone."

He frowns, some awareness coming back into his eyes, and a veil of worry moves over his face. "Wait, what? What did I call you?"

I take a deep breath. Okay. He's drunk. He's out of his head. I see that. But it doesn't mean I have to like or accept it. I grab his hand and tug him away from the group. Some of his normal instincts must be kicking in because he follows me without protest. The other guys are watching, so I keep my voice low and my focus on my boyfriend. "Hawk, you're drunk, you're acting like an ass, and you're . . . hurting me. You're hurting *us*."

Those killer blue eyes of his go soft. "Baby, I didn't mean anything. I'm just having a good time—"

"Like you've had every weekend these past few months? You know how many times I've had to help you walk into your apartment lately?"

His eyes glint with something ugly. "You're not my fucking mother, Chris."

I rub the spot between my eyebrows, a headache brewing there, and take another breath. "No, but I'm your girlfriend. And I deserve better than this."

He scowls. "Just because we play games in bed doesn't mean you get to tell me what to do outside it."

"Is that what this is about? You proving you're still the big man? Because remember who wanted me to be in that role. I didn't ask for this."

Frost hardens his features, the man I know disappearing beneath the icy layer. "No, you didn't. I'm the fucked-up one, right? You're just taking pity on me."

I stare at him, the barbed words puncturing me at first, then pissing me off. I want to shove him, pinch him, do something to knock some sense into him. But I know he'll like that too much. "Are you being serious right now?"

He shrugs and looks away.

"Fine. If that's what you think, then go back to your friends."

"Whatever, Chris." He turns on his heel and heads back toward the group. I'm almost ready to end everything right there, but then he looks back over his shoulder and this forlorn look passes over his face—this anguish. He covers it quickly, but I see it. I *feel* it. Right in the center of my chest.

And that's when it sinks in. What Hawk said is exactly what he believes. He thinks he's fucked up and that I'm doing this whole power-exchange thing because I feel sorry for him. Goddammit. I thought we were past this crap. I mean, yes, when I found out how he is, I was a little freaked-out. Who wouldn't be? But I'd been willing to give it a try. And after training with Kelsey and learning more about the whole lifestyle, I've actually been enjoying the role. It's nice that everyday me—the play-by-the-rules girl who's going to school to be an elementary school teacher—can take off that hat and become something totally different at night with my boyfriend. A hot, sexy guy wanting to serve me and indulge my every whim? Yes, please—one heaping order, thank you. I'll take that any day over some guy who wants to be aggressive and gropy in bed.

My last boyfriend, Bryan, had been the other type. Lots of steamrolling make-out sessions and him murmuring directions that I guess were supposed to be sexy—*I know you like that, baby. Yeah, do it just like that.* And he seemed to have no conscious control of his hands once he was turned on. It was a free-for-all—him grabbing whatever was available. Sex with him had been like engaging in hand-to-hand combat. Not my idea of a good time. But I think we just weren't a good fit. He's had no shortage of girlfriends since we broke up, so someone's into that kind of thing.

The whole experience taught me that the bossy bad-boy types didn't work for me at all. Nope, what works for me is the sweet, protective guy. The guy who, despite confidence in other areas, may be a little shy when it comes to girls. There's something so endearing about that. And when Hawk, this big, burly football player, had found me working a late shift in the university library and had offered to help me shelve books so I could get home earlier, I'd been hooked.

At first, I'd thought he'd made the offer as a come-on for a quick hookup. I'd seen him around campus and knew he was a big deal on the football team. I figured he'd be cocky and suave like the other jocks I'd come across. But instead, he had let me show him how to shelve things and then had been determined to get it done the right way for me. And if I tried to lift a heavy stack of books, he'd rush to my side and take them from me. By the end of the night, it had been *me* who'd asked *him* out.

But that guy I know him to be is disappearing on me—hiding. Something is wrong. And I'm running out of ideas on how to fix it. But if Hawk thinks I'm going to give up that easily, he's underestimated me. Because he may be able to pull that crap with other people—get surly and rude to scare them off—but that's not going to fly with me. You don't give up on the disruptive kid in your classroom. And you don't give up on the guy you're in love with when he suddenly starts acting like an ass. Hawk is going through something, and I need to tackle it head-on.

But even though I'm not ready to give up, I know that I'm out of my depth with this now. This is going to require reinforcements. I head back to Amaya to get my purse. She peers up at me, concern creasing her forehead. "You all right?"

"No. I need to go outside and make a call." I rifle through my purse to pull out my phone. "I'm done with this shit."

She frowns. "I can give you a ride if you need one."

"No, I have Hawk's truck and I'm not leaving yet. But text me if he passes out before I get back. I don't need one of those wasted guys driving him home. He'll be going home with me."

"Got it. I'll keep an eye on him. That guy monitoring the front door isn't going to let any of those guys get their keys back anyway until they sleep it off."

"Good. Back in a minute."

I push my way through the mass of sweaty bodies, cigarette smoke, and booze breath to find the door to the backyard. The temperature outside has dropped significantly since I arrived, and the contrast from the humid body heat inside and the crisp air out here makes me suck in a breath. I wrap my arms around myself, wishing

I'd remembered to grab my jacket. But of course the weather hasn't stopped a few kids from jumping into the pool out back. The blue water glows in the dark, and there are sounds of "Marco! Polo!" and awkward splashing. As I get closer, one of the girls squeals because a guy grabs her from behind and steals her bikini top.

I shake my head. How did I end up at this kind of party? Not that I'm opposed to having a good time. But I haven't exactly run in the same circles with the girls-gone-wild group during my years at Dallas U. My friends are the ones who prefer to go out and listen to a local band in a bar or have margarita and queso night at Dos Gringas. Skinny-dipping in forty-degree weather? I'll skip that chapter of my college experience.

"Hey, baby, why don't you come on in?" one of the guys in the pool calls as I walk by, my heels clicking on the concrete. "Swimsuit's optional."

"Thanks, I'm good," I say, not even glancing his way.

"Aw, don't be shy," he teases, and splashes water my way. "It's Friday night. Even librarians need to let loose sometimes."

My jaw clenches, and I turn my head. The guy's braced on his forearms on the side of the pool, grinning up at me. His dark hair is slicked back but I recognize him. He's a business major who came into the library earlier this week to find sources for a last-minute econ paper. I'd helped him look up a few things and had shown him how to use the printer. He'd seemed like a really nice guy. Apparently, alcohol distills his personality down to the most unappealing elements. He and Hawk have something in common.

Which only makes me more determined to do what I came out here to do.

I ignore pool boy's second invitation and head toward a quiet spot on the other side of the house. But the closer I get to the secluded flower garden, the more my nerves start to invade. Maybe this isn't a good idea after all. Maybe this is going too far. My step falters, but then I look back toward the house. If I go back in, what am I going to do? More of the same, that's what. If I walk back in there right now, I'll chicken out and do what I've been doing. Babysit. Get mad. Take care of Hawk. That's not helping either of us. This repetitive dance is turning us both into people I don't like.

I force my feet forward until I'm in the garden and far enough away that the music and voices won't make it too hard to hear. When I put the phone to my ear, my heart is beating so fast I'm beginning to sweat despite the cool weather. She picks up on the third ring.

"Christina?"

I lick my dry lips. "Yeah, hi, sorry to call, but—"

"Is everything okay?" Kelsey asks, her tone instantly alert in that way people get when woken out of a sound sleep. Damn, I should've thought about the time.

"Yeah, sorry. I mean, everything's mostly okay. I didn't mean to wake you up. But, um, remember how you told me I could call you if I ever needed help with Hawk?"

"Yeah, sure, hon." There's a rustling of sheets. "What do you need?"

I look toward the backyard, making sure no one is close enough to hear me. The plan that's forming in my head is crazy. I know it is. But I don't know what else to do. In my gut, I know that if I don't do something, my relationship is done. Hawk is in sabotage mode for some reason, and he's going to be successful unless I do something extreme. So I swallow hard and tell her exactly what I need.

She's quiet for a long few seconds, and I think she's going to tell me I'm crazy, but finally she releases a long breath. "Okay. Give me the address."

I rattle it off and she makes me repeat a few things.

"How much time do you need?"

I check my watch. It's almost three in the morning. "An hour is probably safe. But I can text you when we get there."

"All right, hon. Just let me know if you need anything before then."

Tension I didn't realize I was holding sags out of me. "Thanks, Kelsey. I'm so sorry I woke you."

"Not a problem. I'm glad you called. Hawk's lucky to have you. Most girls would've bailed on him by now."

"I've thought about it a few times lately. But I love the guy."

"I know you do." I can hear the smile in her voice. "And you know him well enough to know he's not such a dumbass normally. Your instinct to push him harder instead of running away shows a lot. You're better at this domme thing than you think."

I laugh. "I don't know about that. I feel like a poser most of the time."

"Not a poser, a newbie. There's a difference," she says, a smile in her voice. "And really, after all the training we've done, you're not even that much of a newbie anymore."

I lean back against a trellis and close my eyes. "I just hope this works."

Because it could go so very wrong. I could rip all hope of fixing this right from under our feet. But I can't stand by anymore and wait for it to get better.

I love Hawk, and I know he loves me.

This weekend I'll find out if that's enough.

TWO

Hawk

I will never, ever, ever drink again. That's the promise I'm making myself as I lie in bed in the darkness. My brain feels like it's swelled to twice its size, possibly putting cracks in my skull, and I know my stomach is going to turn inside out the second I attempt to move. So much for my teammates' claims that I can hold my liquor better than anyone.

I keep my eyes closed, willing the mother of all hangovers to go away and lying as still as humanly possible. Maybe I can go back to sleep. Maybe I can stay in bed until . . . wait, what day is it? Saturday. Yes, I think it's Saturday. I can't remember most of last night. I know I went to a party. Clearly, there was lots of alcohol. Chris was with me. *Chris.* I groan as the memory rushes back. I did something to piss Christina off. That's where the night blurs for me. I can remember walking away from her but not what the fight was about or what happened afterward.

God, did she leave? Did we break up? I rub my hands over my face. Suddenly my hangover feels like nothing compared to the twist in my gut as I think of all the possibilities. Maybe it happened. Maybe she finally realized that a relationship with me is too fucking complicated. Because God knows it is. Honestly, I'm shocked she's lasted as long as she has. Chris is beautiful, smart, and sweet. There isn't a mean streak in her. And expecting her to change that because my wires are all crossed when it comes to sex isn't fair. I knew it from the beginning. It's why I didn't tell her about my secret when we started dating. Instead, I went to The Ranch, the kink resort my dad (of all people) found for me, and did paid sessions with Lady K. It wasn't a relationship. Hell, it wasn't even sex. But it fed a need in me that I've never been able to fully shake.

Then Chris found out.

The fact that she stayed with me after that, forgiving me and asking to learn how to dominate me, had only made me fall harder for her. But I should've known better than to take her up on the offer. Asking her to change something for me wasn't fair then and it's not fair now. Every time we do a scene, guilt presses down on me like a wet mattress. She's having to play this role for my benefit, and it makes me feel like a selfish asshole.

My thrill in the D/s dynamic comes from knowing I've satisfied and taken care of my girl, and there's no way I'm doing that for my girlfriend by making her perform for me. In a way, it was so much easier when I was doing sessions with Lady K. I could look at it like going for a service or seeing a doctor, clinical. I went in, got dominated, then paid and went home. I didn't have to worry about what Lady K thought of my bent needs. I didn't have to worry that I'd freak her out. I didn't have to stress about losing her because I never had her.

My lungs squeeze. Fuck, I don't want to lose Chris. But maybe I already have. And if I haven't . . . well, I know I need to let her go anyway. She deserves someone who doesn't come with an instruction manual. She deserves someone who lets her be fully herself in all arenas. She deserves better than some jock with a C average who doesn't know how to be normal.

With that morose thought, I rub my sandpaper eyelids and attempt to open them. All of my muscles seem to be working on tape delay, responding a few seconds after I request them to, but when I finally lift my lids, I find I'm in near darkness. It's jarring for a moment. I figured it was morning already, but I can't find my alarm clock shining back at me. What the hell? Did it come unplugged? Maybe the electricity is out.

I turn my head to look toward my window, but instead of the small square one I expect to find, there's a wide one outlined with a yellow glow—like sunlight peeking around blackout curtains. Wait.

I sit up too fast. *Where the fuck am I?*

My stomach protests the sudden movement, and I put my hand over my mouth with a sick groan. *God.* Never. Drinking. Again.

Hungover, possibly dumped by my girlfriend, and waking up in a strange bed? I'm now the poster child for why one shouldn't binge-drink.

"Need a bathroom?" a cool female voice asks from the darkness.

I jolt like I've been hit with a cattle prod. Oh, shit.

No, no, no . . .

If I got in an argument with Christina last night that's one thing, but if I went home with some other girl . . . *Christ.* I'd never fucking forgive myself. I may be a lot of things, but I was not *that* guy.

"I, uh . . ." I shift in the bed, noting that I'm wearing boxers and T-shirt—a sliver of good news.

A lamp clicks on, the shards of light stabbing my eyeballs and blinding me for a moment. I shield my face on instinct, but after a second, I lower my arm, blinking frantically. And what—or rather who—greets me when my vision clears is even more bizarre than waking up to a stranger. I gawk at the lithe blonde perched in the armchair near the end of the bed. She's not in the kind of outfit I'm used to seeing her in—the jeans, deep red sweater, and bare face making her look younger—but she wears the same attitude that used to make me sink to my knees. *"Lady K?"*

Kelsey presses her lips together, more than a little displeased, and leans forward. "Good to know you at least remember your manners."

Confusion swamps me. "What are you doing here, mistress? And . . . where *is* here?"

"You're at The Ranch."

The Ranch? "What? How?"

The resort is a solid hour from town. And I know I didn't drive out here. I gave my keys to Chris last night when we got to the party.

"How?" Kelsey crosses her legs. "Well, it took both Wyatt and Grant to carry your drunk ass out to the car last night. And you didn't wake up the whole way here. You've been out for hours."

Panic moves through me. Wyatt and Grant brought me here? Wyatt is Kelsey's husband and Grant is the owner of The Ranch. Why in the hell would they be involved? "Where's Chris?"

Kelsey's eyebrow lifts. "So you care about that now? You didn't seem to be concerned last night when you called your girlfriend a bitch in front of your friends and pretty much told her to go to hell."

I wince. *Bitch.* Had I done that? That would've hit Chris like a brick to the face. "I don't remember—"

"No, of course you don't," she says, cutting me off with a tone as sharp as honed steel. "That's the allure of getting shit-faced, right? You can do all kinds of crap, let ugly words fall out all over the place and then you don't have to remember them. Believe me, I know. I've ridden that bus. Round and round and round."

I rake a hand through my hair. "I didn't mean what I said. I wouldn't hurt Chris on purpose. You know that."

Kelsey sighs, some of the starch leaving her spine, and I get a flash of the woman instead of the mistress. The one who I know fought hard to get clean and sober not so long ago. She leans back in the chair, looking tired. "I know that, Hawk. But getting drunk and saying it still counts. How often are you drinking?"

"Just on weekends."

"Could you give it up?"

My shoulders tense. "Is this an *intervention*?"

She frowns. "Not necessarily, but you're going to tell me if you have a problem. Because I refuse to stand by and let you go down that path. I'll tie your ass up and drag you to an AA meeting before I let that happen."

I sink back against the headboard. "I'm not addicted. I could give it up."

"Then do."

"Wait, what?"

"That's not a request, Hawk," she says, pinning me with a hard look. "Three months. No alcohol. Prove that it doesn't have a hold on you. If you find you can't do it, you come to me and I'll bring you to a meeting."

Part of me wants to rail against the order. She's not my mistress anymore and has no right. But the other part of me, that bone-deep submissive side, wants to obey—especially when Kelsey has been nothing but good to me. She's not doing it as a power trip. She cares, and that means something.

And really, I don't crave alcohol or think about it outside of parties. It's just sometimes easier when I'm out on the weekends to go along with the group and get numb for a while, especially when it means I won't have to face the awkward should-we-or-shouldn't-we conversation afterward with Christina. I always want to say yes, but then once we're in a scene, that guilt hits me again and I don't know what to do with it. It's probably been a month since I've let Chris do more than some light bondage on me. I always stop her from doing more. I tell her it's enough. Even when it isn't. "Yes, ma'am."

She nods. "Good."

"So where is Chris? Obviously, she's talked to you."

She considers me, drawing her hand over her long, blond ponytail, then tightening the band around it. "What if I told you she left you in my care?"

I look down at my hands, the words punching me right in the stomach. Chris would never do that willingly. Not if she planned on staying with me. She likes Kelsey and has done some training with her on occasion, but there's always been a lingering thread of jealousy because of my previous arrangement with Kelsey. "I'd say that if she left me, I don't blame her."

"Why?"

I scoff and peer up at her. "You know why."

"Because you've been a jerk to her?"

"Well, that, but more the other stuff."

"Because you're submissive," she says, her voice flat.

I shrug. "She's not like us, and it's not fair to ask her to be. Just because Chris and I love each other doesn't mean we're compatible."

She gives me an exasperated look. "Hawk, how can you know if you're compatible or not if you don't even let her give it a real shot? Christina told me what you guys have been doing so far and that you stop her from taking things further. You're too scared to even let her try."

"I—"

"And you're topping from the bottom, which she's letting you get away with because she's treading so carefully." She points a finger at me. "I should take the bullwhip to you for that shit."

I swallow hard. Normally the thought of a whip would get my blood hot, but no interest stirs. All I can think about is Chris. Kelsey doing those things to me doesn't flip that switch anymore. "I'm not trying to top—"

"You're trying to protect her from what you see as some flaw in you. I get it. But she's a grown woman with a solid head on her shoulders and an iron spine. She's not some girl who's going to do something just to please her boyfriend. Give her some credit, Hawk." Kelsey shifts forward. "That girl cares about you and deserves to see the real you so she can decide one way or the other. If the D/s stuff is not for her, I promise you she'll end things. She's not going to put either of you through that if she doesn't think it can work long term. But don't shut her down before you give her an honest chance."

I groan and tap the back of my head against the headboard. "You don't understand. When we started dating, she fell for the guy I am at school—the football player, the tough guy. That's the type she dated before me. You should've seen her last boyfriend. That guy walked around like he was God's gift to the female population."

"But she's not with him anymore," Kelsey points out.

"No, but clearly she was into him for some reason. So when we get into a scene, all I can think about is how let down she must feel, how I pulled a bait and switch on her. I can barely let her do the bondage much less tell her the other things I like—the humiliation stuff, the pain, the denial. I mean, how am I supposed to ask for dark stuff from someone so full of light?"

Kelsey stares at me for a second, then bursts out laughing. "Jesus, Hawk. You've put your woman on quite a high pedestal there. No wonder you can't relax in a scene. You've got it in your head that you're asking some white-robed angel to do these things to you. That'd ruin the mood for anyone."

I clench my jaw.

"And you're wrong about her. Your angelic girlfriend is the one who called me last night to ask if I'd basically help kidnap you. And she didn't blink an eye when Wyatt and Grant carried you out to the car like a side of beef. So you might want to rethink your image of her. Christina is a nice girl. But she's also a force to be reckoned with."

"Is she here?" I can't decide if that'd be a good or a bad thing.

Kelsey points toward the door. "Go shower and get dressed. There are clothes on the counter. Meet me out front in twenty minutes."

"But—"

She puts her palm up and stands. "Shut up, Hawk. We're done talking for now. Unless you call your safe word, you're not in charge while you're here. Get moving."

With that, she strides toward the door and shuts it behind her, leaving me staring after her and more than a little confused.

I guess I'm officially kidnapped. And Chris is behind it.

For the first time this morning, my body stirs with something other than dread.

My girl *is* an angel. But it sounds like today she may be a vengeful one.

The thought gives me more hope than it should.

THREE

Christina

My hands tremble as I smooth them along the confining corset one of the dommes helped cinch me into, and I take a deep breath before stepping into one of the public play spaces at The Ranch—an area I've never dared venture into before. Grant is waiting for me, which should be a relief since I won't be alone in here, but the big cowboy intimidates the hell out of me. Not that he's ever been anything but helpful and friendly toward me, but it's impossible to forget that he's the master of this whole frigging place. That gentlemanly Texas charm is only the surface layer of a very powerful and dominant man. It makes me wonder how I could ever come close to carrying that kind of swagger into a room.

He glances up from his cell phone and notices me standing there. His gaze takes in my outfit in an almost clinical way and he gives a nod—as if he's a high school principal approving dress code—but then his eyes linger on my face. He frowns. "What's on your mind, darlin'?"

I shake my head. "Nothing really."

The corner of his mouth lifts. "Try again."

Dammit. Doms are worse than my psych major roommate—always, always analyzing. "Okay, how about everything is on my mind. I've never done anything in a public room. I feel like everyone can tell I'm inexperienced. And I was just looking at you and thinking I'll never be able to stroll into a room with that kind of intimidating presence." I let out a huff of frustration. "No wonder I haven't gotten things working well with Hawk. He's probably laughing on the inside at my attempts."

Grant smiles then. "I assure you Hawk's not laughing. And I promise all the other worries are very normal ones. Every dom feels like they're faking it for a while. It's a lot for our minds to accept that we're worthy of that role. Who deserves to have that kind of power over another person?"

"Right?" I say, the last question hitting a chord for me. "It seems unfair. It's like getting to be queen when you've done nothing to earn it."

"Ah, but that's the thing you need to realize. You *have* earned that spot in Hawk's life. The power that we have is only as strong as the person who entrusted it to us. You get to wear that crown and wield that authority because he handed it to you."

I look down, the tightness in my chest having nothing to do with the snug corset. "But what if he doesn't really trust me? He holds out that crown for me, but he hasn't let his fingers off it yet. I know he let Kelsey do things that he would never let me—"

Grant steps forward and reaches out to give my shoulder a squeeze. "He's scared, darlin'. With Kelsey, there was no emotional risk. Paying someone to give you a flogging is very different than trusting the person you love to see you stripped down to the most basic parts of yourself. What you're asking of Hawk is to let you see the things he's fought hardest to keep hidden from the world. Not many of us would be brave enough to show someone else that secret part of ourselves, the part we're not convinced is lovable."

I peek up at that, the words resonating. "But how can I show him that I'm not scared of what I'll find? I know who he is. What turns him on isn't going to change how I feel about him. I mean, I already know a lot of those things anyway. Kelsey showed me the forms he has on file here. I know that he doesn't have a lot of limits."

His blue eyes soften and he lowers his hand. "But I'm guessing Hawk doesn't know you've seen all that information."

I blow out a breath. "No. I mean, he gave Kelsey permission to share stuff about him with me. But he thinks I just did a few intro training sessions with Kelsey and didn't get too deep into anything. He doesn't know I've been out here weekly, working with her."

Grant steps back and motions for me to sit with him at one of the tables on the edge of the main play space. Only a few people are in here at the moment and there's no active play going on since this room doesn't officially open for another twenty minutes. I sit down and Grant takes the chair across from me. "I'm glad you've been training so much. It shows me that you take this seriously and are committed to trying this with Hawk. But how are *you* feeling about the training, the role?"

I cross my legs beneath the table, a feat considering the short black skirt I wiggled into, and try not to feel like I'm on a job interview. "It's been a little strange practicing with subs who aren't Hawk, and I'm always worried I'm going to mess something up. But once I get over the initial I-might-throw-up nerves, it becomes . . . a rush. I mean, I'm used to taking charge in a situation. I do student teaching and work in a library, so I'm good with structure and enforcing rules. But this is so different. Knowing I have this guy bending to my will, that he enjoys it and finds my control sexy, is really exciting."

My cheeks go a little hot at that. Grant has probably heard everything under the sun before, but it still feels odd talking to a guy who's probably only a few years younger than my dad about this stuff.

"And has Kelsey had you try out the submissive role at any point?"

"Yeah. She told me it was important to understand both sides. I did one group class and then a private session with your head trainer, Colby."

And I'd protested about that last one before giving in. For one, Master Colby is hella gorgeous and the last thing I wanted to do in any training was feel attraction to someone else. That would feel like a betrayal. But in the end, the worry hadn't been necessary. Colby had kept it focused on training, and Kelsey had stayed in the room. I'd even been allowed to keep my sports bra and underwear on.

"And what was Colby's verdict after training?" Grant asks.

I smile. "He said, 'Good student, terrible submissive.'"

Grant chuckles and leans forward on his forearms. "I would've guessed the same. You're quiet, which some people might mistake for submissiveness, but I know they're not the same thing. And any insecurity you're feeling is more due to your age and inexperience than anything. But, having said that, I want you to make sure that if you go forward with things tonight, you're doing it because it feeds you as much as it does him. This kind of dynamic only works when the reward is flowing both ways. Otherwise, one person will suck the other dry." He folds his hands on the table, his unrelenting gaze holding mine. "Don't try to fit into this mold to save the relationship. Make sure this lights you up, too. If it doesn't, you're not doing right by either of you."

I swallow hard. "I know."

And I do. But how am I supposed to know if this fills me up if I've never really gotten to do it with the guy I love? Sure, I've practiced with subs here under Kelsey's supervision, but I was just learning skills. I didn't feel any emotional connection or investment. And the few things I've done with Hawk have been great, but I know we've barely moved beyond the line of vanilla. We've been playing without taking the bubble wrap off.

But today would be different. If he shows up, I'll find out for sure. We both will.

"You ready?" Grant asks.

I take a deep breath and look toward the mostly empty room, the room that will soon be filled with people. "I have to be."

He gives me a reassuring smile. "Feel the fear and channel it into purpose. And trust your gut. No one in this place knows Hawk better than you do. If you stay focused on him, your instincts will kick in and guide you. He probably won't make it easy on you, especially when he sees what you have planned. But if he's not calling one of his safe words, then some part of him is still on board with you. Don't be afraid to push. Kelsey will help monitor things so you have backup, but I think you're going to do great."

"Thank you," I say, nerves rumbling through me like an oncoming storm.

He checks the time on his phone. "You've still got a few minutes to prepare. And it looks like your partner in crime just walked in."

He cocks his head toward the door as he gets up from his chair, and I turn around. My breath catches at the sight of Julian, the sub I've practiced with a few times, standing in the doorway. He gives me a friendly smile, but I'm having trouble responding because seeing him in just an open robe and a pair of very short, very fitted black boxer briefs is a little too much for my mind to process.

Not to say the view is bad because good God, the man is beautiful. He looks like some dark-haired, dark-eyed Italian swimmer—all long, lean, and tan. But I consider him a friend and seeing every part of him, including the obvious outline of what those shorts are confining, makes my face go hot. The outfit is standard issue around here. It's what many of the male subs wear. But I've only seen him in street clothes. During training sessions, he only took off his shirt. So I'm kind of tempted to put my hands over my face like the one time my friends dragged me to the male strip club, but I manage to keep my composure.

Grant tells me good-bye and nods at Julian as he walks past him. Julian heads my way and his grin only goes wider as he gets closer. His obvious amusement breaks my momentary lapse of brain function. I straighten in my chair. "What's so damn funny?"

He smooths his smile, but the humor lingers in his eyes. "Forgive me, mistress. But you are literally red from hairline to corset. Is something wrong? Would you like something cold to drink?"

"Don't tease me. I'm fine. It's just—well, I expected to see you. Just not . . . so much of you."

He glances down, obviously comfortable in his state of undress, and his shoulder-length hair falls forward. "Would you like me to close the robe?"

"Please. At least while we talk. And tie your hair back. I don't need it getting in the way during the scene."

Okay. Good. The words come out sounding authoritative enough.

"Of course, mistress." He fastens the robe closed and then pulls a rubber band from the pocket of it to secure his hair. "Sorry to be so distracting."

I narrow my eyes. "Don't be cocky, Jules."

A hint of a smirk appears. "Never, mistress. I have better manners than that."

"Uh-huh." I don't believe that for a second. Even for the limited amount of time I've been around The Ranch, I know Julian has quite the reputation. He's deeply submissive and up for most anything, but he knows exactly how enticing he is and uses it to his advantage. Kelsey told me he can run over a mistress who doesn't keep her wits about her because all that charm can let him top from the bottom before you even know it's happening.

He's been nothing but obedient and helpful in our training sessions, but he's going easy on me because I'm new to all this and already have a boyfriend. And though he's a relentless flirt, I know he's not attracted to me that way. He's just one of those people who flirts with everyone.

I stand and adjust my skirt, getting used to both the feel of the snug clothes and the height of the boots I'm wearing. At first, I thought the whole idea of wearing a special outfit was kind of silly, but I can't deny that the clothes give me a layer of confidence I wouldn't feel in my normal clothes. There's power in this getup.

Julian lets loose a low whistle as he gives me an appreciative once-over. "Wow, mistress. You look . . . hot. Has your guy ever seen you in anything like this?"

"No."

Julian shakes his head. "That boy is going to lose his shit."

I glance at the door on the other side of the room, knowing Hawk could be showing up anytime in the next few minutes. "I'm not sure that's what will make him lose it."

Julian turns his head, following the direction of my gaze. "Should I have packed a weapon? I've heard he's a big dude."

I smile. "I think that's why Kelsey suggested cuffing him before bringing him in. Just in case."

Julian snorts. "Great. I volunteer for the mistress with the linebacker boyfriend."

I turn at that and pat Julian on the shoulder. "The sign of a true masochist."

"Only at the hands of a beautiful woman, mistress. Hits from a fistfight aren't quite as satisfying."

My eyebrows lift. "Get into those a lot?"

He shrugs. "I used to box in college and still put on the gloves with the guys at the station every now and then."

"Station?" The question is out before I realize it. "Sorry—you don't have to answer that."

"Nah, it's fine. Most people around here know I'm a firefighter. They had a fire in the kitchen here last year and I kind of outed myself."

I blink, the answer catching me off guard. I hadn't really considered what Julian might be in his everyday life, but I wouldn't have guessed that. I pictured something that required a suit. But maybe despite my experience with Hawk, I still had my own stereotypes about submissive guys. "That's awesome."

"I know."

I take in his deadpan expression and shove his shoulder, laughing. "You're ridiculous."

"Yes, probably. But seriously, if today goes well and your boyfriend doesn't try to kill me, you can tell him if he ever wants to grab a beer or something and chat, I'm game. I know what it feels like to have two sides of yourself completely at odds with each other."

The offer touches me but also makes my heart hurt for Hawk. Is that what it feels like for him? Like two internal forces going head to head in some death match? I reach out and grab Julian's hand, giving it a squeeze. "Thanks, Jules. I'll be sure to do that."

He smiles and cocks his head toward the main floor. "So, mistress, ready to torture me?"

I nod, trying to swallow back my nerves. "Are you sure you want to do this? I know there are much more experienced dommes here tonight who could give you more than I'm going to be able to."

He looks down, his expression going wry. "You're better at this than you think. And knowing I can't cross any lines because you have a boyfriend kind of adds a different flavor to it—like invisible restraints. So believe me, I'm a willing victim."

I tilt my head, considering him. So Julian liked the deprivation part of it. He knows even if he gets turned on, there won't be an outlet for release because I won't touch him that way. Well, then. I know how I can return the favor for him helping me out.

I grab his chin to make him meet my eyes, some reserve of confidence bubbling to the top. "Do you have plans to scene with someone else after we're done?"

He seems surprised by my shift in mood and my hand on him, but he holds my gaze. "No, mistress. Nothing set."

"Good. Then after we're done, you owe me one more hour. When I walk away from you, no one else is allowed to touch you for that hour—including yourself. Understand?"

His dark eyes flare, and I can see I've hit a button. A very good button. The reaction gives me a little thrill. I've actually picked up on a cue and used it effectively. Go, me.

He wets his lips, the cocky firefighter shifting to the background and the submissive part of him kicking in. "Yes, mistress."

I release his chin. "Very good. Now let's do this."

When I head toward the main floor, I'm not yet blazing with the confidence Kelsey or Grant walks around with, but I'm not half as scared as I was when I walked in. Instead of nerves knotting inside me, it's anticipation. My guy will be here soon. And I'm ready to fight for him. For me. For us.

Hawk may think he's shoehorned me into this role, but I'm ready to show him that this pair of boots may have been a perfect fit all along.

FOUR

Hawk

Kelsey has kept me busy all afternoon. I gave up on asking her where Christina is because she gave me a note in Christina's scrawling handwriting that said, *We need to talk. But I'm not dealing with you hungover. See you tonight.* The note had left me with a stab of worry. *We need to talk* were never good words. But I know that I'm the one who fucked up, and I should be thankful that she's willing to talk to me at all. But obviously I'm not going to be allowed to see her until I'm clearheaded and able-bodied. So I've followed Lady K's orders, which involved eating and hydrating, taking ibuprofen to shake off my booming headache, and going on a walking tour of the vineyard side of Grant's property to get my head on straight.

Apparently, Kelsey's cure for my hangover is food, pain relievers, exercise, and fresh air. It's not what I want to be doing at all. Staying in bed all day in the dark seems like it'd be a much better idea. But if I want to get to Chris, I need to play by these rules. It's a test of some sort. And honestly, as I open the gate that leads from the Water's Edge Vineyard back to The Ranch, I do feel mostly normal again—physically at least. Mentally I'm all over the place.

Once I find the right walking path, I head toward the cabin Kelsey told me she's staying in as the sun sinks toward the horizon, orange and pink streaks painting the big Texas sky. Despite my morose mood, it's hard not to be awed by the beauty out here.

Maybe that's why Kelsey wanted me to go on the walk. I pull in a big gulp of the country air and try to get my thoughts together. I know that whatever is going to happen here will be tonight. Chris didn't have them drag me out here for a vineyard tour. But I have no idea what to expect, and that unknown element has me gnawing at my already ragged thumbnail.

Annoyed with the old habit that won't die, I shove my hands in my pockets. Lights are blinking on in the cabins dotting the property, and my gaze goes to the main house. It's a large cedar building that blends into the landscape during the day but stands out more at night with the lighting. People seeing it perched in the distance from the main road would assume it's just a home of a wealthy landowner. No one would suspect that behind those walls, Dallas's kinky elite were having the time of their lives.

I so don't belong here. I'm anything but elite. But my dad paid the crazy high membership fee last year when he found out how I am. Worst day ever. If asked beforehand, I would've told you I'd rather die than have anyone, especially my dad, find out about my twisted sexual fantasies. But when I'd gotten stupid, experimenting with hot wax solo, and ended up with second-degree burns in less-than-ideal places, my dad had figured it out. He'd admitted to me that he'd dabbled in the BDSM scene when he was in law school and didn't want to see me get hurt.

I'm not sure I've ever been more embarrassed, and my dad and I have never talked about it since. But he set me up here, got me the sessions with Kelsey, and, thank God, never breathed a word to my mom. My mother can barely stand to watch me play football since she's always so worried I'm going to get hurt, so I can only imagine how'd she feel about me getting tied up and beaten on a regular basis. But regardless, I'm thankful my dad stepped in back then. Things are still beyond complicated, but at least being at The Ranch has shown me that I'm far from the only one with these desires. It doesn't make me feel normal, but it makes me feel less like a freak.

Maybe my only mistake has been trying to hold on to Chris

through the transition. I wanted the best of both worlds—the girl I love and the submission I need. But maybe it's time to accept that I can't have it all. This is who I am. If I thought I could shut it down and be vanilla to keep Christina, I so would. But I can't. I'm wired this way and those needs aren't going to go away. I've tried to do it the other way.

And that's what I'll tell her when we talk tonight. I'll absolve her of any guilt if she needs to walk away. I can't imagine my life without her, but I also can't justify putting her in this position any longer. Christina's a perfectionist and a hardheaded optimist. If someone tells her something can't be done, she'll do everything she can to prove them wrong. And I think that's what she's been doing with us—seeing it as some challenge from the universe. *Okay, this guy I love isn't who I thought he was, but watch me make it work.*

I don't want her to *make* us work.

"There you are."

I look up, finding Kelsey standing in the doorway of her cabin. Her cheeks are a little flushed and her eyes bright. And with her husband, Wyatt, standing behind her, I'm guessing I know why that is. Wyatt nods my way. "We thought you'd gotten lost in the grapevines."

"Sorry. Guess I was out there longer than I thought." I shift and pull my hands out of my pockets. I've been around Wyatt a few times, and he knows that I used to be one of Kelsey's clients, but it still feels awkward. Plus, it's weird to know that he's Kelsey's dom. I have a hard time imagining her in anything but the dominant role. "Hey, uh, I'm also real sorry about last night. I heard that you had to help carry me out."

Wyatt considers me, adjusting his dark-rimmed glasses, a frown touching his lips. "You had Kelsey worried. I suggest you don't make a habit of that."

I look down at the gravel path, the cool authority in Wyatt's voice ringing through the night air. "Yes, sir."

"Don't give him too hard a time, babe," Kelsey says. "That's my job. And Christina's."

I glance up.

Kelsey has turned toward Wyatt and he's smiling down at her. He kisses the top of her head. "Fine. But don't be too late tonight. I've got plans for you."

Kelsey grins. "Ooh, I love plans."

They share a quick embrace and a lingering kiss, and all I can do is stand and watch and be jealous. It's so easy between them, so effortless. I'm happy for Kelsey. She deserves that love. But I can't help the envy. She and Wyatt don't have to be anything but themselves with each other. It just works.

After they separate and Wyatt shuts the door, Kelsey turns back toward me. "All right, sub, you ready for this?"

"What exactly is *this*?"

She reaches in her purse and pulls out something. I can't see it fully in the twilight, but she tosses it my way and my reflexes react automatically. I catch it. A leather collar. Not the personalized ones that mark you as belonging to someone specific, but the standard-issue ones here at The Ranch that identify you as a sub. "Put that on. We're going to the main house."

My stomach knots. I've rarely walked around the public rooms and never with a collar. Knowing I'm submissive is one thing. Advertising it is another. Which is why I've always stuck to a private room. I can already feel that crackle of embarrassment moving over my skin at the thought of others looking my way and knowing what I am.

"Am I going to get to talk to Chris?"

"Collar on, Hawk."

I swallow hard and force my fingers to loop the leather around my neck.

"And Mistress Christina is busy right now, but maybe if you're a good boy, she'll be ready to talk to you afterward."

"*Busy?*" The word comes out harsher than I intended. But busy at The Ranch without me? Nothing about that sounds good.

Kelsey cocks an eyebrow. "Follow me. No more talking."

I want to ask a thousand more questions, but I know I won't get anywhere. The way I get what I want is to obey, so I will. For now. But if I don't get to see Chris soon, I'm calling my safe word. Enough of this stalling. I feel sick thinking about the kind of conversation I'm going to have to face tonight, and delaying it is not the kind of torture I'm into. Even a masochist has his limits.

So I follow Kelsey up the path toward the main house, fighting hard to keep my mouth shut. There are a few people milling around the paths and a few exchange greetings with Kelsey, but no one talks to me. I'm the one with the collar. I'm the property. It's the role I choose for myself in private, but being seen like this is making me sweat.

We reach the main house, and Kelsey leads me into a small room on the right side of the hallway. It looks to be a locker room of some sort—though swankier than any locker room I've ever been in. Kelsey opens one of the dark wood cabinets, pulls something out, and turns to me. She hands me a folded piece of black clothing. "Strip down and put these on. You can leave your things in one of the lockers."

"What?" I take the item from her and hold it up. It's the smallest, tightest pair of black shorts I've ever seen and there's an O-ring at the waist where a leash could be attached. "Oh, no fucking way."

"Excuse me?" Kelsey says, giving me a look that could melt steel.

"Mistress, I'm sorry," I say, stumbling on my words. "It's just— you can't expect me to walk out in front of people only wearing this."

"*I* don't expect you to. This is your mistress's request. She thought you'd prefer those over the thong or leather jock strap. Though I can tell you, she was *very* tempted by the jock strap."

My jaw goes slack. "*Chris* wants me to wear these?"

"Yes. Tonight I'm doing everything per her instructions. So disobeying me is disobeying her."

I look down at the stretchy fabric again, having a hard time believing my girlfriend would want me to wear this in front of people. God, it's going to be like walking around naked because this scant piece of material is definitely not going to hide any secrets. I can feel my face flushing at the thought. But if Chris wants me in this, that has to mean that this is going to be more than some breakup talk. We're going to scene. A frisson of hope goes through me. Maybe all is not lost yet.

I take a deep breath. "Okay."

Kelsey gives a quick nod. "Good. I'll wait outside for you. Don't dawdle."

She leaves me alone in the room to get changed, which I appreciate even though she used to see me naked in our sessions. It would feel weird now—for both of us, I'm sure. Without giving myself more time to think about what I just agreed to, I strip down and pull on the shorts. The material slides on and hugs every part of me like a second skin. In a way, it feels good, more comfortable than I thought it would be. But after I adjust everything and catch a glimpse of myself in the mirror, my fear is confirmed. There's no hiding anything. The bulge in the front is prominent and the fabric clings so well that I can make out the size and shape of every bit of me. If I get even a little turned on, there will be no detail missed.

I can't imagine walking into a room of people in this. Not that I'm ashamed about my body. The relentless training schedule for football has served me well for that. But I've never put my submissiveness on such display. My throat wants to close. But then I stare at my reflection longer, taking in the collar around my neck and remembering that Christina has chosen this for me. She wants to see me like this. It's not about anyone else here. At that, an electric feeling that has nothing to do with anxiety moves through me.

I inhale a long breath and turn around. I can do this. I will do this. For her.

When I step back out into the hallway, Kelsey gives me a quick glance of approval, then wraps leather cuffs around my wrists, hooking them together in front of me. After she checks that they're not too tight, she beckons me to follow her again. "This way."

I follow a few steps behind, my now-bare feet silent on the carpet. "Can I ask where we're going, mistress?"

"The second floor. There's a demonstration I'd like you to see. We need to hurry, though. We're a few minutes late."

A demonstration. Okay. Maybe that's where Christina will be. Maybe we're going to watch something together.

But when Kelsey leads me into the large playroom, there's already a crowd gathered and the sound of leather on flesh is prominent. The familiar sound moves over me like hot fingers against my skin. *Hell*. I roll my shoulders and try to rein in the involuntary reaction. Last thing I want to do is stroll into the room with a monster hard-on.

But any burgeoning arousal quickly flatlines when we make our way through the group and get a peek at what's happening on the main floor. Because when the last person steps out of my way, I finally find out the answer to the question I've been asking all day. Where is Chris?

Now I know.

Christina, my girlfriend, my mistress, is currently taking a flogger to the bare back of some other dude. A dude who looks to be having a *very* good time.

Everything inside me cracks open, and I rush forward.

But Kelsey must've been expecting my reaction because before I can step past the invisible barrier the onlookers have created, she has a firm hand on my shoulder. "Don't you dare."

She's not nearly strong enough to hold me back, but her hard tone makes me instinctively pause. The guy on the receiving end of my girlfriend's flogger gasps when she lands another blow. I can see his profile, the way his eyes slip closed, his head sagging forward. The fucker is flying high. And his dick is hard as a rock.

Blood rushes through my ears. "Let me go, Kelsey."

"Get on your knees, Hawk," she says calmly. "You need to see this. And interrupting a scene will get you kicked out of here."

I look back at her, seething. "Kelsey, I mean it."

Her jaw is set but there's a sympathetic note in her eyes. "You need to get on your knees or call your safe word, Hawk. Those are your two options. If you want to talk to her tonight, this is the price."

It feels like there's a weight pressing against my chest. Like someone forgot to spot me during lifting and the bar is pinning me to the bench. I don't think I can do this. I don't think I can watch Christina with some other guy—not like this. But when I look back toward Chris, I find her watching me, her gaze burning into mine.

For a moment, we're both held there in suspension, and I can't move or look away. She's wearing full mistress gear—corset, skirt, heavier makeup than normal, and her dark hair is pulled back in a long braid down her back. She always looks great, but right now she looks like she's stepped straight out of just about every fantasy I've ever had about her—sexy, yes, but more than that . . . dangerous. And mean in the best way possible.

My voice comes out in a soft plea. "Chris."

She lets her gaze trace down my body to the barely-there shorts. Unmistakable interest flickers in her eyes, but she keeps her expression smooth. She tips her head my way. "On your knees, sub. I'm in the middle of something right now."

Her voice is quiet but no less compelling than if she'd shouted. I feel the eyes of those around me gliding my way. Now's the time to decide. Am I going to safe out or am I going to subject myself to the girl I love giving some other guy pleasure? The thought makes my teeth clench, but Chris is telling me this is what she wants. This is my penance for last night . . . and so much more. Yesterday, I called her a bitch in front of my friends and treated her like shit. Today I would show her I'm sorry. I take a deep breath and lower to my knees.

Something passes over Chris's expression—relief, maybe—and she turns back to the guy, dismissing me. The other man is glistening with sweat, and his tanned skin is covered with raised red welts from her flogger. My back tingles, memories of exactly how those welts feel awakening my senses and making jealousy burn in my gut. It's been so long since I've had those kinds of marks on me. I've never let Chris take it that far. I didn't even know she was capable of wielding that much strength.

Apparently, I don't know shit.

Chris strolls over to the man bound to the St. Andrew's cross with a swaying, haughty walk, and I can't take my eyes off her. Where has my girlfriend gone? She's been replaced by someone who looks like she's been brandishing this power for years. She steps behind the guy and pulls the band from his hair. Her nails rake over his scalp and he moans softly.

I want to vomit.

"How you doing, Julian?"

"Excellent, mistress. Green," he says, his voice dreamy as he delivers the all-clear signal to Christina.

She drags her fingernails down over the welts on his back, and Julian visibly shudders beneath her touch. "You're doing a beautiful job."

"Thank you, mistress. You're the one who's beautiful."

I'm going to fucking break that guy in two.

"Don't hand out the compliments so soon," she warns. "I'm not finished with you."

She reaches down into her bag and pulls out a long, thin cane. The vicious tool makes my whole body lurch. Son of a bitch. I didn't know Chris could pick a cane out of a lineup much less know how to use one.

She drags the tip over the back of Julian's thigh. "My boyfriend doesn't trust me to use things like this on him." She looks over at me. "Assumes I'm too sweet for such violence."

She flicks her wrist and the cane snaps sharply against Julian's thigh. The guy cries out, and maybe I make a sound, too. Because man, I know what that agony feels like, and I want to be the one feeling it from her. *I'm* her sub. Not some pretty boy with a pony-tail. "Please, Chris."

I don't intend for the whispered plea to come out, but I know it must've when a few people look my way. Chris heard it, too. I can tell by the way she's peering at me. She doesn't move her gaze away, but she flicks Julian again in a spot just below the last strike.

Julian's cursing now, but it's just another form of begging. I can hear the need in his voice, the crazy high of that intense pain twining with the pleasure of all those endorphins. And what is he picturing? Is he imagining sinking his cock into my girlfriend? Or maybe burying his mouth between her thighs until she screams? The thoughts make me murderous, but my body is responding to the scene against my will. My cock is pushing against the thin fabric of the shorts, my heart beating fast and my blood pumping hard. My mistress is something to behold.

And when she hits Julian again, she doesn't look squeamish or scared or uncomfortable. She doesn't look anything like I've imagined she does when she's dominating me. I've always asked her to blindfold me in scenes because part of me has been afraid to see any of that on her face. But now I can see how very wrong I've been. Chris is enjoying this. She likes it. In fact, when she looks down at the marks she's made, a deliciously evil smile touches her pink lips.

And that's when I realize why I'm here, why she's making me watch. She's making me see what I would never let her show me.

She's not just good at this. She *digs* this.

And when she turns and saunters my way, her dark eyes predatory, I know nothing is going to be the same again.

Because I can tell by that gaze that she's not coming for her boyfriend, she's not coming to talk, she's coming for my surrender.

And finally, I'm ready to give it to her.

FIVE

Christina

Holy. Hell. I can't even process how amazing Hawk looks. My body is already running hot from doing a scene in front of all these people. The rush of power is like a drug pumping through my veins. But to see Hawk kneeling before me, that perfect body of his quivering with restraint and his hard-on pressing against his shorts, I almost can't keep it together. He's like some fantasy slave delivered to my doorstep. And all I want to do is drag him away and devour him.

I know it's been torture for him to watch. The anguish on his face when he first walked in hit me hard, and it took all I had not to end the scene right there. But like Grant told me, I had to trust my gut. And something had told me that I needed to push Hawk to a breaking point. I needed to get myself there, too. Because he wasn't going to buy into me being a domme until he saw I was truly capable. And maybe *I* hadn't totally believed I was capable until I took the training wheels off and went for it. But now that confidence is surging through me, and seeing what it's doing to my dear boyfriend is a very, very potent thing.

I step close to him, the tips of my boots almost touching his knees, and grab a fistful of that dirty blond hair. I tip his face toward me. "Ready to play by my rules, sub?"

His eyes lift to mine, and I know I have him. He's right there with me. "Yes, mistress."

I tilt my head. "Why should I bother with you after you disrespected me? I have a very nice sub over there who knows how to properly treat a woman."

Hawk winces like I've slapped him. "I'm so sorry, mistress. Give me another chance, and I'll make it up to you. I promise he can't do for you what I can."

"Oh? And what exactly do you think you can do for me?"

Those blue eyes heat, the smoldering look enough to make me forget the crowd around us, and the most sincere confidence I've ever seen fills his face. "Everything. I would do *everything* for you, mistress."

Warmth coils low and fast in my belly, and I fight hard to maintain my impassive expression. Hawk may be submissive, but there's no lack of male bravado in his gaze. The guy knows how to please a woman. And he knows I'm well aware that he can back up those lofty promises he's making.

But he probably doesn't expect me to exploit the true meaning of that offer of everything. Before now, I've let him off the hook. I've let him guide things even when I was presumably in charge. But not tonight. Tonight, he needs to see that I expect nothing less than his full surrender. He's not going to like what I'm about to say.

I let go of his hair and drag my knuckles over his cheek. "You want to replace Julian tonight, sub?"

He lets out a breath. "Yes, mistress. Please."

I nod and reach down to unhook his cuffs from each other. "Fine. Then grab the cooling cream out of my bag and apply it to Julian's marks. You can release him from his restraints once you've taken care of that. And you will thank him for serving me in your place tonight."

Hawk blinks—once, twice, as if the words haven't quite registered. "You want me to give some other dude a *rubdown*?"

I lean down and get face-to-face with Hawk, channeling every bit of badass I can muster. "You will do it because I requested it of you. And you should be thankful I don't ask you to rub something else for him because I'm sure he'd happily take the offer of a slick hand for some relief right now."

Hawk's eyes go wide, his Adam's apple bobs, and I can feel the shift as if the whole room has tilted beneath us. He's just realized that I'm not fucking around. This is real.

And just when I think he's about to call his safe word, his tense shoulders soften and his eyes get this resolute look. "Of course, mistress. Sorry for the outburst."

I stare at him for a second longer, trying to gauge what's going on, but when he gets to his feet and moves past me to do my bidding, I'm left looking at Kelsey. My expression must be screaming— *Am I screwing this up?*—because she gives me a small smile and leans forward to whisper in my ear. "He's all yours, girl. You've got him. He fights that shame button, but when it's pressed it sends him halfway to subspace."

I peer over my shoulder to where Hawk is now rubbing gel over Julian's back, and I can see from here that Hawk's level of arousal hasn't flagged. And I know for a fact that he doesn't harbor any attraction to guys. So what's got him hard is me, the act of being forced to do what I asked. The sight sends this lightness fluttering through my chest.

I give Kelsey a quick nod and then head back to the main floor to supervise—and enjoy—what my boyfriend is doing. Hawk may not be attracted to other guys, but I can't say that the sight of two very hot, half-naked men touching each other isn't doing it for me. I guess I have my own hidden kinks, too.

Hawk finishes attending to Julian's welts and wipes his hands off on a towel before unfastening the man from his restraints. Julian steps away from the St. Andrew's cross and rolls his wrists and neck. When he turns to me, I have to fight the blush from rising to my cheeks. Julian is damp-skinned, sultry-eyed, and aroused as hell. Even though I see him only as a friend, knowing I did that to him gives me this strange sense of pride. I am mistress; hear me roar.

I walk over to him and put my hand on his shoulder. "Thank you, Julian. You did a fantastic job for me tonight."

He gives me a lazy smile. "Sure you don't want me to stick around, mistress? Lots of fun games to be played with three."

The offer catches me off guard. Julian's a flirt, but he's never propositioned me. I don't think he sees me like that. But I guess everybody has their breaking point, and he's turned on enough to forget any boundaries we've set up in the past. I let my fingernails dig into his bare shoulder. "You know you're not allowed to touch me, Julian. We both agreed to that."

He wets his lips. "Rules can change."

In the corner of my eye, Hawk is bristling, and I'm sure it's taking every bit of his self-control not to charge Julian and tackle him.

But I maintain my poise, and pray that Hawk will maintain his. I push onto my toes and kiss Julian on the cheek. "Thank you for tonight. But the rules haven't changed."

The smile he gives me this time is resigned. "I'll keep my promise of one hour. Best of luck with your boy, mistress."

I nod and Julian retreats back into the crowd, drawing the hungry looks of more than one dominant in the room. No doubt the guy won't be left alone for long.

My attention goes back to the man I'm most concerned about. Hawk's gaze is firmly on me, his body stiff as a soldier's. And though his expression is stoic, I can tell he's uncomfortable standing in front of the crowd wearing next to nothing. I know him too well for him to hide that from me.

Part of it is because he's an intensely private person. We both are. Having all these eyes on us is not a natural feeling for me. I can definitely scratch exhibitionism off my list of potential kinks. But I know that another part for Hawk is that shame he still carries about being submissive. So though I'm craving some privacy with him, I know what he needs right now more than that.

"Hawk, stand on the X on the floor and lift your hands above your head. Back to me."

My sharply delivered words seem to snap him out of his soldier

stance. He glances at the spot on the floor and moves to stand on the
X. When he lifts his arms above his head, I grab a step stool and
move it next to him so that I can climb up and lock his cuffs to the
chains hanging from the ceiling. I draw the slack out and his arms
stretch a little farther. After checking everything to make sure I'm
not putting too much strain on his shoulders, I climb down.

He looks gorgeous stretched out like that, muscles flexing and
broad back on full display. I let my fingers trail down his spine. I
could just bite him.

Wait, I *could* bite him. Realizing he's mine to play with gives me
a silly little thrill. I lean forward and press my teeth into the meat
of his shoulder. He groans and the sound zips right through me, so
I don't stop there. I trail small bites down his side until I reach the
firm curve of his ass. I drag my lips over the thin black material and
then bite down hard.

Hawk jolts beneath my touch and the desperate noise he makes
sends my body pulsing with heat. There is nothing sexier than this
man. Nothing. I want to hear those sounds again and again. I want
to hear him beg.

I straighten and rub my palm over the spot I bit. "I'm going to
take these off."

The chains above him jangle. "No, Chri—mistress. Please. Not
here."

That kind of plea would normally stop me. I'd adjust, do something he's more comfortable with. But I'm running on instinct now.
"You have a word, Hawk."

"Please," he says, an edge of fear in his voice.

"That's not it, babe." I tug his shorts down to his feet, leaving
him naked in front of the onlookers, his cock standing proud.

There are murmurs of appreciation from the people in the room,
but I'm not listening to them. All of my focus is on Hawk and his
reactions. I step in front of him and slide my hand down his chest.
He's shaking a little. I press my hand to the spot over his heart.
"Look at me."

He forces his eyes open and peers down at me.

"Don't you dare be ashamed. You should see how perfect you look. I bet half the women in this place would beg to touch you. But they don't get to." I let my palm drift down his chest and stomach until it dips low, gripping his balls. "Because you're *mine*. Every part of you is for *my* pleasure. And right now, I am very, very pleased with you."

"Yes, mistress. Thank you." He swallows hard and the apprehension in his eyes is giving way to that starry look I've seen other subs get in their scenes. It's something I've never really witnessed in Hawk. He's never let me get him to that mysterious place called subspace.

I push up on my toes and press my mouth to his, enjoying the familiarity of those lips in such unfamiliar circumstances. He gives over to the kiss like a man starved for touch, and I hear the chains clink above him as he tries to reach for me, but I pull back before he can deepen the kiss. I give him a *not-so-fast* smile and move away from him.

His eyes follow me, his head turning with my movements, but soon I'm behind him again just out of his view. "Eyes down, sub."

He lowers his head and presents me the lovely view of his naked, chained-up form. There's a faint red mark on his ass where I bit him through his shorts. Very nice. I plan for it to be the first of many. But before that, there's one more thing I want to add to the mix. I pull a few items from my bag and move close to him again. He shudders as if sensing my presence right behind him.

I touch the curve of his ass and he startles. "Easy now."

"Sorry, mistress."

"You're going to want to relax for this." I take the plug in my hand and draw the tip down the crack of his ass.

He arches away, on full alert again. *"No."*

I give his hip a harsh pinch. "Don't move away from me. And *no* isn't the word that will do anything for you."

"Mistress, please. I can't . . ."

The plea is hard to hear. I know this is going to be difficult for him. He's never let me go there, but I've seen his Ranch documents.

This wasn't checked off as a hard limit, and I need to break down the last of his walls so that they can't stand between us anymore. He needs to know I own all of him. I lubricate my fingers and rub them against his opening, preparing him. His entire body seems to clench, and he's shifting on his feet. But from where I'm standing, I can also see his cock leaking fluid as I rub. His mind may be fighting it, but his body's responding.

So is mine.

"You won't deny me this pleasure, Hawk. Do you know what it does to me to feel you hot around my fingers? One day soon I'm going to take one of those fat strap-ons and fuck you until you're screaming my name."

He groans and I feel his muscles giving way against my touch, surrendering. I don't even know where the words came from, but now that they've spilled out, I can see the scene painted before me. Never in my life have I thought of penetrating a guy, but suddenly the thought of doing that to Hawk has me going hot and slick against my panties.

But not here. Not tonight. When I take him that way, it will be just between us.

I give him a few more strokes, sliding my fingers inside him and making sure he's ready. Then I take the plug and push the tip against his opening. His muscles resist at first, but I use gentle pressure and coax the plug inside. He lets loose a gasp as the toy seats deep, the bright blue flared base the only thing left in view. Then, because I'm evil, I hit the button on the remote in my pocket and the thing hums to life.

"Oh, Jesus." Hawk's knees buckle for a second and I put a hand on his hip to steady him. The plug is angled to gently stimulate his prostate, and it's going to make it near-impossible for him to hold back his orgasm. He starts to involuntarily pump his hips forward. "Please, Chris, not like this. I'm not going to be able—"

I lower the setting on the vibrator slightly and step around the front of him, lubricating my other hand. Without looking up to see the plea in his eyes, I slide a silicone ring over his erection, drawing it all the way down to the base—a snug fit that makes his cock look even plumper and more obscene. "This should help you out."

Hawk makes a desperate sound, but I ignore it and walk to the sink against the wall to give my hands a wash, taking my time and letting him suffer a little. The longer I draw this out, the better it will be for both of us. I don't even look his way as I head back to my spot.

Once I'm positioned behind him again, I reach into my bag and pull out a cat-o'-nine-tails Kelsey has been training me to use. The tails are braided and have little knots on the end. I know it can hurt like a son of a bitch because I asked Kelsey to try it on me once so I knew what it felt like. I lasted for a whole two strokes before I cried uncle. But she'd said it was the one that Hawk responded to best.

And I want to see the real Hawk, the one who craves that level of pain, the masochistic side he hasn't trusted me with yet. I test the weight of the cat in my hand, getting a feel for it again. "Tell me your words, Hawk."

A muscle twitches in his back, and I can tell he's caught in some suspension between pleasure and desperation. "Yellow for check in. Red for stop."

"Can I trust you to use them if you need them?"

"Yes, mistress," he says a little breathlessly. "You can trust me."

And I do trust him. But more than that, for the first time since we started on this adventure, I trust myself. I know what I want. I know what my guy needs. And I'm not afraid to give it to him.

I lift my arm and let the wicked braids stripe across his back.

SIX

Hawk

By the time Chris lands the last blow, I can barely feel the sting. Instead, I sway on my feet, the rush of endorphins so strong and the ache in my cock so pronounced that I know I must be begging. The vibrator is humming, humming, humming on a spot inside me that makes everything feel like I'm going to explode, and the pain has only amped up my need further. There are words coming out of my mouth, but I can't make sense of them. And I don't care that there are people around. I don't care that they see how desperate I am for her. I just want her. I *need* her.

The swishing tails of the cat stop, and I suck in a lungful of air as her boots click along the floor—closer, closer. My entire backside is on fire and I'm hating the inventor of the cock ring with a deep abiding passion, but when Chris presses her body against me, I never want her to leave. Lips brush my shoulder. "Still with me, babe?"

Her scent fills my nose—honey shampoo and peppermint gum. *Chris.* I come back into my head for a moment.

"Yes," I whisper, my voice hoarse. "Please, I need to touch you."

Her fingers drift over my hips. "You need to come?"

"I need to make *you* come."

And that's the God's honest truth. I'm desperate to see how this is affecting her. Is she hot and wet beneath that short skirt of hers? Has topping me excited her? Or has she ventured too far outside the fence? Is she regretting trying this?

Chris backs away, and I'm ready to beg for her to return. But before I can, she's in front of me, sliding the cock ring off. The rush of sensation and the feel of her fingertips on me is almost too much for me to take. I grind my teeth, doing everything I can to stave off my orgasm. I refuse to lose it like some inexperienced kid—especially in front of all these people.

"I know you need to come," she says, eyeing me. "You have my permission."

My muscles quiver. "No, mistress. Not here, not like this. Please, let me have you. I'll make you feel good."

"Yes, you will. Later. But right now, you don't get to make that decision. I want you to come." She tucks her hand in her pocket and the vibration of the plug goes from slow hum to steady, persistent, rolling waves.

I buck in the bindings, the feeling so intense inside me I can't hold back the moan. My hips thrust forward involuntarily, like I'm going to fuck the goddamned air. I feel the control slipping and panic wells in me.

"No, Chris, please." I squeeze my eyes shut, fighting, fighting. But it's useless.

"Just let go, Hawk."

Her hands cup the head of my cock and every thread of resistance snaps. Her touch, God, her touch. I pump into her palms with frantic, jerking motions—the chains rattling and my body betraying me, demanding relief. People are watching. *Everyone* is watching. I'm tied up, beaten, penetrated, and rutting like a goddamned animal. I can't imagine how I must look, what people must think, but when I look up into Christina's face, that all fades away. Because there's something there I can barely fathom. Something beautiful and wondrous. There's rapture.

And love.

And bald-faced, hungry desire.

She wants this. She wants *me*. Just like this.

And before I can do anything more to stop it, my release is

jetting out, spilling over her palms and draining me of any fight I have left.

"That's good, babe, so good," she soothes, nuzzling my neck as I pant my way down from madness, my softening cock still gliding over her hot palms. "You're so fucking sexy. You're driving me out of my mind."

I lift my head and for the first time I know she means it. The simple compliment sends a tidal wave of satisfaction and pride through me. Confidence. I've pleased her. She's into this.

She gives me a soft kiss and then grabs a towel to wipe her hands and remove the plug. I can't even follow her movements or get embarrassed about her cleaning me off. I'm flying high and coasting on the fact that I put that smile on her face.

Soon, she's got the stool next to me again and is unhooking my cuffs. She eases my arms down to my sides and I sink to my knees, my muscles going jellylike from all the adrenaline and arousal running through me.

"Whoa, there." She hops off the stool and hurries to the spot in front of me. "You okay, babe?"

I look up, knowing I must have some punch-drunk expression on my face, but I can't help it. Her dark eyes are lit with concern, but the swells of her breasts are rising and falling behind that corset and her face is flushed. And when I inhale a deep breath, the tangy scent of her arousal hits my senses. *Yes.* My girl is breathless and beautiful and completely turned on. I want to bow at her feet and thank the universe for this woman. I want to worship. I want to taste her.

"I'm fine, mistress. You've made me weak."

She smiles and runs her hand through my sweat-slicked hair. "Not possible. You're the toughest guy I know. Though, I think I finally know what subspace looks like on you."

Mmm. I close my eyes and bow my head to let her touch me however she pleases. I'll stay here on my knees all night if that's what she wants.

She kneels down in front of me and lifts my chin in her hand, her eyes searching mine. "Come to bed with me, Hawk. I need it to be just us now."

The words move through me, filling me up and making everything feel right in my world for the first time in longer than I can remember. I climb to my feet, taking my time to make sure I'm steady, and then put a hand out to help her to hers. "I'm all yours, mistress."

A slow smile touches her lips. "Aren't I a lucky bitch?"

I shake my head and pull her close. "No, Chris. You could never be a bitch. You're the best woman I've ever known. And I'm so sorry . . . for everything. For how I treated you. For what I said. For not trusting you to see me like this. You should be dumping my ass."

Her face softens and she reaches around to pat my ass right over the welts she left there. The sting makes me wince in the best way. "Then I wouldn't have the chance to beat it."

I grin. "Sadist."

"Glad you finally noticed." She backs away and hands me a robe to put on. "Ready?"

"Yes, mistress."

"Good." She leans close and puts her lips against my ear. "Because I'm not even close to done with you."

No sweeter words have ever been spoken. We're not done. Not for tonight. And not in our relationship. For a night that I thought would mark the end, we instead get a new beginning.

And later, when Christina ties me to the bed in our cabin and straddles me, taking her pleasure and telling me she loves me, I know there's no looking back. There's no more shame or embarrassment. I no longer care if people find out how I am. Because there's nothing ugly or wrong about this.

My name is Hawk Nichols—C student, star running back, and sexual submissive.

And I love this woman.

Not just because she's smart or beautiful or kind.

But because she owns me—body, heart, and soul.

I am hers.

I surrender.

Turn the page for a sneak peek at the
next Loving on the Edge novel

CALL ON ME

Coming July 2015 from Berkley Books!

ONE

"Are you touching yourself?" The voice in Oakley's ear sounded labored and overeager—like a Saint Bernard attempting phone sex. He was probably drooling, too. Lovely.

"Yes, you make me so hot"—she quickly checked the sticky note she'd put on the kitchen island—"Stefan."

Stefan. Literature professor. Single. Six foot five.

That was the info he'd given her. Which probably meant: *Steve, unemployed, married, and five-six on a good day.*

He groaned. "You're so sexy."

Sexy? Two points off for lack of originality, Mr. Lit Prof. Though even the suave guys tended to forget their vocabulary when they got to this point in the conversation. Oakley covered the mouthpiece on her headset and turned off the timer on the oven. If nothing else, she was impressed the guy had lasted through the full baking time.

"Thanks, sugar," she said, letting her tone drop into a lower register.

"God, your voice is so fucking hot."

That she heard a lot. A record company exec had once deemed her voice "smoky, X-rated perfection" when he'd heard her demo. At the time, she hadn't considered how inappropriate it'd been for a grown man to tell a fifteen-year-old kid that. But her raspy voice had gotten her the gig then, and it'd gotten her this one now. Though, admittedly, the bar wasn't set quite as high for this current one.

"I'm gonna give it to you so hard, Sasha," Stefan ground out. "I can feel your hot mouth closing around me."

Oakley donned oven mitts and leaned down to pull out the tray of brownies. The smell of chocolate and the heat of the oven hit her with full force. She inhaled deeply. "Mmm, that's *so* good. I could just lick up every last bit."

"Yeah," he panted, the sound of his slick, pumping fist obscenely clear through the receiver. "That's right. Show me how much you want it."

There you go, Steve, you go on and get your money's worth. Oakley set the tray of brownies on a trivet and tugged off the mitts. Her stomach rumbled. She'd stayed up late enough that her body was looking for dinner number two. But these weren't for her.

She glanced toward the darkened hallway and the stairs beyond. Well, maybe one little corner piece wouldn't be missed. She cut a small square and dipped her fingers in to grab it. But as she lifted the brownie, her knuckles grazed the searing hot pan.

"Ah, shit!" she hissed, jerking her hand back.

"Oh, yeah, let me hear it," Stefan said on a moan. "Come with me, baby."

Oakley shook out her hand, sucking air through her teeth, and tried to keep the pain out of her voice. Her phone companion thought she was mid-orgasm. She threw in an *oh, oh, oh* and ran to the sink to plunge her fist into the dishwater she'd drawn to soak the mixing bowl.

Stefan made choked sounds as he reached his own release. In another world, maybe it could've been an erotic moment. She'd talked a guy into an orgasm. He was calling her name. But the name was fake and so was the talk. And though she held nothing against the guys who called—they helped her pay the bills—her libido had long ago crawled into a dark corner to die a peaceful death. Even if she imagined the guy on the other end of the line looked like Johnny Depp or Justin Timberlake or something, she couldn't drum up one ounce of interest.

Stefan panted heavy, wet breaths right against her ear, resuming his resemblance to a Saint Bernard. Maybe she should offer him a "good boy" or a Milk-Bone.

"That was amazing," she said, using her husky, after-sex voice as she soaked her hand in the water. "Thank you, Stefan."

Panting. Panting. That was the only response.

Then a tight, high sound—whistling.

No. *Wheezing.*

Uh-oh. "Stefan? Are you okay?"

Those squeaking breaths continued for a few seconds, then: "Yes . . . I'm . . . fine."

He didn't sound fine. "Stefan, if you're having an asthma attack or chest pains or something, you need to call for help."

"Can't . . ." He gave a ragged cough. "My wife . . . can't know . . . I'm down here this late. She'll know I'm up . . ."

He coughed again.

Jesus Christ. Oakley shook the water off her hand. "What's she going to think when she finds you dead in the basement? Hang up the phone and dial 911."

"I—"

"Stu?" a sharp voice said in the background. "What are you doing down here? *Stu?*"

"Oh, shit," Stefan/Stu said between wheezes.

The dial tone buzzed in Oakley's ear a second later.

She pulled off the wireless headset and sagged against the fridge, exhaling a long breath. Okay. It would be all right. Stu's wife might kill him when she found him with the phone to his ear and his underwear around his ankles, but at least the guy wouldn't die of a heart attack on Oakley's watch.

She could handle a lot of stuff—callers threw all kinds of bizarre shit at her—but she couldn't be responsible for helping kill one. It was bad enough that she'd just contributed to strife in another marriage.

Gold star for her.

It shouldn't bother her. The guys who called were grown men making a conscious decision to seek out paid phone sex. She was simply the tool of choice. Another night, they might download porn and watch a dirty movie instead. If she'd learned anything during her year of doing this job, it was that it wasn't personal. She had a job to do. The callers needed a faceless someone to fill in for their fantasy that night. The relationship was purely transactional. And hell, she'd been used for free by enough men in her past. Now she was at least paid for it and not getting emotionally annihilated in the process. But, still, sometimes she felt like the drug dealer, giving addicts easy access to their vice.

She rolled her shoulders, trying to shrug off the stress of the call, and dug a tube of antibiotic ointment out of the junk drawer to slather on her burned knuckles. It was past two and she really needed to get to bed, but there was no way she'd be able to sleep after that burst of adrenaline from the call.

Plus, she'd never gotten her dessert. And right now, she could use a big honking piece of chocolate.

She went back to the brownies. They'd cooled enough by now, so she cut herself a bigger square than the original corner she'd planned and took a bite. She closed her eyes. *Yeah, that's the stuff.*

After pouring a big glass of milk, she brought that and the rest of the brownie to the table. She glanced at the walkie-talkie she'd placed on the table, the soft white noise relaxing her, and leaned back in the chair to enjoy the solitude. She was used to pulling the night shift by now, but usually she fell into bed after the last call, grasping for any shreds of sleep she could get before the alarm went off to start her real job. But it was nice to sit for a moment and simply be.

She polished off the last bit of brownie and milk and brought her glass to the sink. The exhaustion was settling in full force now. She braced her hands on the edge of the counter and eyed the soaking dishes. Her mother had always had the rule to never go to bed with a dirty sink—as if a bright, gleaming, empty sink was some sign of how together the household was. Maybe it was.

Oakley turned away from the dishes. They'd have to wait until tomorrow. She didn't have it in her.

She put plastic wrap over the rest of the brownies and grabbed the walkie-talkie and her headset. She should be able to get at least four hours of sleep. But right as she flipped off the light, the walkie-talkie beeped.

"Mom?"

Oakley halted, startled by the sudden voice in the quiet. She pressed the button on the side of the device. "Yeah, baby?"

"What's that smell?" Reagan asked, her voice groggy from sleep.

Oakley shook her head and smiled. She should've known the bionic nose would pick up that scent even in her sleep. "It's just the brownies for your bake sale tomorrow."

"It's not my bake sale. It's the school's," Reagan corrected.

"That's what I meant."

"But that's not what you said."

Oakley leaned against the wall in the hallway. This was an argument she'd never win. Reagan was into exactness. "I'm sorry I said it wrong the first time. Now go back to sleep, sweetheart. I don't want you to be tired in the morning."

"Did you put nuts or caramel in them?"

"Of course not. I know you're a brownie purist."

"Okay. Good," Reagan said, and Oakley could almost hear her daughter nodding. "Thanks, Mom. Love you."

Oakley pressed the walkie-talkie to her chest for a moment, warmth filling her. "Love you, too, Rae. Good night."

Oakley headed to her bedroom, listening to the footfalls upstairs and the flush of the toilet as Reagan made a quick trip to the bathroom. She must've really had to go because Rae hated getting out of bed in the middle of the night. And she outright refused to come downstairs after dark because there weren't enough places for nightlights.

Hence the walkie-talkies. Oakley had gotten tired of Reagan yelling from afar anytime she needed something at night. And leaving every light blazing through the house all evening wasn't an option either. The electric bill was already high enough.

Bills. No, she wouldn't think about that now. Even though she could see the stack staring at her from her desk. The gas bill. Rent. The quarterly installment for Reagan's private school and therapies. She couldn't face that tonight. Plus, she knew the due dates by heart so she could hold on to her money until the very last minute without being late.

She closed her bedroom door and walked over to her computer to wake the screen. Her sign-in page for the service she used to get her calls was still up. It showed how many minutes she'd logged tonight. Not bad. But she was six minutes shy of hitting the bonus level where she got an extra fifty bucks for the night. Stu's health scare had cost her more than stress.

She sighed and sagged into her desk chair. Fifty extra dollars could pay for that pair of lime green Chuck Taylors Reagan wanted for her birthday.

Oakley yawned and checked the box that indicated she was available to take a call. Her cell phone rang within seconds and she slipped on the headset again. "Hello, this is Sasha. Ready for a fantasy night?"

"So ready," said the deep-voiced caller. There was male tittering in the background.

Great. A frat-boy call.

"What are you wearing, Sasha?"

Oakley looked down at her oversized T-shirt and yoga pants. "A sheer robe with nothing underneath."

"Aw, yeah," the dude said. "How big are your tits?"

Oakley put her head to her desk. Six minutes. She only needed to keep them on the phone for six more minutes.

Six.

Five.

Four.

Three.

They hung up at two, laughing in the background as the phone went dead.

Their Truth or Dare game complete.

And she was short.

She lifted her head and checked the *Available* box again.

"Hello, this is Sasha . . ."

TWO

The chick in his living room was taking a selfie next to his gold record. Pike leaned back, watching her through his half-open bedroom door. "Fantastic."

"What's fantastic?" his friend Gibson asked on the other end of the line. "Did you even hear what I said?"

"No, I didn't. And what's fantastic is that I have a seriously hot B-list actress in my living room, who was all kinds of cool after the show tonight, but is now snapping duckface selfies in front of my shit."

Gibson snorted a laugh. "At least she's not using you just for your body."

"That I'd be okay with. But this . . ."

"Hey, if there's no selfie for proof, the event never happened. At least that's what my niece tells me. It's like a tree falling in the woods."

Pike sighed. "Observation: Duckface is a friend to no one."

The longer Pike watched, the more he regretted his decision to bring this woman home with him. He'd been buzzing off the energy of the performance tonight and had wanted to keep that feeling going. Darkfall had kicked ass onstage and had impressed the promoters putting together the big Summer Insanity tour. If Darkfall landed that spot, they'd have a chance to recapture some of the traction they'd lost when their lead singer had to take extended time off between albums to get surgery on his vocal cords. In some ways, tonight felt like a rebirth of the band, and he wanted to celebrate.

And usually the only thing more exciting than pounding the drums, making thousands of fans scream, was making just one scream. But as he watched his date take another photo of herself, he was losing his enthusiasm for his plan.

Maybe a chill night at home with the dog would've been a better idea.

Monty barked from somewhere in the living room, protesting the fact that Pike hadn't given him his requisite belly rub and dog biscuit when he'd come home. He'd been too busy pouring a drink for his guest.

"What's her name?" Gib asked.

Pike scrubbed a hand through his damp hair. "Why does that matter?"

"Come on, tell me that you're not that big of a dick and you remember her name."

Pike grimaced at Gib's tone. This is what he got for hanging out with businessman types instead of fellow musicians. The suits had a different code of conduct. With the dudes in his band, remembering names was only expected *after* you slept with someone. Luckily, Pike's memory was good. "Lark Evans."

"All right. Hold on a sec." The clicking of a keyboard sounded on the other end.

"Gib, look, can we talk about whatever you were calling for tomorrow? I'm ignoring my company." He walked away from the door and dropped the towel from around his waist to pull on a fresh pair of well-worn jeans. "I told her I'd only be in the shower for a minute."

"Ha! I knew it," Gibson said, triumph in his voice.

"What?"

"Your girl's on Instagram. And guess what pics are making their way around the world as we speak?"

Pike sighed.

"Damn, she is hot, though," Gibson said. "Duck lips notwithstanding."

"Which is why—"

"Ah, shit. You're gonna love this. Wait for it . . . caption to the pic: *Hanging out with Spike, the drummer from Darkfall!* Hashtag: *hawt.*"

"Hold up. *Spike?*"

Gibson burst into laughter. "Spike! Man, she doesn't even know *your* name. How very rock-star of her."

Pike looked to the ceiling, letting that sink in. Karma's a fucking bitch. "You are totally ruining my hard-on here."

"Now don't kid. I know my deep, brooding voice makes you hot," Gib said. "Want me to talk dirty to you, Spikey?"

Pike grinned. "So it's finally happened. You're going gay for me. I'm flattered. Of course, it was inevitable. I mean, have you seen me? But I hate to break your heart, Gib, I only play for one team."

He sniffed. "If I were gay, I'd have way higher standards than you. That record would need to be platinum."

"Aw, love you, too. I'm even making my duckface for you." He made a loud kiss sound. "Now I'm letting you go because, unlike you, I'm about to get laid, son."

"Fine. But call me back in the morning. I have a charity thing I need to run by you."

Pike tucked the phone between his shoulder and ear and pulled his bedside drawer open to check the condom supply. "The Dine and Donate event? I told you the band's in again this year, if you need us."

"No, this is for something different. More of a favor than anything else."

"Sounds ominous. But yeah, call you tomorrow."

"Cool. Now go rock her world, Spike."

Pike snorted and disconnected the call. He tossed his phone on the chair by the window and padded to his closet to grab a T-shirt. But when he stepped out of his room, ready to block out all the information he'd learned—selfies, Instagram, Spike—in order to enjoy his date, he was greeted by a shriek instead.

Lark hadn't seen him come in because her gaze had zeroed in on a growling Monty.

"Give it back, you stupid mutt!" she yelled, and jabbed a closed umbrella at Monty. Monty yelped.

"What the fuck?" Pike hurried forward and grabbed her wrist, stopping another poke. "What the hell's going on?"

She pointed at Monty, rage twisting her pretty face into something ugly. "Look at him! Your idiotic dog is eating my *Jimmy Choos*!"

She said it like Monty was murdering her kid. Pike glanced at Monty who was in defense mode, baring teeth, two little paws on one of Lark's high heels. Pike shrugged. "Well, the brand does say *Choo*. Maybe he's just following directions."

Lark gasped and looked at Pike like he'd lost his mind. "Do you know how much those *cost*? What is wrong with you? Do something!"

The grating tone of her voice made his teeth clamp together. Being yelled at by anyone pushed his buttons. But messing with his dog pushed the ugliest of them. He took a breath, trying to keep his cool. "Do you know that my dog was *abused* as a puppy? And that jabbing him with a sharp object is fucking traumatizing to him? I'll buy you another pair of your goddamned shoes."

Her head snapped back a bit at that, and she had the decency to look chagrined. She glanced down at the umbrella still clutched in her hand. "Oh. Shit, I'm sorry. I didn't know."

And he didn't care. Abused or not, you don't poke an animal with something that could hurt them, especially over something as stupid as a shoe. He could put up with her using him for his fame or whatever. They would've both been using each other. They each knew the score. But he wasn't going to let anyone fuck with his dog.

"Monty, release," he said, in the firm, dominant voice that worked best on the feisty dachshund/schnauzer mix. Monty looked up with big, sad puppy eyes and backed away from the shoe. But just when Pike was about to send him off to his bed, Monty trotted over to Lark and gave her the *I'm sorry* look.

Lark's expression softened, and she reached down to pat his head awkwardly. "It's okay, buddy . . ."

Monty lifted his leg and pissed all over her bare foot.

"Monty, no!" Pike said.

But chaos ensued after that. Lark hopping and shrieking. Monty barking and spinning in a circle. And Pike doing his damnedest not to laugh.

He wasn't entirely successful, and that earned him a glare from Lark and a happy, yipping bark from Monty. Finally, he gathered himself together enough to direct Monty to go to his crate so he could help Lark.

He showed her to the bathroom so she could rinse her leg off in the tub, and he cleaned up the mess in the living room—after sneaking Monty his treat and a belly rub.

He was halfway through a beer when Lark stepped into the kitchen a few minutes later, wearing nothing but a pair of lacy pink panties and a bra that made her breasts look like icing-covered cupcakes. His dick jumped to attention—the response automatic.

She leaned in the doorway, posing like she was at a Victoria's Secret cover shoot, and gave him the inviting smile she'd given him from the audience tonight. "Sorry about all of that. How about we start over and get back to why we're here, hmm?"

Pike still had the bottle of beer pressed to his lips. He lowered it and set it on the counter.

Lark's smile spread wider and she sauntered over with a heavy sway in her hips. She pressed her hand to his chest. "I have all kinds of ways we can apologize to each other. For getting mad at your dog, I was thinking this would make it up to you."

She dragged her hand down and lowered to her knees. Pike stared down at her. She looked like a fucking porn star at his feet. Pouty lips with a fresh coat of pink lipstick, blond hair flowing down her back. A wet dream of a woman. But when she put her painted fingernails to the zipper on his jeans, he put his hand over hers. "Stand up."

She blinked, the sultry look shifting to a perplexed one. "What?"

He helped Lark get to her feet. "Be right back."

Her smile returned, though it had a confused tilt to it. "O-kay."

He headed back to his bedroom for a minute, then returned to the kitchen. She was drinking his beer, putting lipstick marks on the bottle. He draped her dress on one of the bar stools, set a pair of his flip-flops on top of it, and handed her a few hundred-dollar bills. "For the shoes and a cab."

She stared down at the money in her hand. "What?"

"This isn't going to happen tonight."

"Wait, you want me to *leave*? But I thought—"

"It's time for you to go." He was tempted to take a co-selfie with her. Hashtag: *HookUpFail.*

She stiffened like a rod had been shoved up her back and made these little sounds of disbelief—like she was trying to come up with a really good insult but couldn't think of any.

When she obviously couldn't string anything worthy together, she shoved on his flip-flops, which looked like flippers on her small feet, and yanked her dress over her head. "I can't fucking believe this."

He dumped the beer in the sink, bored.

His lack of response brought a new level of hatred glowing in her eyes. "Is this about the dog? Because that's just stupid. How was I supposed to know he was abused?"

He walked to his front door and pulled it open. "You never know where anyone's scars are. Doesn't mean you get a pass to hurt them."

She reared back like he'd slapped her. Then her lips pressed together and she flounced out the door, muttering something about hoping that the dumb dog kept him warm tonight.

He shut the door without watching her go and leaned against it, absorbing the quiet of the condo, relief instead of disappointment settling in. Hookup fail, yes. But even he had standards. He'd rather fuck his fist than spend another second with Duckface the Puppy Poker.

A year ago, he might've just written it off and taken her to bed anyway. What did it matter if a woman was shallow? It wasn't like they'd be seeing each other again. Plus, he'd always hated sleeping alone in a house. But now he couldn't stomach the thought of spending another moment with a woman like that.

Maybe he was getting used to being by himself. After his roommate, Foster, had moved out to live with his girlfriend last year, Pike had felt that old need to always have people over. Mostly of the naked female variety. But for the last few months, he'd been so busy with band stuff and working at his music studio on the side that he hadn't sought out that brand of companionship very often. He hadn't even gone to The Ranch, the kink resort he and his friends belonged to, in at least three months. Tonight had been the first night he'd done the hookup-after-a-show thing in a while.

Now he remembered why he'd backed off from this kind of thing. He had no issue being someone's one-night stand. Most of the time, he preferred things that way. But now that he'd seen how Foster and Cela were together, how explosive the chemistry could be when two people connected like that, he could see how superficial this other shit was in comparison. Women fucked his type. The bad boy. The drummer. Whatever. They didn't fuck *him*.

And he'd been guilty of the same. He'd fuck the groupie, the model, the B actress. If not for Monty chewing Lark's shoe tonight, he would've never known that the woman was capable of hurting a dog for something as inconsequential as a shoe. Because he didn't *know* her.

For some reason, that dug into him like a burr, annoying the shit out of him.

He sank onto his bed and Monty jumped up to join him. He scratched behind Monty's ears. "Good job, Monts. You're making me grow a goddamned conscience."

Monty licked his chops. There were pieces of red shoe leather stuck in his teeth.

Pike chuckled and kissed the top of Monty's scruffy head. Monty rewarded him by releasing some noxious gas and dog-grinning at the effort.

"Jesus, Monts." He put his hand over his nose and mouth. "Take that stuff somewhere else."

Monty, of course, took that as his cue to settle next to him on the bed. Pike waved the poisonous fumes away, coughing, and grabbed his cell phone.

Gibson answered on the second ring. "Please tell me you last longer than that because, seriously, any thoughts of going gay for you are definitely out of the question otherwise. I require stamina."

Pike let his head fall back to the pillow. "Shut the fuck up and stop flirting. It's not going to work."

"So you kicked her out?"

"Yeah."

"Good. You're better than that," Gib said, no sarcasm in his voice. "You need to stop dipping into the groupie pool, anyway. You're too old for that shit. Find yourself some normal women who are your own age."

"Normal women have too many expectations."

"What? Like remembering their names and calling them the next day?"

"Exactly. Plus, I'm best in limited doses. I'd send normal women running for the hills after too long."

"I don't know. You haven't scared off your friends yet. I mean, yes, I thought you were an egotistical douchebag when I first met you, but now you've grown on me. Like a fungus."

"So you're saying I should try to infect some normal woman with my fungus? Good talk, buddy. Good talk."

"Dr. Phil gets all his best stuff from me."

"Just tell me about this charity thing so I can get to bed and think about the sex I won't be having tonight."

Gibson paused as if ready to push the topic, but then relented. "Fine. The charity project would involve music."

"Excellent."

"And would be helping my lovely sister-in-law-to-be out."

"Making sexy Tessa happy. Good."

"You'd be working with kids."

"And . . . I'm out."

Gibson scoffed. "You have something against kids?"

"I'm inked up, curse like a convict, and have piercings in questionable places. Parents don't want me near their children, and the kids freak me out."

"Bullshit. How can you be freaked-out? You're one of them."

"Sorry, Gib."

"Are you being serious right now?"

"I'm not a kid person." He could still smell the stench of the house he'd grown up in. The overstuffed diaper pails. The spoiling government-issued baby formula. His younger siblings seeking him and his sister out when their mom couldn't keep up.

"This would be the older group, not the little ones."

"Can't I just write a check or donate proceeds from a show or something?"

Gibson blew out a breath. "No, they need your expertise, not your money. Just hear me out. Tessa has a great idea for a fund-raiser, but she needs someone with experience in producing music. All the money would go toward the college fund and resources for the after-school program. You know what the charity's about. These kids don't have a lot, man. You and I both know what that's like."

Fuck. "You're really going for the jugular here, Gib."

"Just speaking the truth."

Yeah, that and Gibson was a brilliant PR guy who knew how to pitch things. Monty laid his head on Pike's chest, and Pike scratched behind Monty's ear. "You've even got my dog giving me the don't-be-a-bastard look."

Gibson chuckled. "I sneak him treats when I'm there. He's on my side."

Pike ran a hand over his face. "What exactly do they want me to do?"

He could almost hear Gibson's victory grin over the phone. "It won't be a big deal at all."

Pike closed his eyes. Famous last words.

Roni Loren wrote her first romance novel at age fifteen when she discovered writing about boys was way easier than actually talking to them. Since then, her flirting skills haven't improved, but she likes to think her storytelling ability has. Though she'll forever be a New Orleans girl at heart, she now lives in Dallas with her husband and son. If she's not working on her latest sexy story, you can find her reading, watching reality television, or indulging in her unhealthy addiction to rock stars, er, rock concerts. Yeah, that's it. Visit her website: roniloren.com.